Out of Time

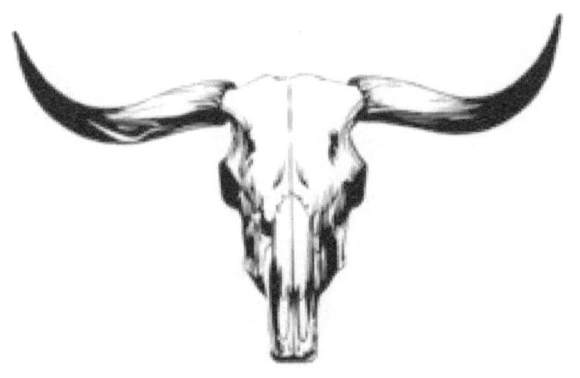

By K.D. Elledge

This is a work of fiction. Names, characters, places, and incidents either are the product of the author's imagination or are used fictitiously. Any resemblance to actual persons, living or dead, events, or locales is entirely coincidental.

Copyright © 2024 by K.D. Elledge

ISBN (Paperback): 979-8-9919381-0-5
ISBN (Hardcover): 979-8-9919381-1-2

Previous books by K.D. Elledge:

Finding Maisy

This book cannot be dedicated to just one person. Therefore, I would like to dedicate this book to all the strong women in my life. The real FMCs. My mother, Judy, who passed away in 2022, and my mother-in-law, Mary, who's the backbone of the family. Two strong females who shaped my life. And to my four daughters, Megan, Cameron, Emily, and Amelia, for having an untamable, wild strength and sense of adventure. Long live cowgirls.

Oh, and thank you to magnesium gummies…
for the lucid dreams.

Trigger Warnings

While I want my readers to revel in the many ups and downs of this novel, I want you to be aware of a few triggering details. This book includes alcohol consumption, smoking, violence, death, stalking behavior, physical abuse, sex, vulgar language, and attempted rape.

If you are about to turn the page…glad you are still here. Happy reading friend.

Out of Time Playlist

Available on Apple Music

To listen, visit the link below.

https://music.apple.com/us/playlist/out-of-time/pl.u-aZb0gg7TPJx91ZZ

Chapter 1: Witchy Woman by The Eagles

Chapter 2: Thousand Miles from Nowhere by Dwight Yoakam

Chapter 3: Fire Away by Chris Stapleton

Chapter 4: Southside of Heaven by Ryan Bingham

Chapter 5: The Bluest Eyes In Texas by Restless Heart

Chapter 6: Wild Horses by The Sundays

Chapter 7: Ten Thousand Angels by Mindy McCready

Chapter 8: Worst Way by Riley Green

Chapter 9: Hippies and Cowboys by Cody Jinks

Chapter 10: Pretty Little Devil by Shaya Zamora

Chapter 11: Do You Love As Good As You Look by Bellamy Brothers

Chapter 12: Blue Side of the Mountain by The SteelDrivers

Chapter 13: Angel in Disguise by Earl Thomas Conley

Chapter 14: Wicked Game by Chris Isaak

**For Out of Time aesthetics
visit the Pinterest link below.**

https://pin.it/Eb5v85LuH

Wicked Witch of the West

CHAPTER 1

March 1878

Samantha

"Hey, Warren, pass me the good stuff," I say quietly through a long, drawn-out exhale. I lace my fingers and prop my chin on my hands. The rough oak bar we sit at is digging into my elbows, matching the numerous aches lingering in my body.

I cut my gaze to my right and see concern building in Warren's chestnut eyes as he says, "This is the last of it, you sure you want to polish it off tonight?" He raises an eyebrow at me.

I bite my lip, lean back in the rickety bar stool, and consider his question for all of two seconds before I nod.

"Okay, but then we are left with piss-warm beer and ancient rot gut whiskey." He grins and slips a flask from his leather duster jacket—discreetly pouring each shot into our empty glasses. He eyeballs the room one more time to make sure no one is watching as he pockets the silver flask.

I look down at my fingers gripping the murky glass and notice for the first time how rough my nails look. My hands are dry and weathered. I cringe at the sight.

How the hell did we end up here? Is this some kind of punishment?

Warren interrupts my thoughts with words of encouragement as usual. "Hey girl, don't look like that. I need your strength as much as you need mine right now…besides, we aren't doing so bad. Look at us," he gestures between us flicking his hand toward me and then himself, "out here making a living and figuring it out. *That* is something to be proud of." He pats me on the back and gives me a soft smile.

Looking over at him now, I wonder what I would've done this past year without him. He is amazingly resilient and cunning. His prepper mentality used to make me laugh and poke fun at him, and now…I'm nothing but grateful.

Warren Mathews has a strong persona, but I can see how this place has changed him too. His face is sporting a few lines it didn't have before, and his deep brown skin is dry like this town. His short curly black hair is speckled throughout with gray, and his beard needs tending to again.

"Yeah, yeah," I mutter as I lift the glass to my parched lips and sip the liquid gold that is Jack Daniels Fire.

Man…I am really going to miss this stuff.

For a while we stay silent, and both enjoy the last taste of our home. I listen to the saloon girl banging away at the piano keys as the men whoop and holler at her. The warmth from the fireplace is almost unnecessary. The nights in Arizona can bring a chill, but it's nearing the end of March, and the days grow warm…hot even, leaving the nights pleasant. All around the room, people are bustling. There are gamblers, ramblers, and frilly saloon girls meandering about. Everyone has one thing in common here…they love a good bar.

I catch a glimpse of myself in the mirror behind the counter and pause the glass as it grazes my lips. My once pale white skin is bronzed from riding long hours outdoors. My blue-green eyes have taken on the gray tone they get in certain lighting. My long, light brown hair has blonde streaks streaming through from the sun.

And to think…I used to pay for those.

One positive thing that I can say about the two of us now is that we no longer need a gym. My once soft, thin figure is now cut with lean muscle—the product of eating *real* food and manual labor. Warren's tummy is slimmed down, too, and thick with muscle. For a fifty-year-old man, he looks much younger in physique.

I give myself another go-over in the mirror. I still look twenty-four but feel much…much damn older.

I slowly savor another sip as I avoid eye contact with a rough-looking crowd that just barreled through the swinging saloon's batwing doors. I can feel Warren tense up beside me. I cross my legs and nonchalantly pretend to straighten out my long blue skirts as I feel for my grandfather's Colt 1911 strapped to my thigh. Warren handmade me a leather strap contraption to hold the heavy piece.

Warren doesn't look my way as he whispers, "Samantha, just calm down and stay cool. If they talk to you, be polite. Don't go looking for trouble this time."

He only calls me Samantha when he is chastising me. I give him an incredulous look, which he mocks back at me. "I never go looking for trouble. It seems to know exactly where to find me at all times," I say before I reach for my hand-rolled cigarette on the counter and strike a match.

He arches a brow and purses his lips. "Uh huh, well, I mean it. We can't afford the trouble. I like having options for supplies, and this town is abundant in that." He pauses and then says, "And you smoking those gets too much attention too." He tips his head at my cigarette.

I roll my eyes and hit the cig again. He is right, and I know that. Most women here either use snuff or smoke from discreet pipes, but I could care less. Let them stare. I am so over it all. As a woman, it's hard not to get attention. Especially if you look half decent and are clean. It really doesn't take much here.

Just as I inhale a long drag, I feel the presence and smell the stench of a man beside me. I look to my left and let the smoke curl from my lips. Then, I purposely blow smoke rings into the stranger's face as he eyeballs me vulgarly.

He wears a worn, wide-brimmed hat that looks as if it has died and come back to life, and his once-white linen shirt is as brown as the bar but *less* clean. His yellowed grin makes me cringe as his eyes trail from my hair to my chest. I don't fail to notice the six-shooters hanging from each hip.

He licks his butter teeth then says, "I ain't ever seen a lady smoking a quirly before. What's your name, honey?"

My brows raise. I assume quirly is a type of cigarette but ignore him and take another drag as I sneer. Finally, I keep my face placid as I reply, "I'm not a lady, and my name is none of your concern."

His eyes darken a touch at my indifference. Then he looks past me to Warren as if he is noticing him for the first time. "What's the problem? You and this darky friendly like?" He levels Warren with a look of disgust as he lifts the decrepit hat and slicks out his greasy, matted brown hair.

My eyes widen, then turn into slits. "You son-of-a…"

Warren cuts me off abruptly, keeping his cool, and says, "No sir, this here is just my friend, nothing more.

Now if you don't mind, we were just finishing up our drinks, and we'll be on our way shortly."

I bristle as I try to hold my tongue.

"Well, that's good to know." The man looks between us one more time before he winks at me. "Be seeing you around." He tilts his head down and curls his lip before he finally saunters off.

Warren releases a breath he was holding and eases his hand away from his holster. "That was too easy."

"Way too easy," I concur, then add, "We may have a problem with these guys." I motion with my head for Warren to look over his shoulder.

Near the back of the saloon, butter teeth makes his way to the group sitting mixed between two round tables in the beginning thralls of a game of poker. At a glance, there looks to be seven or eight of them. The burgundy filagree walls and dim lighting create an ominous vibe around the cowboys in this smoke-filled room. One man in pristine clothing methodically rolls a silver dollar across the tops of each of his knuckles as he plays.

All the men's eyes raise and are suddenly watching us...except one.

In the corner sits a man with his faded black cowboy hat pulled down low over his eyes as he casually sips from a large beer tankard. From the looks of him, he is tall, maybe a little over six feet, with a slim strong build. He has a dark presence to him. I can't place why I feel that way. He stays to himself, hiding in the shadows, not participating in the game, but is clearly with the others.

I can only see the lower part of his face with a short black or maybe dark brown beard and mustache. Just as I start to turn away, his cowboy hat tips up, and his eyes catch mine for a brief second. Long enough to see the anger that resides in them. I try to turn away, but something keeps me from doing just that. One of his eyebrows arches, almost in a challenging way. I break the connection and turn my head to avoid that penetrating stare.

I down my last bit of Jack and curse under my breath. "I will *never* get used to this—the way they talk to you! It's bullshit!" I try to ignore the unease I feel building and that menacing man behind me. It's like I can feel his sharp gaze burning into my back. I glance at Warren who is rubbing his beard and looks lost in thought.

Eventually, his eyes flit my way, and he says, "You think I don't feel the same? I can't stand the way you are treated any more than me, but this is the hand we were dealt, Sam. We have no choice but to make the best of it."

I roll my shoulders, attempting to relieve some tension. "Are we making the best of it? Really? We've tried befriending locals in three different towns. On every supply run or hunting trip we've taken, it always ends the same. People don't accept strangers, and especially not us. Other than our few friends in Tombstone, we have *no one*."

"Yeah, well, look at us. Old black man and a young white woman. We bound to get stares and confrontation." He shakes his head subtly.

"You're not old, just...seasoned." I feign sprinkling seasoning on him and nudge his shoulder, which gains me his warm smile.

"Then *you* must be spicy seasoned," he throws back at me.

My mouth drops open, but then I can't help the laugh that bubbles out. My smile fades. I worry my lower lip as I think about Warren's words more carefully. Have we really tried to make a life here? We made a home, yes, but a life...We travel only long enough to gather the supplies we need, and then we are back to hiding out in the canyon—never engaging with people long enough to make lasting relationships.

The bartender and owner of this "fine" establishment strolls by. "Need another round?" he asks, shifting his worried eyes behind us and then back to ours quickly. That small gesture told me that we should probably leave.

Warren and I cut our eyes to each other and silently agreed. It's time to go. "No thanks, we appreciate it." I slide my glass toward him and hop off the stool. I don my leather riding duster as we make our way out of the saloon. I try not to, but my eyes dart of their own accord to the man in the corner. His head is tilted down, but he watches me. What is his deal? I look away and move quickly through the doors.

The night air is cool against my face compared to the roasting fireplaces indoors. We check our saddles' girths before mounting. I reach into my saddle bags and pull out the canvas pouch full of flowers and leaves that I harvested along the way…making sure that they're not spilling out inside. I carefully wrap them up so as not to crush the leaves from the oleander plant. Those little devils are very poisonous. I also secure the bottle of chloroform I scored from a local physician. Here's hoping I never have to use it, but I feel better having the anesthetic just in case. I reach down to pat Clint, my big brawny dappled gray gelding. I nudge his sides, bringing him to walk on. He is the one thing I have fallen in love with here.

Maybe the only thing.

Warren rides a red roan mare with an attitude almost as spicy as mine. He named her Halle. We both had a good laugh over picking names for these horses based on our favorite movie stars, Clint Eastwood and Halle Berry. We had an even bigger laugh when Warren was learning to ride. I was certain he wouldn't survive a week on horseback. Now, he looks like a natural. I was fortunate enough to have been raised on horses. My parents spent every last dollar they had to purchase a farm when my sister Jenna and I were kids.

I shake away the thought of Jenna. The breeze tonight is soft and comforting, and the sky is like looking straight into a massive kaleidoscope. Billions of stars linger overhead. The colors that traverse above us are unfathomable. I never knew a sky like this before.

Okay, so maybe there are two things I love here.

Just as we pass the town's edge and start our journey to our home, I hear the steady beat of hooves behind us. My blood runs cold.

Warren picks up the pace, trotting Halle, and I follow suit. "What are you thinking?" I whisper.

"Don't panic, and don't jump to conclusions, Sam. Let's stay calm. Maybe it's not them." He looks back over his shoulder the same time I do then we swing our heads back to face each other.

"It's definitely them, Warren!" I grind out.

"I can see that!" he spits. "Listen to me, Sam, do not pull out that gun. If they see it we will have a hell of a lot more problems. Here take one of mine." He hands me his 1873 Colt.

I try to steady my breathing and keep my wits about me. He is right…how would I explain my gun? "You know I haven't shot anything in a long while. I'm not sure I could hit the broad side of a barn." I say as I tuck the pistol into my holster.

"Ah hell, Sam, you could shoot a hair off a possum's ass from a mile away before we came here. You'll be fine. Do *NOT* pull it out unless we're in a life-or-death situation! Let me handle the talking." He angles his head and stares straight into my soul until I finally nod at him.

I lean my head back and take in a deep breath to calm my frayed nerves, but it doesn't help. It seems we are a beacon for trouble for just…existing. I keep my fingers lightly grazing over the Colt as I hear the hoofbeats coming closer.

"Hold up there, honey, what's your hurry?" I hear a man call out from behind me. "We just wanna talk."

Warren looks at me and nods, and we slow our horses down, spinning them to face the men. I trust him completely, and if he thinks we can talk our way out of this, then so be it. Besides, if we run now, they would find us eventually or kill us right here on the spot. My optimism died out long ago. People here are ruthless, and it seems *no one* can truly be trusted.

The gang staring back at me brings chills down my spine out here in the absence of witnesses. I quickly count eight men. My heart begins to race, but I never show it. I hold my head high and scowl at the lot of them while Warren does the good cop routine and smiles politely.

"How can we help you, gentlemen?" Warren asks calmly.

Butter Teeth is eyeing me with a look of longing, and it makes me want to vomit, but he doesn't speak up. The man beside him does.

This man is tall and wiry with a thick brown mustache and the rest of his face cleanly shaved. He is a little more refined than the others in the way he dresses. I recall that he was the one rolling the silver dollar, flipping it smoothly across his knuckles in that saloon. His tailored vest, clean derby hat, and pristine neckerchief elude to money. "I am just curious as to who *you* are." He looks directly at me, ignoring Warren and making my brows rise, then continues, "We know everyone around here, but we've never seen the likes of you before. Where are you two headed this time of night? Do you live around here?" His voice matches his clothing in that it is a little more upscale than the company he keeps. I can see his right hand resting on a revolver, and his left hand is slicking down his mustache.

Warren gives him his most earnest smile and says, "Well, we just came to Tucson not long ago, so we don't know many folks yet. My name is Warren, and this here is Samantha. We only come this way when we need supplies. We were just heading back out to…"

I cut my eyes at him in warning. We agreed to never lead *anyone* to where we live.

"To make camp," he finally says.

The leader of the gang's lips form a tight line as he looks between us. His face is intrigued, as if he loves a challenge, and we are *the* riddle to be deciphered. Just then, I notice a loner off to the left. His black horse is fidgeting and stomping the ground. Even in the dark, I can tell it's *him*. The man from the corner of the saloon. When my head lifts to meet his face, his eyes are already on mine. I see something in them—something that feels like a warning. My brow raises again along with all my curiosity, but I quickly avert my gaze as the leader speaks.

"To make/camp…why not stay here, in Tucson? There's plenty of rooms available." He leans forward in the saddle as he talks. "It's not safe around here at night, you know." He tilts his head with a sly grin.

Warren keeps up the good manners, replying, "Much appreciated, sir, but we must be on our way. We have quite a ride ahead of us. Now, if there was nothing else you wanted to know…besides who we are, then I bid you farewell. You folks have a good night." Warren tips his hat toward the men and looks at me—motioning me to go ahead of him. Whilst he plays it cool, I know the real Warren, the one that would smash them all into the ground if it meant keeping us safe.

The man speaks again, halting our exit. "We heard a tale a few towns over of a strange couple coming through there." He pauses, looking between us, then continues, "A black man and a white girl with strange accents and even stranger mannerisms. It was said that the girl made potions for women to use." He chuckles. "Strange, right? Not that we believe in that kinda thing, but still strange." He sneers at me, making my blood boil. "There was even a tale that she was marked by the devil himself." His eyes narrow in on me—gauging my reaction.

I keep my composure…only barely. My hands begin to shake, but I plead for these men to see nothing but strength. I inhale slowly and straighten in the saddle, holding my chin high. Out of the corner of my eye, I see the man on the black horse ease closer.

"That sounds a bit like the looks of you two, doesn't it?" The leader leans back in his saddle cocking his head to the side.

I can't hide my distaste and fury as I curl my lip.

Warren shakes his head and laughs, causing us all to turn his way. "That is some story, but no, sir. That couldn't be us, you see. We heard the same tale when we came through the last town. I assure you we don't fool with the devil's work. I'm a Godly man myself."

The leader cuts his eyes my way and raises an eyebrow in question. "And you...what do you have to say? You are certainly not mute and *do*, in fact, speak. I know that because you insulted one of my gentlemen in the saloon."

"*That* is not a gentleman." I point at Butter Teeth. His face reddens with anger, but I continue speaking to the leader. "Are you a deputy?" I cock my head at him. "What business do you have questioning us? Who are *you* exactly?" I hear Warren swear under his breath.

The man levels me with a glare, but after a few seconds begins to laugh. Slowly, the other men around him laugh along with him...all except for the scary one on the black horse. "You are a fiery one, aren't you...I like that." His smile fades as he says, "I ask the questions here, not you." His eyes darken. "However, I will indulge a name. Everyone calls me Bill, but you...*you* can call me William."

Good, I think I've pissed him off.

Bill continues as if I am not leveling him with rage-filled eyes. "Rumor has it that the girl had a devil's mark on her hip. There is a simple solution to rid the doubts and speculations. Now, if you would be so kind as to show us your hips, we will be on our way."

My mouth drops open with my sharp intake of breath. Panic seizes my lungs as I try to rationalize how to get us out of this. If I get Warren killed...I might as well die myself. I couldn't live with it. I can see the men all shifting in their saddles expectantly, all except that one. He is as still as if he was made of stone. His eyes are burning a hole through the leader, Bill. I wrinkle my brow at him.

Who is this man? Why is his attention now focused on Bill?

Warren bristles beside me, and I can see the calm fade from him, and the Army Vet comes out to play. "Now you listen to me. You *will not* disrespect my friend like that." His voice rumbles. "She is *not* going to expose herself to the likes of you." He blatantly lays his hand on his pistol in warning. All the men around do the same. Tension grows in the air.

"Well, he does have a backbone after all," Bill says to Warren. "I was starting to think she was the only one who did." His eyes shift between us but land back on Warren. "I'll tell you what, you can pick *one* of my men to witness that there is *indeed* no mark on her, and we will be on our way, or we can force it, which won't be pretty." He pauses, looking me up and down. "Although...it. Would. Be. Fun," he says, dragging it out.

These men won't let this go. I can tell by the excitement in their faces. Whatever rumors they have heard have piqued an interest in me. If I deny them, trouble will follow and there's only two of us and eight of them. I don't know what comes over me, maybe insanity, but I find the menacing look in the eyes of the cowboy riding the black horse comforting as he pierces Bill with it. There's clearly animosity there. For some unknown reason, I feel I can choose him, and maybe, just maybe…we live to see another day.

Or maybe I've actually lost my damn mind.

Warren starts to speak, and I quickly interrupt him. "Deal," I mutter. The look of shock and outrage on Warren's face kills me, but his life is in my hands. I will not have him die for me.

"Absolutely *not,* Sam!" His eyes bulge as he yells at me, then looks to the men gathered around. "I will not have this! You are disrespecting her privacy!" he spits.

"Warren, stop," I plead. "It's going to be okay." I nod slowly at him, trying to silently convey that I have a plan. His eyes are wild and sweat beads on his brow even in the cool air. We have a standoff with our eyes, but he eventually relaxes his features.

"Are you sure about this?" he whispers.

I nod and see Bill smile with a shit-eating grin as he asks, "Well then, darlin', who will it be?"

I hesitate for only a second before I point to the man on the black horse. His face is stoic, showing no signs of shock or hesitancy. The leader spits to the side in aggravation, clearly pissed he wasn't the chosen one.

"Okay, get on with it then Jake." The rest of the men huff out complaints and slurs.

So that's his name…Jake.

I turn toward him with my head held high to find his unrelenting gaze already on me. I ignore the trembling in my body and dismount my horse quickly before my good senses return. Looking around, I find a few boulders to our left, far enough away from the others for sight or sound.

"Don't do this, Sam," Warren whispers as I walk past his horse. "You can't."

"It's going to be okay," I whisper back. "Trust me…please." I see the hurt in his eyes.

If I am wrong about this man and the looks he was giving Bill, then we will both likely be shot out here in this God-forsaken place and for no reason other than ignorance and misunderstanding.

I hand my reins to Warren and walk toward the boulders. Every step beats in time with my heart. I can see a faint glow of a light heading my way from a lantern Jake is carrying. My heart pounds in my chest, threatening to burst free.

What if I have made a colossal mistake?

As he rounds the stones, he places the lamp on top of one. For the first time, I can see him up close. His tall frame towers over me. His tanned face is lean with a strong jawline and full lips show through the short mustache and beard—a single straight scar, a few inches long, transverses his left eyebrow. It makes him all the more intimidating. I squint as I look into his eyes. They appeared dark and perilous in the saloon, but up close, they are golden flecked and bright in the lamplight—reminding me of whiskey in a crystal glass at sunset. His hair is dark brown, almost black, just like his beard and tuffs of it curl from below his hat. Underneath his black duster, he wears a brown linen shirt with a navy neckerchief rolled loosely around his neck. Hung low from his hips is a double holster sporting two peacemakers. This close to him, I can smell leather and sandalwood.

I stop my scrutiny of him and raise my chin to give him my spiciest bitchy glare, only to find he has beat me to the punch.

"Get on with it, show me," his deep voice growls out. The kind that rumbles in your chest and somehow makes it all the way to your toes.

If I misjudged the looks he was giving Bill or the situation, we are finished.

"You don't even buy me a drink first, but okay." I try to make light of the situation, but he doesn't break a smile.

Now I think I have *really* made a mistake. I take a deep breath and pull my skirt hem up slowly, baring my left thigh, but pause when I see Jake looking at my hands, not my exposed leg. They are trembling. For all the strength I'm trying to feign right now, my body is telling on me—calling me a liar.

His face is placid as he takes my tattered skirts from my hand and proceeds to lift them himself. I gasp and flinch away, but he ignores me and proceeds. His hand grazes my thigh, and goosebumps spring up along the length of my leg. He stops suddenly, and I feel his finger move ever so slowly against my skin, and his brows wrinkle, but then he continues. By the time the skirt reaches above my hip, my chest is rising and falling faster. His brows furrow more with confusion. I peer down and see the purple lace of my panties.

My face instantly heats, and his eyes meet mine. There are so many questions in them. All of which I am praying that he doesn't ask.

I see his chest rise and fall a little too quickly, then he composes himself and drops my skirt. He clears his throat before saying, "Let's see the other side."

This is it, the moment where I have either doomed us or spared us another day.

I grasp the lower hemline of my skirts again and drag them slowly upward. My heart feels like it is beating in my brain as I near my Colt 1911. The fabric moves above the gun, and I see more confusion mar his face. His jaws clench slightly. I don't stop pulling up the skirts until they are clear above my hip.

There, plain to see, is a tattoo curving from my inner thigh around to the top of my hip bone—a mix of flowers and vines I got when I turned twenty-one. And smack dab in the center...a Taurus Zodiac symbol—pointed horns that could be mistaken for something sinister.

Like the devil.

Jake freezes, and I hold my breath. Seconds pass that feel like minutes. All of a sudden, he does something strange. He gently touches the tattoo.

I feel like I might be sick. Sweat breaks out on my brow as I release a shaky breath I was holding. I can feel the anxiety climbing inside me. He continues to smooth his fingers across the design, but he doesn't say a word. He simply looks...*mesmerized*. I can smell the heady aroma coming from him again. His gentle caress is at odds with his imposing presence.

What is he thinking? Why won't he say anything? What is going through that head of his?

Finally, I break. "What are you going to do?" I whisper. "Are you going to tell them? This is not what you think it is. It's...I..." I stumble over my words as his fingers trace the tattoo again.

Jake gently drops the fabric of my layered skirts, and they sway to the ground. Oddly, the warmth I just felt leaves me, and the cold reality seeps in. His hand still rests lightly on my hip. I back a step away, letting his hand drop. We are only a foot apart as he devours my eyes for information. Information that I have *no* intention of sharing with him.

"Say something!" I whisper fiercely.

His stare roams down to my now covered hip slowly and then back to my eyes. "What would I tell them? I didn't see anything." His voice vibrates through my skin.

My mouth drops open, and my brows pinch together as I try to figure out this man and his intentions. I was right to choose him, but what keeps him silent? His face gives nothing away as he leans in close to my ear. His breath along my skin brings new goosebumps to the surface, and I can't seem to form words.

"But now...you owe *me* a favor," he whispers.

Reminiscing

CHAPTER 2

Samantha

"I want to know how the hell you *knew* that man wouldn't turn on us, cause damn it Samantha, you about got us both killed tonight." Warren burns a hole through me with his eyes as he chastises me by the fire.

I bristle at his tone. "I'll have you know, there was *NO* way out of this one. Those men had it in for me and would have stripped me down had I not made that call!" I bite a gamey piece of rabbit from my skewer and chew aggressively to match my temper.

"Ah shit…you're probably right about that, but still…that was bullshit!" Warren tosses his skewer stick into the blazing campfire. "I don't get how you knew he wouldn't tell the others." He looks at me expectantly.

The entire ride back, we didn't talk. We had to make sure we were not being followed. Warren decided it would be best for us to camp elsewhere for the night rather than chance someone following us toward home. I just knew Warren was dying to question me about several things that happened tonight.

Number one being Jake.

I glance at him and then back to the fire before finally answering, "I don't know how to explain it. He didn't seem to enjoy the company he keeps. He was staring at Bill as if he'd rather shoot him than hear another word. There was just…something in his demeanor."

"You mean to tell me that you had a "hunch" based on a mean look he gave that other man? Are you losing it, Sam? We could have been killed tonight. Oh, and where on earth did that story come from about your tattoo?" He swings his head toward me and purses his lips.

I drop my heated face into my hands in embarrassment and mumble, "I may have been bathing by a river some months ago…not long after we got here, actually, and a man was peeping." I feel Warren's shock without even looking at him. "I caught him, and he bolted."

"Oh my God, woman, you gonna give someone a damn heart attack. You should have told me! What if he meant you harm?"

I finally lift my head and peek out at Warren. "He probably *did* mean me harm, but then saw the 'devil's mark' and ran like a bitch."

Warren chuckles lightly. "What did Jake say to you back there? Are we gonna have trouble out of that one?"

I could lie, but what good would that do us? "He said he didn't see anything and that...now I owe him."

Warren's eyes bug out of his head. "Holy shit. That man doesn't look like the type to let this go, either. If he comes near you, I *will* put him down. You hear me!"

I have no doubt in my mind of what Warren is willing to do to keep us alive. He has proven that over and over again. "I know, and I am not some damsel in distress. I can handle myself."

He nods and says, "I'm sure you can, but that's one big asshole out there with a debt he's holding over you. I'm just saying."

"Yeah, it's definitely not good," I sigh loudly.

I can see the moment Warren gives into the night and finally relaxes. His shoulders slump and he stretches out by the fire. I quietly do the same, and we both watch the sky and all its glory. An hour of silence ticks by before Warren speaks again.

"Hey, Sam," He whispers.

"Yes," I mutter.

"I think I am forgetting what home feels like."

Of all the things he could have said...I wish it wasn't that. Tears burn the back of my eyes, and I struggle to keep them from falling. I hate crying, fucking *HATE* it. It makes me feel weak and vulnerable, and I swore I would never feel that way again. But in this moment, with no one around to see me, a single tear leaks down my cheek.

I know how he feels because I, too, am forgetting what home feels like. "You wanna talk about it?" I whisper.

I hear him sigh, then he says softly, "I miss my son."

A knot forms in my throat, and I try to swallow it down. We have talked about the past and what happened several times, but we've both refrained from talking about family. It's too hard and not helpful to reminisce. Here in this breezy desert with no one around to hear us but the stars, I let him relieve some of the ache inside.

"Sam, I wish you would've known him. He was almost finished with med school when...we..." He pauses, then continues, "He was handsome like his father, of course."

A choked giggle comes out of me. "I knew he was in school but had no idea he was almost finished. I know you're one proud papa. I wouldn't knock his looks by comparing them to you, though," I jest as I look his way.

He laughs, but it doesn't quite reach his eyes. "Yeah, you're right. He is much better-looking than me." Warren turns his head to me, too. The fire dances across his skin, and I can see a wet streak down one cheek, and my heart breaks entirely. I can't handle a grown man's tears. "Do you think we are missing persons back home? Do you think we've been forgotten by now?" he mutters.

I turn away and let the sky claim my attention again. "I think that we're probably on an awesome episode of *Dateline*," I feign a laugh, "but forgotten—*you*—no way! You were a legend."

"I don't know about that." He chuckles.

"Are you kidding me? Warren Mathews, master gunny and war vet? Owner of the best damn armory and shooting range ever?"

He beams at me but still shakes his head as if he is as mundane as anyone else. Then he asks me, "What do you miss, Sam?"

"Pizza from Joel's place." I moan loudly for added effect.

"I'm serious, Samantha," Warren huffs.

This conversation is getting too deep, and even my untimely humor isn't helping. I don't want, nor feel the need to reminisce on what I miss. The list is devastatingly long. "I am serious too, *pizza*," I say softly.

"Yeah, yeah, yeah, I know. Anytime the conversation gets too personal, you shut down," he mutters under his breath and turns away from me.

Yes, I shut down. Our entire belief system has been shaken to the core. Any feelings I have about our former life are irrelevant. Conjuring up all these emotions will only lead to depressive thoughts. I have armor around me for a reason. I earned it.

I lie there awake for another hour until I hear the even breaths coming from Warren, indicating he's asleep. Only then do I let myself drift away.

That night, for the first time since we came here, I dreamt of the day it happened. Relived it like a damn sci-fi movie.

Guns, Men, and Cosmic Problems

CHAPTER 3

17 months ago
August 21, 2017

Samantha

I race down the deserted highway, my 454 Big Block roaring louder than the Chris Stapleton song on my antique radio. I crest the ridge and see the signs for the armory. A renewed sense of rightness flows through my veins.

This is what I needed today.

A few minutes later, I park my '68 Chevelle under the one and only tree in the lot to block out some of the sun that will, no doubt, have my ass burning on these leather seats later. It's a massive Frémont Cottonwood tree. I always liked this tree. It's huge, imposing, and a loner, somehow surviving in this heat year after year. The parking lot is barren outside of

Deadeye Armory and Shooting Range today. The Arizona heat is blazing enough to fry an egg on the hood of my car. It could give hell a run for its money. I throw on my boots and socks, cursing under my breath from the scratches on my feet. I hop out and lean into the back seat to grab my duffle bag. It's packed to the brim and hefty to shoulder it. I prop against my car and light up a Marlboro, inhaling deeply.

Today was hard, but from now on, my life belongs to me again. I lean my head back, closing my eyes, and let the warmth envelope me and the nicotine calm my nerves.

"Well, well, back again, are we!" Warren's voice startles me back to the present. He is the range owner and, as of recently, a great friend. "You done got hooked, didn't you." He grins at me.

I smile warmly and toss the cigarette to the ground and smash it out with my boot as I make my way toward the door. I pull my aviator sunglasses down from my head to cover my eyes the closer I get to him. Warren is dressed in his usual tactical green pants and his old military boots that he can't seem to part with. His cadet hat sits low over his eyes and that beaming smile of his is contagious.

"You got me, Warren, I'm hooked." I glance around the parking lot and again notice its barren state. "How am I the only one here today?" I wrinkle my brows. This place is a hot spot for gun enthusiasts.

"Today is the solar eclipse." When he sees my confusion, he blinks and is taken aback. "Do you live under a rock, girl? Everyone is out on the town or having parties on the water somewhere. I know I'm fun and all, but what are *you* doing here?"

I push past him, and we head inside. The air conditioning hits me, and I breathe a sigh of relief. "Damn, it's hot today!"

"You are avoiding my question, Samantha. What are you doing here? Young, pretty girl like yourself should be out having fun."

"It's just an eclipse, what's the big deal? Besides, I thought I'd get in another practice run out back with the targets if that's okay. I didn't really have any plans today..." I keep my head down and fidget as I try to look anywhere but directly at him.

Warren shuffles two chairs over for us by the counter. "Take a load off and cool down. I'll get you set up to shoot in a bit."

I drop my pack and slide into the seat. "Why are *you* not with family today?" I ask.

Warren's lip pulls up into a half smile before he says, "Miles is off in med school, so he's not around much lately."

"That's right, how's Miles doing." I look down and pull out a string from a ripped, frayed hole in my jeans.

"He is so damn smart...acing everything they throw at him," he gushes.

"Must not get that from you," I say, causing him to laugh out loud.

"Nah, must've been Birdie."

I can see the light dim in his eyes whenever he mentions his late wife's nickname. In some of our long talks over guns this past year, we have shared some life stories, too. Bernice was Warren's everything. His whole world wrapped in one person. She passed much too young at the age of forty to breast cancer. The way he talks about her—it's the kind of deep love that people long for to truly exist. And it did for him.

I lift my glasses to wipe away a bead of sweat and see Warren's whole demeanor change. "What in God's name is that?" He points to my eye.

Here it is. The moment I was dreading. I had hoped we would go straight to shooting shit and not have to have this conversation.

Warren stands and moves until he is in front of me. "You take off those glasses, or I'm going to do it for you!" he spits.

I stand, too, backing away a step as I say, "You are not my father, Warren, so stop treating me like it."

"Well, someone has to! What is really going on, Sam? You show up here with a pack and shadows under your eyes. Take off those glasses!" he yells at me. Warren is normally a friendly man, but right now, I see the intimidating veteran in him coming out…and he is terrifying.

"Fine!" I yell back and sling the glasses to the floor.

"What the hell happened to you?" His voice lowers to almost a whisper as he surveys my black eye and then seems to drop his gaze and finally notice my bruises and random scratches.

I hate pity parties, and this is beginning to mirror one. I know what my face looks like. Hell, I stared at it for those few minutes in the bathroom before I forced myself to run.

Warren raises his eyebrow at me expectantly.

I rub the back of my neck while I pace the floor. My black tank top is sticky from sweat, and my jeans are plastered to me. Even my long braid is damp underneath. As uncomfortable as all that is, this conversation is WAY worse.

"It was Trevor," I mutter under my breath.

Warren is silent, I can see his Adam's apple bob as if he is trying to swallow what I'm feeding him. His eyes trail my arms, and I can tell by his furrowed brow when he makes out the faint handprints marking them in several places.

"Damn, Warren, say something. Don't just stare at me!" I yell.

He rolls his shoulders and walks behind his register counter. I see him lift a bottle of Jack Daniels Fire out and two glasses. "*You*," he points the bottle at me, "are going to sit down and have a drink with me, and *then*…you are going to tell me everything."

"You know what? I came here to shoot shit, not have a heart-to-heart!"

"SIT DOWN, SAMANTHA!" his voice booms in the armory.

Well, fuck.

I level him with a glare that would have most men running for the hills, but he just gives it right back to me. "Fine! Let's chat like clucking hens, shall we!" I dramatically flop down into the seat as he ignores my temper and pours us some whiskey.

I sip mine and gratefully let the burn sear my parched throat. Feeling something is better than feeling nothing right? Warren stares at me with round eyes and then nods for me to get on with it.

When I don't say anything for several seconds, he starts without me. "Let me see if I can decipher what you're not saying." He rolls his shoulders, then continues, "The boyfriend, Trevor, that you have told me about before…he put that shiner on you along with all those other marks." I start to say something, but he holds up his hand, stopping me. "You have been coming here for a year and all that time, I've *never* met him. You came to me wanting to be able to protect yourself last year, and I never thought to ask…why." His eyes lose the anger and soften a touch.

"Don't feel bad. I didn't tell anyone," I say as I sip my liquor.

"How long has this been going on?" His eyes bore into mine.

I hesitate, but only briefly. We are in this now, might as well spill it to someone. I sigh heavily. "He changed a few months after we started dating. It wasn't all at once but more like a progression. If you would have asked me in the beginning stages if he'd ever harm me, the answer would have been a resounding no."

Warren rubs his stubbled chin and releases a long, raged breath. "Damn, Sam, I had no idea."

"Well, like I said, no one did." I shrug.

"You didn't even tell your friends? What about your parents or your sister?" He leans in closer, placing his elbows on the glass tabletop.

"No, he alienated my friends, pushing them slowly away from me. I was such an idiot because I didn't see it happening until it was too late. And as for my sister, Jenna moved to Phoenix, and we haven't seen each other much lately. We talk on the phone, but since her move, not as often. And as far as Mom and Dad go...I didn't want to disrupt their new lives. They're running the farm and traveling more—really living."

I can see Warren scrunching his brow in thought as he pours us a little more whiskey. "Living and traveling aside, they're your parents, Sam. You should've told someone; had someone to lean on."

I roll my lips together and look at the floor. He's right, but hindsight is twenty-twenty.

"So, the pack you have." He points to the large black tactical duffle bag on the floor. "Does that mean you left today?"

I nod.

"Are you in trouble? Will he come after you?"

I shrug. "Probably...at some point."

Warren scowls. "You are staying with me today. I welcome the thought of him showing up here." His eyes take on a predatory gleam.

"Let's not get too trigger-happy drunk. We may both very well end up in jail. Anyway, this is my mess to fix. I let it go on too long." I pause and raise my chin higher. "But no more. I'm taking my life back."

"Well then, that *is* something to celebrate, at least." He gives me a reassuring smile. "Let's finish our drinks, enjoy a beautiful creation from God in the sky, and *then* we'll shoot shit." He taps my glass with his.

That's what I love about Warren. He is fiercely loyal and straight to the point. If I'm being honest with myself, I *have* treated him like a father figure for months, probably because I was hiding from everyone else. I can't berate him for acting like one. I have no doubt that this conversation is not over. Warren is a mister-fix-it of all problems, whether it be a jamming gun or a life lesson. He will not stop until he inserts himself in my future well-being.

Thirty minutes later we are prepped for the range. Warren stuffs the bottle of Jack into my pack and gives a sly side smile. "You keep this bottle. I have plenty."

"Thanks," I say as I shoulder my pack and follow him through the armory, grateful for the change in atmosphere. The band Korn plays Coming Undone loud on the outdoor speakers.

Over his shoulder, he asks, "What do you want to start with?"

"I brought something different to shoot today," I say as we step into the inferno that is the desert. I look up briefly to the sky and quickly avert my eyes. The eclipse must be close because my pupils burn, and I see spots behind my eyelids.

He stops short and looks at me with excitement, his eyes crinkling as he grins. "Really! What do you have for me?"

I adjust my bag and unzip the side pocket to reveal my pistol tucked neatly inside. I gingerly pull it out and hand it over to Warren's greedy hands.

"Colt 1911. This is really nice, Sam. Where did you get it?" he asks as he turns the gun over in his hands, examining every inch.

"It was my grandfather's, passed down to me."

He nods his approval as he unleashes the magazine and then pops it back in. "You know, I have something you might wanna see too." He hands me the pistol, and I drop it back into the pouch. "Wait right here, I'll grab it." Warren scurries off into the shop with a distinct pep in his step, bringing a grin to my cheeks. This is his element, this shop, and all these guns.

A few minutes pass, and he emerges from the doorway smiling from ear to ear, holding a rifle. "This here is a Winchester 1876 model lever-action rifle. It was passed down in my family, *always* to the eldest son."

He lays the rifle in my hands. An odd tingling feeling creeps up my forearms. I shake my head. This heat must really be getting to me…or the liquor.

I caress my fingers along the rich color of the walnut stock. It reminds me of dark amber on a tree. "It's beautiful. This must be worth a fortune."

"You have no idea. The first person to own it in my family was a Buffalo Soldier." Pride pours from his face.

I, however, scrunch my brow with curiosity. "What's a Buffalo Soldier?"

"Ah, well, that is a history lesson not taught in all schools." He shakes his head in disapproval. "They were regiments of all-black soldiers created after the Civil War for the peacetime army. One of my ancestors was in the forty-first unit that set out to man the Mexico border and enforce laws in the Texas frontier." The pride in his voice only grows stronger and moves into his eyes.

"To have something like this still in your family all these years later…it's incredible," I whisper. My voice sounds strange and muffled even to my own ears. The tingling feeling in my arms has increased; it's like when your limbs fall asleep. I shake one hand out before I turn the rifle over and see a name engraved on the inner stock. I squint my eyes to try and read the marking, but it blurs. I press my eyelids with one hand, trying to clear my vision.

"You alright, Sam?" I hear Warren's voice, but it sounds far away.

I look around as the desert begins to darken, a clear sign the eclipse is upon us. "I'm fine," I lie and try to shake off the unease streaming through my bones like molten metal. "Who was it…your ancestor?" I ask, pointing to the engraved name.

Warren reaches out and touches the name, gently grazing the stock of the gun. A humming sound feels my ears gradually getting louder. I see Warren trying to answer me. His mouth moves, but I can't hear anything over the humming. It becomes deafening, but then a deep gut-curdling howl mixes in with the noise. I force my eyes open to see Warren drop to his knees as he screams, both of our hands still firmly latched onto the gun, unable to let go.

Seconds seem like hours as my screams join the chorus of his! Every cell in my body is set on fire. I can't move a muscle. Panic seizes my breath and my heart.

Time stands still as we burn.

All of a sudden, I feel my body, my being, combust. And I am no more. Just particles burning through a tunnel of colors and lights.

Take me Home

CHAPTER 4

Samantha

"Samantha, wake up!" I hear someone shout from above me, making me jolt. My eyes pop open, chest rising and falling rapidly. A face comes into view…Warren's panic-stricken face to be exact, and it's hovering.

"Jesus, get off me!" I sit up, pushing him away.

He curls his lip as he stands and shuffles away. "You were screaming in your damn sleep! I was only trying to help," he lashes out.

My shoulders slump, and I lean my head back, soaking up the morning sunrise. Sweat drips from one temple even in the cool morning air. "Sorry," I mumble.

"You wanna talk about that?" he asks, obviously still grumpy that I yelled at him.

"No," I say firmly. That is the *last* thing I need—a pointless conversation that leads to nowhere. If he knows I'm dreaming about that day, he'll worry. Besides, we discussed it enough the day it happened. Nothing new surfaces. We are here and may never know why. I try to leave it at that. Why hope for anything different at this point?

It's been almost *two* years.

Anyway, hope is a bitch that can let you down.

"Alrighty then." He scoffs and begins packing up camp a little too aggressively.

I stumble to my feet and reluctantly begin packing as well. Everything about me aches. My body...my heart. I feel a touch guilty when I see coffee over the fire and salted pork. Here he is, trying to help me in every way, and I can be such as ass to him.

"I'm sorry, Warren...thanks for the food and coffee." I run my hands through my hair to release the knots from sleep and quickly braid the waves.

"It's okay, but I don't see why you feel the need to be so closed off with me." He tosses his saddle across Halle's back with a grunt and continues, "We are in this together. If something is bothering you, then talk about it. Hell, we have *no one* else to talk to but each other."

I roll my eyes and huff but finally give in. "I dreamt of the day we came here."

He stops short, and his eyes soften. His worried brows pinch together, and I can see his mind has wandered back there, too. "Did you remember anything that might be helpful? Anything new?"

I make my coffee and chew on a piece of the salted pork. "No, same as always. The burning felt so real. It's like I was nothing more than specks blazing through a tunnel. It kinda felt like evaporating." I shudder.

Warren runs his hand over the back of his neck and looks haunted as he says, "I can still feel it, too, sometimes."

We pack the rest in silence as the morning sun grows higher in the sky. We both felt like we had eluded the gang from last night and didn't seem to have any indication that we were being followed. So, we ride—heading toward home. That is strange to even think.

Home.

Being on the outskirts of Tombstone, Arizona gives me a small amount of comfort…it's where I grew up, after all. This boomtown officially got the name Tombstone last year. It blew our minds to be here when Ed Schieffelin, the miner who discovered the silver, laid claim. We witnessed a moment in history. The awe of it is not likely to wear off.

We will stick around for as long as we can but knowing the history of this place…there's no way we can stay forever. However, tempting it might be to meet the famed Wyatt Earp and Doc Holiday.

We steer clear of people for the most part—keeping to ourselves unless supplies are needed. The Wild West is a rough-and-tumble place where justice is a touchy thing. We are supposed to be able to trust in the law, but not here. Here, you trust no one. After the Civil

War, most were expecting everything to resemble a reflection of peacetime, but between the Apache conflict and civilians taking the law into their own hands, this place is anything but peaceful. Some of the same men wearing the badges are the dirtiest of them all.

My thighs burn from many hours spent in the saddle and gathering supplies. Clint has immense stamina, but even he seems to hang his sweet head a bit lower as we crest the last hill. I reach down and rub his thick black mane, give him all the praises for being a good boy, and whisper to him, "Take me home, boy."

I can see our house in the distance. Small, but made with purpose and drive. Every bit built by our own hands. It's secluded on all sides by mountains. One would have to be intentionally coming this way to find us. Building here was Warren's idea, and I have to say, it was the right call. We haven't had one straggler come along…so far.

Everything we've acquired has come from selling the jewelry I had stashed the day we came here. Somehow, everything on our persons came with us the day we were zapped from our reality and deposited into another. We made a decent amount to get us started with horses and building supplies, but it took most of a year, all of our wits with bartering, and many wagon loads to get us where we are today.

Warren and I part ways at our makeshift barn. We both share various duties—both trying to pull our own weight around here. I clean the stalls and tend to the horses and other livestock we've acquired. I also make all of our toiletries by hand and laundry the clothes. Warren works the land and restocks the wood and feed bins we built. He also creates new and impressive ways for us to feel more at home. The most impressive things being indoor plumbing and a hot water reservoir. Not prevalent in these parts, it would likely turn a head or two if people were to see his double-tanked contraption constructed off the ground.

We built a bathtub inside and have an extra-large tin tub outside with the hot pipe meeting through the wall between each. This way, we have hot water in both if needed. I have white curtains strung from clotheslines, forming a square around the one outside for privacy. We spent the better part of two months perfecting water filtration with charcoal and creating effective ways to stay clean and healthy. We even mined for zinc ore and then roasted it carefully to obtain the powder form, zinc oxide. I add nut tree butters and oils extracted from flowers to form aromatic deodorants and much-needed sunscreen, among other uses.

After trial and error, I have perfected a paste for our teeth and many medicinal tinctures. Some of those oils and lotions I make have become popular with the saloon girls in surrounding towns. I love to see the smiles on the women's faces when they try new, alluring scents I've created to entice men. Doing this reminds me of my apothecary back home and what it could have been had I been there to continue my renovations. It brings me a little peace to continue doing something that has always interested me and been such a passion of mine.

While finishing up chores, I run the outdoor bath to the brim with steaming water. My hands ache from crushing and bottling each and every different plant I've harvested lately. I make a few tinctures and leave the rest to dry out. By the time I have cleaned the stalls and unloaded all the supplies from the saddle packs and wagon, I am exhausted. The day's errands have left me beat down and yearning for that bath. I tip-toe through the house to find Warren out cold in his bedroom. Creeping through slowly so as not to wake him, I gather my nightgown and toiletries. Right before I slip out the back door, I snatch a biscuit and the whiskey off the counter.

It's no Jack Fire, but it will do.

Twilight is settling into the desert, and the last rays of sunlight paint the sky in brilliant shades of orange and yellow with streaks of red streaming through. It is breathtaking.

Seeing as I am quite alone, I turn back the curtains allowing me an unencumbered view of that sunset. I drip several drops of lavender oil into the tub, then hang my hat on the closest rusty nail I can find. I shed my clothing piece by piece. Lastly, I place my toiletries and Colt pistol on the wooden table beside the bathtub. Inch by inch, I ease myself into the fragrant bliss. The cool evening breeze mixed with the heat of the water is pure bliss and welcoming to my sore muscles. I drop below the surface long enough to thoroughly soak my hair and then rise again to lather myself from top to bottom.

Once my body and teeth are scrubbed profusely, I finally relax into the flowery scent and sip from my whiskey bottle as that sunset holds me captive.

Strange Wild Creature

CHAPTER 5

Jake

It's late in the day by the time I reach the edge of a ridge, following the hoof tracks imprinted into the dusty earth. I managed to keep my distance last night as I watched her sleep.

Samantha…that's her name.

She tossed and turned, crying softly, trapped in some hell inside her mind. Temptation almost gave me away. It was torture not waking her from whatever nightmare plagued her sleep. I stayed hidden, if for no other reason than to just watch her. This strange, wild creature.

Bill's obsession with her has me concerned. I don't trust him as far as I could throw the bastard, but I need not jump to conclusions. I heard the rumors too, but everyone's a damn gossip and thrives on talking shit. I paid it no mind, until last night. We sauntered right into that saloon, and there she was like a beacon in the night…and so obviously out of place. I'm still not sure why I bothered lying for her. Maybe it goes back to the trust issues I have with Bill. He did hire me to track them. He's still curious as to who these two are and why they're so elusive and standoffish. Even if Bill hadn't hired me, I would have gone willingly. I need to learn more…to know who she is.

Where did they come from?

Everything, from the curious mark over her hip to the smooth silk of her legs, has me absolutely wrecked. I simultaneously want to condemn her for her wickedness but also bask in it. Her eyes are hauntingly bright—not quite blue, not quite green, but somewhere in the middle.

As my mare crests the ridge, I see the mountains give way to a small hidden valley. Nestled in the center is a farm. Animals meander about in the pastures. I've ridden all over this desert and never encountered this house before. Smoke billows from a chimney. Other than the animals, everything is quiet. I can just make out a distinctive dappled gray horse in the fence.

This is it. This is where she lives.

After tying up my horse, I go the rest of the way on foot to inspect the surroundings—careful not to disturb the ground and shake loose any stones. I weave in and around boulders and wild brush until I finally reach the valley below. The sun is setting lower on the horizon. I have precious little time before I'll need to venture back out and make camp.

I hunker down and creep along the property, listening for any sounds—hearing nothing but animals at first…then all of a sudden, I hear the faintest moan, then an alluring sing-song voice. It reminds me of sailor's tales of sirens in the night. My mouth goes dry and my entire being goes rigid as I peek around the corner of the barn.

There…for all the world to see, is Samantha. Naked. In an outdoor bathing tub.

Sunsets and Revelations

CHAPTER 6

Samantha

I sing *Wild Horses*—what words I can remember— as I soak up the calm moment. A simple tune from home gives my heart comfort and my mind clarity. Sometimes, I feel like my former life never happened, but then I remember a song or the distinct taste of a favorite food. That's when I know for certain that I'm not crazy—that this is real.

I sink down into the water until it covers my head, and I hold my breath. Thirty seconds go by before I surface, sucking in a gulp of cool evening air. Blindly, I swipe at my eyes to clear them while reaching for the bottle of whiskey. Just as I blink and regain my vision…my heart slams into my chest.

There's a man standing over me. I hear the click of the hammer going back on his revolver. The dark figure is shadowed by the sun setting behind him, and his black hat is pulled low over his face. My chest rises and falls rapidly as I locate my gun, *sadly*, a few feet away.

"Hello again, witch," the man says in a gruff, familiar voice.

I hold absolutely still as his head lifts, revealing those golden-flecked eyes with slivers of amber. They pierce my soul with an intensity I've never known. The scowl on his face is at odds with his wandering gaze, which is lazily traveling the length of my *very* naked body.

Immediately, I regain self-control and take a reassuring breath. I mask my features and force myself to relax, resting my arms along either side of the tub.

"Witch huh? Am I in the wrong decade?" I internally laugh at how *right* that question is. "Thought burning witches at the stake died out years ago…guess not." I raise one brow as I gauge his every move. I take a long sip from the whiskey that I still hold in one hand. Voices are screaming in my head to yell for Warren, to grab for the gun anyway, but I hold steady. The past me would have covered my body—screamed for help. Not anymore. I am no longer her. She died the day the world was eclipsed in darkness.

"That's debatable." He gives a sly side smile, then continues, "I personally don't care for the smell of burning flesh, but a bullet to the head…" He gives a sinister grin.

I peer at him through my wet lashes and remain as still as possible. He is either here to harm me, here to collect his debt for not outing me, or out of sheer curiosity, but one thing is for sure…someone sent him.

"Bill sent you…to follow me." I can tell I am right by the slight shift of his body. "What exactly do you hope to discover out here? Séances and sacrifices?" I smirk at him. "I quite like my animals alive and of use to me, and I don't converse with the living, let alone the dead."

He remains stoic. "Where did you come from?" He lowers his voice but not the gun, which is still aimed with a steady hand at my head.

I move the bottle to my lips and take another sip. There's no way in hell I am telling him anything. When I move a little too quickly to set the bottle down, I see Jake tense up. I hold my hands up and ease down lower in the tub, hoping the murky water is covering most of me.

"Easy cowboy, I *am* an unarmed woman, remember."

He glances at the gun near the tub. "Where did you come from, and where did you get that…gun? It is a gun, that much I'm for certain," he growls out. His eyes grow hard the more silent I remain. "Answer my questions, witch."

"If I was a witch, you would know it…I'd probably curse you first." I slant my eyes at him and watch a smirk play at his lips. Good. There's a little humor buried in him. "*And* if you wanted me dead…or Bill wanted me dead, I would be *dead* by now." I lean my head back and stare into those piercing whiskey eyes.

He will get nothing out of me. I decide to divert the questions.

"Why did you help me? Why not tell Bill and the others what you saw? Would have saved you the trouble of coming all the way out here for little old' me."

Jake's demeanor changes slightly; he clenches his jaw and uncocks the hammer on his pistol, holstering it, but doesn't release my stare. My breathing becomes easier the moment I am no longer facing a loaded weapon. The sun has fully set behind him, and the glow of my lantern illuminates our surroundings. The steam barely rises above the rapidly cooling water that I am submerged in.

He cocks his head to the side and squints his eyes. "I haven't decided yet if you are, in fact, worth this trouble or not." He rubs his beard. "I'm not in the business of killin' women," he admits. "I knew what would happen if I told them. Let's just say…killin' wasn't the only thing on their minds."

A shudder works through me at his implication, but I hide it the best I can. "You are not in the business of killing women…yet your gun was aimed at my head. You are decidedly confusing."

"I never said I *wouldn't* kill a woman…just don't care for it." He grins, and it almost looks genuine before his usual scowl replaces it. "You gonna tell me where you come from, or are we going to have problems?"

I laugh, gently throwing him off guard. "Problems…troubles, they fight for my company, cowboy. I am no stranger to this song and dance." I pause, biting my lip before saying, "Would you like a dance?" I curl my lip as I taunt him.

His gaze has dropped to my mouth and seems frozen there. Heat blossoms in my face. Taunting is one thing, but if I've pushed him too far…who knows what this man is capable of? His eyes move over my face and notice the blush on my cheeks. He smiles knowingly.

"Wipe that look from your face before I do it for you," I snap.

"What's the matter, witch? You seem flustered."

My mouth drops open. "Men who point guns at my head and ride with a gang of assholes don't do it for me…so don't flatter yourself," I sneer at him, wishing the heat would disperse from my blasted cheeks.

All of a sudden I hear Warren fumbling around in the kitchen, most likely brewing some coffee. I shoot a panicked look over my shoulder and then back to Jake. I could scream. Now is the time to scream…so why am I silent? What am I waiting for?

"Until next time…Samantha," Jake whispers. The sound of my name from his lips rolls over me like molasses.

My brows furrow intensely as I watch his dark silhouette eventually blend into the night. He's nothing more than a shadow in the deft way he moves about the land. I take a gulping breath in. My hands tremble as I dry myself off and hurry into the house. Still being as silent as possible so as not to alert Warren, I sneak to my room.

Once I am under the covers in my bed, I grip my gun tightly and try to calm my shaky breaths. For all the strength I portray, the danger is not lost on me. Baiting Jake and teasing may have gotten me by tonight, but he will be back; he will not stop until he has answers. Once again, I worry that I misjudged him initially. A revelation sinks into me…he could lead the rest of them straight to me—could be doing it right now.

All of this trouble because of a damn tattoo.

To Unpaid Debts

CHAPTER 7

Samantha

Two weeks later, Warren and I are traveling with our wagon into Tombstone for supplies. Some still call it Goose Flats. We had only one reason to stay close to this area and that reason was hope. We thought if we stayed near the spot where we arrived, maybe one day, we would hear the humming again—be able to go home.

But, as I have said before, hope is a bitch.

I am weary from tossing and turning each night. The unknown plaguing my thoughts and—as much as I hate to admit it—Jake inhabiting my dreams. I play out every word we exchanged as if I will discover something new.

What is his end game here? He lied for me of his own volition, but of course, Bill had to send him my way, still not trusting our odd duo. Why lie for me twice? By now, if he told the others where we live, surely they would be stalking me out. I roll my shoulders, trying to loosen up some of the tension gathered there. Why does Bill care anyway? Herbal remedies are abundant throughout these parts nowadays. I'm not that strange in comparison to other women healers. Although, the real problem is that dick that saw my tattoo spreading rumors.

"What's up with you?" Warren says through a bite of jerky. "You been acting weird for days." He cuts his eyes at me.

I quickly avert mine as I roll my lips together. "I'm good, just tired." An ache forms in my chest from guilt. I never told Warren about Jake following us. If he knew, he would be sitting by the window with a gun every night. I didn't want to cause him to lose sleep, and maybe I just wasn't ready to tell it yet. Something keeps me from outing Jake. However, we worked too hard to make a life in those canyons and I can't have anyone ruining that. We are nice and secluded out there and plan to stay that way until we can figure out what happened to us and maybe…just maybe, get back to the future.

Ugh, there goes that hope again.

Regardless of whether my decision to keep it to myself proves to be detrimental or not, the guilt is there sitting in me like curdled milk.

"Uh, huh," he mutters. "I've been with you long enough to know when something's up…and something is *up*." He shoots me a glare and jabs a finger skyward.

"Eat your damn jerky, Warren, and quit analyzing me."

He scowls but drops it, thankfully. We ride in silence for a while, opening space in my head for all manner of worries to scurry about. While the most pressing is Jake and his band of assholes, there is comfort in the fact that there's been no sign of him since that night. Although I have had the eerie feeling of being watched for days.

I get goosebumps just thinking about it, and my pistol never leaves my side.

Today is all about adequate supplies to get us by so that we can stay secluded from people. I shove aside the anxiety I feel building as we round a bend in the trail and see the town shimmer into view like a mirage. It's hard to believe that this place will remain relatively the same, become a tourist town for people longing for gunslinging actors and saloon reenactments, while the rest of the world will move on.

Warren breaks the silence again as he shifts in the squeaky wooden seat and says, "Have you thought about it anymore? How we could get back," Warren whispers as we get closer to the people bustling about.

Of course I have. Even when I try hard not to. I have replayed that day over and over, hoping to have a clear-cut answer to what occurred. "I remember every detail, yet none of it makes sense." I lower my voice more as we pass a lady carrying a crying child across the street. I pull my distressed leather cowboy hat lower over my eyes. My hair is tucked in nicely today so as not to draw too much attention. I went for the breeches and button-down top with my lighter duster jacket, hoping that I would be less noticeable to the opposite sex.

"We know we were both holding that old gun of yours—" I mutter.

"The 1876 Winchester," Warren interrupts me.

It's the only thing that made sense really. We went back to the same year that *particular* gun was made. "Yes, well, if you recall, we have tried over and over again to recreate that day, with no success." I huff. We've held the gun together, even tried other items from our time period. We even built our house near the property where Warren's gun range will one day be, just to be in the same location. In case history does, in fact, repeat itself.

And every time, I felt like a fool. Standing there waiting on something…anything to occur. We both knew the eclipse was the key. There was a total solar eclipse the day it happened and one here in this time when we "landed."

"Maybe some cosmic event happened during the eclipse. Whatever it was, there's no way to know for sure and only one true way to try and recreate it…and that would take an eclipse. Better to not dwell on it," I grumble.

"Don't lose hope, Sam. You just never know how any day will go. Maybe we were meant to be here…for a greater purpose. You have to have faith that we are doing what we were meant to be doing." He grins at me as we pull our horses up next to some hitching posts outside of Myra's Baked Goods.

"You have enough faith for the both of us...so hush and let me be the sour one," I mutter as we dismount and tie the horses.

I hear his chuckle as we part ways. Warren always goes straight for the elderly man Clifford, who sells the grain and seeds beside Myra's place. We have hidden away a pretty penny from the items we've sold. We never bring much with us. Robberies happen every day. No. We keep ours hidden at home and bring only what we need from our list.

In the wagon, I grab out a pack of the goods I brought to exchange. I can see inside the bakery that Myra's busy with an ornery customer, so I take a seat on the bench beside the front door. I remember the first time that I met Myra. She was so warm and humble. She never had personal questions for me. She seemed to know I didn't want to be asked. Instead, she welcomed me with open arms and has been one of the very few people that I communicate with regularly.

Men and women walk the dirt streets today. Some of them are clearly pioneers, some gamblers, and a few lawmen. Three women across from me are laughing and fanning themselves in their fancy dresses and finery while two gentlemen charm them with tales of bravery that sound a little far-fetched. I can see the balcony of the saloon from where I sit, and a girl in a low-cut dress leans over, waving at a cowboy passing by—her breasts barely contained. I cover my grin as the cowboy almost falls from his horse, trying to watch her.

Leaning my head back, I enjoy the warm breeze of the day. I'm glad the weather is changing, but not sure that I am quite ready for the Arizona heat in the dead of summer.

I shudder at the thought.

"Nice damn day, isn't it?" a crackly voice says to my right.

I lift my head and look to find a tiny old woman, not even five foot tall, who has taken the seat beside me. Her fluffy gray curls are haphazardly sticking out around her silk and lace-covered cap. She is meticulously folding a napkin over and over again as her vacant hazel eyes stare into the street.

I clear my throat and finally answer, "Yes, it *is* a nice damn day." I wait for her to giggle or respond, but she stares out into the streets at nothing. "What's your name?" The little old lady doesn't say a word. "You live around here?" I try again.

Nothing.

Okayyy. What the hell? About that time, Myra Benton comes through the door swinging a cloth over her shoulder and patting her flour-covered hands on her cream-colored apron. Her dark hair, with its few gray streaks in the front, is up in the usual chignon. Flour dots her sweet face.

"Oh! Hello there, Sam…did you bring me some goodies today!" she belts out before wrapping me in a quick hug. I am *NOT* a hugger, but it's hard to tense up when she has such a loving aura about her. She must be a Pisces, with her empathic abilities and creative nature. She is my biggest fan when it comes to my handmade lotions and toiletries. I've been trading with her for a few months now.

"I did. Can we go to the back?" I ask, looking around. I don't like to dabble and trade with too many people. That caused a stir near Prescott already.

"Absolutely! Follow me," she whispers.

Beside us, the strange old lady swings her head in my direction and stops me with her vacant glare. "You are not from here, traveler!"

My blood chills. "Excuse me?"

"Travelers have to pay their debts!" she mumbles.

I gape at her, but before I can reply, Myra shakes her head at the lady and steps in. "I see you've met Judith Lambert, my great aunt. You'll have to ignore her. She's a little…off." Myra looks at me and rolls her eyes, and sighs. "She's also half-blind and can get *very* mouthy. God love her. Pay her no mind, dear, and follow me."

I look back to Judith, but she has turned her attention toward the dirt road. I get an eerie feeling about her but shake it away. I turn and follow Myra through the bakery until we reach the backroom. As I lay out everything on the counter, I ask, "How have I never seen her…Judith?"

"Well, for one, you are a recluse deary, and for two, she doesn't get out much either. I look after her now that she has no one left. Her husband Ray was the love of her life, and he passed a few years ago. She hasn't been right since. He was the life of the town, always had an improper joke to tell but a warm smile for Miss Judith."

I grin as I mull that over while I watch Myra excitedly pick up each and every item inhaling deeply the fragrant scents. I finally perfected the craft of making a shampoo that actually cleans and doesn't leave my hair feeling like sticks. I have dabbled in a few medicinal tinctures but need much more practice.

Back home, I was the proud owner of Emerald Moon Apothecary. My parents helped me save and taught me the ropes of running your own business. It was a rundown, lonely building near the edge of town needing renovations and lots of TLC. Either way, I had a shop and a name for it. The rest would come with time and hard work. Mom and Dad were so proud. I could hardly keep Mom from hanging out there daily to brag on how successful I would be one day when it was finished.

I had planned to incorporate an area for reading and coffee in the back that led out to a deck with a view of the stunning Arizona landscape. I dreamt of plants hanging everywhere, full bookshelves, dark and moody vibes, with herbal tinctures and teas. I was mostly accustomed to making lotions, shampoos, conditioners, chapsticks, and body butters, but I envisioned the shop to be so much more. A place for peace and enlightenment. Living here now, I really wish I had studied more about medicinal plants. The business wasn't open yet. Mainly because Trevor was a controlling asshat who rarely allowed me the time needed to work on it.

What an idiot I was.

As Myra selects each jar and vial she wants to try for herself and sets aside a few to sell, she blurts out, "Oh my, I have some exciting news…the whole town is celebrating in a few weeks. Tombstone is growing day by day, and the mayor decided, in a town meeting, that the local business owners need to come up with some ways to bring in even *more* business to our area. Debates were had, and many ideas were thrown around, but this is what was settled upon…next weekend will be an auction, the week after that will be a fun-loving celebration for artists, musicians, and anyone of talent." Myra pauses to dab some rosemary lotion into her palm. "The weekend after that is more geared for inventors and scientist. Later…into June, we are having a Wild West Show! Ladies will all be dressed in their finest attire, and the gentlemen clean up nice, too." She winks and laughs. "The silver mining is still profiting, and the mayor has declared we are in desperate need of many celebrations." She pauses, beaming at me. "Would you want to attend one, if not all?" she asks hopefully.

My mouth opens, but nothing comes out right away. I…*we*, don't do those types of things. We steer clear of crowds. Too much attention is never a good thing. "Umm, I don't think that's a good idea. Besides, I don't have anything to wear." I look down at my dusty breeches and scuffed boots. "I have like one dress, and it's tattered." I pick at my duster nervously. I haven't cared one bit what I look like since the day we came here until this moment. It would be kind of nice to dress decent for a change.

"Oh, honey," she grasps my hand in her warm ones, "I have the perfect thing for you. It was my daughter Milly's; she's outgrown some of her dresses since childbirth, and you can have a few of them if you want."

I look at her hands wrapped in mine, and out of nowhere, my eyes burn with unshed tears. The last time I felt that kind of comfort was with my mother. Shaking it off, I look to her. "I couldn't possibly."

"I'll not take no for an answer, dear!" She smiles broadly. "Besides, you are an absolute catch. Why you are still single is beyond me...if I looked like you..." She trails off, eyeing me up and down, and then waggles her eyebrows. We both giggle together.

What else can I say, I will not turn down such a compliment and generous gesture. Warren and I could use some adult interactions other than each other's. I feel like this is either a monumentally terrible idea or just what we need...change.

Two hours later, we are finished with trading and purchasing what we need. It will get us by for a time anyway. I stored the lovely dresses in the wagon last and made sure they were wrapped carefully.

I take a seat in Big John's Saloon and flag down Big John himself, propping my boots on the rail lining the bottom of the cherry bar. He takes a napkin and blots his plump red face. John is one of few townspeople who's taking a liking to us besides Myra. The feeling is mutual. It's hard not to like his contagious smile and kind brown eyes.

"You want your usual Sam?" He wipes a glass and nods toward the line-up of whiskey. "And one for Warren too?"

It's sad that we have a *usual* drink. "Yes, thank you, that would be lovely," I say as I relax on the worn stool. John passes me two double shots of whiskey. I slide one to my right, knowing Warren is never far behind.

The saloon is quieter than usual this evening. A few patrons looming about the room—one stumbling up the stairs. There are a few frilly girls dressed far too nice for the likes of the men that will—no doubt—fill the room tonight, searching for someone to warm their beds.

I watch John tenderly wipe the wood counter and meticulously line up the liquor bottles. For a humble establishment, he's made this place a touch more charming with its brighter tapestries and drop-down globe lighting twinkling due to the array of crystals dangling from the bottom. A smile graces my face at the pride I see in Big John. It's clear that he's doing something he loves.

My smile fades because I recall with vivid detail what that feeling was like.

Just as I take my first sip of the liquid gold, the stool beside me creaks when someone sits down.

"For me? You really shouldn't have." That voice curls around me like barbed wire, caging me in.

I lick my lips and sit the glass down without looking his way. "Considering you've lifted my skirts *and* seen me naked." I lower my voice to a purr. "I'd say you owe *me* a drink…and you're welcome for the view, by the way."

Big John chokes on some water across from us, and I instantly regret what just blurted from my mouth. Why does his presence provoke me so?

I finally turn my head toward Jake. His beard is a tad thicker than last week. His handsome face and whiskey eyes are alight with what looks to be… amusement.

"You're right…I owe you for the enticing view, but don't forget who the debt really belongs to here," he whispers. He takes a large swig from what was supposed to be Warren's glass.

I sit a little straighter, perturbed at his flippant attitude. "My mind is a bit foggy, wanna tell me what it is, *exactly*…that I owe you," I reply, keeping my voice low so that no more bystanders get an ear full.

Jake gives a lazy side smile that has my body warming in places it shouldn't be. What the hell is wrong with me?

He bites his lower lip before saying, "To. Be. Determined."

I have to forcefully remove my eyes from his lips and turn away. "Well then." I grasp my glass and clink it into his. "To unpaid debts." I down the whole thing, coughing slightly after the burn.

"To unpaid debts," he repeats and takes a drink. I see him watching me the whole time from the corner of my eye.

I'm stewing inside at how ridiculous my body is reacting to this man...this literal gunslinging asshole. I'm over this cat and mouse game he has going on. Who the hell does he think he is anyway? I push a coin across the counter to Big John and begin to rise from the stool, but a hand clamps down on my arm.

"Remove your hand before I remove it for you," I growl. Flirtatious jibes and quirky banter are one thing, but touching is another.

"I think you better sit down, wouldn't want you to cause a scene, and perhaps townspeople may get the wrong idea about you." His voice is low but commanding. His brows are lowered over his threatening glare.

With a huff, I reluctantly sit back down. I take a deep, settling breath to calm my frayed nerves and ask, "What do you want from me, Jake?"

"Not sure yet, but the pleasure of your company and witty conversation will do right now," he says languidly.

His hand still rests on my arm, burning into it like a brand. I look down at it and then yank my arm away. "Isn't there loads of women in this town willing to babble on to you endlessly?" I raise my hand for John to slide me another.

He leans in, whispering into my ear. "None that carries a foreign weapon strapped to her hairless leg and a mark like none I've *ever* seen."

I refuse to look his way as I try to school my features. My pulse quickens, and my hands tremble slightly as I reach for my glass. Hairless leg, he said. I had laser hair removal several times in the years before, but I also squirreled away my razors in that duffle and can't help but indulge in using them once in a while. Then my brows pinch together, and I swing my head toward his. "You've seen tattoos...I mean...um markings?" I blurt out—that part of his statement finally registering.

He smiles, no doubt enjoying that he lured me into conversation. "Very few. Asians working the train tracks sometimes have ones representing something in their culture, and natives too, but I have never seen *anything* like what you have."

I stare bewildered. I had forgotten that needling was rare but happened in native communities in the Wild West and some sailors, too. I look away and fiddle with my nails. This is good. At least I'm not *that* unusual.

Albeit people would still want to either light me on fire or avoid me altogether if they saw the zodiac portion of mine. The fact that I'm a woman having one at all is still strange and looked down upon. I think about the first part of his statement, the foreign gun. I can work with that. Maybe it could be from another country. That could explain it.

He picks my silence apart, reading me far too easily. "You thinking of more lies to tell, trying to weave them together?" He cocks his head to the side as he towers over me, even on the stool.

"A lady's business is her own."

"Maybe so, but secrets tend to have a way of revealing themselves. They never stay buried forever." Jake leans over me, and it's suffocating, his proximity.

"No, but bodies do." I sneer at him.

His laugh has me struggling not to smile, too. His face relaxed and happy is at odds with the shadowy figure I'm used to. "Well, I'll be damned...he laughs," I mutter and roll my eyes. When his grin fades, the light still lingers in his eyes. That heated look he gives me is too much. I need this man far...far away from me. I can't have anyone digging into my life or Warren's. I decide on a more straightforward approach. "Jake, I need this to stop."

"What needs to stop?"

"This." I gesture, flicking a hand between us. "I am no one. Nothing. Definitely not worth all this trouble."

There's a hint of humor in his tone as he says, "It's no trouble at all. Did you think that you are my only reason for being here? I do have a life, Samantha."

I blink a few times, warmth burning my cheeks, feeling self-centered. I look down at the bar. Why is he so unnerving and such an ass? "Well...that's good. Go, do whatever it is that you are here for. Don't come looking for me any longer."

Suddenly, he grasps my chin with his long fingers, forcing me to look him in the eyes. Shock is an understatement. Although his grasp is gentle, it's the command in his eyes that speaks volumes. His face is inches from mine, and I can smell a mix of whiskey and mint on his breath. I try to pull away, but his other hand rests on my shoulder, keeping me close as he leans in. My eyes skirt around the bar, but no one is watching. I can feel panic rising.

"I don't know who you really are or where you come from, but I will. Time reveals everything." He leans in as if he's about to kiss me. My mouth drops open as a soft breath releases.

I should pull away. I should slap him.

His eyes cut through me as he says, "We will never be done, you and I; I look forward to our encounters...dream about them," his voice low and enticing.

Suddenly, the spell is broken as he tips my hat down in the front and winks at me. He tosses some coin down for John and gets up. I notice enough coin for both of our drinks sit on the counter. My chest rises and falls quickly as I try to regain my composure.

"Until next time, witch," he mutters softly as he leaves the saloon.

I sit there far too long, imagining two scenarios. One where I punch him in his smug face, and two where he closes that minuscule distance, and his lips touch mine.

It's official. I have been lonely far too long, and the prospect of human touch is alluring, even from that asshole.

Fucking Beans

CHAPTER 8

Samantha

"Fuck this place!" I rage as I try to repair a broken fence. Halle decided today was a good day to kick the shit out of a pole when Clint tried to get fresh with her.

After several more minutes, I finally got it secured in place. Sweat trickles down my spine, even though it's just April. I removed my jacket hours ago and am left in tan breeches and riding boots. I'm wearing my navy tank top that Warren has bitched at me for keeping. I refused to part with clothing in that duffle bag that I keep hidden. Besides, no one will see it out here in the middle of bum fuck Egypt.

After finishing my chores, I go into the house and put on a pot of beans. "Yay, more fucking beans," I gripe. I cut up some bread I made yesterday into chunks and leave the knife and homemade butter on the table.

I've been in a right pissy mood since the encounter at the saloon with Captain JakeAss a week ago. He has no right to question or stalk me, for that matter! Why do I let him get to me? What is his deal? I should have told Warren about both incidents. Let him shoot him in the face, and we could toss him over a cliff. Okay, maybe I need to take a break. My anger is sitting inside me like a caged beast.

Where the hell is Warren? I peek out the window and look around the valley and toward the distant mountains but see no signs of him. He left on Clint hours ago to hunt but normally isn't gone this long.

I twist my long hair into a messy bun and use an old hair tie from my bag to secure it as I stir the beans. It's been three days since I saw Jake. His words are making it impossible not to think of him and wonder what's next. What are his intentions? Why do I even care?

I vow to myself that he will take up space in my head no longer! And with that, I smile and give a little nod for no one to see.

The sun is low in the sky…four o'clock, maybe. The light streams in through the windows. I start a fire in between cooking. The nights here still bring a chill into the house, but soon, we will be roasting out here.

I can't seem to sit still, so I begin cleaning and organizing what little we have. As I do, my stress slowly starts to abate. I just need to keep my mind on something...anything else besides *him*. Shit...there I go again!

I shake my head and focus on the house. Looking around while I clean, it's hard not to appreciate everything we built in a little over a year. This place is small, rustic, and would probably be considered a shit hole in the future, but it's home to us. It is a result of desperation, drive, and pure survival. It makes me realize how blind and naive we are in the future. We took so much for granted.

Not now. *Now*, we know the difference between needs and wants. Our home is small but sturdy, comfortable, and logical. We used adobe bricks on portions of the house and logs where we could. The clay mixture we made the bricks from has helped with insulation in the extreme temperature differences the desert can bring. The kitchen and living room are open, but the restroom we built is secluded beside my bedroom on one side of the house, while Warren's is on the other. I am grateful every damn day that Warren is a handyman. I have no idea where I'd be without him.

I make a bowl of beans. Just as I plop down in the squeaky dining chair and take my first bite, I hear the sound of boots scuffling outside on the porch. I curse under my breath and gently place the bowl on the table and tiptoe to my holster thrown haphazardly on the counter. I ease out the pistol and creep along the house to peer out the window. I would've heard Warren ride up. Clint nickers whenever he lays eyes on Halle, so he's a dead giveaway if he's near. My heart races, my chest rising and falling fast, but I see no one. I wait a minute…then two. Nothing.

I slip quietly to the door, but just as I reach for the knob, a voice sounds from the other side. "Nice place you have here. Mind if I come in?" Jake casually asks.

I don't move or breathe. He sure has balls; I'll give him that. Warren is somewhere out there. He could be here at any minute, and if he sees Jake…someone may not survive it. For all the niceties Warren shows to the townspeople, he would bury a body if it meant keeping me safe.

"Come now, open up. I know you're in there." He sounds almost playful.

I clench my teeth and mutter a curse word. "What do you want, Jake? Warren will be here any second."

"I just wanna talk. I'll leave my guns outside if that makes you feel better."

I hear him move on the porch, and I sprint over to the window to see him laying his guns on our rocker. His eyes meet mine, and he raises his hands in a gesture of surrender. What the hell? There's no peace in this God-forsaken place. I huff and move for the door, collecting myself before slamming it open and aiming my pistol straight for his head.

"You are crossing several lines. What. Do. You. Want!" I emphasize each word as I yell at him.

Jake's hands are still raised, but he doesn't even bother looking at the gun. His brows are knitted together as he looks at my chest.

I glance down to see my low-cut tank top.

"Eyes up here Jake." I wiggle the gun for emphasis.

He finally drops his hands and raises his eyes to my gun. "I'm an unarmed male…you gonna shoot someone unarmed?" He throws back at me what I said to him the night I was bathing.

"Clever, and maybe. Look, I don't know you, nor do I trust you." I hold steady. "Say whatever it is you're here to say and leave before Warren gets back and we have a mound of shit on our hands."

He moves a step closer like a predator. I back up a step on instinct. "Stop right there." My voice is shakier than I would like.

He cocks his head to the side and stares me down as if he is testing me. "Warren bagged some hares a few miles from here. He was lounging on a rock smoking a cigar when I saw him last. Way I see it, I have another half hour." My mouth gaps open, but he continues, "so, stand there until your arms give out, or…you can indulge me." That side smile rises on his face.

I could shoot him. I could scream and hope Warren's close enough to hear me. I bite my lip with aggravation, and then my gun lowers as if my arms and brain are not on the same page…or chapter even. Deep down, I realize I may not have what it takes to shoot someone. I tuck the pistol into the back of my breeches which gets me another curious look from Jake.

"I'll give you ten minutes." I turn on my heel without another word and sit back in my dining chair. I casually continue eating as if his presence means absolutely nothing to me. I quickly swipe the knife that's beside the butter, sticking it into my boot…just in case.

Jake's eyes shift around the room as he takes a step in. His tall frame seems to take up so much space. Before he can make it three steps, I mumble through a mouthful of beans, "You now have nine minutes."

I see the smile he tries to hide. His glowering eyes rake over me, but then he moves through the house, not toward me, ignoring my warning of time. I pause my next bite, watching as he heads straight for my room, opening the door as if he already knew which one it was. Alarm bells go off in my head.

I swig a shot of whiskey and then slam my bowl down, and march in after him. "You said you wanted to talk, not plunder through my personal things. Get the hell out of my room!" I yell.

He looks at the dresses hung on the wall and glances back to me, squinting his eyes and pursing his lips in thought. Then he kneels to the clothing I have stacked on the floor beside my dresser and, to my absolute horror, lifts my purple lace underwear. My face burns with embarrassment but also rage. I snatch for them, but he simply raises his arm, bringing them just out of reach.

"These…I remember. Very odd indeed." His voice is low and guttural. "I've never seen ladies wear *anything* like this before." He spins them around his finger.

"And you never will." I take his distraction and use it to pluck them away from him. I quickly chunk them into a drawer, then turn to face him. "What do you want, Jake? Really? I can't have you showing up every time you get the urge to disrupt my life. If it's a debt I owe, then tell me, what is it? I'm sick to death of this cat and mouse game."

His smile broadens, "I don't think you are. I think you like this game." Before I can retort he adds, "As far as the debt goes, I haven't decided. I'm here because I *know* you are hiding something." He walks closer to me. Every step he takes is slow and deliberate. I take one back.

"Bill *did* send me that first day, but I lied again. Told him you were a nobody…no one to concern himself with." He steps again, and so do I.

"I *am* a nobody." I swallow hard. "So, you are stalking me, unpaid and unprovoked? Isn't there anything else you would rather be doing?" I whisper. He stalks forward again, but this time, my back hits the bedroom wall. I can smell that earthy scent that emanates from him, like sandalwood and leather.

He looks down his nose at me, his hat seated low over his hooded eyes. "I can think of one thing," he whispers, and his heated gaze drops to cover the length of me slowly, "that I would rather be doing."

My lips part in a gasp—my chest rising and falling erratically. Suddenly, my clothes feel as if they are smothering me. He is smothering me, and I need to be far, far away from him.

He moves even closer until we are only inches apart. I should move. I should bolt from this room, but I stand absolutely still as he leans into me, placing his hands on either side of my head. I have a strange urge to touch the scar on his left eyebrow. He whispers into my ear, "Maybe you are a witch…Samantha, because you have most certainly cast a spell on me. I can think of nothing else, no one else. What is it about you that has me so vexed?"

Heat blossoms low in my belly, and I clench my thighs and fight against my traitorous body. I should shoot him. Right now. I should do it. Rid myself of this torment. I move my head to look away, and he grabs my chin with one hand and forces me to look at him. The heat from his grip is scorching.

"I can see it in your eyes, you know. You think of it too," he says against my lips. The hand, once on my chin, now moves to cup the back of my neck with his fingers, his thumb moving lazily against my throat. I close my eyes, trying to break the hold he has over my senses, but to no avail. If I moved just an inch, I could kiss him. I could taste him.

What the fuck is wrong with me? Maybe there's a thresh hold limit for loneliness, and I have maxed out, making me susceptible to any random asshole.

I finally open my eyes. "Stop, Jake. I don't know you. You don't know me. Please…just stop." My voice sounds small and vulnerable. I hate it. My hands have been stuck to my sides like glue, but now I place them against his chest to move him, but he doesn't budge. I can feel how solid he is through his shirt—a wall of muscle earned by real work and hard living.

I meant to drop my hands, but there they were, still on his chest. Traitorous bastards!

"I'll make you a deal; you tell me one true thing about you, and I will do the same. Then…we know each other a little better." His breathing is ragged, the first sign I've seen that he's as shook as I am.

"You first," I whisper.

That cocky side smile appears, sending butterflies rampant through my stomach. "My last name is Evans," he says as he inches closer, our mouths almost touching.

My body is lit up like a furnace. Jake's scent is so overwhelmingly wonderful that I can't help myself from inhaling deeply. I'm not sure at what point I lost this little battle with Jake, but now I'm surrendering—waving the damn white flag. "My last name is Thorne…Samantha Camille Thorne, to be exact," I say against his lips.

"Lovely, now we know each other Samantha Camille Thorne." My breath halts completely as he presses me into the wall. I let out a squeal when he lifts my legs until they wrap around his torso, and then his mouth is on mine. I tense up. I try to resist, to move away, but I can't. My body has a mind of her own and has been deprived of affection for too long. All logic leaves me, and I finally release the tension in my taut limbs. My stiff kiss relaxes, and he groans when I open for him. His tongue sweeps into my mouth, and the taste is sweet, like cigars and whiskey. The soft tickle of his beard has me writhing against him. I moan into his mouth, and he loses all control. Time ceases to exist as we devour each other in a greedy fight for domination. I move my hands into his soft hair and hear his cowboy hat clank to the floor. His lips leave my mouth and move to my jaw. I toss my head back as his tongue and teeth rake down the side of my neck.

Jake squeezes my hips in a delicious way. He pulls his face back for a moment and watches me closely as he presses himself into me. He looks to be savoring the moment—savoring my reactions. His lips find mine again, and this time, I deepen the kiss. I'm rewarded with a rumbling growl from deep in his chest. An ache forms low in my body. I'm about to give this man anything and everything he wants…

All of a sudden I hear a soft nicker of a horse nearby.

Oh shit! Clint!

Jake stops, hearing it too. We breathe hard, gasping breaths. I can see the strain in his eyes as he reluctantly lowers me until my tip toes touch the floor. He leans into me, lowers his head, smells my hair deeply, then grabs my chin and kisses me fiercely before forcing himself to back away. "We are far from finished, witch." He snatches the hat off the floor and disappears. I never hear him leave the house, nor do I hear his horse outside. The window in my room is open and I still hear nothing.

He really is like a shadow.

I stand there far too long, looking at the floor. I hear Warren when he finally comes into the house, muttering about having to eat fucking beans again. I don't snap out of it until he yells for me.

I stumble over my words, "I'm here, just putting…ugh…things…away."

What did I do? I just made out with a perfect stranger who's been stalking me for weeks and has literally held a gun to my head! Okay, I've held one on him, too, but still…it's not right. What if he's playing with my emotions just to get more information or to use something against me later on…like that debt? Either way, this *cannot* happen again. You would think I would've learned my lesson with Trevor.

How long was Jake watching me? He walked straight to my bedroom as if he knew which was mine. Okay, there's only two bedrooms. It was a literal 50/50 chance, but it's the way his eyes were alight as if he was *finally* getting to see inside. I peer out the open window but see nothing. My eyes close, and I lean back against the wall and slide down until my bottom is on the floor.

I gently touch my swollen lips from the punishing kisses we shared. Heat is still coursing through my body. His words from the saloon haunt me.

"We will never be done…you and I."

Nice Damn Day

CHAPTER 9

Samantha

It's the weekend, and here we are, all dressed up and heading into town. The last day we were there, I told Warren about Myra's excitement and anticipation for the month's up incoming events and about all the frilly dresses she gave me. He wasn't sure it was a good idea but relented and bought himself a new vest and jacket with breeches. It's the beginning of May, and the sun is screaming that fact as it beats down upon us.

I flit my gaze to him now, bouncing along on the wagon. He is suited for this life more than he realizes—more than me, for sure. He puffs on a sweet cigar; his fitted brown vest compliments the striped shirt underneath and is made even sharper with the gold chain watch hanging from the pocket. He shined his holster and boots with oil and his fedora hat is tipped forward a touch.

"You look very handsome, Warren." I grin.

"Hell, don't I know it." He smiles, and it is contagious.

"WOW, full of yourself today, huh?" I nudge his arm.

"Maybe…you are stunning too, you know. I don't know that I've ever seen you look like *this*." He waves his finger, gesturing to all of me.

I ruin the moment by rolling my eyes, stealing his cigar, and taking a huge puff, making him chuckle. "No, for real," I say through the smoke, "why haven't you tried to meet anyone here?" He cuts his eyes my way for a second, then looks back to the trail. His eyes grow distant as I continue, "You are handsome, in the best shape of your life, and very intelligent. You have a lot to offer someone."

He looks at me as if he is seeing me for the first time—his brows wrinkle. "That's very nice of you to say, Sam." He stops and turns back to the trail, exhaling forcefully. "I had someone…back home, or at least I almost did."

I tilt my head, looking at him with confusion. His sad tone pinches my heart. "I had no idea. I'm so sorry! Why did you never mention her?"

He flicks the reins, making the horses move into a trot. "We met at the armory and kinda hit it off a few weeks before it all happened. I was planning on officially asking her out on a date the day of the eclipse." His cheek lifts into a sad half-smile. "Her name was Carla."

I take another puff off of his cigar and then pass it back to him. We both lost family. We both lost friends. We both lost our homes and careers. I had no clue he had fallen for someone. That is a different kind of lonely pain—a different kind of loss.

"Well, I'm very sorry. She would've been fortunate to have had you…but I still think you should mingle today. We've been here a long time, Warren." I wave my hands at the scenery. "Maybe it's time to move on. You can't take care of me forever. You deserve happiness."

"I would never abandon you, Sam, for nothing. We are in this together." He wrinkles his brow again and then stares at me hard. "Why are you mushy all of a sudden? Did the fancy dresses go to your head? Where's the bitchy Sam I know and love that keeps me grounded?"

I avert my eyes and laugh it off. "I'm still me, just thinking about the future I guess." He doesn't buy it, but he leaves the conversation at that.

Why am I being this way? I think I have an idea, but I shut that thought down entirely. I do wonder if I am holding Warren back, though. I'm helpful in ways for sure, but he thrives here. I feel I am a burden.

We put the wagon in a secure place and stable the horses since the evening is early, and there's no telling how long we will be in town. I pass a few extra coins to the stable hand for watching our horses and for the feed.

The moment we walk into the dusty streets eyes fall upon us. As much as we've traded here, we have *never* been here to "have fun" per se, and we have *never* dressed as such.

I peer nervously down to the gown given to me by Myra. The deep teal bodice shines in the Arizona sun. Black lace and silk line the edges of the corseted center. The layered skirts are also teal with a top layer of soft black lace. The back of the dress flares out with a small bustle, the ends dragging slightly on the ground. I have matching gloves on my hands and soft leather button ankle boots. I was at a loss as to how to fix my hair, so I improvised and spun half my mass into a clean French roll, and the rest of my hair hung in waves down to almost my lower back. I left a few pieces delicately framing my face. I'm second-guessing my decision to wear my old makeup that I kept hidden, but my desires won the battle. It has been too long since I felt…pretty. I decided on just liner, mascara, and lip gloss to keep it as simple as possible. I pat my thigh, making sure that the knife Warren gave me is still secure. I opted not to wear the heavy strap and pistol all evening in a dress.

Now, looking at the glares I'm receiving from women and the lustful looks from the men…I may have made a mistake coming here like this. Too much attention is never a good thing, and it's not just me. Warren is drawing eyes from several bystanders when they see me arm in arm with him.

"Maybe we should just leave," I whisper.

"Absolutely not…and give these pricks the satisfaction. No way." He pats the hand I have wrapped around his arm. "You deserve this too, you know—to mingle—to meet someone."

I swallow the lump in my throat and look anywhere but into his eyes as he continues, "I mean it, Sam. We both deserve happiness, but that doesn't mean we are giving up, *or* gonna lose each other."

I know what he is insinuating…giving up on getting back home. As far as losing each other, I'll never let that happen and neither will he. Maybe I've treated him too much like a father, but now…it feels like he's stepped into that role, and I'm okay with that.

Today, we will ignore the gawkers, the whisperers, the curious glances, and enjoy ourselves.

Moseying through the town streets, I see there are performers and tricksters out and about earning a coin for their entertainment. A band plays upbeat tunes and children are dancing and running amok. Gunshots are ringing out periodically, and I follow the sound along with the other people flowing in that direction. The entertainer catching my attention is a slim young gentleman in a paddock to the side of the local hotel. He demonstrates quick draw techniques as he blasts away bottle after bottle. He appears to be nineteen or so by the looks of him but holds himself confidently. He has haunted blue eyes and a sly shit-eating grin that makes me think he's a lot of trouble in one small package. I lean against the fence and watch his marksmanship. It's like nothing I've ever seen. In the blink of an eye, he takes out six more bottles several yards away, then spins his guns dramatically before holstering them and doing it all over again. He never misses. I am observing his skills attentively—Warren a few feet away doing the same—when a voice to my side startles me.

"You're not from here, are you?"

I glance to my left and am forced to look up at the man beside me. He is tall and lean with a clean-shaven face and dark blue eyes. His hair is light brown and short under his flat-crowned cowboy hat. He has quite a handsome face and kind eyes.

"I get that a lot," I say and continue watching the show.

"My name is Henry Fletcher; can I ask your name, ma'am?" His voice is cool and proper.

I give him my attention again. "Samantha."

"Nice to meet you, Samantha." He smiles.

"Likewise." I muster a smile of my own. I struggle to try and relax. That's why we are here after all, to mingle—meet new people.

"You enjoying the show?" He laughs. "Well, that was a silly question. I can tell you are. He's rather good, is he not?"

"Very," I say. Almost too good, I think. Where did this kid come from?

"I'm sorry if I am impeding on your time. It's just that, well, you are a vision." He has my full attention now as I arch an eyebrow at that statement. "I apologize if that was a bit too forward, but I could not hold back the blatant words no longer."

My mouth is slightly open as I try to form a conversation out of that. "Thank you and no…not too forward at all." I am terrible at this. He is handsome in a scholarly kind of way. I should consider this a win. A moment to meet someone new. So, why do I feel like walking away right now?

"Would you consider a dance with me later this evening at Big Johns? I hear that is where everyone will end up when the sun sets."

I hesitate a few seconds, and my eyes move about the town, looking for something or someone. I shouldn't, but I *have* been looking for *him*. My eyes scan the crowds one more time. Finally, I nod. "You know what, that would be lovely."

His lips pull back in a huge grin, and he tips his hat to me. "Perfect, I will leave you to your show. See you this evening…Samantha." He bows his head subtly before sauntering off.

I watch him as he weaves through people in the town. His attire suggests money and good breeding. He seems nice enough. So, what is wrong with me? He's obviously a good catch, and I need to come to the realization that it's time to move on and actually *live* my life here. I cock my head to the side in thought as Warren slides closer to me.

"Was that what I think it was." He elbows me gently.

I scowl and glare at him. "Oh, for God's sake, Warren. It was nothing."

"It was something…so you gonna dance with him later?" He winks at me.

"You dog, you were listening the whole time!" I huff. "And I don't know…maybe."

Warren nods his head repeatedly in little bobs while grinning from ear to ear.

"Quit meddling in my affairs and find *you* someone to talk to!" I gripe.

He laughs it off as we watch the gunslinging kid exit the paddock and make his way to a bay Mustang hitched near us. He has several guys in his posse waiting by their horses. He looks me up and down brazenly and then winks.

The absolute confidence this little shit has. I laugh as he yells, "Mount up!" to his posse.

I nudge Warren, grinning, and say, "*Regulators… Mount Up!*" quoting an old Warren G song from the nineties causing Warren to laugh out loud.

The kid suddenly swings his gaze to me and raises both brows, then gives that shit-eaten grin and winks again. He slings his leg over the horse, and the men take off—galloping away, leaving a dust cloud behind them.

"He was a strange one, huh," I say.

"Definitely strange," Warren concurs, then says, "Back to our conversation…you gonna dance with that man later?"

"Ugh." I roll my eyes and stomp off in search of more entertainment, hearing his laugh trail off behind me.

I walk the streets for two hours, enjoying the music and occasional tasty treat. Along the way, I encounter Myra sitting in the shade of a tree with Judith beside her. Myra is lovely today in a yellow and cream dress, and her dark hair is curled in ringlets. The gray streaks in front swirl into the mix. "Hello, Myra…Judith!" I hitch my dress hem up and pick up my pace until I reach them. Myra bounds out of the chair and smashes me with a hug. I stand awkwardly, patting her back.

"Oh, my WORD! Honey, you look amazing!" she gushes, holding me at arm's length. "I *knew* this would be a perfect fit! My Milly had a tiny waist and bigger hips like you."

I blush as she cups my face in her hands. "That's too kind, and the dress *is* perfect. I really appreciate it."

"Well, I am glad you didn't back out! OH, lordy, the eligible men meandering about today," she fans herself dramatically, "are everywhere and on the prowl." She waggles her eyebrows at me, making me giggle.

"Not sure if I'm ready for all that, but I *am* having fun," I say honestly. For once, I really am. The twangy music fills the air, and my confidence is thriving in this dress. The weather is tolerable, not too hot just yet. Maybe this is the beginning of moving on.

Suddenly, Judith pipes up from her silence. "You remind me of my mother...she was a traveler too. Didn't belong here."

My mouth drops open, but then I gather myself. Myra cuts her eyes at Judith, but I chime in before she can chastise her. "It's okay," I whisper to Myra. "Let her talk. It's fine." I look to Judith and speak louder. "What do you mean, Judith?"

She ignores me as usual. I try another tactic. "Nice damn day, isn't it, Judith." She smiles at me. That lets me know one thing...she has some memory. Maybe everything she says isn't that crazy.

"Nice damn day!" she spits. "Momma always said you need to pay your debts to go home! *A piece of home, of where you belong*," she sings, "*debts to be paid in a day, ohhhhhh, and the Lord's work!*"

She continues chanting it over and over until Myra lays a hand on hers. "It's okay, honey. You want a beer?"

I'm still reeling over her strange words when beer catches my ear. "She drinks beer still?"

"Oh, yes, this one," she points to Judith, "can be a lush." Myra nudges me and whispers, "I really only give her one whole beer, the rest I water down, or I'd never get her home!" We laugh out loud.

Myra links her arm in mine. "Come dear. The evening is growing dim, let's go have a drink, shall we."

"Sounds amazing." I hold her tight as we walk toward Big John's Saloon—Judith walking slowly behind us. Her words played havoc in my mind. Maybe I'm just trying to make *something* out of *nothing*.

After an hour of chit-chatting with Myra, I've learned a few things. Number one, she is no one to mess with. She once shot a man dead who tried to touch her daughter Milly inappropriately. Number two, she is still virile. She has unabashedly gawked at every man that has come through the door that looked half decent. Number three, she can probably out-drink most of the people in here tonight.

I have also learned an interesting fact about Miss Judith…when she drinks, she becomes more lucid.

The moment Myra starts pressing me about needing a man in my life, I hear Judith say, "Momma always said love will stop a traveler's journey…cut it short. She said if you want to go back home, don't fall in love."

The hairs on my arms stand on end. "Tell me about her home," I try to coax her into that line of thinking.

"It was different," she mutters.

"Different how Judith?" I ask excitedly.

Myra is staring at me with skepticism, probably wondering why I'm bothering to converse with Judith. Judith never gets to answer my question. Instead, she yawns and says, "I think I want to go home."

"I'm sorry to leave you so soon, honey, but I've stayed longer than expected, and I should be getting her home," Myra says as she hugs me goodbye.

We say our farewells, but Judith's words bother my soul. She was so close to telling me about her mother's home. Still, I feel like a fool for indulging in the hope that her words come from some truths. I sigh and sip my beer alone with my imaginative mind spiraling.

Pretty Little Devil

CHAPTER 10

Jake

"Holy hell," I curse. The pretty little devil herself. I watch as Samantha waltzes into the bar, arm in arm with Myra—Judith not far behind as usual. What the hell is she thinking coming here looking like that. My eyes skim the dress. The bodice is pushing her breasts up, and her hair is flowing behind her. Every single man in this room is gawking at her, making me want to bash their heads in. She is either blissfully unaware or hiding it well.

I tip my hat down lower to hide my face as I hunker down at a corner table playing poker. I hold a royal flush, so I'm about to ruin Doug's evening. Everyone else done folded. Not my fault, though, dumbass shouldn't gamble if he's broke.

My eyes drift back and forth from the game to her. I can taste her still…there on my lips. She's torturing me every waking hour. I need to have her body, and maybe that will get her out of my system. I never intended to move that fast in her home. I couldn't resist. She blushes so innocently, and it gives her true feelings away. She wants me as much as I want her, but she's stubborn. She'll not admit it. I close my eyes briefly, remembering her legs wrapped willingly around me against the wall.

Someone says "call," and it brings me back to the game. I toss down my cards to the dismay of Doug. Everyone grumbles as I rake in the winnings.

Dusk settles outside as more patrons enter the saloon. Soon this place will be crowded. I light up my walnut pipe and take a puff of the tobacco, letting it roll from my lips. Crowds are never good. It always starts off fine, but then some jackass gets too drunk and picks a fight.

Maybe I should just leave. I don't need this shit.

After a few hours of watching her from the shadows, in walks a man I recognize…Henry Fletcher, a wealthy businessman from the north. Bill has mentioned his endeavors for a time or two. They are in cahoots these days. The man portrays the perfect gentleman, but I know the truth. He's as dirty as they come, and he's walking straight for Samantha. She smiles up to him at something he says.

My hackles rise, and my blood boils.

The thought of Henry *Fucking* Fletcher being on the receiving end of her smile has me wanting to march right over there and beat his face in.

Doug says something to me, but I'm fixated on the vixen that is steadily ruining my life without even trying. Henry leans in and whispers something only the two of them can hear, and Sam blushes.

I grind my teeth and watch from the shadows.

Making a Scene

CHAPTER 11

Samantha

I cross my legs and lean back on the stool as I sip my whiskey; Judith's words are still bothering me. My mind travels back to the moment we came here. The excruciating pain, the blinding lights, and the piercing noises are something that I'll never likely forget. I rewind it in my head like an old VCR tape.

"You look like you could use some company?" I startle as Henry Fletcher pops up from nowhere and takes the seat beside me. He strikes a match and lights a pipe. Smoke billows around us.

"You are probably right." My torrent mind is no place to be right now.

"You still up for that dance later?" he asks, his eyes alight with hope.

I smile up at him. "Of course. I said I would, and I meant it. Although, I have to admit. I am going to be terrible at it. I have no clue how to dance other than swaying back and forth like the pendulum of a clock."

He laughs and then leans in closer. His eyes turn heated as his voice lowers. "No worries…you have my hands to guide you."

I instantly feel my cheeks redden and turn to stare at nothing or *anything* except him.

"Have you enjoyed your day thus far?" he says, pulling me back into conversation.

"I can't complain. It was just what I needed." I turn my eyes to his. "And you?"

"I feel this may be the highlight of my day." His wandering eyes devour me as he sips his liquor.

He is more brazen than I thought, much more than his earlier, gentlemanly demeanor. I'm sure several drinks have brought about this side of Henry. I take a breath and force my shoulders to relax. I am overthinking things as usual. I need to experience life again, real dating, and companionship.

"You know what?" I clink my glass into his. "It's the highlight of mine too." I give him a soft smile.

We shared small talk for a time, and it was…normal and exactly what I needed. It's what I'd hoped for when this evening began, but hope is still a bitch. The color blanches from my face when a group of men saunter in that I recognize instantly. William and his gang of assholes linger at the batwings doors for a moment before heading to the back area designed for the poker players.

My heart hammers away in my chest. It's not just the fear I feel; it's anger. I will *not* let their appearance ruin this day! What the hell are they even doing here? I was sure they lived near Tucson. Jake said he got them off my back, but still, I feel with certainty they will be a problem for me. I eye them again, searching for the one person I shouldn't be searching for, but Jake...he's not with them.

"Is everything alright, Samantha?" Henry's worried eyes roam over my face. "You look like you've seen a ghost."

"Something like that," I mutter and peer into the back to make sure Bill is *far* away from us.

Henry glances in the same direction as me, and he chuckles. "You mean William Evans and his crew. They are some old friends of mine, more like business acquaintances really, but good chaps."

"Evans? You said, William Evans?" I ask, narrowing my eyes.

His brows wrinkle. "That's correct. Everyone calls him Bill. Do you not know them because you seem like you do?"

Evans...Jake Evans and William Evans. I clench my jaw. "I don't know them really, they just..." I pause, searching for the right words, but I don't know Henry and definitely can't tell him anything but the basics. "I saw them when they were passing through Tucson one day, seemed like they could be trouble."

"I shouldn't think so. They are prominent players in the growth of this area. I've had many dealings with them. They're important around here."

Uh, huh? I don't like the sound of that. Maybe Henry can be of use to me. Now is the perfect opportunity to learn more about my stalker and his gang.

"I met a Jake Evans once," I say and nonchalantly sip my whiskey. "He was in town the same time as those guys. Are they related?"

His eyes crinkle with humor, but his mouth is in a tight line, as if that name bothers him too. "Yes, they are. Jake is his nephew."

Nephew. I think back to the way Jake looked at Bill that night as if he could rip his head off at any moment. Maybe he has bad blood there, or maybe it's none of my business. I just want them *all* out of my life, especially today when I am finally letting go and ready to move on. But…I can't help myself. I want to know more about the band of assholes. "Is Bill their leader or something? He seems like the one in charge, and the rest follow suit."

"Leader is a way, yes. They are each well paid for their services," Henry says as he leans in closer to me and points to each person around Bill. "That one to the left of Bill, they call Denver—not very creative, as he is from Denver, Colorado." He pauses as we giggle and he briefly drops his eyes to my lips, then clears his throat before continuing, "To the right of him is Tom

Whitmore and the rough looking one is Lennard Sands."

"Butter Teeth," I whisper, recognizing his greasy, unkempt appearance instantly.

"I'm sorry, did you say something?" he asks.

"Oh, no, please continue." I swig the whiskey.

"The other three across from Bill are the brothers, Kelvin Mack, Charlie Mack, and Bobby Mack. Charlie and Kelvin are twins, and the younger brother is Bobby."

I tilt my head, analyzing each one. Denver is rail thin with a clean-shaven face and graying slicked-back hair. Tom Whitmore is a large, burly man with a menacing scowl and flaming ginger hair cropped short to match his mustache. Butter Teeth remains looking as if he believes cleanliness is a sin. The youngest Mack brother is indeed…young. He looks to be no more than eighteen years old, the proof of it in his patchy beard and doughy face. The twin Mack brothers have near identical long beards, brown with a reddish tint. Their beady eyes are haloed by thick, bushy brows. They're all dressed nicer than our last run-in, but only Bill stands out—his tailored gray suit is sharp and clearly expensive. He would be handsome if it wasn't for the evil lurking in his vacant eyes. They are each betting with more money than I've seen in two years of being here. There is no way that's legitimate earnings.

The one called Kelvin sports a shiny brass pocket watch that he spins seemingly out of habit. He stands, saying something to Bill, and hurries out of the bar. My curious glare follows him. "What do they do? For a living, I mean?" I ask, my eyes still on the doorway.

"Odd and end jobs really, except, of course, Bill. I'm not sure how you are unaware of this, but he's the constable."

My eyes dart to Henry's. "*He's* a constable?"

"Why yes, I assumed you would know that if you live around here." He cocks his head in a questioning manner. "No wonder I've never seen you around...you really haven't been *around*, have you? Where are you from?"

My brain fails me in that instant, and I reply to quickly to stop myself. "I live near the canyons outside of town." Oh shit. Why did I say that? "I don't get out much," I mutter under my breath. I have royally screwed up. Our number one rule is to tell no one where we live. I redirect the conversation. "What about the nephew...Jake? What does he do?"

"You are awfully curious about this lot...and especially *him*. Is there something I should know about?" His eyes are a bit guarded.

"No, of course not. I'm just that—a curious person," I lie and avert my eyes. "Being that I've lived away from civilization for so long, I just want to get to know the people I live around."

Henry nods and sips his drink again before he responds, "I don't know much about Jake, except that he used to be a scout during the Civil War. It has been said that he lived with the Apache for a time and learned his tracking skills from them. However, those could be rumors."

A scout and tracker…makes sense as to why he reminds me of shadows. Henry definitely knows more than he's saying and seems to have had a nefarious run-in with Jake in the past.

Henry nods toward the corner to a saloon girl who is hanging on Bill's every word. "If you want the best gossiping hens, go for the girls that work the town." He winks at me. "They know everything that goes on here and everyone involved. Her name is Lonnie. She runs the brothel. She has quite the knowledge…for a price, of course."

Lonnie is a *very* pretty woman. You can tell that she knows how to work a crowd to get what she wants. Her dark hair is gathered up in a fancy bun with tendrils around her heart-shaped face. Her slender figure is packed into a snug green corseted dress with gold embroidered leaves throughout the skirts. Her dark cat like eyes are zoned in on whatever Bill is saying. "She sounds interesting," I muse.

"Ah, that she is," he says in a way that lets me know he's done more than talk to her. "As riveting as gossip can be," he changes the subject, "I would much rather cash in on that dance I was promised." Henry stands and holds his hand out for me.

I prefer the gossip, but…ah, why the hell not, I think as I grasp his warm palm in mine. I toss back the last sip of whiskey and stand, coming to his side to lace my arm into his. We move across the adjacent rooms until we reach the open dance floor. A few other couples are already moving in tandem with the music. I feel the eyes of patrons upon us. Henry takes my hand in one of his and lays the other on my hip as he spins me around. I lean my head back, laughing out loud as he ends the spin and pulls me close to him. Henry's hands move lower on my back as he sways and guides me around the floor.

I suck in a breath when my eyes make the mistake of drifting to Bill. He has not only noticed me but now the whole group is watching—their poker game at a standstill. His fingers rolled on his right hand—flipping the silver dollar across his knuckles, like the first time I saw him. Bill leans in, whispering something to the one called Denver as he smooths down his mustache. I notice the three Mack brothers are nowhere to be seen. My stare moves away and back to the man beaming down at me.

I will not let anyone ruin this night. I chant the mantra in my head.

He spins me at the end of the song and ends in a dip. It has me feeling breathless and giddy. My laugh is genuine. It feels good to do something as normal as dancing.

Henry clears his throat, gaining my attention. "Round two?" he asks as he pulls me closer. The next song begins, and I hear a lovely, tortured voice belting out a bluesy western tune. When my eyes find her, I am a bit shocked. It's Lonnie, belting out each note with her soul.

I give Henry my full attention. "Yeah, I mean… yes."

He sways me gently in time with the song. For a moment, I'm not here. I'm anywhere but here…if only in my mind. I close my eyes. When I open them again, he is mere inches from my face—the desire to kiss me is written all over his. I think back to the face that haunts me, the whiskey eyes. I quickly step away, breaking the moment.

"I am *so* sorry, Henry. It's just that I…" What do I say? Sorry, Henry, I have a stalker asshole that has me questioning my sanity and taste in men.

Henry takes my hand in his and places a kiss on the back. "The fault is mine. That was presumptuous of me to move that quickly."

I dart my eyes about the room, embarrassed to have backed away like I did. That is the moment I see Lonnie leave the stage and head toward the back exit near the privies.

"Parden me. I need to use the ladies' room, be back shortly," I say as I'm already walking toward the exit. I glance behind me to see Henry's lips pinched together, but he simply nods and winks at me.

Once Outside, I lean against the building and let the cool night air caress my skin. I wait impatiently for Lonnie to exit the privy. No one is out and about behind the building; however, I hear hoofbeats. A few seconds go by before I can make out a brown and white painted horse moving down the back street. The rider looks an awful lot like Kelvin Mack. I can almost make out the gleam of that pocket watch he always has on him. Behind him, a girl is slumped against his back. She appears to be sleeping. It's dark, but I can make out her long black braid hanging over her thin shoulder. There's a large turquoise gem at the end of the braid that almost glows in the moonlight. After a few minutes, Lonnie is out and walking toward me. I pull my attention back to her and away from the bystanders.

"Hello there, Lonnie, is it?" I stop her by stepping into her path.

Her sharp gaze drags over quickly. "That's correct, and you are *Samantha*."

My eyebrows pinch together, but I don't bother asking how she knows my name. Henry said she knows everything about everyone. "Yes, I am. I heard that…for a price, you were pretty knowledgeable about everyone in this town."

She purses her lips and crosses her arms over her chest but doesn't say anything.

I pull out several coins and grab her hand dropping them into it as I close her fingers over them. I step closer and whisper, "What can you tell me about Jake Evans?"

She rolls her eyes at me with a smirk and looks away but finally brings them back to mine. With a sigh, she says, "I don't tell whole life stories for a few measly coins, darlin', be specific. What is it that you want to know? And I have things to do, so you get one question."

What do I want to know? "Is he dangerous?"

She laughs and brushes past me toward the saloon doors. She stops at them, looks over her shoulder, and simply says, "Yes."

I stand there a few more minutes gathering myself. That one simple word has me unhinged.

Back inside the bar, I don't see Henry right away, so I lean against the wall beside the exit and watch the poker players. Lonnie continues to hang on Bill and then move around the room, shmoozing the men and they're eating it up. She leans in close to each one, giggling and dragging her hand over their backs as she makes her way around the table to Bill. Before long, he throws down a winning hand. Men curse and sling their hats as Bill rakes his winnings into a pile.

I laugh out loud and then slap a hand over my mouth. She's colluding with Bill. They are dirty little cheats. I bet if I watched closer I could find the hidden cards she slips to him. I make a mental note to never pay her for information on Bill Evans...it's likely she would never cross him.

"What is so amusing, my dear?" Henry walks up to me and places one hand beside my head as he leans in close. His glassy eyes tell me that he has slammed a few more drinks while I was outside.

"Nothing," I lie and try to move away, but he places his other hand on my hip.

"I enjoyed your company this evening." His gaze moves to my chest. "Would you like to take the evening somewhere more private?"

"I think I need to find Warren and call it a night." I go to move his hand, but his fingers tighten on my hip.

Just as I am about to lose it, I hear an unmistakable, low, rumbling voice that all at once annoys me and excites me. "Get your hands off her *now*." Henry immediately drops his hand from my hip and straightens, getting eye-to-eye with Jake Evans. I stare open-mouthed. My corset makes it hard to breathe. Jake stands to my right with his burning stare aimed at Henry. On one hand, I wanted Henry's hands off me, but on the other, I didn't need rescuing.

"What the hell do you think you are doing?" I rant to Jake.

Instead of answering me, he looks down his nose at Henry, which is a feat considering both men are tall. "I think you're finished here." Then his eyes move to mine as he grabs my arm, pulling me along. "You are too! You're coming with me...*right* now!"

Henry makes the mistake of reaching out to pull me back. "You let go of her this instant!"

Jake releases my arm and whirls around in a blur, punching Henry square in the nose. I hear the crack of bone. Blood spurts out as he grasps his face and falls to his knees with a gurgling sound emanating from him.

I stand in shock, hand over my mouth, as Jake grabs me again. Around us, the music has stopped; I hear John yelling at someone to get Henry out of there and find him the doc. I try to yank and move from Jake's grasp, but to no avail. His vice-like grip is unbreakable as he pulls me along. "You can't do this!" I look around for help, but no one seems concerned except John, but his attention is more on the bloody Henry. "Jake, let me go...NOW!" I yank some more. He disregards me as the batwing doors slam behind me. The brisk air hits my skin, still glistening with sweat as I continue attempting to free my arm from his grasp.

They all just watched me being dragged away by a man. Does no one in this *fucking town* have a decent bone in their bodies? My brain tries to rationalize the actions of Jake and of the whole damn event.

Where *the hell* is Warren?

"Jake, stop!" I yell. "Talk to me. What the hell are you doing?"

He slams to a halt beside his black horse and bends to get in my face. "You have no damn clue how reckless you are for even being here tonight." He pauses at my confusion but doesn't elaborate. At that moment, I hear the banging sound of the saloon doors behind us. I see Jake clench his jaw in frustration and I look over my shoulder to see Bill and Denver moseying over to us. Bill's face alight with humor.

"Everywhere we see you, every town you have been through...there is always a stir." Bill tsks at me. "Why is that, huh?" Then he looks up to Jake and says, "Your actions tonight are interesting indeed."

Jake sneers, but he doesn't say a word.

"It's none of your damn business what is transpiring here!" I spit. "I think it best for you to give us our privacy." I back up a step into Jake and feel him against me. I glance back at him and see shock in his eyes at my "sort of" defensive words for him.

"I would watch your tongue if I were you, girl!" Bill steps toward me, curling his lip in anger. "Everything that goes on in this town is my business. You'd do well to remember that."

Jake moves around me until I'm partially behind him. "Goodnight, Bill," is all he says.

Bill chuckles and swaggers back a few steps, Denver never leaving his side. "Y'all be safe out there in those canyons, gets wild sometimes." He dips his chin down and cocks his head menacingly.

My body trembles as I watch him turn and walk away. Denver keeping his hand near his pistol as he finally follows. Bill knows where I live. Does that mean Henry told him?

My breath huffs out of me as Jake dips down, suddenly lifting me off the ground and slinging me up and onto his horse. I let out a squeal. "Oh, no, no, no, JAKE! What are you doing?" I yell. At this hour no one is in the street who cares. Only a few drunks stumble around the alleys. "Warren will kill you! Do you hear me? Speak damn it!"

He mounts the horse, settling himself against me. He wraps his duster around me, and the smell of leather and sandalwood reminds me of our last encounter. My traitorous body reacts to that scent even as I feel for the knife I have hidden, hoping to stab this bastard.

Jake leans into my ear. "Keep your voice down. You are making a scene."

My eyes narrow in anger. "*I'm* making a scene. *ME*? Are you..." My words die out as he kicks his horse, and I'm slung back into his chest. We speed out of town. The shock has me holding the saddle horn and horse's mane for dear life. I lean forward to get a miniscule bit of distance between our bodies as I curse Jake repeatedly. Jake brings one arm around, forcing me to scoot back flush against him.

I feel for my knife again strapped under the dress and breathe a sigh of relief when I find it still there. He may have the upper hand right now, but not forever. I'll catch him off guard, and then...then I will what...kill him? Could I actually kill someone? I wanted to kill Trevor, but I know deep down I never would have. So, could I now?

My heart is still hammering away in my chest as panic begins to settle in like fog on a valley. Where is he taking me?

A Truth for a Truth

CHAPTER 12

Samantha

An hour later, Jake stops his horse near the base of a mountain—one I recognize. "We are near my home," I whisper. I hadn't spoken to him any more during the ride. Instead, I let my stormy mind weave all manner of vile things.

"Yeah," he grumbles as he dismounts.

He reaches for me, and I slap his hand away. "Don't fucking touch me...and *yeah*, that's all you have to say?"

"You have a foul mouth," he says blatantly.

"Go to hell, Jake Evans!" I dismount myself and storm away, heading in the general direction of home. It's pitch black out here, and the light of the moon only helps in the slightest of ways. I reach down, slip the knife from my garter, and hold it close.

"Already there...every damn time I'm around you!" He growls out right before he grabs my shoulders and spins me to him.

I've had enough. I slam my body into his and offset him enough that he hits the ground, and seconds later, I am on top of him with the knife to his jugular. I begin to shake with anger, frustration, confusion...it all slams into me at once.

Jake lies beneath me, seething, but doesn't move. "You want me dead, witch...do it then." He presses his neck harder against the knife.

My lip pulls back as I bare my teeth in anger. "What the hell is wrong with you?!" I yell. "You can't just barge into my life and do with it as you please!" He leans into the knife more as his jaw flexes. I see a bead of blood and gasp—my senses return to me, and I move the knife away from his neck—body shaking.

His chest rises and falls against mine as his eyes burn me alive with their intensity. I start to ease myself off of him when all of a sudden, he grabs me, flips me onto my back, and presses his weight into me. The knife I was holding is now lying useless a few feet away as I gawk at him. "You can't walk aimlessly through the desert in the dark. I'll take you home, but not until I make sure we're not being followed." He leans in almost nose to nose with me. "And if you ever pull a knife on me again, you better damn use it, or I'll bend you over my knee and make you wish you had!"

"How dare yo—" I start to say when he shakes me gently.

"Try me, witch!"

I bite my tongue to keep from lashing out. He finally releases me, gets to his feet, and turns, walking toward the mountain surrounding the canyon below. I notice his horse follows him without being led. I lie there in defiance for a minute before I hear a strange animal sound that raises the hairs on my arms. I bound upward from the ground and jog to catch up with him. He doesn't say a word, just keeps walking. He stops at the edge of the mountainous structure and takes a large canvas bag and lantern from his saddlebag then lights it with a match, slinging the bag over his shoulder. After walking a while longer, he slips behind a large, overgrown area of bushes and disappears. My brows wrinkle as I follow, pushing them aside curiously. There, hidden away neatly, is a cave. The mouth wide enough for us, but not his horse. The black mare walks away into the night, nibbling across the ground in search of food.

"Will she not run away? Your mare?" I ask as I follow. The lantern brings to life the orange and red walls of the cavern—some with smooth surfaces and some with jutted stone, sharp as knives.

"No," his voice echoes.

"You really are quite the conversationalist," I huff.

He stops when we reach an open area. There are already rocks in a circle with ashes in the center—a stack of wood against the far slate wall. He stays here. I wonder how often? I glance above us nervously, seeing the points of stalactite aimed down upon us. "Is it safe to be in here?"

"Safe as anywhere else around here."

"Okay, well, that is *not* comforting in the least," I whisper. "How long will we stay here?"

"'til morning," he mumbles as he begins making a palate on the floor with blankets and lighting a fire.

"What? Jake...I can *NOT* stay here until morning. Warren is going to lose his mind looking for me— probably already is!"

"Warren is fine. He got drunk with Clifford. They were down by the paddocks when we left. I sent word to him that you were safe and would be home in the morning."

"He won't believe that. We *never* leave each other."

"He will, because I had a girl write it...as if it was you...said you met a man and decided to spend the evening with him."

I pinch my lips together and cut my eyes to him. "Even if he does buy that bullshit, why did you do this anyway." I gesture around to the cave walls. "Did you know that this was the first time we, Warren and I, had decided to make this place feel more like home?" My voice breaks a little, and I clear it. "I was finally letting go—having fun and meeting people." I walk in a circle as I get more and more pissed at the thought of what everyone now thinks of me. "How can I show my face there again?"

"*Fun.*" He laughs.

"Of everything I just said…that is the one thing you picked from it?" I rant at him.

He glares at me with a scowl, and I see his jaw flex. "Not only did every man in there have one thing on their minds, but you chose Henry Fletcher to flaunt yourself to. He is the worst kind of man. The kind that hides their true selves behind fancy clothes and slick talk."

"Flaunt myself, ughhh, I did no such thing. He simply asked me to dance, and I obliged!"

He smirks, throwing my words back at me. "Flaunt, out of everything I said, that's the one thing you picked from it."

We are at a stand-off—glaring at each other. Him, now lounging by the fire and me standing as far away as possible. I hide the shivers from the chill, but apparently not well enough. He motions for me to sit by the fire—more like points in a demanding way. I tuck away my pride and sit on the blanket.

Jake grabs the bag and pulls a small pot from it and a jug of water, placing it over the fire. "Would you like some coffee and something to eat?"

My stomach growls at that exact moment. I want to say no and starve until tomorrow, just to be as obnoxious as possible, but I cave in at the second growl my tummy makes and say, "Sure." I can feel the fight leaking out of me. The day has been long and tiresome, but the evening's events really did me in.

He remains quiet as he works the fire and unwraps the meats. I watch him curiously. He removes his duster and neckerchief, laying them aside next to his holster, keeping them close to him. As he should. I may very well decide to shoot him depending on how the rest of this night goes. I notice for the first time an intricate dagger holstered beside one of his pistols. There's a leather strap that hangs from the hilt, and colorful beads and feathers dangle from it. He removes his hat and tosses it aside next. His thick dark hair reaches almost to his chin in the front and a tad longer in the back. The fluffy and silky strands gleam in the fire. My eyes veer back to his face and that scar that runs through his eyebrow. It somehow suits him. Like it was meant to be there. I'm sure whatever story comes with it is a proud one, as with most men. I feel like I know less about him now than before if that is even possible. Lonnie says he's dangerous. How much can one trust her words, though? She works for Bill.

I adjust my seating and realize my feet are killing me in these boots. I remove each and place them neatly beside me, along with my cumbersome gloves. Then, I remove my French roll from my hair. I close my eyes in instant relief when my bound hair falls, and I can stretch my fingers and toes. When I open them, Jake has stopped stoking the fire, his eyes are on my hair. He quickly looks away.

I grow tired of the quiet awkwardness we're sharing and decide to pry something, *anything*, out of him. "Why do you think Henry is a bad man?"

Jake pours us two little tin mugs of black coffee and hands me one before saying, "I don't think, I *know*."

"So how do you *know*? What happened between y'all?"

Jake looks as if he won't respond but then surprises me by doing just that. "He laid hands on his wife; I beat him to within an inch of his...should have killed him that day, big regret of mine."

I gasp. "What happened to her?" I ask, assuming he's no longer with her.

"Not sure. She left years ago and never came back." There's something in his eyes that makes me question that statement.

"Smart girl," I mumble under my breath. That was not what I was expecting. I keep my eyes on the ground as I churn that over in my head. I know the kind of pain she must've been feeling, the kind of betrayal when the person who is supposed to love you relishes in dominance and control. The type that thrives on your misery. I really am a magnet for the shittiest of men.

"You've known a man like that." Jake looks at me knowingly.

I nod, shifting uncomfortably then clear my throat. "It was a long time ago."

"Who was it?" Jake's murderous look tells me he would not hesitate to kill this time. Too bad that douchebag is in another time and place.

"His name was Trevor, but he is long gone. Nowhere near here."

Jake hands me some meat he warmed over the fire, and our hands touch briefly, he pauses before pulling away, then says, "Henry frequents the brothel, Lady Grave's, at the edge of town…just so you know."

Wow, I *really* know how to pick them. "Gross. I get the point. He's an abusing, womanizing bastard…stay away." I sigh loudly. "Why is it called Lady Grave's?"

"Because Lonnie Grave runs it along with help from Bill and Henry." He looks at me pointedly, then says, "You cannot trust her. She is one of them."

"Are you not one of them, Jake?" I meet his gaze sharply.

He just scowls and says, "No," but then he doesn't elaborate.

It just gets worse and worse in my head when I mull over everything. I chew on the mystery meat and moan appreciatively, letting my mind drift. I can almost understand Jake's reasons for dragging me out of there tonight, even if he acted like a barbarian. The question is, why? Was it that one kiss we shared, or was it something more? I decide to ask him straight out. "Why bother taking me away from Henry? I seem to crawl under your skin…piss you off regularly for just existing. So, why?"

Jake cocks his head to the side and has a wolfish grin on his face. "I enjoy your verbal abuse so very much. I couldn't bear to share it."

"You think you are funny, huh? Do you always redirect questions you are uncomfortable with?"

Both his eyebrows raise as he says, "Now, that is *the* question between us, is it not? You give me nothing, so I give you nothing."

"Touché." I purse my lips in thought. "Come on…tell me something true about you. If I am forced to stay in your company for the night, the least you can do is indulge me."

"Not much to tell, really." He finishes his coffee and sets the cup down.

Ugh. He can be so damn frustrating. "What is the real reason you helped me that night leaving Tucson?" I throw at him.

Jake glances at me and says, "I give you something. You give me something…remember."

"Fine. A truth for a truth," I say.

His eyes soften. "Bill is my uncle." He stops, noting that I am not shocked, and then continues, "He would've done some really bad things to you just because you are different. I couldn't have that on my conscience."

"My, my, my…Jake Evans answered my question *and* seems to have a heart in that chest somewhere," I give him a devilish grin before I ask the more serious question, "But why are you with them? If these men are such bad people, then why ride with them?"

"I'm *not* with them. I do some odd jobs for people here and there, tracking and such. I am working…sometimes even when it looks like I'm not."

That's interesting, I think. He waves his skewer at me, indicating it's my turn, and asks, "Where did that gun come from?"

Instantly, I tense up and look away. I see him shake his head in aggravation, so I alter the truth. "It was my grandfather's and is not from here. I keep it because it's special to me." Even though that statement is truthful, I still feel the choke of guilt. I fucking hate liars or being lied to.

"You are being somewhat forthcoming tonight, but don't think that I buy that *that's* the whole truth." Jake chews on some more meat.

"Well, let us see, you have held me at gunpoint, stalked me, forced yourself on me, and dragged me from an establishment in front of witnesses...I think I have the divine right to say or not say whatever the hell I want." I stare relentlessly at him.

Jake pins me with his eyes. "I never forced myself on you."

I smirk, knowing that would hit a nerve. He just smiles back and bites his bottom lip, drawing my attention there before saying, "Your tongue slid into my mouth willingly, and those legs..." he trails his eyes down to my bare feet, "couldn't wrap around me fast enough."

We wage a war with our eyes, but I lose the first battle and turn to look at the fire. "You are ridiculous, you know that?"

I can feel his gaze still upon me. Suddenly my skin is too sensitive for even the touch of my clothing. He really is the most frustrating man. I finally stop berating him with questions and just enjoy the silence. Besides, the more I ask...the more he asks, and that's not a good thing for me. He moves slowly around the fire, stoking it, and then tosses his bag behind me. "Use this as a pillow for tonight." I nod as he passes his duster over to me. "And this as a blanket."

I lie down and try to get as comfortable as you can be on a stone surface. I hear him do the same a few feet away. I'm not sure that I can sleep this close to him. He's still a stranger to me. His scent hits me from the duster coat, and I inhale deeply the manly smell of him I've come to know so well. The scent of Jake. The eerie silence of the cave becomes comforting after a while. The warm fire eases my tension, and sleep is not far away now.

My lids grow heavy. I don't know why I ask, but the thought hits me, and I can't hold it back. I whisper softly, "The other day…why did you kiss me, Jake?"

He's silent for a moment and when he does answer, it's not what I expected. "There is no universe in where I wouldn't have kissed you in that moment."

The honesty in that answer has floored me. How can he be such a complete brute one minute and then bust through every stitch of armor I have the next? What am I going to do with him?

Choosing Chaos

CHAPTER 13

Jake

What the hell was I thinking? I keep inserting myself where I do *not* belong. I had no business hitting Henry in front of half the town. Although, I'd gladly do it again. That don't matter as much as the message Bill will take away from tonight. When he sets his eyes on something he wants or wants to destroy, it never ends well. All those years away from this place, only to come back to the same old' shit. Well, except Sam, she's something else entirely. She's otherworldly, and anyone with half a brain can see it. Whatever secrets she and Warren keep must be big, or they wouldn't have lived secluded from people for this long. It's almost like they force themselves not to have relationships. I can relate to that. It will all come out in the wash, as Momma used to say. Nothing stays secret forever unless the only people harboring the secret die.

One more job, that was all this was supposed to be. Here I am, in the middle of a heaping pile of shit to deal with.

A soft moan escapes her lips, pulling me from my thoughts. I lean over and gently finger a strand of her silky hair that's billowing out around her. This woman is going to be the damn death of me. Already, her blueish-green eyes haunt me when I try and sleep. I've moved closer to her. I'm just close enough now to feel some of her warmth and catch the scent of her herbal bathing oils on her skin. She always smells like them.

Tonight, I watched her closely as Henry leaned into her in conversation and seethed as he spun her around the floor and while she may have smiled, it wasn't in her eyes. When he made a move to kiss her, I wanted to throttle him then, but I needed to see if she would— I needed to know if she wanted a man like him. I knew I had to get her away from that abusive piece of shit either way. I took time to pay one of Lonnie's girls to write a false note to Warren. I followed her outside to make sure she was safe, and what did I find but the curious and devious little Sam paying for information about me. I was impressed.

In the beginning, I had all intentions of tracking her down and threatening the truth from her. The truth of where she actually came from—where that pistol came from...and that marking. The day I showed up, gun drawn, she kept her cool and even managed to sass me while naked for all the world to see. I was done from that moment on. She could lie to me forever, and while I wouldn't like it, I would settle with it if it meant being near her.

Suddenly, her face twists in pain while she dreams of what I do not know. She whimpers and moves restlessly—her breathing rapid. Against my better judgment, I scoot beside her and pull her to me, placing her head under my chin. Within a few seconds, her breathing calms—becomes steady. Her body relaxes into a deeper sleep. I relish in the fact that she calms in my arms. I breathe in her scent.

I'm now a lost man. I would choose her chaos over peace any given day.

Tortuous Ride

CHAPTER 14

Samantha

My eyes are heavy as I peel them open. My shoulders tense up in an instant when I feel the press of a body against my chest, arms laid over me, and slow, even breaths. I raise my head ever so gently and see Jake's resting face. I'm not sure why he has me wrapped in his arms, but I don't pull away as I should. I simply watch him sleep. His square jaw is relaxed, unlike the usual tension I see there. He's quite possibly the most handsome man I have ever laid eyes upon. His tan skin glows with health and vigor.

The fire has long since died out, and the only light comes from the dim lantern a few feet away. His words from last night roll endlessly through my weary mind.

Why would he say that to me? We don't know each other—at all, really. We're from different worlds entirely. He can never know the truth. If he did *really* know me, then he would surely assume I was insane. This is the reason I've stayed far away from any sort of companionship since coming here. I'm sure Warren feels the same. It can never work between two people when there are so many secrets stashed away.

I'm not a blind woman. I know he lust for me, but that's all this is—some infatuation that would surely pass after his body was sated. I believe he has good intentions. Like the night he lied for me, or even last night's attempt at keeping me away from a dangerous man, but he has still crossed boundaries by stalking me in the shadows of my life the last few weeks.

As I lie here. I can almost pretend—live in the fantasy for the moment. I reach up and gently touch the scar running through his brow. His dark eyelashes flutter open, and those whiskey eyes catch me red-handed. I suck in a quiet breath, but I don't move my hand. Instead, I run my finger over that alluring scar. He watches me closely with his eyes at half-mast.

"You were having nightmares." His deep, low voice vibrates through me.

I nod, catching his meaning. That's why he held me last night. My heart feels that one statement so deeply. I need him to be the asshole I met, not this…this is much harder to handle. "Thank you," is all I can muster to say back.

Jake's eyes linger on each and every inch of my face. I can feel heat blossom in my cheeks and the warmth spreading lower. "What happened here?" I whisper as

I point to his scar, maybe to distract from what is transpiring between us.

I can see with certainty I've made a mistake. His eyes grow distant. The mask he uses when he needs to hide emotion is pulled back on. He leans toward me, shocking my senses, when he plants a gentle kiss on my head. Then, his warmth is stripped from me as he pulls away. He stands, stretching his arms over his head. His sleeves are rolled up, and I can see every vein in his taut, muscled forearms. "I'm sorry, I shouldn't have asked." I stand, turning away to fold up the blanket we had laid upon.

From behind me, he shuffles around, packing his things. "It's a genuine question, nothing to be sorry about. It's just not something I like to dredge up," he says.

I glance his way and nod. "I understand, I have those too." I shove the blanket into the pack. "Scars so deep, they seem to run completely through your soul, leaving a trench behind." He stops for a moment as if he's debating telling me something, but then he continues preparations to leave.

The moment passes. Whatever he intended to say, I may never know.

Once we are out of the cave and into the glare of the morning sun, I see Jake's mare a few yards away. She stayed here *all* night…just lingering around waiting on him. It's beautiful and sad at the same time. "She's a loyal one," I muse. "What's her name?"

"She doesn't have one."

"What?" I ask shocked. "But she *needs* a name. All horses need a good name, or all good horses, at least." I nudge his arm, smiling.

He laughs under his breath. His smile is something to see, something not seen often enough. "I got her a few years ago. She's a Mustang mixed with something…and I guess I just never thought of anything."

I look her over now more carefully. She's at least sixteen hands, much taller than your average Mustang, but has the head shape. "She's stunning, and a girl that fabulous needs a name, Jake," I reiterate. "What do you call her when you want her to come to you?"

He gives me that side smile, the one that men seem to have down to a T when they want women to swoon, and then he calls out to her, "Come here, girl."

The mare's head raises, and she doesn't walk…no, she gallops to him with ears forward—excitement clear in her big brown eyes. "You know, if I let Clint go in the middle of the night, he would probably be across the country by morning." I laugh.

"Clint, huh?" He grins. "Where did you get your name from?"

Internally, I giggle. Externally, I just smile and say, "It's just a name."

Jake doesn't seem to buy that but doesn't question me further. He walks his mare to me, stops, and reaches toward my face. I flinch slightly, but he ignores me and moves a stray piece of hair behind my ear. "If you want to, you could name her for me?"

Again, I feel I can't handle this side of him. He's breaking down defenses I have spent a couple years building up. I ignore the goosebumps his touch inflicted and nod. I don't need time to think of a name...I already have the perfect one. There's no hesitation in my voice, "Shadow," I whisper.

His brows raise, and he tilts his head to the side. "That was fast...I like it, witch."

I ignore the witchy comment as I roll my eyes. Yeah, me too, I think. I *really* like that name...he is my shadow. She is his.

I grab the reins and mount first. Jake swings up behind me, and, like last night, he takes my waist and pulls me flush against him. Only this time, there seems to be so much more tension between us. It's palpable in the air. The hostility between us has dimmed some and in its place is an electric current flowing. I feel the ache of need course through my retched body with that simple act of pulling me to him. As if I couldn't be more flustered than I already am, he doesn't move his hand. He splays it across my tummy, his thumb fingering the fabric of my dress as we ride.

We ride for the better part of an excruciating hour of sensory overload. I question whether this ride is as painful for him or if I am simply overdue for affection and my mind is permanently in the gutter. Eventually I try to relax into him and stop thinking about that kiss we shared. His solid chest is against my back. He leans his head down, and I feel him inhale the scent of my hair. His hand tenses on my stomach. The chemistry between us is dangerously close to causing an explosion. Every fiber of me wants to throw caution out the window and take this man out here in the desert. I can feel his need as strong as mine, tight against my backside. What is he doing to me? My chest rises and falls erratically.

Suddenly, as if he internally makes a decision, his hand moves down to my leg, and, without a care of whether I will mind, he rolls and bundles my skirt until one leg is exposed. I turn my head to look into his eyes...big fucking mistake. The heat in them could scorch the Arctic. I quickly look away.

I close my eyes and tremble at the touch of his calloused hand on my thigh. "What are you doing, Jake?" I whisper. He's playing with my emotions, and I'm not sure I can take much more.

"You want me to stop...say so," he challenges me, just waiting to see how far I am willing to go. Suddenly, his hand glides higher. He pauses as if giving me time to process what he wants or to protest it.

What he doesn't realize is that I am a grown-ass woman who just loves to be challenged. I turn my face back to his, seeing the desire behind the question he is silently asking. I don't say a word. Instead, I take my hand and guide his hand higher before releasing it.

"You really are going to be the death of me, woman," his husky voice whispers into my ear and has my mouth dropping open a touch. His rough hand plays havoc on my nerve endings as he lazily trails his fingers up and down my thigh. He knows *exactly* what he is doing. My brain screams at me that this is a horrible idea, but my body is blocking out those screams. I become putty in his meticulous hands that he can form into whatever he wishes. It's loathsome how pliable I am. I can't breathe, let alone speak, as my heart races inside me. His jaw clenches, and he worries his lower lip with his teeth as he moves his hand, sliding it in between my legs. I see the momentary shock there in his eyes…the laser hair removal was not just for my legs. His shock passes, and my body goes rigid the moment his fingers graze my center. I gasp out loud and watch his eyes roll closed as he groans internally. I lean back into him more. My back arching and my eyes close. I feel his mouth propped against my hair, breathing rapidly. His fingers move in slow, languid circles.

"Jake," I moan.

"What do you want, witch…tell me." He huffs the words out breathlessly into my hair.

I can feel my long-deprived body tremble as he moves over me. The slickness between my legs guiding his exploration. "I want you…all of you."

This seems to be his undoing. He lays Shadow's reins on the saddle horn, and with his now free hand, he holds my chin captive. He turns my head away from him so that my neck is bared. I feel his tongue move across my skin, sending chills up and down my body. My breasts become tight in the already confined bodice, nipples rubbing against the fabric. His fingers never stop their wonderful torture.

"Jake...I..." I sigh a breathy sound, feeling the build inside me all too soon.

"Just let go," he whispers as he moves his fingers faster. I can't take anymore as the pressure becomes too much. I reach back and grip his hair in my hand as he bites playfully on my neck. His cowboy hat tips from his head as I do, but the stampede string keeps it from hitting the ground. I hold his head captive there as my body becomes taut. Heat coils low in my belly and my mouth drops open in a loud moan as the orgasm hits me like a ton of bricks. My body trembles as I ride the waves until there's nothing left of me. I am a panting mess. I can't open my eyes or move in fear that reality will smack me in the face. Jake kisses my head in the most delicate way as his hand slips from my dress, letting my skirt's layers fall back to cover my leg. I now remember vividly why I like the song *Wild Horses* so much; the movie *Fear* comes to mind, and that blasted roller coaster. Loving that film may have been my first sign that I have red flag taste in men.

I look into his eyes and see the torment there. I still have one hand streaming through his soft hair. "Do you...want to...can we stop for a moment?" I stumble over my words.

Jake simply plants a small kiss on my brow and says, "We have all the time in the world. No need to rush. I told you, we will never be done, you and I."

Neither one of us talks the rest of the way. It is *most* tortuous.

Ugh...this is going to be a long ride.

Played Like a Fiddle

CHAPTER 15

Samantha

Now that my head is clearing, and my home is in front of me, I feel guilt settling into my chest like cement—guilt for making Warren worry, which I surely did, and guilt for leading Jake on. I could've stopped this flirtatious back-and-forth banter at any time but didn't…because I clearly didn't *want* to stop it. There was something about him from the moment I met him. I still feel that way, but the reality is the last thing I need is to entangle myself with him.

What future could we possibly have?

We stop Shadow by the fence and dismount. Jake tosses her reins over the horn instead of tying her. No need when you have a horse as obsessed with you as she is with Jake. I giggle when she rubs her head against him roughly while he scrubs behind her ears. Clint and

Halle come galloping over to see the new horse and slide, causing a cloud of dust to surround us. I guess Warren got them home okay. We are waving the dust away when I hear Warren step out of the house.

"Sam, Sam, Sam…" he says as his footsteps get closer, heading our way, "I take it your dance with Henry Fletcher went well considering it's the next morning." He chuckles as he turns the corner around the edge of the barn. His eyes land on me first with a big smile splayed across his face. That smile drops instantly when those eyes move to the man behind me. Warren's six-shooter is in the air and pointed at Jake in an instant.

My heart slams in my chest. "WOAH, WOAH, hey, calm down!" I yell and get in between them. Over my shoulder, I can see that Jake simply has his hands raised with his head cocked to the side. That stoic mask I know so well is in place. "Warren, put your damn gun away…*NOW*! I can explain."

He stares me down. His steady hand is unwavering. "You better get to explaining." He reluctantly lowers his gun and holsters it. I hear Jake drop his hands behind me.

"Jake saved me…in a way," I mutter.

"In what way!" he spits.

"Henry is not a good man—not like we thought." Warren pins me with a skeptical look. "It's true…he abused his former wife, *and* he runs the brothel in town." Warren's eyes widen then his mouth turns in disgust. "Jake took me away from there last night to warn me about him," I finish.

Warren shifts his gaze back and forth between us. "That may be the case, but this man right here," he points at Jake, "was riding with the same damn men that meant to strip you down in front of God and everyone…and who knows what they planned that night!"

"I know what it looks like, but he was a perfect gentleman last night." I hear Jake snort behind me and am thankful Warren seems to miss it.

Warren burns us with his scowl for a beat before he says, "There's more here." He waggles his finger between us. "I wasn't born yesterday. How long has this been going on."

My cheeks burn as the image of what just transpired on the horse flits through my mind. "It's not what you think. We've had a few run-ins. It's *nothing* more than that. Absolutely *nothing* at all." I glance back and see anger plastered all over Jake's face. I didn't mean for my words to come out so harsh, and *instantly* I regret them.

"Come inside, the both of you," Warren demands. "I got some food on the boil and coffee." He walks away grumbling, "Sounds like we need to have a little talk."

"You do know I'm a grown-ass woman, right! Ugh," I huff as he continues walking and ignores me. I could throw a rock at him right now like a petulant child.

I wait until Warren is out of hearing range before I turn to Jake, intending to apologize. Before I can speak a word, he is on me in an instant, backing me against the fence until I slam into it. He grasps my chin gently in his hand and leans over me. Grazing his thumb against my jaw.

"Nothing at all, huh…*absolutely* nothing at all." He tsks. "Your flushed face and fast beating heart say otherwise." He lays his palm across my hammering chest. He inches closer as if he is about to kiss me. My eyes close in anticipation, but then he backs away. I feel the instant void there. He's playing me like a fiddle.

"Seems I've overstayed my welcome." His voice sounds like gravel. "Tell Warren I appreciate the offer of food and him *not* killing me today, but I must decline."

My mouth is flailing like a fish, but nothing comes out.

"Goodbye, Samantha…until next time." Then the bastard kisses his fingers, the ones that *also* played me like a fiddle and swings himself onto Shadow and darts out into the rising sun.

"That motherfu—" I start to say, but I hear Warren yell, "Sam, you coming?"

One hour later, Warren and I sit on the porch, sipping coffee. Our bellies are full, but our hearts are troubled. I spilled the proverbial beans with him about…*almost* everything. He knows now that Jake has followed me, that Bill is in town and—of all things—a damn constable, and I told him that Bill may very well know where we live. I told him everything *except* the part about Jake being in the house, the whole make-out session that transpired, and of course…the ride home.

Warren clears his throat. "So, you are saying that Bill and his guys were playing with large amounts of cash after just coming into town, and that girl Lonnie is helping rob patrons?"

I nod. "Looks like Bill has several people in his pocket around here."

Warren purses his lips in thought. "The gambling is small-time stuff. It's dirty money for sure—a classic hustle. Somewhere else, he's doing bigger things and bringing the cash back to here," he rattles on as he sips from his mug, "could be robbin' banks or trains."

"Could be." I tap my fingers against my mug repeatedly. "Why is he trying to meddle in my affairs though?"

Warren groans and says, "You are an anomaly to him—a curiosity. Maybe he is determined to pick you apart and figure out what you are hiding."

"Way to make me feel better, Warren…shit." I sneer at him.

"I'm just saying we need to keep an open mind here. If he wields power over this town, then he can be very dangerous. He could have dozens of men working for him, willing to do *anything* he asks of them." He pauses and lays his hand on mine. "If it comes down to it, we *will* leave here—pack what we can and go…I'll not have you harmed."

My heart squeezes at his words. I pat his hand back. "I hope it never comes to that. We worked hard for this semblance of normalcy we have out here." I gesture to the barn and land that is so very peaceful this evening.

"That we did." Warren moves his hand, and we slink back into our chairs, sip our mugs, and enjoy the rustic view of the landscape. "You should have told me about Jake the moment he came here. You could've put us both in grave danger."

I pinch my eyes closed. "I knowwwww. I'm so sorry."

"From now on, no secrets in this house…you hear me?" he bites out.

"No secrets." I tip my head to him.

"Perfect, cause now let me ask you this…*and* you be perfectly honest with me." He cuts his eyes my way. I hesitate but nod anyway. "Is there more going on between you and that Jake Evans?" He cocks an eyebrow at me.

I open my mouth to lie but then stop myself. "I don't know…maybe," I answer truthfully. "He's frustrating and elusive. One minute, I think he's a creep, and the next, I'm hanging on to his every word, which, by the way, are few and far between," I ramble on. "Annnd he is a smartass most the time, Oh and cocky as hell." Warren starts laughing. "What the hell is so funny?" I demand, turning in my chair to fully face him.

"You have it bad and don't even realize it." Warren holds his hand over his mouth, muffling his laugh.

"I do not." I swat his arm. "Oh, what would you know."

"I know plenty. I couldn't string two words together when I met Birdie. I sounded like I was born with a stutter," he continues, laughing at me.

I roll my eyes dramatically and sigh. "Ah hell, who am I kidding." Once Warren calms down, I add, "It's just that I don't know anything about him, and I can never tell him about us. You know what I mean?"

"Do I ever?" he huffs.

"On a serious note, I want to go back to town…and soon," I add.

He raises a brow at me. "What for?"

"I've never thought to ask Myra about Bill or Jake. I still have *many* unanswered questions, and maybe she can answer a few for me."

Warren nods his approval. "Keep your friends close and enemies closer. I like it."

Hours later, the chores are complete for the day, and I have had my bath...indoors this time. I'm never one hundred percent sure my shadow isn't out there lurking. I move the oblong rug in my bedroom and roll it out of the way. Underneath, I wiggle loose the three un-nailed plank boards and smile when I see my duffle bag. I yank it from the floor and swing it over and onto my bed. Taking a jump, I bounce when I land behind it.

I haven't done this in a long time, but after last night and then today's events, I feel like I need a reminder of home—a reason to cling to it. I shuffle through until I feel a plastic bag crinkle. A smile pulls at my lips when I open the zip lock bag with my pink silk sleep shorts and tank inside. I am now thoroughly thankful that my mother always packaged her items in bags because my silks still smell fresh, unlike some of the other things that have been in this bag for far too long. I quickly undress and pull on the jammies. It's like heaven against my skin. I fumble through the contents of my past/future and find my mother Camille's necklace. I put it away months ago, fearing something would happen to it, but now I roll the Labradorite pendant she gave me in my fingers and watch the light from my lamp catch all the brilliant colors. I latch it around my neck.

The next thing I grab is the framed photo of my parents, taken with me and my sister on the farm. The absolute joy on my mother's beautiful face as she kisses my sister's head always tugs at my heart. Jenna looks so much like her. They both have dark hair and dark eyes and high cheekbones like the native side of my family, while I get my lighter features and blue-green eyes from Dad and his Irish/English side. Mom and Jenna sit on the farm's bench seat made from a tree off the land. My dad and I stand behind them. I'm leaning against him, grinning from ear to ear. Christmas tree lights twinkle in the background, lining the porch.

I remember that day well. Jenna's boyfriend Ryan snapped the picture, and right after that, he dropped down on one knee and proposed to Jenna on that front porch. It was perfect. One of those instant memory moments. The kind that you know will linger in family conversations at every holiday. I found out later that Ryan had even asked Dad's permission…old school style and respectfully. I can recall the smells wafting from the house. Ryan helped Dad grill steaks while Mom and Jenna made the side dishes. I always preferred baking, so I made homemade chocolate chip cookies.

Everything in the world felt right. I had a new business to establish, Mom and Dad got to live out their dream of running a farm and traveling, and Jenna was in college and engaged…it was all so *normal*.

All except that it wasn't.

My secrets were hidden behind that smiling face in the photo. I glare at her now…me. How could I be so stupid? I was hiding the discoloration of healing bruises with long-sleeved shirts, but here I was, grinning with my family and *pretending* everything was fine. I swallow the lump in my throat, threatening to choke me, and lay the picture back in the bag.

Maybe a trip down memory lane is not what I need right now.

I flop back on the bed and stare at the ceiling…within minutes, my eyes grow heavy. The day catches up to me, and sleep claims me.

I stand barefoot in the bathroom of my apartment. Trevor is screaming at me through the door. My body is shaking uncontrollably as tears pour down my face.

"Get the fuck out here, Sam! RIGHT FUCKING NOW!" He slams his fist into the door, and I jump backward when I hear the cheap pressed wood board crack. I wrap my arms around my midsection as if I can hold myself together literally.

I am no weak woman; I have held my ground in the past, but today is different. I've been preparing myself for months, even going as far as to take shooting lessons, because I feared him that much.

Today, I told him I was leaving.

To prepare, yesterday, I put a duffle bag in my car. Inside, I packed only the necessary clothing I needed, toiletries, cell phone, makeup, and all the money I had been stashing back over the last six months. I stuffed any of mine and my mother's jewelry in there, too, not trusting leaving it there with Trevor. I grabbed my favorite photo off the dresser and wrapped it in a hoodie so the glass wouldn't break. Lastly, I slipped my pistol in the side pocket of the duffle. Once I had everything ready to go, the plan was to leave before he got home from third shift. I was done—

done with being talked down to and ridiculed. I had been docile long enough; it was time to stand on my own two feet again.

I awoke today, late, to the clock showing six and scrambled to get showered and dressed, knowing he would be home by seven. The minutes on the clock taunted me as I rushed around the house. Not even taking time to put them on, I tossed my socks and boots in the car and ran back in to pour my coffee. Then I glanced at the clock again...six thirty. I was heading for the door right when it swung open, and I gasped.

Trevor was early.

His sandy blond hair was mussed, and he looked tired, but when his eyes landed on me, he stopped dead in his tracks and demanded to know where I was going. He knew I had no plans to work on my shop today. So, I looked him directly in the eyes, lifted my chin, and stood tall when I said...it's over.

Next thing I knew, he slammed his fist into my eye. I stumbled back and hit the floor, coffee going everywhere. The pain didn't set in right away. Instead, adrenaline kicked up a notch, and I scrambled to get away from him as he stomped forward. Trevor is a stocky guy but fast. Before I could regain my feet, his meaty hands grabbed me and yanked me to standing.

He yelled and screamed in my face as he shook me. Demanding to know who I was leaving him for, things like that. At one point, he shoved me into the wall, and I could feel the plaster buckle. He laid his head on mine, pinning me there, begging me not to go.

There was a brief moment, through my tears, when I almost said...okay, I'll stay.

My watery eyes shifted around the dull prison that had been my apartment, and I couldn't find anything of me here. No Sam.

Everything was distinctly Trevor, down to the beige walls and cream couches. He had me caged here in his image.

I took a deep breath and rammed my knee into his groin as hard as I could. The moment he hit the ground with a strangled cry, I realized he was blocking my exit...so I bolted for the bathroom.

Now, here I stand, wiggling my toes on the cool tile floors, holding my abdomen, while Trevor tries to break the door down. I move to the window and peer out. Maybe if I can climb down that metal rose trellis...I think. I slink my legs over the side of the windowsill and glance down to the ground. Luckily, we are only on the second floor. I lace my fingers into the metal swirls of the trellis and then the toes of one foot. I take a breath, praying this thing holds, as I move my other foot to the metal, placing my full weight on it. So far, so good. I ease down, one foot and one hand at a time. My hands and feet are being pricked by the thorns as I descend. I'm almost there, just a few feet away.

I hear the door smash in completely. I jump the last few feet, twisting my ankle, but I keep my balance and make a beeline for the car. I can hear Trevor yell from the window and his footsteps retreating. He's no doubt on his way down those apartment stairs.

I lunge around the corner of the apartment complex and see my lovely flat black '68 Chevelle, just waiting to take me away from this hell. My feet pound the pavement. If they hurt...I don't feel it. I grab the door handle at the same time that I hear Trevor shout my name from the doorway. I peer over the hood and see him running for me. I slide into the car, push down the clutch, and hold the brake. I turn the key, and the engine roars to life...but sputters out. "Shit, shit, shit! Now is not the time, girl...come one!" I plead. She's old and can be testy to start. I try again, and this time, when she roars to life, I rev the engine over and over to keep her going. Trevor grabs for the passenger side door right when I slam her into first gear. Smoke boils from my screeching tires as I sling my car onto the street sideways. I can see Trevor in the rearview, stumbling and cursing. Then he is running back toward the building.

I don't let up until I am miles and miles away. I don't want to go to Jenna's and have a good cry. I don't want to see the anger on my father's face or sadness on my mother's. I want to release this pent-up stress, give myself time to think of the future. I need time to decide where I go from here...and I know just the place.

I barely notice how difficult it is to change gears with bare feet. It's okay. I will take this moment of freedom any which way I can get it!

The Sound of Silence

CHAPTER 16

Samantha

I awake to my heart beating erratically. The dream still replaying fresh in my mind. It feels like a lifetime ago, but in reality, it was only close to two years ago for me, but many years into our future. I think if I had Trevor in front of me right now...*this* Samantha would shoot him in the face, not just knee him in his balls. I giggle. I have no remorse for leaving him. The only regret I have is not slamming my fist into his face and doing it sooner.

My mind is restless, and I highly doubt I'll fall back to sleep after that dream, so I scramble out of bed. After tucking my duffle back into its safe little hiding spot, I head for the fresh bread we baked today on the counter. I take that and some whiskey to the porch, along with my homemade butter and a blanket.

The air is nice and cool against my skin, especially in these silk PJs. I swing the blanket around my shoulders and unbraid my long hair to let it breathe. A sigh escapes my lips as I dip my bread in the butter and savor that first salty, smooth bite before washing it all down with a swig of liquor. It is usually quieter out here in the middle of the night, I muse. The animals seem shifty and more vocal. I hear the horses nicker every now and again and the chickens are clucking about, not roosting as they should be.

Maybe they are just as restless as me.

Out of nowhere, I hear a strange clinking sound coming from the barn. I can see Clint slinging his dark mane side to side and trotting in circles. The silver of his dappled areas almost glow fluorescent in the full moon tonight. My worried brows pinch together. "What the hell has you all worked up," I whisper as I pick up the whiskey bottle and carry it with me toward the barn, dropping my blanket on the steps as I go.

The barn we built has three stalls on one side, a place for feed on the other, and a loft with stairs above that. It's simple, but all we needed at the time. I open the gate, letting myself into the fence, and creep slowly to the front of the barn. Clint is still prancing around—puffs of steam huff from his nostrils, and Halle has her ears pinned back...which is her everyday face. It's hard to tell if she's ever happy or just always pissed.

I hear the clink again. It sounds as if it's coming from one of the stalls. I weave my head side to side as I check out my surroundings. Everything gets quiet. I peer over the stable door into the first stall…nothing. The hay on the ground crinkles under my bare feet as I walk to the second and look over…nothing. My nerves kick up a notch as I tip-toe to the third stall and raise on my toes to see in…*nothing*. It's the sound of silence that's unnerving, but I shake it off.

I take a deep breath and sigh out loud. "Clint, you are such an ass. You're gonna give me a damn heart attack," I mumble.

Suddenly, someone grabs me from behind. A hand wraps around my mouth, stifling my scream. The whiskey thuds as it·falls to the ground, and I hear a man grunt as he struggles to contain me. My heart thrums haphazardly in my chest with my fear. I scream continuously, but it's muffled. I try to kick, but he's dragging me backward into the feed room—my feet scraping uselessly on the ground, trying to find purchase. I feel myself falling forward as he wraps one of his legs around mine, tripping me to the ground. My arms are pinned behind me as he pushes my head in the dirt. His weight lays upon me, hindering my legs from moving an inch.

"Do *not* scream again, or I'll walk right in there and shoot your colored friend in the head…do you understand me?"

I know that voice. Henry Fletcher. I recall my blunder of telling him the general direction of where we live. That one simple mistake may now haunt me forever.

"Nod if you understand me, girl," he growls into my ear, his once proper voice now monstrous and distorted with anger.

I nod with my face turned sideways and my cheek pressed into the ground painfully. Before I can react, I feel a noose go around my neck and then one around my hands in the back. My body panics, and fight or flight kicks in. I struggle with everything I have, but every time I move an inch, he tightens the noose. I flail side to side. Fear washes over me.

"I want you alive, so stop moving. Every time you move, I tighten this rope." I hear his ragged breathing, either from exertion or excitement.

"Why are you...doing this?" My voice breaks as tears leave trails down my cheeks.

He chuckles beside my ear, and I feel his hands sinking into my hair, and I want to vomit. He reaches around and shoves a cloth into my mouth as I sling my head side to side, then he ties it around in the back. I throw my head backward in one quick motion and hear a satisfying crack when it makes contact with his face.

He grunts and groans and then slams my face harder into the ground. "You little bitch!" He bites out against my ear. "You will pay for every move you make against me tonight."

I can't move and can only breathe through my nose; I feel like I'm having a heart attack even though I know it's a panic attack.

Breathe...just breathe. I keep saying it over and over in my head. He roams his fingers over the silk of my pajamas from my back and then veers down slowly. "I'm doing this because I can and because I know it will *piss off* Jake Evans to know that I took you from him. You're coming with me tonight," he grunts as he tightens the ropes on my hands. "But first, maybe we'll have a little fun."

My blood runs cold at his implication. Jake tried to warn me. Now I understand why he was adamant about taking me far away that night. Henry is much worse than I could've ever imagined. Oh my God…Jake and Warren. What will they do when they find me missing? I can't let that happen, my worry for them briefly overshadowing my own fears.

His hands slide into my shorts. I try to buck him off, but he pulls the noose tighter, making me gag. All of a sudden, he flips me over and slaps me so hard that my head snaps to the side. I see stars for a minute, and my ears are ringing. I blink rapidly, trying to clear my head.

"You're a worthless whore like the rest of them, you know that? Like my bitch wife, God rest her filthy soul."

His wife is dead. Oh my God, his wife is dead. He killed her. That is a certainty screaming in my head. Breathe, just breathe…I say again and again. The face I once thought was handsome comes into focus. His features are marred by rage—his crazed blue eyes look psychotic. His right eye is black, and his nose looks to be broken from Jake's punch and now my headbutt. The light is gone from his eyes. It's like his soul is gone, and his entire being has dimmed and is void of humanity.

He leans down, grasps my chin in his rough hands, and licks my face. "I want to taste your fear," he says with a smile.

I squeeze my eyes, trying to clear them, but the tears flow, blurring my world. I feel faint as the rope mixed with the gag begins to take its toll. I'm not getting enough air. My eyes roll back into my head, but I pry them open again. I vaguely feel my top being ripped away. Air hits my chest a second before greedy hands do. The rope Henry holds is slowly getting tighter around my neck.

Everything goes black.

When I come to, I see the shape of Henry. He fumbles with his breeches. I no longer have the strength nor breath left in me to struggle. My shorts are gone. I can feel the rough ground of hay and dirt under me digging into my skin.

"Well, well, well, Bill will be surprised to learn that his nephew is a filthy liar." I don't catch his meaning until I feel the sharp point of a blade graze my tattooed hip. I close my eyes, drifting away again.

A sharp point on my neck forces me back to consciousness. "You will watch me, girl." I moan through the gag. Henry rears back and slaps me again. This time, the gag comes off my mouth. I don't hesitate as I release a guttural scream just seconds before Henry yanks on the rope, cutting off my air supply completely. I feel his body settle between my legs. I gasp for air and squirm my body—arms numb from being strapped underneath me. I feel him press against my center. My world begins to fade again as my oxygen depletes.

I'm going to die.

A deafening shot pierces through the barn. Warmth spreads over my face and chest. Slowly, air begins to enter my lungs again. It takes a few beats for me to realize the warmth I feel is blood. I gasp as soon as Henry's limp body falls lifeless beside me, releasing the pressure on the rope completely. Air struggles to move through my wounded throat.

"I got you, Sam…It's gonna be okay." I hear Jake's voice, the ground crunching under his boots. I squeeze my eyes closed to keep the blood from running into them. "Stay still—don't move—I need to cut these ropes." His voice is different. It's calming but with a heavy dose of worry dashed in the mix. I keep taking in each and every precious deep breath as I feel my bindings slowly fall to the floor one by one.

I hear the click of a gun and then, "What the hell happened here?" Warren's voice booms through the rickety barn.

"Henry Fletcher happened," Jake's voice sounds vicious. I feel something tossed around my nude body and a cloth of some kind gently wiping my face as I flex my arms and wiggle my fingers.

"Holy shit…*Sam*?" Warren's strong voice breaks as if he's seeing me for the first time. A few seconds later I feel his hand clasp mine.

"I'll be fine once his blood is off of me." My voice creaks.

"Warren, go draw a bath outside. I'll carry her over." Jake says as he continues wiping the blood from my face.

I finally dare to open my eyes. My first sight is Henry's head. It has a gaping hole—his lifeless eyes still on me. A shiver creeps down my spine. I flit my eyes to Warren and wish so badly that I wouldn't have. Tears stream down his cheeks as he takes note of the marks going around my neck. I reach my hand up and wipe his wet face.

"I should have gotten to you sooner. I'm so sorry," he cries.

"You couldn't have known what was happening. I'm alive, and that's what matters," I whisper.

Jake interrupts us by grabbing Henry's legs and pulling him out of the way and into a corner. "I'll deal with this piece of shit later…Warren, can you run that bath?" Jake's agitation is evident in his stride and tone.

Warren stands to leave, shock written in his weary expression. He doesn't trust Jake or seem to particularly like him, but he may have gained some respect for him tonight because he does what he asks and heads for the house.

Once we are alone, Jake comes to my side and kneels down to examine me. His jaw clenches, and his lips form a tight line. He reaches out and threads his hand behind my neck and into my hair, then pulls me against him. I shake violently with release as I sob against his chest. He doesn't say anything. He just holds me until all the monsters go away.

Sometime later, I hear Warren call out that the bath is ready. Jake scoops me into his arms and carries me to the other end of the house. The curtain sheets are drawn around us as he gently sits me in the warm water. "I'll be right back." He walks away, slipping through the curtain. I hear him discussing something with Warren, but I can't make out their words, only that it's a heated conversation based on the pitch of their voices rising and falling. I grab the closest bar of shea soap mixed with lavender and begin viciously scrubbing my body from the face down.

Jake flings the curtain back when he returns carrying a nightgown and the whiskey I dropped in the barn. I sink lower to hide my breasts…not that he hasn't now seen them covered in blood, but still, I drop into the water. He pauses, noticing my reddened skin as I still scrub my arms raw. He tosses the gown aside and then sets the whiskey on the table.

"Give me that," he says, not waiting for a reply. He simply takes the soap from me.

I try to make my voice as soft as possible. "I can do that myself." Everything in my neck is on fire.

His eyes dart to mine, and my heart aches in my chest as he says, "Doesn't mean you have to."

He reaches into his pocket and pulls out a cloth. He dips it in the water and then lathers it before bringing it to my cheeks. On one hand, I feel exposed and defenseless as he washes my face, like a child. On the other hand, it feels nice, like he truly cares about my well-being right now. When he gets near my neck, he hesitates. "You want some whiskey first?" he asks.

"Yes, please." I take the bottle from him and down three large gulps, coughing a little after.

"Easy, a little for the pain, but I need you awake." He takes the bottle from me, setting it aside, and eases that cloth back to my neck. He moves so very slowly, trying his best not to hurt me. It brings fresh tears to my eyes.

"What were you saying to Warren out there? Sounded like you two were arguing," I whisper.

Jake doesn't look at me when he says, "Told him I'm staying tonight." He lifts his gaze to me and sees my confusion. "Henry might not have been alone."

The thought did cross my mind. What if Bill sent him? Either way, now I understand Warren's raised voice. Then, another thought takes over. "How did you get to me in time, Jake?"

He continues cleaning every inch of me as he moves to my hands and arms. "When I left you today, I didn't get an hour's ride away and noticed tracks crossing my path. They lead toward the canyon." He finishes one arm and moves to the other. "I almost walked away, but then I wondered if it could be Bill coming to nose around."

"You almost walked away?" I ask even though I know the reason. I wounded his pride today with my careless statement.

"I wasn't sure if you really wanted me around," he admits.

I feel embarrassed by his admission, but I can't find the right words to express it. They lump in my throat and refuse to budge. I never meant to make him feel like that, even though we have both steadily held back from each other—never fully giving in to this weird connection we have.

After I've soaked all the remnants of Henry off of me with two baths, Jake leaves me alone to dress in private. Inside the house, he tucks me into bed. He turns to leave, but I clutch his hand to stop him. I see a war raging in his whiskey eyes.

"I'm glad you came back," is all I can manage to say. I release his hand as he heads to the living area to sleep.

Uncle Bill

CHAPTER 17

Jake

I flick the pad of my finger over my knife checking for the sharpness of the blade—still too dull. I continue pressing the blade outward on the whetstone as Bill rambles on.

"You haven't seen him nowhere, then?" Bill says as he shuffles documents around on his desk.

"Nope."

"Henry was supposed to be here three days ago for a meeting—a *very* important one. It just proves my point that you can't rely on no one." He pulls out a key from the top drawer in his desk and shoves his chair away as he walks to a safe beside his entry door. "That whoremonger is probably out doing what he does best."

My eyes stay low, but I watch carefully as he opens the safe and inserts a document. From the corner I sit in, I can just make out the shine of gold bars and currency notes stacked to the brim inside. Interesting…where does one acquire that much money these days?

Bill locks the safe and turns to me. "What's going on with you and that girl?"

"I don't know what you mean." I slick the knife across the whetstone with a little more vigor.

"You know exactly what I mean, Jake." His voice holds a touch of animosity. "I ask you to follow her, not fuck her!"

I roll my lips into a tight line to keep my temper in check. Today is not the day for Bill to *piss* me off. "What I do with women is *damn* sure not your business."

He eyeballs me for a few seconds. "No, it's not. However, you are my nephew, and contrary to popular belief, I care about your life choices."

That is bullshit, but I continue working my knife and keep my thoughts to myself. William Evans has only ever cared about himself. He is strategic in that everything he does is for his ultimate benefit.

"How were you *unable* to find out any information about those two? It's odd that she lives with that black man, but even stranger that they have kept to themselves for this long." He rubs his mustache, slicking it down. "I do *not* like a mystery, and especially not one in *my* town."

I'm not sure what all manners of shady shit he's into, but one thing is for sure…he better steer clear of

Samantha. "There's no mystery out there, just people trying to make a living."

Bill cuts his eyes to me. "If you do find out anything unusual, you will let me know right?"

"Of course," I lie. After what happened to her, I would never allow this asshole near her, let alone provide any information on her. Sam's bruised neck comes to mind every time I close my eyes, and I have to take a reassuring breath—keep reminding myself that she's alive and unharmed. If I'd been a few minutes late…ugh, I can't even think it.

I stayed with her for four days—took watch every night. Warren wasn't in love with the idea, but in the end, he appreciated the added protection. I'm still not certain if Bill sent Henry or if Henry came on his own. Bill does appear to be genuinely pissed with Henry's sudden disappearance.

Either way, I stayed. I bathed there, ate there, and slept when I could. I questioned Warren about his strange piping system and his setup for heating water. I've seen something similar once before at a hotel in Kansas, but never like his. It was impressive and just added to the questions piling up in my mind. After days of being around them, I'm no closer to understanding their strange relationship or way of living. It was absolute torture being near her but also keeping my distance. It was never meant to happen anyway. I crossed lines that I shouldn't have even been close to.

I peer out of the window at the people below walking the streets. Today, Tombstone is bustling with scientists and inventors from all over. The excitement is thick in the air. I couldn't care less. I need to distance myself from everyone, including Sam. I never intended to get close to her. I promised myself a long time ago that I'd never get close to another human being. They never stick around. Death follows me through life, taking away anything and everyone I care for.

"Where are you off to today Jakey boy?" he asks.

I fucking hate when he calls me that. I'm a thirty-year-old man, and Uncle Bill has called me that since birth. I turn back to face him. "Not sure, maybe to the farm."

"How's your parents' place these days?" he mutters without meeting my eyes.

"Barren. I don't have time for it…not with my line of work anyway." What's there to go back to, I think—an empty house with tainted memories. Nah, I much prefer the open land.

Bill nods and swivels in his chair to watch people lingering in the streets below. "I understand," he says, then his smile grows as his brow raises. "Look there, Jakey…is that not the peculiar Miss Samantha?"

My heart picks up a notch as I look out the window and see her walking with Warren. What the hell is she doing here? It's been a week since she was almost raped and killed, and there she is, parading the damn streets. I clench my jaw.

Bill turns his tilted head to me and smirks. "You still going to the farm today?" He chuckles.

Lost and Found

CHAPTER 18

Samantha

Warren won't let me out of his sight today, and it's beginning to irk me to no end. I had every intention of coming here with or without him. Normally, just this environment alone would be enticing, but that's not why I'm here. I came to have a little chat with Myra and Judith. I've yet to tell Warren about the weird things that Judith has said recently that piqued my interest, mainly because it could be utter nonsense. I would much rather decipher her rantings thoroughly before involving him, but here he is…not leaving my damn side.

Today, I am wearing another of Milly's hand-me-down dresses. The deep navy fabric is accented by cream lace and the corset is a little on the tighter side. I feel like my breasts may explode. I opted for a cream silk scarf to hide the red marks still healing on my neck. My hair is rolled into a chignon with only a few tendrils down to frame my face. My heavy pistol is strapped with Warren's handy contraption he made for me on my thigh.

Warren is in his brown vest today, paired with a cream linen shirt. His fedora is tipped low as usual. He carries two peacemakers and a bandolier of bullets around his hips. He has been in a murderous mood for a week now. His guilt for not getting to me earlier is eating him alive, no matter how much I've tried to ease his troubled mind.

"Why don't you go see Clifford?" I nudge his shoulder. "You need to loosen up." He begins shaking his head. "It's broad daylight, Warren and look around you." I gesture to the crowd. "Nothing is going to happen to me today."

"I think it best if we hang together," he mutters.

"Henry is dead and buried where no one will ever find him. You need to stop beating yourself up. Last week, you said we needed to live more, to move on." I give his arm that's laced with mine a gentle squeeze. "We can't let what happened change that."

His eyes soften around the edges, but his body shows tension. "I still believe that, but we can't let our guard down again. We're a team, you and I."

"That we are." I smile up at him. "I want…no, I need a little girl time, though. I will only be with Myra and Judith, and we can set a time to meet up after. How does that sound?" I try my most persuading grin and doe eyes.

He huffs and releases my arm. "Five o'clock…In the stables. NO later than that. Understood?" He looks at me pointedly.

I give him a terrible salute and sashay away toward Myra's before he can change his mind. I look back after a few feet to see him still staring after me. It breaks my heart. I love that man more than he knows.

I lift the hem of my dress and pick up my pace when I see Judith in her usual chair outside of Myra's bakery. I walk right up to her and plop down on the chair adjacent to hers. "Hello there, nice damn day, isn't it?"

She turns to me, squinting her blind eyes, and says, "Nice damn day."

I cover my mouth and try to hold in the giggle. "You know what else is nice…whiskey." I bite my lower lip and look around to make sure no one is watching and pull out a flask from the pocket I built into my skirt. I take Judith's small hand in mine and press the flask to it.

Without hesitation, she unscrews the cap and takes her a long pull from it. "Ummmm," she mumbles as she smacks her parched lips.

Myra may throttle me for this, but I need to find out if it was a fluke last time or if, in fact, Judith does find clarity after inebriation. I make small talk to myself for half an hour, letting her continue to sip away. She keeps quiet other than the occasional ranting or cursing a child who gets too loud near her. She's a feisty one.

All of a sudden, Judith flits her unseeing eyes to me and says, "My mother was a traveler too, you know?"

My heart picks up its pace. "Why yes, I believe you mentioned it before." I tip-toe my way into this conversation.

She nods her head, making her gray ringlets bounce. "She fell in love."

"With your father?" I ask.

She bobs her head again. "Daddy," she whispers.

Guilt eats at me suddenly. Here I am, getting this poor old woman drunk and making her relive the people she's lost. All for what? I'm grasping for straws with some random crazy talk.

"Momma always said you needed the Lord's work to get home," she blurts out, interrupting my thoughts.

I dart my eyes around us, making sure we are still out of earshot to bystanders. "What else did she need to travel?"

Judith smiles real big. "A piece of home and to pay your debts." She pulls her hand from mine and shakes a bony finger at me as if she is about to say more and then stops.

I clench my trembling hands and ask, "What was your mother's piece of home?"

"She kept it hidden away." Judith's eyes close, but her smile is still there. "Where Daddy wouldn't see it."

I blow out a deep breath I was holding and ask, "But she told you about it?"

She nods her head again.

"What was it, Judith?" I pry.

She hesitates but then downs the last of the liquor, squishing her face at the taste, and says, "She called it a tape." She laughs. "A case tape."

My brows wrinkle, and tears burn behind my eyelids as I watch Judith go from laughing to singing the way she did the last time I saw her. She's chanting away manically while I feel like I can't breathe. I'm not sure if it's from her words or the damn corset. Could she mean what I think she means?

"Oh my, Sam, I didn't know you were out here!" Myra's voice pulls me back to the present.

I try hard to drag a mask over my emotions. "Myra! It's so good to see you." I stand quickly and distract her with a hug as my hand snatches the flask from Judith. I slip it into my pocket before pulling away from her. "I couldn't come to town and not see my favorite baker."

She purses her lips. "Ah hell, I'm the only baker," she says, making me giggle along with her. "Come in, dear. I have a new pastry I'm throwing together. You are going to love it!"

"That sounds spectacular."

As I follow Myra inside, I see Judith's eyes narrow in our direction, clearly pissed I swiped the flask from her.

I shake it off and make my way to the counter—the aroma immediately making my mouth water. Fresh bread, flakey pastries, and cookies line the counter. Other folks are wandering in from the streets to purchase the goodies, all while Myra talks a mile a minute to me about every stitch of gossip in town, which gives me the gumption to tackle the other task I had set my mind to…learning what I can about my shadow and his uncle.

I wait until we are alone for a spell and pop some questions on her. "Myra…do you happen to know anything about Jake Evans?"

She stops with her rolling pin and shakes more flour around, but her dimple is showing on her cheek as she looks me up and down knowingly. "I might know a few things…is there a reason you're asking? Maybe the scene last weekend has something to do with it?"

I pinch my lips together second guessing this conversation, but then curiosity was always my downfall. "Yes, it has something to do with it." My face reddens.

She continues rolling, but now her smile is beaming. "What is it you want to know, dear?"

I consider what I want to know first… "Is he…I mean, can he be trusted?"

She cuts her eyes to me and scrunches her face as if that's a bizarre question. "Of course. He's a good man, honey, or at least he was." She looks down at her flattened dough. "He's been gone for many years. I heard tales of his life here and there, but I've known him since he was a baby. He had a rough life, that one."

I don't fail to notice her eyes sadden on that last part. "What tales have you heard?" I ask.

Myra tips her head to the side in thought as she dusts her hands on her worn apron and says, "I heard that he lost many friends in the war…and after that, he left society for a while. They say he was living with Apache's out near the Mexican border."

I look away from her. The thought of him adrift after losing people is too much. It makes me wonder again about that scar that, not so long ago, I was tracing with my finger. "Wait, wouldn't he have been too young to be in the army during the Civil War?" I mentally calculate the time frame. I'm not sure his age and can only guess, but it still seems less likely that he would be old enough.

Her eyes grow sad again. "Honey, if you are this curious about him, maybe talk to him sometime." She's holding back something but suddenly changes the course of the conversation. "Everyone in town was hen pecking about you two," Myra blurts out. "They said that after I took Judith home, you danced with Mr. Fletcher but *left* with Mr. Evans." She waggles her eyebrows in her signature way.

"Ughhh." I rub my hand down my face. "Well, while that *is* true…it played out a little differently."

"Oh! Do tell honey, I need to live vicariously through someone!" She chuckles.

While I can't tell her everything, it's nice to have this simple girl talk. It makes me realize how very much I missed it. "Henry was a little too forward with me and Jake didn't care for it." She looks at me expectantly. "What? There's really not much to tell. Jake took me home. That's all."

"I wish I would've been there later and not left when I did." Her tone becomes serious. "Because I could've warned you that Henry is the one that cannot be trusted." Her lips tighten.

"I wish so, too," I whisper. She has no idea how much I wish we had that conversation before things ended like they did.

"Anyway, good thing Jake pulled you away from that man. He is a looker and all, but the ladies around here talk, and most of what they have to say is scary stuff," Myra says with a sigh and continues working her dough.

Was a looker...I think. He is now *very* dead. I feel nothing about it—not guilt, not shame, not anything. Maybe this life has hardened me more than I realized.

Just as I am about to ask more pertinent questions, several people waltz into the shop and pull the conversation away from me. After a few minutes, I realize the crowd is increasing, not dissipating. I guess this interrogation can wait until another time. "Myra...you'll have to excuse me; I have some errands to run. See you next time." Someone asks her about a purchase, so she throws a hand up, waving as I head out the door. As I pass Judith, she watches me with those vacant eyes but says nothing else.

Outside, the crowds are a buzz with life—a little too much for me. I briskly walk toward the barn at the edge of town. I need a moment to gather myself, and Clint always helps ease my torrent mind. Along the way, I pass by the brothel and stop abruptly when a girl on the balcony catches my eye...and she is a girl—very young, maybe between fourteen and sixteen. It makes my heart skip a beat the moment I can see her face more clearly in the daylight. She reminds me of my sister Jenna when she was a teenager. I could almost mistake them; the resemblance is so uncanny. She's looking out toward the sun. Her deep tawny skin and black hair stand out against the creamy-colored ruffle dress she wears. What is a child doing there?

My breath catches when I follow her long braid down to the end and see the large turquoise stone there. She's the girl I saw on the back of the Mack boy's horse that night. Her eyes must be the saddest I've ever seen. I wonder what sort of events could make a person's eyes hold such sorrow. I wave to her, catching her attention, but she bolts inside the moment she sees me.

What the hell? I have an eerie feeling crept over me, but I can't place it.

My mind is reeling after my conversations this morning and then the unease I have about that native girl. I feel a sense of panic in my chest, like a shift in the trajectory of life. It feels like two trains about to collide. On top of everything, today is my birthday. Warren and I don't celebrate those. I don't like the reminder that we have been trapped in another time...for another year, while our families move on without us.

All of a sudden, the crowd proves to be smothering. I pick up my pace to a fast walk, and then eventually,

I'm jogging until I end up in the barn with Clint. I recognize my symptoms immediately. It's the second time I've had a panic attack since the night Henry almost...

Clint lowers his head to scratch it against me as I rub behind his ears. I breathe in his scent deep, or as deep as I can, and curse the tight corset.

"Well, boy, what do you think? Am I losing my marbles?" I sigh... "Probably." I talk to Clint as if he understands me. His deep brown eyes see into my soul. I lean my head against his neck and gently caress his coat. "What am I doing here?"

A voice I know all too well startles me. "You talk to your horse often?"

I turn to find Jake leaning against the barn's stall gate. His black cowboy hat is sitting low over those golden, amber eyes. His long duster is hung open, showing both six-shooters and a bandolier stacked with bullets splayed across his chest. He must be as paranoid as Warren today. They both look prepared for war. "Clint is a very good listener," I say as I turn away from Jake and run my hands through Clint's mane.

I barely hear him move, but the scent of leather and sandalwood surrounds me, letting me know he's behind me. "What *are* you doing here...that *is* a good question," he asks.

"I'm just enjoying the festivities like everyone else."

Jake places his hand on my arm and gently turns me to face him. His eyes are searching mine for the truth. "Everyone else is not hiding in a barn talking to their horse." His fingers graze my silk scarf, and his eyes darken. "You shouldn't be here today."

"Where should I be, Jake? I will *not* cower. I will *not* stop living because one bad thing happened." I try to pull away, but he holds steady, not releasing me. I feel the sting of unspent tears. Why does his presence affect me so?

"You need more time to rest—to heal."

"What I need is for you to quit following me." Anger begins to take over, to tamp down the other emotions I'm trying so hard to contain. "What are we, Jake? You're all over me one minute and cold the next. You have hardly spoken to me, even while staying in my home this past week! Then you show up wherever I happen to be and make me feel..." I stop and take in a shaky breath.

"What do I make you feel?" His deep voice caresses my senses.

"Lost and found at the same time," I whisper. The truth of those words sting inside me. I was lost in an endless sequence of surviving, and I was perfectly fine with that. Then he came along and turned my world upside down. It made me realize that I *could* feel something again. The problem is...I don't want to. It hurts too much, or at least it will when it all inevitably comes to an end. "I wish I would've never met you," I choke out.

He pauses, staring at me, then pulls me into his chest and whispers, "The feeling's mutual witch."

A Special Place

CHAPTER 19

Samantha

Warren and I are on our way home. He's lost in his head as much as I am, and neither of us has chosen to open up to each other about those nagging thoughts. Jake held me for a few minutes, and then we parted ways when Warren walked into the barn and caught me awkwardly in his arms sobbing. That was a week ago. I don't know what to make of us—of him. He's fighting this attraction as much as I am, but why? Maybe his reasoning is as strong as mine. I'm beginning to have hope again that we will be able to get back home one day, but where does that leave Jake and me? I've denied myself friendships and relationships all because of the idea that one day, we will leave this place. What if Warren and I have been merely wasting precious time? What if we never go back?

"Warren, can you take me to our special place?" I ask as we bounce along the trail. The landscape gives way to the familiar and I realize how close we are to that very spot. "I haven't been there in months, and I need to see it, to feel it and *know* that it was real."

"Sure thing…I wouldn't mind seeing it myself today," Warren says.

I worry my lower lip with my teeth as I watch him drive the wagon. He is unusually quiet and distant. We stay that way, in our tensed silences, until we reach the landmark that we can see from a great distance. It's a Frémont Cottonwood tree. The same one that grows outside the gun range that 'future' Warren owns. As we get closer, we can see the stacked stones around the bases of the three enormous Saguaro cactuses surrounding our 'landing site.' These specific cactuses loom between fifteen and twenty feet into the air with each containing numerous branches.

I get off the wagon and take a seat in the center of the massive spiney plants. There's no humming, no pain, just nothing. I sit there staring off into the dry land. I close my eyes and bring back the memory to analyze it, to keep it forever welded inside my brain. Because the fear is that one day, I will forget.

Everything burns! I scream until my throat is raw. My vision slowly returns to me, and instantly, I grab my abdomen as nausea wells inside of me. I feel like I'm being ripped apart. I crawl on my knees, searching for Warren. I hear him near me…both of us moaning. Then my stomach lurches, and I heave out all the contents onto the ground. My whole body trembles with the exertion, but I eventually drag myself to him and grasp his hand in mine. I don't know how long we lie there, but eventually, the pain recedes, my vision clears, and my senses return.

We sit up at the same time and survey our surroundings, only to find that we are alone—no armory, no people, no cars…nothing. We are surrounded by an empty desert with only my pack and Warren's gun beside us.

"Alright kid, tell me what's got you feeling nostalgic," Warren interrupts my memory as he grunts and lowers himself to the ground beside me and pats my leg.

"Where to begin…ugh." I huff out a sigh. "This is going to sound crazy…like really crazy, but I believe that Judith's mother was a time traveler."

His eyes grow wide as saucers. "You're going to want to go back a little further and explain why you think that."

I do just that: I tell him everything she has said up until today and then end with, "Today I asked her what her mother's piece of home was, and she said a tape…a *case* tape."

Warren ponders that for a minute before saying, "A cassette tape," Warren mumbles. "Do you really think that's what she means?"

I shrug. "She sang or rather chanted that you need the Lord's work, a piece of home, and a debt to be paid. We have pieces of home but not much else to go on."

"I wouldn't be so sure." Warren suddenly stands and begins pacing the circle, piquing my interest immensely. "Some lady scientist was in town today talking about the next total solar eclipse." He ignores my gasp. "She said that the day before it happens, the town will gather for a pre-celebration. They'll have everything set up outdoors. Then, the next day, towns people will gather together for the event. There is a whole group of female students set out to study the phenomenon up north."

Now I understand why he's been so quiet. I bound up from the ground and grabbed Warren to make him stand still. "What's the date?!"

Warren grins from ear to ear. "July 29, 1878…about two months from now."

"Holy *SHIT,* Warren! The piece of home…check, the Lord's work must mean the eclipse…check, now what do we do about the debts to be paid?"

His face falls. "Hell, your guess is as good as mine. *Also*, if you remember, my gun was made in 1876, the year we came to. If we pick a random item from home, we may go back to a different time and place, or worst case scenario…it doesn't happen again. What if it was a once-in-a-lifetime cosmic fuck up?" I turn and stomp away, kicking the rocks as I go, and he yells after me, "I don't mean to sound negative, Sam, but we have to ease into this idea. I don't want either of us getting our hopes up. It could shatter us both if we do."

He's right, as usual. It doesn't mean I'm not entitled to be pissed off at the universe right now. I have every right to be. I…no, *we* didn't ask for this shit!

"The other thing is," he swipes his hand down his face, "we left on an eclipse and came here during one…so chances are, we can only travel from one point in time to the other while an eclipse is actively happening."

"So, to go back to the exact time, we need something from 2017."

"It makes sense," he mumbles.

We stay silent for a few minutes, the weight of that possibility making us both question everything. I scan through my memory bank for the items in the duffle bag. Do we even have something from that year? Or was it the gun all along, and there's truly no way of returning home?

"What else is there, Sam? Something else is bothering you today."

"It's Jake," I admit as I climb onto the wagon and adjust my dress.

Warren leaps up beside me and clicks his tongue to get the horses going. "You like him, that's easy to see, and he likes you. What's the problem?"

"It's the unknown for me. What if we get the chance to go back? If I let myself fall for him…then what? Do we just part ways like it never happened?" I spew it all out to him—feeling the release of it deep in my gut. "If I tell him the truth, he will think I'm nuts. If I don't tell him and we stay here, then I'm just a liar, giving him only a piece of me and never all of who I am."

Warren nods and pulls out his pipe to light it, mumbling awkwardly with it in his mouth, "What is Jake's deal then? This doesn't seem to be one-sided here."

"That is the million-dollar question, isn't it? He acts truly infatuated with me at times but keeps a certain distance between us. He's got demons, that's for sure. I'm just not sure that *his* can ever play well with *mine*."

We discuss ideas and theories along our way home. I shut down the Jake conversation because it's going nowhere—like we are. We are into May now, and the land is heating up to an uncomfortable degree. Today, the dry desert dust kicks up behind us in a cloud as we round the base of one of the mountains surrounding our canyon below. Literal tumbleweeds roll by, but other than that, the only sounds out here belong to the steady beat of our horse's hooves.

I flinch as a sharp whizzing sound zings past me, followed by a thud. My breath stutters, and my heart hammers in my chest when I see the culprit. A lone arrow protrudes from the wood siding of our wagon. Warren's eyes find the arrow and then hold my panicked gaze. Before I can react, Warren's pistol is out and scanning the ridge. I lift my skirt, pull out mine just as fast.

Warren places a finger over his mouth indicating for me to be quiet. "Stay calm. Maybe it's a warning shot." He halts the horses.

"Apache?" I inquire.

"Most likely, by the looks of that arrow." Sweat beads on Warren's brow.

"What do we do?" My voice trembles while my eyes dart around wildly.

"They had a clear shot...we are out in the open. I don't think they'd have missed if they wanted us dead." I swallow the knot in my throat. I pray he's right. There's a bone-chilling silence all around—like the world paused for this moment.

Out of the shadowy crevices of the mountain a man appears...alone. His bronze skin, high cheek bones, and midnight black hair tell me that he *is* most likely Apache. Oddly, his hair is lopped off in an oblong slant hanging loosely about him. His dusty cotton tunic is belted around the waist with a thick leather strap and his moccasin boots go up to just below the knee. They're adorned with vibrant beads—the only colorful thing about him, really. Peeking out above his shoulders I see a quiver full of painted war-type arrows and in his hands a bow with one arrow already notched.

I hold my breath as Warren says, "We mean you no harm." He holds his hands up in a peaceful gesture and continues, "We're just trying to make it home."

I notice Warren's finger never leaves it's spot hovering over the trigger, even with his hands raised in a show of peace. I keep my gun lowered beside me, but ready to fire if need be.

He continues walking forward without speaking. All of a sudden, the mountains seem to be moving. I glance around and blink several times before I realize it's not the mountains, it's people in them. "Warren," I whisper in my panic and nod for him to look up. I hear his ragged breath as we come to terms with what we are seeing.

We are completely surrounded.

"What do you want?" I ask—holding my head high and feigning strength. I'm beginning to think he doesn't speak English after several seconds pass.

Warren's arm lowers a touch as the man gets closer. I look over, shaking my head for him not to do what I think he is about to do. Warren belts out, "Don't come any closer. We mean you no harm," he says again but with more force this time. "I will do what it takes to protect this woman beside me, so I suggest you stop moving." Warren's voice has taken on a deadly calm. He lowers his arm more when the man continues, placing the aim of his pistol back on the stranger.

Out of nowhere, we hear hoofbeats pounding the ground behind us. The man in front aims his arrow in that direction just as we turn our heads around. There's Jake with a rifle pointed at the man and Shadow barreling toward us. When Jake locks eyes with him, though, he yanks back on the reins, lowers his rifle, and

Shadow slides to a stop beside us. A cloud of dust rolls through the air.

"What the hell do you think you're doing, Tai?" Jake barks out at him as the dust clouds around us start to settle. My mouth is hung open—gawking at him. Warren has yet to lower his pistol, which is still aimed at the man Jake called Tai's head.

The man releases his hold on the bow and slips the arrow back into the quiver as he cocks his head at Jake and shocks me even more by speaking clear English. "I could ask you the same thing, Chato."

Chato? Tai? What the hell is happening here?

Jake drops down from his horse and looks toward the mountains. Scanning the area, I notice the others have mostly retreated. The ones still there have lowered their arrows. As Jake saunters past me in the wagon, he mutters, "You really are a magnet for trouble, witch." Jake walks right up to the man and stares him down for a beat, but then a sly grin pulls at his cheek. The man returns the smile. The cold demeanor changes instantly as the two men have their silent interaction. "It's real good to see you, partner," Jake says.

"Very good to see you alive and well, Chato," the man replies slowly with an accent.

Warren has lowered his weapon but is still tense beside me. I interrupt their odd reunion with, "Someone care to explain to me what is going on here?!"

Jake looks at the me then back to the man he calls Tai, "I was wondering the same thing. Now, why did you have an arrow aimed at my friends here?" I feel a little flutter of something inside when I hear Jake refer to us as friends. It's strange given the chaotic situation.

The man purses his lips and looks away from Jake to face us. "My name is Taiyin izé, but you can call me Tai. Me and my people are here looking for someone who was taken from us. I meant only to question you. We needed to find Chato." He turns back to Jake.

Needed to find Chato? What the hell? "And the best way to question us was with arrows aimed at our heads?" I blurt out.

"She has a point, Tai." Jake levels him with a glare. "And why did you need to find me? Who was taken?"

Tai looks to the heavens and sighs before meeting Jake's skeptical eyes. Worry and strain are evident in the man's features as he says, "It was the only way. I tracked you here. I didn't know if these two could be trusted. I knew *you* could help me find her...my daughter."

"No...not Nalin." Jake lifts his cowboy hat and runs his hands through his dark hair in frustration.

My heart is breaking for this stranger, even though he held us at the tip of an arrow a few short moments ago. Simultaneously, my brain is trying to wrap around the idea of these two men and what kind of history they must share. The stories of Jake spending time with the Apache is obviously true. My eyes flit to the beaded and feathered dagger that is positioned near Jake's pistol. I wonder, was that a gift from Tai? It makes my curiosity peak even more. What brought them together in life?

Warren's still pissed beside me. However, hearing that a man's daughter is missing has taken some of the fire out of him. Warren has already holstered his gun. He climbs off the wagon, approaches Tai, and surprises the man by saying, "My name is Warren, and this," he points to me, "is Samantha. How can we help?"

This is the side of Warren I love and hold dear. He would give the shirt off his back for anyone in need. He's a fixer of problems…and people. I can tell this is something that sits in his chest and pains him because he knows what it feels like to lose a child, even if his son is just not born yet.

Tai shifts his gaze between both men before saying, "My Nalin was taken from us a week ago during a raid. We were out hunting buffalo when they descended upon us. Nalin was supposed to stay at the camp, but she didn't. These were not men from another tribe nor from the border of Mexico. They covered their faces and bodies to hide their true selves, but not well enough. They were white men. One had hair like the setting sun. They stole horses and pelts and killed five of my people, but it wasn't until the raid was over that we realized she was missing."

I listen to the men discuss what the raiders looked like and their horses. I hop off the wagon and move to stand with Clint—running my hands through his thick mane. Tai tells Jake and Warren about his harrowing night of loss. My heart aches for him. I can almost understand his extreme behavior moments before Jake showed up. What lengths would I go to for the people I love?

"Sounds like this was planned. They were most likely looking for your camp but found the hunting party instead. Have you moved your location?" Jake says.

"We are safe…for now," Tai replies.

The conversation between them continues, but it's not until I hear her description that Tai is giving Warren that I drop my hand from Clint and suck in a raspy breath.

Jake swings his head my way. "What is it, Sam?"

"I know where she is!"

Mischief Maker

CHAPTER 20

Samantha

I pour over the details Tai gives of his daughter, Nalin. He describes her face and size, and her long midnight hair braided.

"Are you sure it's her you saw?" Jake asks, and I don't fail to notice the glimmer of hope shining in his and Tai's weary eyes.

I hesitate. What if it's not her? It would shatter this poor father. I scrape up my memory of her riding through town on the back of one of the Mack brothers' horses, then of her leaning over that brothel balcony. "It's her, Jake. I just know it." I look at Tai and ask, "Did she have a large stone fastened to the end of her braided hair?"

Tai's eyes light up, "Yes!" He says excitedly and then proceeds to describe it to me.

I nod. "It's her." The men listen as I recap the times that I saw her. I want to sugarcoat it for Tai, but I don't. When he hears where I last saw her, I can see unspent tears in his deep brown eyes. "I'm sorry, Tai…truly sorry."

He tips his head to me with respect, then looks to Jake. "Chato, do you know the man she speaks of? The one who rode her into town." Jake's jaw clenches, and he nods once.

I make a mental note to ask him where he got the name Chato.

"We must get to her tonight. My mind will have no rest until she is back with her people. Will you help me?" Tai asks Jake.

"Of course, you need not even ask me that."

"I want to help too," I add.

Warren is shaking his head as Jake protests loudly, "No damn way, Samantha! I don't want you anywhere near this mess."

"You can't tell me what to do, Jake Evans! And I *can* help. I know some of those girls that work there." My brain begins working overtime, and an idea hits me. "I have something—a tincture that can make a person feel deathly sick." They all stare at me like I've lost my mind as I recall the samples of oleander I gathered in Tucson and the chloroform. "I can use my tincture to incapacitate Lonnie, or I have chloroform if need be…we could take Nalin without bloodshed and chaos. We could devise a plan to simply walk in and take her back."

Jake tries to hide his side smile, but I catch it before it's gone. Warren curses under his breath, probably because he knows my stubborn ass will never listen to reason, and Tai full-on looks at me with curiosity.

"Are you a medicine woman?" he asks.

"No, no, no…I mean, I dabble in herbs and their uses, but I mainly make soaps and lotions," I babble on.

Tai crinkles his brows together and says with certainty, "No. You are a medicine woman. I can see these things." I feel my face warm at his comment. There's something so deep and intuitive about this man.

"So…let's make a plan," Warren interrupts Tai's scrutiny of me. I'm floored by how quickly Jake and Tai nod in unison. I expected more of a fight from them, but it warms my heart that they are putting trust in me.

Now, I just have to *not* screw this up. A young girls life is a stake.

The four of us gather around a blazing campfire not far from Tombstone. Tai instructed his men to stay in the mountains and await our return. Night has fallen, and the desert is blanketed with stars. It would be a magnificent scene and a most relaxing evening if it wasn't for the nature of this meeting and the tensions that are running high.

So far, the only thing we have agreed upon is the timing of our extraction. We all decided that the middle of the night would be best—too soon in the evening, and more men would be lingering about—too late into the morning, and the ladies could be a problem. Tai is bound and determined to slaughter Kelvin Mack and whoever the other three men are; however, Jake believes that it's unlikely they're even still in town.

I learned that Nalin is fifteen years old…just a baby, really. I can't imagine how scared she must be. She can speak English also, but not as well as her father. I just hope she can understand enough to trust me when the time comes.

The men begin to argue, catching my attention.

"If it was Kelvin Mack…then it was likely his brothers with him and one other person." Warren levels Jake with a glare. "You ride with them. What do you know that you ain't tellin' us, Jake?"

Jake's lip pulls back in a snarl. "I don't ride with them, and I don't take kindly to your insinuations." He sits next to me with the firelight flickering on his face—illuminating his sharp jawline that in now clenched.

Warren spits, "Bill is your damn uncle, is he not? What do you know?"

Tai looks to Jake but doesn't hold the same animosity that pours from Warren. There's a certain amount of understanding that passes between them. "Would your uncle have done this?" Tai asks.

Jake's face is unreadable. He keeps that mask in place. "I'm not my uncle's keeper. If I had to guess, I would say it was the Mack boys' decision to take Nalin. Bill is money-hungry, but I've never seen him do anything like this."

I decide to derail the interrogation and get back to the plan. I stand abruptly and dust off the tan breeches I am wearing and kick a pebble with my tall riding boots as I start babbling off facts. "Jake...you said that the brothel has two men—three counting the bartender, that work there late at night." I pause as he nods. "Then Lonnie is usually there most hours of the day...or at Big Johns. If we go in after midnight, we may bypass several customers..."

I tap my chin in thought. "If we hide our horses and split up, that could work best." I see Jake and Warren tense up, but I continue and ignore their body language. "I can divide out the chloroform, ensuring we each carry one." I motion my hands to myself, Warren, and Jake. I look to Tai. "You can't come with us. There's no way people will *not* notice an Apache man wandering the streets in the middle of the night. If anyone sees you, they will assume the town is about to be overrun."

My eyes trail to the worn hatchet along Tai's side and the bow across his back. He would cause a panic for sure. Apache's are feared right now, in this era. People have relentless aggression and believe there will be a great uprising. More and more Native Americans are being put into reservations. It makes me wonder how his tribe has skated the infantry's reach for this long.

Tai holds my stare, making me nervous. "What do you believe I *should* be doing…Naiche?" he asks.

My brows pull together. Naiche?

"What does that mean…Naiche?"

Jake answers for him with a smirk, "It means mischief maker. Looks like you've just earned your tribal name."

I hear Warren holding in a chuckle, so I walk over to where he sits and kick his booted foot, which only makes him laugh more. I go back over to Tai, disregarding Warren, and say, "Anyway, I think you should watch our horses and stay hidden." I point to Warren. "And you giggle box. You should man the rear exits of the building while Jake man's the front lookout."

Jake pulls out a flask and takes a sip before passing it to Warren without making eye contact with me. "And what will you be doing, *Naiche*?"

I grit my teeth at him. "I need to go in first and locate Lonnie. I've heard that she makes her rounds at Big Johns every night. She needs to be my first target. We can't have her going back to tell Bill what happened."

"You're not going in alone. Forget it," Jake says sternly.

"I never said I would be alone. I just need to take out Lonnie first. After that, we will play it by ear...together. We won't know who's around until we get in there." I stop and ponder this mission for a beat. Then a thought hits me. "Maybe I can go to Big John's now and scope it out. Lonnie's usually there early to lure men to the brothel, so I may be able to slip her the oleander in the bar before she ever returns to Lady Grave's."

"Or we could go in, grab Nalin, and shoot everyone who gets in our way." Venom laces Jake's voice.

"You would have a world of shit in your hands, and you know it! We can do this without being seen." I pace the ground some more and say to no one in particular, "Revenge will be had to the ones that decided it was okay to kidnap Nalin. I have no qualms about that; however, we need her out safe and sound and back with her people first. That's what's important."

They all stare at me, making me uncomfortable. Tai smiles, and so does Jake, even though his cowboy hat is hung low, and he tries to hide it. "Well...who's ready to save Nalin?" I stand tall with my chin held high.

"I shall follow your lead, Naiche," Tai says and bows his head.

"I'm with you, Sam, no matter what," Warren adds.

I turn to Jake. His head lowered to the ground. He nods. "I'm wherever you are, witch."

I can feel my chest twinge at Jake's words. There's a feeling forming inside that I do *not* want to explore.

Wherever You Go

CHAPTER 21

Jake

I followed Sam again today...for a few days now.
It wasn't my intention when we parted ways at the
barn, but something inside was pushing me to—like a
force beyond my control. Every fiber inside my body
was on edge. I meant what I said to her. Sometimes, I
wish we had never met that night in Tucson. I was fine
with being a loner. My job requires a certain amount of
distance from people. Now my brain is captivated by
my mysterious little mischief maker.

I'd stayed far enough away that I wouldn't have
been seen and stuck to the fresh tracks. I almost gave
myself away today when I rounded a bend to find their
wagon stopped in the distance. I strained to see what
they were doing, but I was just too far. After they

loaded up and headed out, I made my way to the area where they were sitting.

Every time that I think I have this woman figured out, she goes and proves me wrong. In front of the spot where the wagon's wheels rested, I could see stones had been placed around the bases of three enormous cactuses. There was nothing special about this place. I searched for any reason they might've come here or moved the stones but came up empty.

While that was strange, it was nothing compared to the shock that was to come. It felt like my insides were twisting when I crested the ridge and saw the lone native man with his arrow raised toward her and Warren. It was a sickly feeling. The world tilted and all I could see was red. There was too much distance to see who held the bow. I took off on shadow as fast as her legs could carry me. I've experienced loss, too much for my short life, too much for any one person. But *never* have I felt what a loss would do to me before it happened. It would've ripped my soul to pieces. I knew right then and there…hooves pounding the ground, rifle raised to fire—I was lost to her.

Maybe it was meant to be, or it was pure luck, but there stood Tai. A friend. A mentor. It had been several years since I'd last laid eyes on him.

Now I sit on Shadow, a few paces behind Sam, Warren, and Tai, headed toward town with an insane plane to save Nalin. Our lives all becoming intertwined by that fickle thing called fate.

I listen as they exchange stories—get to know each other. As usual, Sam tells very little about her past, only basic generic information that gives me no details regarding who she really is at her core. Warren is just as guarded with his tales of life. Warren seems like he could be in the infantry. It's written all over him in the way he presents himself...maybe a Buffalo Soldier, but if so, why is he here and not with a regiment? The two of them are intelligent and cunning. I've seen the way they work and live. Warren's ideas on homesteading and Sam's uncanny ability with herbs are learned behaviors. Their life-preservation skills on the farm are beyond anything I've ever seen.

Which begs the question...where did they learn these things?

Seeing her debate strategies to save a girl she doesn't even know tonight made me weak in the knees. I watched as she'd paced around that fire—her eyes alight with determination. My mind could hardly stay focused on the task at hand. She was distracting in the worst way. Her breeches clinging to her curves, her whisps of hair falling around her shoulders under her cowboy hat, she's too much for me...too good for me. Her beauty inside and out, mixed with her witty but frustrating charm, is intoxicating. The flame from the fire would catch her irises at times, and they would glow from within, just like the flame inside her.

I've held back, only allowing myself a taste of her passion, but it's becoming harder to do the longer I'm in her presence.

Sam breaks off from the two men and slows Clint until she rides beside me. She doesn't say a word but doesn't have to. Her face tells a story as worry bleeds through her expressions. "Having second thoughts, witch?"

I see her slight eye roll at the pet name before her face falls again, and she whispers so that only we can hear, "This will be my fault if it goes south." She pulls her lower lip into her mouth, nibbling it, then says, "We could have done this several ways, but now everyone is relying on this plan to work and…"

"And what?"

She sighs heavily. "And I don't think I can live with myself after if I'm the cause of something horrible." She looks at me with heart-wrenching, saddened eyes. "What if it doesn't work?"

I don't know why, but I reach over and take her hand into mine. I need to stop this connection between us before it gets to a point of no return, but my body is far from listening to my brain. Her stunning eyes round a touch with her shock as she gazes at our intertwined fingers. Her tiny hand fits so perfectly in mine that my chest aches just looking at it.

"What if it goes right?" I ask. "You have a good plan here—one that, against my wishes, leaves everyone alive in the morning. I'd say that's something to be proud of." I trail my thumb over the soft skin of her hand. "Who's to say it will work out any better if we go in guns a-blazin'."

She looks off into the distance, my small lamp hanging from the saddle horn, causing a flurry of colors to bounce on her skin. When she looks back into my eyes, her chest is rising and falling with fear and trepidation. Again, I don't know why. I can't seem to control my impulses, but I reach across our horses, take the back of her neck, and pull her to me. I press a small kiss to her forehead and flourish in the breathy sound she makes before I let go of her neck and hand. Her warm scent of some kind of flowery soap invades my senses even after I pull away.

Her face is flush as she whispers, "I could deal with you better when you were an asshole."

I smirk. "That can be arranged." I am blessed with her beautiful smile that erases some of the sadness from her eyes.

We stay silent for several minutes, and then, out of the blue, she asks, "How did you get the name Chato?"

I laugh a little. "It means 'lively one.'" She raises her delicate brow and smirks. "Yeah, I know. I didn't know the Indians could be sarcastic people, but Tai is. I was…maybe a little withdrawn back then."

"Back then…" she grins.

"Okay, now, too."

In the distance I can see the lights from the lamppost in town flickering in the night. I douse the lamp light and break up the conversation about me. "Where did you learn to dabble in herbs?"

Her interest has peaked, but I see hesitation in her when she says timidly, "My mother," she mutters. "I grew up on a farm with my parents. My mom used to grow a large variety of flowers, both native and foreign to this area. She has a green thumb like no other." She beams with pride. "While she was into growing magnificent gardens for the beauty of it, I was into researching the properties from a young age." She laughs quietly. "I would experiment with the roots, leaves, and flowers, sometimes to my own detriment." When I raise an eyebrow to her in questions she adds, "I once mistook Poison Ivy for my mother's Blackberry Bush that was just beginning. I was only twelve, but those leaves looked *exactly* the same to me." She giggles again. "We were scratching ourselves raw for weeks."

I can't help the genuine laugh that bubbles out. She flits her gaze to me and creases from at her brow. "What?" I ask. "I *do* laugh occasionally, you know."

"Not nearly enough." Her voice is low and spreads over me like butter. She laughs again as another memory surfaces. "There's this plant called Solanum Elaeagnifolium, commonly called Silverleaf Nightshade. It has a purple flower that has little points on the end, and I thought it was the coolest plant until the day some of the juices from a leaf caused me to almost pass out." She giggles. "Later, I discovered how poisonous that particular plant was!"

We laugh together. I marvel at her beauty, made even more apparent when she's happy. She beams brighter than the sun. Her smile fades as we take in each other. I break the heated connection of our eyes when I look up to see our rendezvous spot looming near. "Here, I want you to have this." I pull out my steal dagger wrapped in soft buffalo hide and the intricate sheath and hand it to her.

"I can't accept this, Jake...it seems important to you. You always carry it."

"I want you to have it." I push it back to her, and she finally relents as she takes it from me carefully.

Her eyes skim the beadwork and feathers that dangle from the tip of the handle. "Did Tai give this to you?"

"Yeah, he gave me the blade, but Nalin made the decorations and the sheath." I smile at the memory. "She was a feisty little one when she was younger but had a heart of gold. She told me that this would always keep me safe." I look away when I see Sam fighting back tears. "Anyway, I want you to have it. Maybe it can keep you safe."

She nods several times, still clutching the dagger as if it may fly away at any moment. Finally, she hooks the sheath into her breeches and slides the dagger in. It looks like it was meant to rest on her lovely hip.

"Okay, mischief maker...it's time. Are you ready?" I ask.

"Ready as I'll ever be," she says through a long exhaling breath.

I reach over and grasp her hand once more and lift it to my lips, placing a kiss atop. I rub my thumb over that spot as I recklessly say, "Wherever you go...I go."

Poison and Whiskey

CHAPTER 22

Samantha

The rendezvous point is a large desert willow tree on the outskirts of town…just far enough away not to be seen but close enough to walk…or run. All four horses are tied there, and an extra bay mare Tai brought for Nalin. Each man carries a cloth with a vile of chloroform, and I carry both the chloroform and oleander mixture. Each man has been designated a spot to linger whilst I manage the task of drugging an unsuspecting Lonnie. I have the mixture diluted so that it should make her rather sick, but she will be right as rain by morning.

Tai is staying with the horses until we signal him to ride to the stables, Jake is on the other side of the street across from the brothel, hidden down a side alley, and Warren is in the back alley behind the brothel. If I end up in some kind of trouble, they will be near. The goal is for it to seem like we were never there. No one can see us near Lonnie's place or suspicions will rise tomorrow with the sun.

I waltz into the saloon as if It's a normal day, not a heist mission involving a young girl. At the bar, I drop my saddlebag that was slung over my shoulder to the seat next to me and order a double shot of whiskey. I make small talk with John as I survey my surroundings. "Business looks slow tonight, John," I state the obvious, seeing as there are very few stragglers hanging about at this hour.

He cocks a brow at me. "It's late, Sam…I don't believe I have ever seen you here at this hour…where's Warren?"

I shrug nonchalantly. "We had some errands to run, and a wheel on our wagon broke today just outside of town. Warren's fixing it now, actually," I lie.

"You be careful. This is not a good time of day for a lady such as yourself to be on the streets." He motions to the few drunks scattered about the saloon, eyeballing me.

"No worries, I'm stronger than I look." I give him a wink as he dips an already dingy cloth into water and begins cleaning the sticky ringed remnants of alcohol from the bar top.

After scanning the area again, I see no sign of Lonnie. Jake was certain she comes here early in the evening to sing occasionally but always dropped by around this time to lure the intoxicated men's full pockets to the brothel. Another few minutes pass, and I begin to get worried.

All of a sudden like clockwork, there she breezes through the door in her finery, looking astonishingly out of place in the dim barroom atmosphere with her pale yellow bustle skirt and cinched bodice a few shades darker. Her eyes meet mine and she gives a coy smile. I remember her telling me how dangerous Jake was. My blood boils when I recall that she saw me with Henry that whole evening but never warned me away from him. She hides her devilish ways behind a beautiful façade. Seeing her for what she is now…I don't feel bad for what I am about to do.

"Lonnie!" I smile back and wave her over. As she nears, I pull out the bar stool beside me and offer her a seat. "Come, have a drink with me. I am in desperate need of a woman to chat with. Warren and I are broken down at the moment, so I have some free time to spare. I could use some refined company." I playfully roll my eyes and gesture to the ruffians throughout the place.

She looks me slowly up and down, taking in my appearance. The worn hat, the breeches, and dusty riding boots. Her eyes linger a moment on my newly acquired dagger before she says, "I am sorry, dear, but I have business to attend to."

The word bitch crosses my mind, but I just grin and yell to John, "John, two more rounds here on me," and then add, "Nonsense. Stay and have one measly little drink with me." I see her eyes move around the room, and she purses her lips. "Just one won't kill you." I swirl the liquor around my glass and entice her to stay.

She rolls her eyes but sits, crosses her legs, and looks at me expectantly. "What brings you here this late?" She observes me closely and then licks her lips. "Looking for work?" Her lip pulls up in a snarky way.

I cock my head and give her back just a touch of the attitude I'm trying so hard to hold back. "Lonnie...I'm afraid you couldn't afford me." I regret it instantly. I am going to fucking blow this mission before it begins with my mouth.

To my surprise, this has her giggling. "Well then, I'll drink to that." She peers down the bar to John. "Hey big boy, where's the drinks already?"

My skin crawls at the tone she uses with him, condescending and flippant. John places each glass in front of us. I pretend to adjust the long sleeve of my linen shirt. Gently, I pop the cork from the vile I have hidden in my sleeve—keeping my elbows on the bar and wrist raised, holding my glass so as not to douse myself in the hidden liquid strapped to my arm.

She sips her whiskey as I slide a bit closer to her. "I really wanted to ask you about someone...Jake Evans." Humor twinkles in her eyes as I add, "Why did you say he was a dangerous man?"

She sets her glass down and folds her arms across her chest as she looks to me knowingly. "He's dangerous to the heart." Something like anger or maybe jealousy flit through her eyes momentarily.

I try to hide the shock from my face but most likely fail. "Well, if that is all, then great," I grin, "I wasn't lookin' for love when I asked…just maybe a roll in the hay." I wink at her, but she scrutinizes me thoroughly.

"Good luck with that. That man is like the wind, here one minute and gone the next. He will never settle down. So, rolls in the hay…very likely. I'm not buying that you are that type of woman, though." Her voice takes on an almost warning tone—void of humor. "You'd do well to keep your heart, *and* your legs closed with that one."

My nerves are grated imagining all the various reasons she feels this way. Were they lovers? Did she fall for him? I pick my moment carefully, and when she smirks at my wide eyes, I lean a little too close and topple her whiskey.

It splashes harmlessly onto the bar. She gasps and looks away just long enough for me to lean my arm down by my side…dripping every—last—drop of oleander into my own shot of whiskey.

"Oh, my! I'm just so terribly clumsy…here take mine. I haven't had a sip from this one yet!" I motion for John to get me another with a wave.

She takes the glass from my outstretched hand as John gives me another. I nod my thanks to him and apologize for yet another mess he must clean up, then I spin back to her. I take a deep breath and hold out my glass. "To keeping our hearts and our legs closed," I say a little too loudly, and John's face reddens.

Lonnie gives the first true sign that she has humor inside and giggles, not faking it this time. She taps her glass to mine, and when we turn them up. I continue drinking to down mine in one gulp. Lonnie, not to be outdone by any woman, shoots her entire contents back as well.

I hold back my cringe as the liquor burns going down, as does Lonnie. Her fleeting moment of humor is gone as fast as the drink. She stands tall and graceful as she murmurs, "This was nice and all, dear Samantha, but I must be off." Her sickly fake sweetness turns my stomach as she says, "Oh, by the way. Henry Fletcher...you know, the one you danced and laughed with *all* night the last time I saw you." She raises her eyebrows. "He's gone missing. Funny thing is, I seem to remember him saying something about heading out to the canyons the next day—where *you* live."

I pull a mask tightly over my features and reply, "What a pity he's missing. He's a grown man. Maybe he left town for a bit."

Her cheek pulls up as she bares her teeth on one side. "Darlin', he lives for money, and he makes his money here in town...he would *never* leave. Anyhow...if you happen to see him, you'll be sure to let me know, right?"

"Of course," I say, but she has already spun around and headed toward the men playing poker in the back, not bothering to hear my reply.

Fucking Bitch.

"Hey, John, can I get one more before I head out?" I ask as he passes, but my eyes follow Lonnie. The oleander shouldn't take long...maybe five to ten minutes. The cramping should get intense enough that she wouldn't be able to hide it well.

John passes me another shot, and I down it instantly as I try to calm my frayed nerves. My hands are trembling. I just drugged someone. Oh my God, I just drugged someone. I had all the confidence in the world before, but now! What if my dosage is off? She could die. Holy shit, I need to get it together.

As I watch her work the men, my eyes land on someone unexpected. Kelvin Mack. His eyes meet mine briefly but turn away. His long beard has been cut shorter, but it's definitely him. My throat goes dry, and my heart threatens to crack through my ribcage. He spins that brass pocket watch as he eyes me. I quickly turn away from his gaze. He's one very dangerous obstacle tonight who apparently has no qualms about killing or kidnapping people. As long as he doesn't follow me out, we're still good, or at least I tell myself that.

Minutes go by. I glance Lonnie's way again and hold my breath when I see her pale face. Her hand is resting on her abdomen as she tries to maintain a conversation with a random man raking chips into a derby hat. She bends and clutches her belly. I can barely hear her apologies as she bolts for the back door, heading straight to the privies out back.

I close my eyes and send a silent prayer that she will be okay when this is all over. She's a vile person but underserving of her part in this deception, nonetheless. I need her out of sight and mind for at least thirty minutes—can't have her showing up at Lady Grave's and ruining everything.

Quickly, I say my goodbyes to Big John, toss my saddlebag back over my shoulder, and make my way out the back entrance. I wait three whole minutes outside the back door to make sure no one, especially Kelvin Mack, follows me. When the coast is clear, I tip-toe to the nearest privy and listen in as I hear Lonnie wretch inside.

This is it. Time for round two.

I stick to the back street, hiding in the shadows as I make my way to the brothel. No one lingers in these areas tonight, and I couldn't be more grateful. Once I am but a few paces away from the back entrance, I pull out a small lantern inside the saddlebag I carry, strike a match, and light it. I take the flickering flame and wave it, swinging it side to side three times in the general direction of Warren's position.

I stay hidden until I see Warren's dark figure move from the shadows. He positions himself at the back entrance and glances my way once, nodding his head, before he goes in. We agreed on six minutes tops. He is supposed to subdue the barkeep and any other man lingering near the kitchens before I get in there. Chloroform is different for each person, but it usually takes effect within two minutes, and they are passed out for around twenty minutes. I don't envy the struggle Warren will have trying to hold a person long enough to knock them out.

I count in my head to sixty, then count again to sixty. I do this three more times. I start the last set and walk forward as I do. Pacing my final steps with my beating heart. When I reach sixty, I open the back entrance.

I'm greeted with a sweaty Warren. His eyes are big as he heaves in breaths. "Two men down, no one out front," he whispers. "Girls are either upstairs or gone for the evening."

I look to the left and see feet, four of them to be exact, protruding from an empty doorway that seems to lead to the pantry. Flour and unknown liquid tarnish the floor where they struggled. I blow out the lantern, tie it to my side, and sling the saddle bag back to my shoulder. I nod to him, and we move through the kitchen, silent as a mouse. As I peep through the nearest doorway, I see a large lounge area—gaudy red velvet chaise chairs line the room. There's a redwood door that looks like it leads out to the main street. A bar off to the left is stacked with freshly cleaned mugs, and various liquors line the wall. I see no one lingering about.

My eyes flick to Warren, and I point to the staircase leading up to the rooms. He tips his head in understanding, and I take a ragged breath as I step out of the shadowy room and into the dimly lit lounge. Warren waits below me for a few beats as I ascend the stairs to make sure we are truly alone. Each stair creaks as I move, making the hairs on the back of my neck stand on end. I clench my fist at each cringe of the old wood—the noise, however quiet it may be, sounds deafening at the moment. I peer back to see Warren following me. Just as I reach the last step, I hear a woman's voice.

"Lonnie, is that you?" the woman asks from somewhere down the hall we have ascended to.

Sweat trickles down my spine as I shift my head. I nudge Warren and point to an open door a few feet away. We dart into it and hide behind the door as we watch through the crack of the frame. No more than a few seconds pass, and a woman dressed in a night shift passes our hidden forms and makes her way down the stairs.

I exhale the breath I was holding and hear Warren do the same. "We need to check the room that has the balcony overlooking the street," I whisper softly. "That's where I saw her."

Warren looks around the room we are hiding in, which turns out to be empty, thankfully. "Then we need to go to the other side." He peers out into the hallway and then points to the rooms that run parallel to the street.

In the hall, we listen carefully as we quicken our steps. I can still hear the one woman below. The clink of a glass and liquid being poured leads me to believe she's having a nightcap. I am one thousand percent having one myself if we make it through this.

I stop abruptly and lean over the railing to check on the woman's whereabouts. She sits at the empty bar, braiding her long brown hair; a drink and decanter sitting next to her. If she goes into that kitchen, we are royally fucked…or if Lonnie comes back too soon. I try and quieten the doubts and possibilities bouncing in my skull as we finally stand in front of the door that we are praying is Nalin's. Moans and men's grunts are faint down the hallway, but thankfully this room is silent.

My mouth drops open, and I hear Warren swear under his breath as we both notice the chain and padlock at the same time. My eyes dart to his. "This is the only door with a lock on the *outside*…this must be her room." I mouth the words as silently as possible.

Warren begins checking the hinges and I run my fingers along the flat metal plate the chain hangs from that's haphazardly nailed into the door frame. "Look here." I point to the small gap between the metal and wood. "My dagger may fit." I unsheathe the blade, press the tip into the crease, and pry it up and down until it slips in a bit further. The nails barely give any. Warren takes the dagger from me and smacks the handle—jarring it deeper into the gap, then uses it as a lever to pry the metal plate even further. With bated breath I watch as each nail protrudes out more and more. Eventually, he's able to pop it hard one last time, and the chain jangles and clangs against the door as it falls loose, nails making dinging sounds as they bounce off the wood floors. Our eyes cut to each other in a panic, the noise wildly out of place in here.

I can hear the lady from downstairs moving and mumbling something I can't decipher. "It's now or never," I say as I crack open the door, and we slip in.

My eyes try to adjust to the pitch-black room. The only light is a sliver that streams in from the moon's glow through the cracked curtain from the balcony door. The first thing I notice is the bed in disarray...but very empty. We move about the room cautiously. The small space has one other door, possibly leading to a closet. Warren nudges me and points to it.

Warren peeps out of her room to make sure we are still in the clear while I tip-toe to that door. I take the handle gingerly and turn the knob. Before I have the chance to pull, the door slams open, slinging me backward to the floor. A wisp of a girl is on top of me in an instant, holding a lamp, ready to strike. I catch her wrists in mine as she tries to smash my face with the lamp. I roll and fling us over until I'm sitting on her. My chest heaving. Warren rushes to my side as I bare my teeth at her. "Your father Tai sent me." She holds deadly still. Her round, deep brown eyes remind me of a fawn. She squints and glares at the two of us, clearly not trusting random strangers...as she shouldn't. "Look down. Look at my waist, Nalin." I nod my head, urging her to look.

Her shock is evident when I use her name, but she slowly lowers her gaze to my hips. I can tell when she's found the dagger adorned with her beadwork and feathers. "Chato." Her soft voice sounds so adolescent and wistful when she says Jake's given Apache name. It breaks my heart.

"Yes, Chato is waiting outside, and your father is too, but we have to go now…do you understand?" She nods—little bobs of the head repeatedly— and I release her wrists.

"We can't go back the way we came," Warren says. He moves to the balcony door and slides it open. "We gonna have to go over the railing." As if on cue, we hear a gut-curdling scream pierce the night from somewhere downstairs.

I gasp aloud. "Oh, shit! I think she found your handy work, Warren!" I say while standing and pulling Nalin up with me. I look to her. "We don't have long to get clear of this town. Be quiet and do as we say…we'll keep you safe." She nods as if on autopilot. Her eyes are round as saucers after hearing the screams from below and her whole body is shaking.

We make our way to the edge of the railing, and Warren lights his tiny lantern and waves it three times before blowing it out and attaching it back to his belt. From the dark alley, I see Jake on Shadow. A creepy fog has settled in the atmosphere, making it hard to distinguish anything clearly. It's like the weather changed just to help aid us in our escape.

A ruckus of footsteps and chatter is now coming from the hallway adjacent to Nalin's room. "We have to move fast!" I whisper with urgency.

Warren grabs a scared Nalin and lifts her over the edge as he says, "We can hold her arms until she is close enough to drop down." Nalin shakes her dainty head in fear, making her long braid bounce. Her body is trembling fiercely. "We've got you. You're going to have to trust us."

She clings to Warren but looks down and sees Jake below. He tips his hat to her, and she smiles sweetly…all her reservations seem to fly out the window. Warren tries to hold her in order to lower her down, but she refuses and, instead, brazenly, climbs down until she hangs on with only her hands—her limbs dangle a few feet from Shadow. I hold my breath as she drops effortlessly, landing behind Jake. Shadow grunts but holds steady.

I see Jake signal Tai, who should be at the stable's edge by now with the horses. Jake hesitates below us. I wave him on. "Get her out of here," I demand. His face is unreadable in this fog, but I can tell he doesn't want to leave us behind. He kicks Shadow, and they are gone in the blink of an eye, disappearing into the fog.

"I'm going to drop down first, and that way, I can catch you. I'm taller. It won't be as much of a drop for me," Warren says midway through climbing over. I watch as he descends the rails until he's hanging by his hands. He drops and manages to maintain standing.

"Okay, here goes nothing." I ease myself over the rails and then turn to face them to get a better foothold. The drop below suddenly looks farther than before. My face pales as I hear the door to Nalin's room slam open and a man's voice growling out slurs. "Shit, shit, shit," I mutter. I hear Warren coaxing me to drop, and finally, I let go right before the balcony door swings open.

My heart skips a beat. Then strong arms catch me mid-fall.

Before I can catch my breath or my wits, Warren's dragging me into the shadows of the alley. From the spot we hide, we can see two men looming over the railing…searching. I can't tell who they are from where we stand. I try to get a better look, but Warren has my hand in his, forcing me into motion. We bolt to the rear of the building and slink through the darkness, heading for the stable's edge. Jake was supposed to pass Nalin to her father and Tai was to meet us back at the willow tree.

We finally make it, and Jake is there with our horses, as promised. He hands me my reins, and I mount quickly. His jaw is tense, and his eyes skim everything around us. "Is everything okay?" I ask. We just succeeded monumentally. I'm still riding that high. I would think he would be ecstatic too.

Shadow is pawing the ground in an agitating fashion. "Something's not right," he whispers.

An eerie feeling comes over me, so I say, "Well then, let's get the hell out of here!"

Before I can nudge Clint into motion, someone slams into me from above the stall door. I hit the ground and let out a garbled scream as pain lances through my shoulder.

The world around me slows.

In the chaos, I hear Jake's curses and guns being drawn from both sides. A man has me pulled tight against him and jerks me into a standing position with my back against his front—the barrel of a gun pointed at my temple. The cold tip of the pistol presses harder as the man says, "Put your guns down, or she's dead!" His arms have me in a vice-like grip. I can't think through the pain radiating down my arm that lays uselessly against my side. I can't tell if it's broken or dislocated, but nausea rolls through me. My eyes finally adjust and shift to see that Kelvin Mack is the one holding me against him. Then my eyes dart to Jake and Warren. I would rather feel a thousand broken bones than see the worry for me on their faces.

"This *is* something…" Kelvin chuckles. "Look at you, Jakey boy, riding with low-lives and Indian trash. I always knew you were a worthless piece of shit." He spits to the ground before saying, "You biting the hand that feeds you, partner." He tsks. "You take my girl, I take yours…by morning, she won't remember your name." His chest rumbles against me as he laughs.

I think I hear Warren cursing and demanding for my release, but everyone's voices are becoming muffled. I grit my teeth through the excruciating pain. Sweat trickles down my spine as I try to remain upright. Every time Kelvin squeezes tighter, I groan and bite my lip.

Jake never wavers. His gun is steady. "You will never live to see morning…*partner*." His eyes meet mine briefly. There's a plethora of emotions going on behind them. He looks at my dagger, then above me to the loft so quickly that anyone else might have missed it, then to the gun pointed at my head. My brain catches part of that, or at least I think it does, but my body is frozen in agony and fear.

My dagger. I still have my dagger. I breathe in and out.

Warren's horse, Halle, fidgets and slings her head as Warren and Kelvin rage back and forth—my body twitching with every heartbeat. Jake is quiet. Calculating. Suddenly, a clatter to our right has Halle rearing. Kelvin's attention darts to the noise. In the Chaos, Kelvin moves his aim for a split second towards that direction. Instincts I never knew I had take over. My dagger is gripped in my hand in an instant. I slam it into his thigh at the same time that I hear shots ring out through the night.

Everything seems to return to normal speed as Kelvin's blooded hand drops the hold he has on his pistol. His screams ring out into the night as he drops me and clutches his hand to his chest.

Jake's aim was true.

I see blood oozing from his shoulder too. Even with my groggy, panic-ridden mind, I imagine that was Warren's shot. I hit the ground on my knees, holding my left arm close to my body. A ragged breath wooshes into my lungs right before I groan—nausea rolling through me. Kelvin growls and curses as he rocks back and forth and then he, too, falls to his knees beside me. My dagger still protruding from his leg.

Out of nowhere, a dark figure flies from the loft and swings down upon Kelvin. A gut-curdling sound that sends chills through me echoes from his mouth and throughout the barn. I look on in shock as a small-handled ax protrudes from his head—colorful beads and feathers flowing around the end, the beauty of the piece at odds with the blood seeping around the blade. The red-stained face staring back at me goes limp and smacks the ground with a sickening thud.

My eyes trail the ax handle as I fall the rest of the way to the earth. The feathers catch the moonlight every now and again with a subtle sheen. Iridescent. Beautiful. Then everything goes dark.

Paid Debts

CHAPTER 23

Samantha

I awake to a scent I've come to know so well, evading my nostrils in such a pleasant way. Leather, mint, and sandalwood. That smell takes me back to the last time I rode double with Jake Evans. Heat blossoms in my cheeks at the mere thought of that day. Although, that time was full of pleasure, not pain.

Every jostle of the horse's stride is felt in my left shoulder. I turn my head to see that a leather strap has my injured arm bound to my waist. I'm cradled in his arms, legs to one side, and my right side flush against his hard chest. I feel Jake's eyes on me without even looking up. That strange connection we have zings between us.

I avoid his gaze and survey my surroundings. The sun is just cresting with the faintest glow on the horizon. Tai and Nalin ride ahead of us—their bodies only silhouettes against that horizon. Warren rides to our left. It takes me a minute to recognize what I am seeing lain over Halle's rump, secured behind Warren. It's wrapped in dirty, old, and tattered fabric, but there is no mistaken what that is…*that* is a body.

"Is that who I think it is?" My voice is hoarse and creaky.

"The one and only," Jake replies.

I shudder as I eye the limp form of Kelvin Mack. My mind drifts to that moment when the two shots fired. It's more clear to me now that the trauma is over. The precision of it is not lost on me. Jake shot Kelvin's hand at the same moment that Warren shot his shoulder—both ensuring that the gun would drop from his grip when the barrel was no longer pressed to my skull. Then the final blow…that ax…ughh. I shudder again.

"No one else saw us, right? He was the only witness," I ask.

"None that we know of."

"Good." I sigh deeply. I check out our surroundings again and realize we are nearing the farm. "Are we going home then?"

Our eyes finally meet. He nods.

Weariness sinks into every muscle and bone contained inside me. In our silence, I replay the last twenty-four hours. How did I end up here…in this moment? How am I calm with a body jostling a scant few feet away on the rump of a horse? I've always known that experiences create your perspective of life and death, but now I truly see it. I'm not the same woman I was before coming here and I'm not sure if that's a good thing.

My eyes flit back to Tai and notice again his odd, angled hair, cut at a slant. I had noticed it the first time I laid eyes on him. I raise my head to Jake, "I meant to ask this earlier when I first met him, but why is Tai's hair cut like that?"

Jake's eyes flit to me, then back ahead, "Apache tribe members cut their hair like that in mourning. He most likely did it the day his daughter went missing."

"Oh…that's awful." Just as my words exit my lips, a bump along the way has me wincing and scrunching my face in pain.

His worried brow creases as he glances at my immobile shoulder. "We need to have a look at that arm and get you cleaned up."

I nod, understanding the pain awaiting me in my very near future. Now that I've had a chance to actually look at my shoulder and access the feeling there, I realize something. "It's dislocated…from the joint." Jake stares at me. "It's happened to me once before when I was thirteen years old. It doesn't feel broken." I palpate my humerus—traveling my fingers from the distal end to the proximal.

"I thought as much," he whispers.

My brows furrow. "You've seen dislocated shoulders before?" I question, but before he can answer I recall he's seen battle in the Civil War. "In the war?" I ask.

He just nods but doesn't elaborate.

I brazenly examine the details of Jake's too-handsome face. I have never asked his age, but if I had to guess…maybe twenty-eight or so. His skin is bronzed from the sun. His full lips peek out through the thick, short mustache and beard that begs to be touched. And that alluring scar that has me hypnotized. It seems like a lifetime ago when he kissed me against my bedroom wall. Does he feel this thing between us? Is it my imagination or deep loneliness that has me wishing for something more?

Jake has gone from being my stalking shadow to the man who saved my life, *twice*. Well, three times if we count the night we met.

His whiskey eyes meet mine. His deep throaty voice creates goosebumps along my arms as he says, "What's going on inside that head of yours?"

I hold back those thoughts—keep them locked inside for now. I have to keep reminding myself that he is temporary. There's no way this works out. I feel an ache in my heart at that thought but push it away. Instead, I decide to pry into a piece of who this man is. Who Jake Evans is.

"You look young but not *too* young. Still…to have gone through a war…" I stop and let the insinuation hang there, hoping he will alleviate some of my insistent curiosities. From my memory bank, I recall the war ended in 1865. So, he had to be a teen then.

He doesn't take his eyes off mine. "You want to play this game, witch? You know the rules…I give you something. You give me something." His side smile is infuriating…but also becoming one of my favorite things.

"You first," I say softly.

His eyes roam the land for a beat before he says, "I'm thirty years old." He pauses, then adds, "I was fifteen when I ran off to fight in the war."

I'm sure the shock is evident on my face. I imagine a younger Jake and all the atrocities he must have seen. He looks at me expectantly. "What do you want to know, Jake?" I ask timidly. Questions make me nervous…for good reason.

He shocks me with the one he chooses. "Why are you closed off from the world?" Before I can look away, he grabs my chin gently and forces me to look at him. "I'm not asking for your life story…keep your secrets if it makes you feel better but give me something to understand why a woman as beautiful and *charismatic* as you," he grins mockingly, "is holed up in some old house in the middle of nowhere. No friends. No family. No husband. No suiters even…"

My mouth goes dry, and I struggle to keep eye contact. His words play havoc on my weak heart. He said to keep my secrets. Again, I think of how easy this would be if he would continue being an asshole. "I could ask you the same thing," I mutter. "Except the husband part…of course," I say, trying to be funny and break the tension.

His eyes don't waver. "Your turn, remember."

Anything I say can only be half-truths. "As far as my family and friends…they live very far away." I swallow the knot that forms in my throat. "Warren is my dear friend and has helped teach me how to live on my own."

All true things so far.

He sees how I dance over the real answers burning behind my eyes. "What about a man?" I see his eyes darken when he asks that.

"Only one serious relationship, but he wasn't very kind to me." That is an extreme understatement.

Jake sneers. "I remember. The one you mentioned who was like Henry."

"Is that anger for me that I see in your eyes? Sprinkled with jealousy, maybe?" My lip pulls back in a smirk. His eyes lose all humor. That was *not* the effect I was going for. "What is it, Jake?"

"I don't take kindly to men who treat women that way, so yes," his voice vibrates in his chest against my shoulder, "anger is what you see."

Myra's conversation takes root in the recess of my mind, and a picture begins to take shape. She said Jake had a rough life growing up. It makes me question where that hatred for men such as Trevor and Henry formed. The silence between us is deafening after that. He seems to have gone somewhere in his head and left me to wander aimlessly about his life before we met.

The ride back to the farm was excruciating at times, but here we are. I'm pretending to be strong, but I'm also a terrible actor. The pain lancing my shoulder is immense. Jake has me sitting on the kitchen table—his body settled between my legs. I bite my lip to dull the ache. I can hear Warren outside speaking with Tai and Nalin, although their words are jumbled.

"Do you trust me, witch?" Jake tips my chin up with his finger, forcing me to make eye contact.

The heat I feel from that simple touch is unnerving. "No," I chuckle lightly, "but what choice do I have? My arm is dangling, and I would very much like it *not* to be."

He ignores my humor and fails to hide the worry I see clearly in his eyes. "This is going to hurt bad, but only for a moment. I got you."

I nod, suddenly fixated on those three words rather than the impending pain. "Just do it before Warren comes in. He will lose his shit if he sees me in pain."

Jake removes my cowboy hat that I'd forgotten was on my head and tosses it aside. He leans in close to me. His duster is thrown over the counter along with his gun belt and he has his linen shirt sleeves rolled to the elbow, displaying his taut forearms. I close my eyes and breathe him in.

"Bite on this," he whispers, causing me to open my eyes. He places a strap of leather into my mouth carefully. His fingers linger there, and he allows his thumb to caress my cheek. "You ready?"

I'm definitely *not* ready, but it's now or never. I give him an uneasy nod. I groan as he moves my hand from my injured arm and places it on his chest. Never taking his eyes from mine, he takes his right hand and arm, pressing along the side of mine, bracing against it. He grips my elbow with his free hand. I start to flinch away.

"Don't move. Look at me," he demands. His face looms over mine, and he hesitates.

Suddenly, he leans even closer—our lips a hairsbreadth away. He removes the leather I'm biting on. "What are you doing, Jake?" My voice sounds breathy.

"What I should have done sooner," he says as he closes the distance between us. My entire body ignites as he presses his lips to mine in a gentle but firm kiss. The initial shock has me tense, but after a few seconds, my body relaxes into him. His tongue slides into my mouth, and I shiver. A moan escapes me, and I press into his kiss—opening for him willingly. He stops to nibble on my lower lip, causing heat to pool low in my belly. The electricity between us is a palpable thing permeating the air around us and encasing me in euphoric bliss. His kiss deepens and becomes all consuming.

I feel more than hear the guttural growl vibrating from his chest right before his arm and hand tighten on me. Lost in that foggy perfection of his mouth, I fail to see what's coming. In a split second, he presses inward and up with his armed that's caged against mine. An excruciating pain shoots through me, and I start to cry out, but he drowns the sound with his mouth and continues his assault on my lips.

My body is trembling against him. Our lips still touching, but not moving as I pant short breaths. He breaks away briefly to assess my face. "Are you okay?" His voice is shaking as badly as my body.

I laugh manically. "Better than ever," I declare as I rotate my left arm very slowly. "It's really sore...but it's definitely in." He doesn't back away as his eyes dart all over my face, trying to access the truth in my words. I reach up with my good arm to run my fingers along his cheek. "I'm fine now...because of you." Those words are loaded with more meaning than I want to decipher at the moment. "I have to say, I wasn't expecting that kind of medical attention." I grin up at him and finally see his features relax.

"It's my specialty." He smirks.

I lean in brazenly, ready to taste him again, but the door bangs open, and we both flinch apart. The three of them barge into the house.

"Sam you okay?" Warren walks around Jake to get a better look at me. "Ready to get that shoulder back in?" Right as it leaves his mouth, his eyes alight on my rotating arm.

I flex it slowly. "All good. I'm going to be *very* sore and may need to make a sling, but...turns out Jake is quite the medicine man himself." A blush burns my cheeks and Jake's grin tells me he notices.

"Holy shit," Warren curses causing odd looks from Tai and Nalin. He pulls me into a hug, careful not to squeeze that shoulder. "I couldn't stand it...the thought of you hurting." He releases me and takes Jake's hand in a forceful shake. "Thank you for this."

My heart fills to bursting when I see these two— hands clasped, smiling faces. Jake tips his hat but seems lost for words at Warren's gratitude.

We spent an hour after that recapping the events— dotting our I's and crossing our T's, so to speak. We didn't feel that we had any looming threats. I mention my worries to the others about Lonnie. I'm positive my dosage was correct and that she'll be fine, however, she *is* the only person who could place Warren and I in town that night. Which was unlike us to begin with. I knew that going into my plan, but hoped she couldn't piece together a reason we would take a girl from the brothel.

No one from Lady Graves saw our faces except one, and well...he's dead. Warren, Tai, and Jake made Kelvin's body disappear to where...I didn't ask. He'll become a missing person who no one will miss at all...except Bill. We'll cross that bridge when we get to it. Bill is now down two men from his band of assholes, and I'm still not sure what instrument Jake plays in that band. I guess time will tell.

By evening we had thoroughly cleaned ourselves and sated our hungers. I donned my clean tan breeches and midcalf riding boots with a high-necked blouse and plaited my damp hair down my back. I created a makeshift sling from an old sheet that I ripped to size and wove around my body—tying it snuggly against my side. Tai and Nalin lingered on the porch talking with Jake as I looked on from the window. His hair was still damp from his bath.

He's in love with our tubs but won't admit it. His dark locks shine in the Arizona sun. Shadows enhance the sharp features on his face. His shirt clings to his chest. He's beautiful. The kind of handsome that makes women feral. I can almost feel my ovaries acting a fool. His eyes dart my way as if he felt me watching. I back away from the window when he catches my eye, but not before I catch him waving his hand for me to come out.

On the porch, Tai approaches me with a deep crease formed between his weathered eyes. "I never got the chance to thank you for what you did. You brought my daughter back to me safe…without a war of bloodshed. I will be forever in your debt, Naiche." He smiles as he says my Apache name.

My chest swells with pride and—without knowing if it is culturally acceptable—I embrace him in a hug with my one good arm. His body tenses, but after a second relaxes, and he wraps his arms around me, too.

Something unexplainable happens inside me. It feels like a puzzle piece has been slammed into place. I gasp when a physical sense of rightness wash over me. Tears sting my eyes, but I hold them back. I have to swallow roughly to remove the lump forming in my throat.

Tai releases his hold on me as Jake asks, "Samantha...are you okay?" My audible gasp from before has everyone staring at me as if I've lost my mind. And maybe I have.

I can't explain the feelings flowing through me to them, so I simply nod and say, "Just overwhelmed, I guess...It's been a long night *and* day."

Jake seems to buy that, but not Nalin and Tai. They eye me knowingly. It's like they can sense the turmoil inside. Tai speaks up, his eyes still on me, "I want you all to join me and my family." He smiles, crinkling the area around his eyes. "We are to celebrate Nalin's return and pay tribute to Ussen." My brow furrows at the unfamiliar term. Tai nods in understanding and points to the sky. "Ussen...the creator. We will ban all the evil spirits that plague our minds." He looks between Jake and me at that, then says, "It will be when the moon is at its fullest."

I open my mouth to object but close it quickly. When will I ever have the opportunity to experience this? To be a part of a lost culture. I've watched many reenactments and performances demonstrating the Native Ghost Dance and similar ceremonies in my time. This is my chance to live and breathe this part of my history. The Apache blood that runs through my family, as little as it may be, longs for this in an insurmountable way. "I'd love to," I blurt out. I feel Jake's gaze on me. "I...*we*," I look to Warren, who's just walking through the front door, "would love to."

I wait impatiently for Tai and Nalin's departure. We offered Jake to stay the night, and he agreed. He's off tending the horses. The need to talk privately with Warren is eating me alive. I grab the Whiskey from the table and sit on the porch. The sun is setting behind Jake as he runs his hands along Shadow's neck. His demeanor is so gentle with her, each stroke of his hand done so with such care. For a rough-and-tumble man so versed in killing, it's remarkable to watch. Annnddd there goes my ovaries again. I groan aloud.

"Whatcha looking at there?" Warren chuckles as he bursts through the front door.

I roll my eyes dramatically while pink creeps into my cheeks and pass him the liquor, ignoring his previous question. "You're going to need this," I insist before he takes the bottle from my outstretched hand.

"That doesn't sound good," he mutters before taking a swig. He plops down in the chair adjacent to mine. "Give it to me. What has you riled up?"

I bite on my lower lip, debating how to even say this. I settle for the straightforward method. "I may have paid my debt."

Warren looks confused, but then it clicks, and his eyes widen. "What do you mean...how so?"

I snag the whiskey back and down another shot, keeping my eyes on Jake to make sure he stays far away from this conversation. "It's hard to explain...may sound crazy even."

"After what we've been through...nothing sounds crazy to me anymore," Warren points out.

I run a hand down my face as I say, "True. Okay, so here it goes...I believe that I have some connection to Nalin and Tai. When I hugged him, it was like a broken piece inside me was fused back together."

He looks at me thoughtfully and then excitement fills his eyes as they light up. "Do you think they could be your great—something or other—kin folk?"

I nod. "I haven't let myself talk one-on-one with Nalin yet because I am afraid my heart can't take the reminder of what I've lost." His confused brow has me adding, "She looks just like my sister Jenna. Remember the picture I showed you of my family?"

"Oh. My. Word," Warren draws out. "She really is a spitting image of her...I don't know how I didn't see it. What does this mean for us though?"

I exhale loudly and slouch into the chair more in defeat. "I have no damn clue. I could be wrong about the whole deal. Or maybe it was fate that we came here. Either way, we saved that girl." My fingernails tap repeatedly on the chair arm. "Do you think saving her was what I was meant to do?"

Warren looks away as he contemplates everything we've been through. "It's possible...hell, anything's possible." Worry creeps into his voice. "I haven't had that same *feeling* as you, so does that mean I haven't paid my debt?" he asks as we watch Jake begin to head our way.

I reach over and pat his hand. "We'll figure this all out...and if we don't, at least today was a complete success." A huge smile breaks out on my face as I watch Jake saunter toward us. "We are badass, Warren Mathews. We saved a girl's life today."

He laughs outright. "Hell yes, we did!"

I let that euphoria flow through my veins, and the whiskey ease my sore shoulder. The two men in my life begin talking about construction and plumbing. Warren keeps his knowledge to the basics but tries to answer anything Jake throws at him. Then, they start on weapons, and I've lost them completely. I smile like a fool as I sit off to the side, giving them their "man time." Every now and again, Jake looks my way as if to make sure I'm indeed still there. It warms my heart.

For tonight, I keep the nagging worries at bay. The full moon is in a little over a week. I'm going to be a part of something amazing, so I don't let myself contemplate the future because whatever the future holds for us now, one thing is for certain...we can handle it.

We Become the 'Gaan'

CHAPTER 24

Samantha

It's a damn good thing that Jake is a tracker. Otherwise, we would've never found Tai's camp on our own. Jake tells us that the Apache move locations every few months to avoid being targeted and forced into reservations. Tai vaguely gave Jake some indication of their whereabouts.

We crossed the plains containing the Saguaro cactuses scattered throughout, then a rugged, rolling, mountainous set of hills. The rocky terrain with its steep incline made me nervous, but Clint never faltered. He's a sure-footed mass of muscle that was made for this environment. Along the way, I found mullein and sage—forcing the guys to stop and allow me time to harvest some.

The heat of the sun beaming down has my blue button top clinging to me right along with my deep brown breeches. My braided hair hangs to one side under my dusty brown cowboy hat. I have my own gun belt on today that holds one peacemaker, and all three of us have rifles hooked to the sides of the saddles…just in case. I manage to ride well enough with one hand while the other arm is propped in my sling and secured to my side.

Suddenly, Jake breaks the silence, asking me something I wasn't prepared for.

"Why did you and Warren stack rocks around those cactuses in the valley…before the run-in with Tai?"

My mouth hangs there for a second before I tuck it in and reply, "You know stalking is actually looked down upon…"

He smirks. "I would consider it more of a necessity. You seem to attract danger everywhere you go. You should be thanking me."

I think back to the moment the arrow was aimed at us. "Okay, maybe just that one time it was helpful, but you're still wildly inappropriate."

He pays no mind to the insult and asks again, "Is this another secret of Sam's that she is unwilling to share? What's so special about that spot?"

I sigh and look away. "It's exactly that…our special place." When I don't elaborate, he nods softly and moves his horse ahead of me. I see his jaw clench, but he has once again let me keep my secrets. I hate doing this, keeping everything about me from him. I can only hope that he stops asking or forgets about me altogether and gives up this…whatever this is between us.

We are heading west…or more southwest based on the sun's position. It's late in the day as we're coming around a bend—following a creek bed when I see the hills give way to the most spectacular view. I gasp open-mouthed. The creek continues ahead before rolling softly into baby waterfalls that cascade into a deep blue lake. To the left, hidden in a small valley, are sets of tepees scattered about. Something moves in my periphery, and my eyes scan the wooded area.

"Don't be alarmed," Jake mutters under his breath. "They have scouts watching for their protection…they won't hurt us," he says with much more confidence than I currently have.

Warren and I share a weary look as shadows emerge from the trees in the form of men. We keep riding, even as they tag along either side of us and behind. I glance at the boy on my right—and he is that—just a boy. At no more than fourteen years old, he carries a bow slung across his back and keeps a small hatchet strapped to his side. His warm, tawny skin glows with youth, and while physically fit, he has the small, softer build of a child. His long black hair hangs to mid-waist. While I am accessing him, he has no shame in accessing me with a shit-eating grin.

An older man following behind yells at him in what I am assuming is part of the Southern Athabaskan language family. I raise one brow in question to Jake.

"He's telling him to stop staring at you." Jake grins.

My cheeks warm along with the boys. I can't help but stare at Jake's demeanor and how relaxed he is among them. I can only assume he spent a great deal of time with them in order to not only learn their language but to gain such trust and respect. He speaks with ease to a few members as we enter the camp. I catch my name along with Warren's. Smiles meet me from all around as families emerge from every point of the camp. There must be thirty to forty people here. I wonder again how they have evaded being forced into a reservation. It's beyond me. The exact year fails to come to mind, but I know that it's not too far in the future that their way of life is shut down completely. An ache forms in my chest, along with that knowledge.

Nalin drops down from her bay mare and rushes into the arms of a stunning woman in a tan leather dress with beadwork in a nature pattern surrounding her tiny waist. Tears stream down their faces. The woman turns to me, and she freezes as her eyes squint. It's hard to read what is going through her mind. Suddenly, her mouth pulls up to the side, and she says something to me.

I've never in my life wanted to speak another language as much as this moment.

"This is Liluye…Nalin's mother and Tai's wife," Jake says as he, too, dismounts and then reaches for my waist to help me down. I baby my arm as he grips me and eases me to the ground. "She says…you have saved her soul, and you *are* one of their Indee."

"What does Indee mean?" I ask.

"People," Jake simply says. "They don't refer to themselves as anything other than just…people.

How beautifully honest that statement is.

We spend the last hours of the day being introduced to the families and learning every speck of information they are willing to share. For Warren and me, this is heaven. It's something unimaginable to have this opportunity to learn facts from a lost culture…part of my own family's lost culture. The children had a field day playing with my hair and watching Warren explain various firearms while Jake interpreted for the both of us. We ate buffalo and watched the sunset with the most real people—Indee—I have ever met. Their lives revolve around family and survival. I think back to my life before and realize just how little we see our families in the future's fast-paced living. It's sad, really.

Dark has blanketed the sky, and a billion stars twinkle above. The men from the camp have a bonfire roaring, and everyone begins to gather for the reason we're here…the ceremonial dance. All the men participating wear elaborate, kind of scary masks that make them unrecognizable. The headdresses are tall and have intricate geometric shapes. Their bare chests are painted, and they carry long decorated staffs. I watch as Jake removes his hat for Tai to paint warrior strips down his cheeks and forehead. Next is Warren, then me. Tai comes over, tips my chin up, and begins making soft strokes over my brow and under my eyes—lines going horizontally, unlike the vertical ones on the men.

"This is our dance. We become the 'Gaan'...the mountain spirits. We connect to the spirits, and they protect us from disease and enemies." His soothing voice washes over me, and cold chills spring across my arms. An otherworldly feeling drapes my bodies senses. "You are Samantha. You are warrior woman. You are medicine woman. You are mischief maker, Naiche. You are a broken wanderer. You are Indee." He says as he finishes painting my face.

Tears spring to my eyes, but I manage to hold them back. Tai nods once and then walks back to join the others by the fire. I startle as a soft sing-song voice comes from behind me. I spin to find Nalin there.

"Thank you," she takes my hand, "for saving...my life." She releases my hand, pulls out the turquoise hair tie from her braid, and reaches for my own.

I stop her hand. "You owe me nothing, Nalin." It's so hard to look into her eyes that remind me so much of Jenna's.

"I want you to have this." She refuses my words and proceeds to place the leather tie with the large turquoise stone at the end of my braid. Two sharp iron spikes create and X behind it—something I failed to notice until now. It's unusual and exquisite. Her English is not as well-spoken as her father's, but she manages. "You," she points at my heart, "are warrior." Then she turns to drift away, but I catch her wrist, halting her in place.

Without saying anything, I remove my mother's necklace. The Labradorite stone gleams wickedly in the firelight. Gingerly, I place it around her neck and squeeze her tiny hand after. I'm rewarded with a beaming smile and what looks like the shine of unspent tears in her deep brown eyes. She turns and walks away as if she and her father aren't ripping my heart from my chest tonight.

Tai comes back to hand me a small wooden bowl containing a dark liquid with mysterious chunks inside. "What's this?" I question as I smell the odd-looking concoction. My herbal brain can't quite decipher the ingredients.

He leans his head back and looks to the sky. "You have many secrets, Naiche." My mouth gaps open as his eyes meet mine. "I see trouble in your future and mystery in your past. This," he taps the bowl I hold, "is for your spiritual journey of healing."

I look to Jake out of habit, but he and Warren are sharing a flask of whiskey and chatting—paying me no attention. "It's just herbs?" I ask, but Tai just smiles and uses his fingertips to raise the bowl to my lips. His face is so comforting...I don't hesitate a second time. I down the liquid and chunks. A bitter, pungent taste hits me, and I hold my breath so as not to gag. After a few coughs, I get myself together. Tai presses his forehead to mine once before taking his place among the other dancers.

I take a seat on a log off to myself and wait for the ceremony to begin, still holding the little wooden bowl.

I bring it to my nose again and take a big whiff. It's earthy, stinks a little. What the hell? I am usually pretty good at placing certain herbs, especially when brewed into a tea as this was.

Rhythmic drums bring me out of analyzing the mystery ingredients. I can feel the beat of them reverberate through my whole being as the men begin chanting and spinning in time. The entire atmosphere changes. I get a foreign feeling washing over me. Each stomp of a boot or moccasin has me mesmerized. The dust they create boils up from the ground slowly. The men seem to move in slow motion at times and then speed up. The full moon above stares at us from its heavenly perch—glowing down with purpose.

Suddenly, a cramp hits my abdomen, cold chills break out and sweat beads on my forehead. I purse my lips on an inhale and shudder.

What the *hell* was in that bowl?

Peyote Dreams

CHAPTER 25

Jake

Tai passes Warren and me a drink and begins his traditional spill about the journey we are to partake in. While he speaks, I cut my eyes to Warren in a warning glare. As Tai walks away, I snatch it from Warren's hand.

"Trust me when I say you don't want to drink this stuff."

"What is it?" Warren lifts it to his nose, and it wrinkles as he cringes.

"Peyote," I say flatly. "If you want to be high off your ass for the next few hours, be my guest, but I'll pass."

Warren chuckles. "Nah, I'm good, but won't Tai be offended?"

"Just dump it out when no one can see and stare off into the sky for the next while."

My eyes dart over to the bane of my existence every few seconds of their own accord. I can't seem to keep them away from her. I'm explaining the ceremony to Warren and translating when I notice Sam sitting alone, gripping her stomach—a bowl clutched in her pale hands.

"Oh hell," I whisper at the same time that Warren notices where my eyes have landed. He begins to push past me with a panicked look on his face. I press my hand to his chest. "I got her!" I whisper forcefully. "I've done this before; I can help her get through it."

"If something happens to her—" his eyes become murderous.

"She'll be fine come morning, but she's about to experience one *hell* of a night."

Warren grits his teeth but allows me to go to her—not that I would've taken no for an answer, anyway.

She's stopped clutching her stomach by the time I get to her and plop down on the log. "Everything okay, witch?"

"I think so." She licks her lips. That small motion has me mesmerized. "Whatever tea this was," she sits the bowl down before continuing, "it didn't sit well when it hit my tummy."

She turns to me fully, and I have to force myself to swallow. Her face is flush—cheeks rosy against the rest of her face that's pale. Her warrior stripes make her look fierce. Her full lips are still moist, and her eyes are glassy in the firelight. I debate telling her now what was in that concoction or waiting until morning. "How do you feel?" I ask.

"Okay, I guess." She rolls her shoulders, careful with the left one, and I can see her body visibly relax. "Better now." She smiles sweetly.

God help me make it through this night with her. She may very well want to kill me come morning for not telling her, but she looks too at ease for me to put fear back into those perfect eyes. She watches the dance in awe for a long time as I monitor her closely. Her body sways to the beat. My eyes follow her hair down to the gem tied to the end. I finger it gently. "Nalin, give you this?" I ask.

"She did. She is quite an amazing young woman…to have gone through—God knows what—and come out with a smile." She looks at me curiously. "How long did you spend living with them, and how did you meet?"

"Remember how we share secrets, Sam…"

"Ugh, sure…a truth for a truth." She rolls her eyes defiantly, making me grin.

I speak anyways, knowing she's unlikely to indulge me. "I was with them for around five years. Nalin was just a little thing back then." I try to stop at that, but she continues to stare at me. I exhale and look away. "I…I met them when I was sent to scout out Indian locations for the infantry to round up."

Her mouth drops open, and I immediately want to obliterate the sadness in those eyes. Never see it again. "So, you obviously didn't turn their location in."

I shake my head subtly. "Nah, I couldn't do it. They were good people trying to…just live…same as me. Years after I was on my own, I came to find them again. I was drawn to them somehow even though I knew it could mean my death." A smile pulls at my lip. "Instead of taking my life, they took me in."

She looks confused—brows furrowed—when she asks, "I've always heard how violent they can be. Why didn't they attack you?"

"They can be violent and are viciously protective of their family and way of life, don't get me wrong, but Tai said he felt Ussen urging him to listen to me. He said we were something akin to kindred spirits." I watch as her pupils begin to dilate. Not long now.

Her eyes close as she lolls her head back not saying anything for a bit. I reach an arm around her to steady her as she almost falls backward off the log, causing her to giggle. I see Warren piercing me with an "I'll kick your ass look" from the other side of the fire. "You good?" I ask.

Her eyes meet mine with a feral gleam in them. "Never better, Jake. To answer your question…my truth would break your mind into tiny little pieces." She cackles.

I smirk not moving my arm from around her waist. "I think I can handle your truths, witch."

"Witch, witch, witch…but am I a *good* witch or a *bad* witch…that's the question." She giggles again. The peyote taking ahold of her senses as her gaze drifts back to Tai and the others briefly before meeting mine once again. "You are handsome," she says randomly. Her fingers move to touch my war paint and then to my jaw. I hold very still as her soft fingers captivate me. My muscles tense with the sensations running through me. She sits back and, unfortunately, breaks the contact. "A truth for a truth," she says. "I feel guilty."

My brows pinch together, "Guilty for what?" I still refuse to remove my arm from cradling her side. The heat of her body is scorching me to my core.

"Guilty for being happy right now."

My confusion deepens. Try as I might, I don't catch her meaning. Why would anyone feel guilt for being happy? I try to push her further. "That doesn't make sense."

"That's because you've never lost people who are still living…people who will never be able to find you but will scour the earth to do so."

My head tilts to the side as my eyes narrow on her in question.

She giggles again and mumbles something about a wicked witch and then says, "It's not tornados you travel on, Jake…did you know that?" She trails off, murmuring nonsense.

This is going to be a long night.

Spinning in circles, looking at the stars, and singing…that's what Samantha has been doing for the better part of an hour. I finally eased her away from the ceremony and into the woods beside the lake near camp. I promised Warren several more times that I had her under control.

I lied.

She is fully invested in the earth and all its elements and skipped out on reality completely. I've built a fire and laid out blankets, food, and water for when she comes down from this.

"*Oh, let the sun beat down upon my face…*" Sam sings a song in a beautiful soft tone, something I've never heard before. "*I am a traveler of both time and space…*"

"Okay, okay." I grab her and force her spinning to stop. "You're going to make yourself sick."

"I'm wonderfully in tune with the universe. Can you see it, Jake?" She points skyward. "We are nothing but particles moving through. We have no control over where we go. It's all fated. I wasn't even supposed to be here, but here I am. And here you are." She stops abruptly and takes my face into her hands. Her glazed stare is intense. "You are beautiful," she says wistfully. Her eyes grow wide when she spots the lake behind me. "Swim with me." She giggles and darts away before I can grab her.

Running after her, I yell into the night, "Samantha, no! Don't you..." Before I can get the words out, she's slinging clothes left and right. "Sam, no." I grab her boots and shove them back to her when she stops, but she's already fiddling with her breeches with both hands, her sling lying on the ground. "Sam," I grab her gently, "your arm needs time to heal...stop trying to undress!"

She leans in and whispers against my lips, "What's wrong, Jake...are you scared of the water or me?" She smiles a devilish grin right before darting away again, and I see her blouse floating behind her. "Come now, Jake...swim with me," she pleads with her back to me as I give chase.

I slam to a stop. My heart threatens to break free from the cage it's in as her breeches are suddenly dropped to her ankles. She languidly steps out of them. Her body is bathed in moonlight just enough to see the contours of her slim waist and lean muscles down to her round backside. My whole body stiffens as she turns to face me. Her skin is smooth and glowing. Water ripples from the lake, leaving shadows dancing across her breasts—pink nipples taut from the chill. My eyes trail to the alluring mark detailing her hip. How many nights have I dreamt of kissing every inch of her? Of tracing that mark with my tongue?

I rub the back of my neck and then look away. "Sam, this...you...we," I stutter. "Damn it, put your clothes back on!" I hear her giddy laugh and turn back to see her wading in. "Sam I mean it…I'm *NOT* coming in after you!"

I really lied to Warren when I said I could handle her.

"You know I once called you Captain Jakeass!" She throws back her head, laughing again. "Like Jackass, get it? But Jakeass instead."

"You're a real hoot, you know that. GET. OUT. NOW!"

She wades further into the water until just her shoulders are above the surface. "Do you see the colors?" She trails one finger through the water then pokes it over and over causing rings to ripple outward. "They are magnificently complex, like the ones in your eyes."

While flattered, I'm still going to throttle her. "Damn it," I curse as I chunk my boots aside and my shirt. I roll my pant legs up a little, making a cuff, and dip my feet into the water's edge. She backs farther in. "Holy hell, woman, I swear…if you take one more step!" I start to hesitate, but then I gasp as shock washes over me when I see her dip below the surface, leaving nothing but water bubbling behind her wake.

In an instant, my body is submerged. I dive into the dark depths. Every second feels like minutes as I swing my arms side to side, searching for her. I can't see a damn thing and panic grips me. My hand grazes skin, and I lurch forward, wrapping her in my arms and pulling her up. We both gasp, and I cough as our heads break the surface. Panting I swim toward the shallower bank with her grinning from ear to ear in my arms.

"I can swim, you know." She splashes water at me once we are near the embankment.

"You almost gave me a damn heart attack!" I sneer at her and set her down to stand in front of me. Only our legs remain in the water now. My whole body is shaking while hers is as still as the night—no care in the world.

Her eyes grow heavy as she stares at my face. "Where did this scar come from?"

"Now is *not* the time, Sam," I say sternly.

"She reaches up to touch it, and I almost flinch away but hold very still as her breasts come within inches of my lower chest. "Sam stop."

"It's beautiful," she whispers and pulls my head down. Shock is an understatement as I feel her lips graze the scar. Her mouth like a flame against my skin compared to the chill in my body. Even with the water's temperature being rather warm tonight, a light breeze still brings that chill, or maybe it's her.

I shudder then move a step back, breaking her connection. "I only have so much control right now, and you are pressing my limit to the very edge."

Her body sways again as she drifts off to somewhere inside her dazed mind. The high can be different for everyone. Mine was bliss in the beginning. Memories of good times and sometimes no thought at all, just glorious peace. Later the painful thoughts buried deep clawed their way to the murky surface. I recall being thrust into my childhood hell all over again and...the war. I'm grateful that she's not fighting demons on her spiritual journey as I did. She seems at peace.

For now, anyway.

"Come now, Sam, let me get you by the fire." She doesn't say anything or resist as I cradle her in my arms and slosh through the water until we are on dry land. My mind darts in every direction as I try to ignore the feel of her soft skin against mine. I'm trying to be a gentlemen but damn she's making it hard for me...in more ways than one. I settle her onto my blanket and wrap another tightly around her before retrieving our wet clothes and hanging them haphazardly around some nearby trees. My breeches will, unfortunately, have to dry on my body.

Her fingers trail in the air before her as she zones out, watching the blaze of the fire. All the paint is washed away from her face. Her wet braid hangs in a heavy clump. I settle down behind her and take her hair in my hands. Gently, I remove the stone from her hair given to her by Nalin and unravel the weave until her long locks hang free in waves. I pull her against my chest and use the cover to attempt to dry her arms.

"Jake."

"Yeah, Sam."

"What do you miss?"

I scrunch my brows and say, "Miss?"

She ignores my question and murmurs, "I miss my Chevelle. It was really fast...and my family most. My sister Jenna. My mom. My dad." Sam closes her eyes and leans back into my chest further, laying her head to the side so that she can look me in the eye. "They are out there looking for me somewhere in time."

What the hell in a Chevelle? Where is her family that they would need to search for her? "Why would they need to look for you?" I ask before the conversation wanders off. I felt like an ass questioning her in this state of mind, but the words flew out before I could catch them.

"I'm missing Jake. I'm just…gone." She points to the sky.

I scrunch my brow and pull her head to rest under my chin. "You're not gone, Sam. You're here…with me and Warren. I've got you."

"Are you gone too, Jake?"

I contemplate her question for far too long. "Maybe I was." I kiss the top of her wet head. "I'm not so sure now." Sitting with her bundled against me second guessing everything I thought I knew about life. I was certain that I was doomed for nothing but loss and grief. Cursed even. She's making me feel otherwise and I'm not sure what to do with that.

"If I was swept away into space right now, would you miss me?" Her dilated eyes rise to meet me.

"I think I might," I say honestly.

While her comments and questions are strange, they are ripping at the walls I've built to keep people at bay. For every day we spend together, I lose a board from that wall. I could ask her anything right now, and she would probably tell me. No more wondering where that gun came from or the marks on her body. No more secrets. Do I dare cross that line?

She reaches up and splays her hand across my cheek, bringing heat to that spot. No. I don't think I can cross that line tonight. Her secrets are hers alone. Maybe one day she will tell me who she really is. Maybe one day, I'll do the same.

Sam's fingers inadvertently move again to the scar on my face that she seems so fascinated with. "You are so beautiful it hurts. *Why*? Who put the whiskey and amber in your eyes? Your mother? Your father? Whoever did, I'm thankful. I could drown in them," she rambles on.

"My mother...I have her eyes."

"And your hair?"

"My mother also."

"And your build?" Her hand moves to my chest.

My eyes dart away before coming back to hers. "My fathers."

"Well," Sam leans in until her sweet breath fans across my lips, "I am forever thankful for their attributes." She begins to close the minuscule distance between us.

I have a brief moment of sanity that screams not to do this. I do *not* take advantage of inebriated women, but the moment of chivalry is lost when her lips touch mine. Fire erupts under my flesh, and I resign myself to let her burn me to ash. Her kiss is sweet and tender until her lips part and her tongue finds mine. Her breathy little moan has me coming undone. I lift her and spin her around until she straddles me by the fire. The only thing separating us is my breeches. All the questions I have about her or thoughts of her strange ramblings die out as we meld into one another. The blanket falls, giving way to flesh as her breasts press against my chest. I feel every inch of her. An invisible current moves between us and I never want to be free of it.

I run my hand through her hair, gripping as I hold her captive. The kiss becomes more impatient. I can feel her nipples tighten against me. I growl against her mouth as I move to suckle her lower lip. Her head falls back, leaving her neck open while her body moves against me. The beautiful torment is almost painful.

Her eyes open, and I see the glassy sheen to them, and it brings me to my senses—slams me to a halt. I'm panting when I say, "We can't...not like this."

She ignores me and continues to place pillow-soft kisses down my neck while running her hand into my beard. She mumbles against my flesh, "You've touched me before...remember, on the horse?" She leans back taking my hand and moving it lower. "I want you to touch me again, Jake."

My entire body is on fire, and I'm about to say the hell with it. I decide, maybe I'm not a gentleman after all. But she would never forgive me. *Never.* "Sam, stop...we can't." I pull my hand from hers and take her hands into mine.

She arches her delicate brow and smirks at me. "Who's afraid of the big bad witch?"

I lean in and toy with her by nibbling her jaw before saying, "Afraid of you…on the contrary. I yearn for nothing more than to ruin you for all men—to watch you unravel, but tonight is not the night."

Seeing as I'm getting nowhere with her, I pick her up, causing her to giggle, and settle her back onto the blanket on her side. I cradle her front against me and wrap us tightly in the covers. I make sure her back is to the fire for warmth. "Try to sleep." I tuck her head under my chin and run my fingers soothingly up and down her back. After several minutes of her singing again, she finally begins to quieten, unlike my furnace of a body. I can't close my eyes without picturing her writhing, her breasts pressed against me.

"How will I ever leave you, Jake?" Sam whispers.

I pull her tighter against me…if that's even possible. "You aren't going anywhere." My chest rises and falls in a steady rhythm while my mind has just been blown to bits. What does she mean, 'leave me'. Why does that one statement make me want to rip the world to shreds? I know that I'm not good enough for her, and she holds too many secrets. We don't…*won't* work. I promised myself a life alone. To never have anyone means no more disappointments. No more loss. Still…the thought lingers there. What would life be like with Sam? It's a useless torment to sit and wonder.

Still, I say, "You and I will never be done, remember?"

She doesn't respond. I can hear her rhythmic breaths indicating sleep. This is going to be a long night.

Teasing Games

CHAPTER 26

Samantha

I run as fast as I can, but my legs move in slow motion. It's like being in quicksand. Trevor is behind me...barreling forward at an unnatural speed. To the left, I see my family off in the distance. None of them see me. They continue laughing and talking with each other as if I am not in mortal danger.

It's all my fault. I hid the dark sides of my life from the ones I should have screamed it to. I feel Trevor gaining on me. When I flick my eyes back quickly, Henry Fletcher is at his side. My heart plummets. Just as their footsteps reach me, Henry grabs my hair. I release a gut-wrenching scream. I fall.

And fall...

And fall...

My body smacks the ground, and I look up, but the sky creates stars in my eyes as the eclipse moves and the sun blankets.

Suddenly, my body is sucked into a vortex of colors, and nausea rolls through my stomach. Two paths appear before me. One leads home—my mother's outstretched arms waiting for me there. The other...I see Jake riding away on Shadow. Tears spring to my eyes as I scream to the heavens to not make me do this! Do NOT make me choose!

My body is violently shaking. I hear a familiar growling voice above me, "Sam...wake up. I'm here. I got you." My eyes blink rapidly but feel like sandpaper as they squint into the sun. Shadows move over me, and I'm finally able to open my eyes fully. I'm met with Jake's weary stare.

"What happened last night." My voice is crackly and foreign to me. "I feel like I've been whacked on the head." As soon as the words leave my mouth, bits and pieces begin to form in my head. Jake cocks his head to the side, and his mouth forms a tight line, unwilling to answer. "What—" I start to ask again as I sit up, and the blanket falls away. The morning breeze touches my skin, and I gasp as I grip the blanket's edges and yank it to cover my naked breasts. My eyes widen, shooting daggers at Jake.

He holds his hands up in mock surrender. "Do you remember anything? Cause there's an explanation for your state of undress." He awkwardly gestures to the blanket.

I scoot away from him as I gather my thoughts. A hurt look crosses his face, but I ignore it. It takes a few moments for some of the memories to come tumbling together in a disarrangement of events. I recall the beginning of the ceremony, the weird, disgusting liquid. Then fragments of what doesn't even feel like my own memories.

A lake, a fire, violent dreams…a kiss.

My face turns crimson. "What was in that drink, Jake?" I grit out.

He runs a hand through his beard, stands, and moves away from me. "Peyote." When he eyes me and my enraged glare, he throws his hands up again. "I would've stopped you from drinking it, but I was too late to warn you."

I wrap the blanket tighter around me and avoid his eyes when I ask, "Did we…you know…"

"No," he says then a shit-eating grin appears on his smug face, "but not for the lack of you trying."

"You ass! I was out of my mind in 'La La Land.'"

His grin is infuriating when he adds, "That doesn't change the fact that you were trying to defile me."

"Defile you? You are the worst, you know that?"

"Not according to peyote Sam…she was insatiable. *She* said I was beautiful."

I sneer at him, but before I can pop off another comment, the image of me running from Jake nude comes to me. The feel of the lake and the fear in his eyes as I backed deeper into the dark depths. I can't remember everything we said. It's like a puzzle with the middle missing, but pieces are there. Then me, wrapped in his arms, straddling him…

"The rose in your cheeks must mean you have some idea of what I'm talking about."

"I'm done with this conversation! Get me my clothes. Now!"

He stands a little taller and tilts his head back in obvious defiance. His arms cross over his broad chest. "I don't take kindly to orders, especially considering you owe me some gratitude." His eyes hold mischief and dance with humor even as he tries to look intimidating.

"What for? *Exactly.*" I glare at him.

"I jumped in the damn water to rescue you." He paces around and begins taking down the camp, trying to hide his smile.

I grin demurely. "You apparently owe me a thank you then."

He stops abruptly, brows furrowed. "What for?"

"The view," I say as I stand, eyes darting around until I find what I'm looking for—my clothes strewn in some branches nearby. I sashay slowly over to them, letting the blanket slip ever so slowly down my back. I peek over my shoulder to see his rigid body and heated eyes following me. I'm not even sure he's breathing. "You're welcome," I add as I drop the cover completely, bearing my backside to him, and dress as devastatingly slow as I possibly can.

My shirt is on but unbuttoned, barely covering me as I pull on the breeches, tugging them over my butt. I turn to grab my boots and stocking socks but slam right into Jake's chest. My heart skips a beat as my face flushes. I never even heard him walking towards me. Damn shadow bastard.

"Last night," his voice rumbles as I take a step back, "you pushed me to the edge of any man's sanity." He stalks forward with every step I take back. "I don't like to admit it, but I was a perfect gentleman." His steps continue with mine as his eyes rake down the open gap in my shirt, showing a sliver of cleavage and my stomach. "Today...I. AM. NO. LONGER. THAT. GENTLEMAN."

My back hits a tree just as his hands dart out on either side of my head to cage me in. "Jake...I...umm—" I mumble, but my words are lost when Jake leans into me and presses me into the tree. I suddenly realize I may have made a mistake taunting him. My breath is choppy as I glare at him. Bark rubs against my back, but all my cares are tossed aside when his mouth meets mine. His soft lips, mixed with the rough beard, create an inferno inside me. Heat pools low in my belly instantly as if he has the combination to my bodies safe. His kiss deepens, and our tongues collide. His rough hands move along the inside of my open blouse, grazing my stomach before ascending to cup my aching breasts. A breathy moan escapes me.

He pauses the kiss, watching my eyes as his hands roam my body. "I could drown in it," he says under his breath.

My brows furrow. "In what?"

His cheek pulls into that side smile that has me biting my lip. "Your desire that you try to hide," he says plainly.

As if I wasn't ravenous for this man before, it becomes almost too much to bear now. The dry spell that I've been in for almost two years needs a monsoon. I can think of no one better to bring down the rain than Jake Evans.

"Did you know that you asked me to touch you last night?" he whispers against my lips. "Like the day we rode Shadow together. His fingers splay against my stomach and then move ever so slowly until his fingers graze the top of my breeches. They move down lower and sink past the waistband. "I want to watch you come undone. Watch you squirm."

I groan. I don't even have the right state of mind to be angry at peyote Sam right now. She was a floozy, but I think I'm okay with that. My breath hitches. His gaze devours me in the most mouthwatering way. "What if someone sees us?"

"Do I look like I care?" His hand settles lower, and when his fingers graze my center, I moan loudly and close my eyes. My arms suddenly gripping him tight enough that I feel the ache in my left one but ignore it. His other hand grabs my chin and forces me to look at him. "Look at me, don't close your eyes, witch," he commands.

My hands move from his back to thread into his hair. He begins making circling motions with his fingers, and I lose composure. Moaning and writhing beneath his touch like a feral animal. His hand releases my face, and his lips press into mine, silencing the loud noises I can't seem to hold back while his other hand continues its slow torture. His kisses move from my lips to create a path down until his lips are suddenly on my breasts, sucking and teasing. My entire being comes alive. His expert tongue and fingers play me like an instrument as I sing out defenselessly against their onslaught. "Jake," I pant, feeling the coil forming deep inside me.

He brings his face back to mine and holds my jaw captive again, sensing my impending orgasm. "I want you to remember that this is how I feel every second I'm around you. Two can play at this teasing game, Samantha… let's see who breaks first." The veins in his forearms, along with his clenched jaw, let me know exactly how much he is holding back. He smiles smugly and then pulls away from me.

I'm left there…breasts out, mouth agape, as he licks his lips and backs further away. "You…you…asshole!" I spit as I deftly fasten the buttons along my blouse.

"Fair is fair, woman."

If he wants a game of blue balls, then I'm going to bring the pain. Suddenly I hear Warren calling for us, so I quickly thrust on my boots and saunter over to Jake leaning against a tree. "You are going to burn for me so brightly that the stars will be jealous," I whisper against his ear as I slide my hand firmly against the bulge in his breeches. He sucks in a shocked breath, making me smile broadly at him. "The ride home is going to be a long...*hard* one, Jake." I grin deviously as I turn and head toward the camp.

A few hours later, we are headed home. My heart is heavy—full of the kindness shown to me and Warren by the tribe. All the awkward looks and banter between Jake and I temporarily forgotten with the weight of leaving them. The same unexplainable connection hummed in my veins when I bid them farewell as it did on our porch the day before the ceremony. I couldn't hold back the tears that sprang to my eyes. I released them freely. It was a feeling of finality. I somehow knew I would never see them again. Children adorned me with handmade gifts of beaded bracelets. I layered them on my arm and felt the love in each and every one of those seemingly simple trinkets. If someone offered me a thousand gold ones for these, I'd turn them down.

Tai and Nalin had pulled me aside before we parted ways, making certain we were out of earshot of Jake. Tai handed me a worn leather-skinned book, handmade—symbols carved into the front that I didn't understand.

"What's this?" I had asked.

"This is my notes on plants and their uses. I've worked on it for many years. It contains recipes for healing all sorts of ailments." He smiled sweetly.

"I can't accept this." I pushed it back to him, but he shook his head in refusal.

"There is a fire inside you." He tapped my chest. "It burns bright and yearns for purpose. This is your purpose, Samantha." My mouth hung open, but he continued before I could reply, "You are Samantha, warrior, medicine woman, mischief maker Naiche, broken wanderer, and one of us...the Indee. Never forget it." He placed his forehead to mine before he asked something of me that had had me riding home in a daze...quiet. He had said, "Take care of Chato's heart. He's a broken wanderer, too."

Broken wanderer. Is that what Tai feels when he looks into my soul? Is Jake just as broken and has he been moving aimlessly through this life as I have been?

Life was beginning to become normal for me a few months ago. I had resigned myself to this life. Now, everything has been tossed into the wind like ashes— blowing haphazardly, never quite knowing where one speck may land that will change your course. I was fine before all this. My eyes flit to Jake and back before he notices. He has thrown my life into disarray unintentionally. It was so much easier *not* having anyone else to care about.

Bits of my psychedelic memories have surfaced along the ride. Never a complete picture, more like a preview, but I vividly remember the dream's ending. The two paths before me.

"What's bothering you, Sam?" Warren asks, bringing me out of my head.

Jake is riding just far enough away that I can speak freely, albeit quietly. "The future," I say simply.

He purses his lips in thought. "It's a hard thing to consider and even harder to comprehend. We don't know that we will even be given the chance to go back, let alone to our exact time." His eyes soften, and he reaches across the gap in our horses to pat my hand. "When the time comes…if it does, we have to go back. You know that, right?" He looks at Jake and back to me.

I gnaw on my lower lip to hold back the sudden lump I feel in my throat. He pulls his hand away as I nod ever so slowly. He's right, of course. If the time comes, I can't *not* try. I have family waiting for me. Miles is without his mother already, and now he's lost Warren.

"You know, last night I was scared to death for you. What if you were allergic to that stuff, or what if you said some things that may raise some eyebrows," Warren says under his breath, changing the subject when he sees the torture it's bringing.

"Not sure if I *did* or *didn't* say something weird, but if I did, Jake hasn't mentioned it."

"That's good."

"For real. Could you imagine?" I giggle.

Just about that time, Jake slows his horse a bit and turns to ask me, "What's a Chevelle?"

My mouth drops open, and eyes widen. Warren glares at me as if he could shoot lasers through my skull. What shitty timing was that question? I would laugh, but then Warren might seriously laser me. My heart thuds a little too hard. I clear my throat and search for a lie. "Um…it was ugh…my horse from my childhood." My words stumble out of me like a drunkard from a bar. "Remember that horse Warren…Chevelle. He was a good one." I nod like I have a tic or something and Warren narrows his eyes at me but nods too. "Why do you ask?" I say as look back to Jake.

Jake looks confused as he tips his head to the side eye balling me. "You mentioned you missed it last night."

"Oh, yeah…he was the best…that old Chevelle." He looks straight through me with those cutting eyes, but he just turns and lets it drop.

Warren blasts me with his round eyes and says so softly I have to strain to hear, "What else did you talk about?"

I mouth without speaking out loud, "I. DON'T. KNOW."

He exhales loudly. "At least we can blame the peyote for it."

"True," I mumble.

As I've said before, I hate lying and liars. Part of me is screaming to tell Jake everything and let him think me crazy as a loon. That would be better than this guilt gnawing in my stomach. It's almost unbearable, the urge to spill my guts to him. Why does he evoke this turmoil inside of me? My mouth drops open a touch on a small gasp when something I said last night rears its ugly head.

"How will I ever leave you, Jake?"

Lies, Lies, Lies

CHAPTER 27

Samantha

The mint leaf tastes divine, even with the earthy aftertaste, as I chew on it lavishly. I finish making my piles of plants, leaves, and herbs along the table in neat rows. My plan for tomorrow is to begin creating some more useful concoctions for survival and healing—dabble in more than just my usual smelly guilty pleasures. With the use of the book Tai gave me, that shouldn't be an issue. I smile, giddy like a child, when I look over to my herbal table and see the leather book lying amongst my array of herbs.

I had vigorously scrubbed my body and teeth from head to toe before refilling the outdoor tub to lounge in. Jake and Warren left out to night hunt, leaving me with some privacy I sorely needed. It's been almost a week since we returned from the Apache camp, and

Jake has been here most of the time. We haven't had a moment alone, and it's probably for the best. This teasing playfulness between us scares me to death. The more I'm around him...the harder it may be to leave.

The whiskey is stout as I sip it simultaneously with the minty flavor left on my tongue, attempting to improve the taste. I chose drops of amber for the tub tonight, creating an aroma that reminds me of a certain someone's eyes.

The sun has just set, and the moon is awake with all her brilliance, casting the world in a soft glow. I have the sheets drawn around me, but a slight breeze makes them ripple every now and again. The night is silent enough to make me temporarily forget everything that has transpired.

Until it is not.

Hoofbeats sound nearby. Seems to be one set, which doesn't make sense. Warren and Jake rode out together. My hackles rise, and I softly set the whiskey down, reach for my old pistol, and grip it tightly while I try to remain as still as possible—thankful that my Colt is hidden in the house under those floorboards.

The hoofbeats slow. Clanking on a loose stone every now and again, giving away the rider's location off to my left. Then they stop.

Silence.

I debate, rising from the tub and making a beeline for the front door, but that thought is smashed with the swish of the curtains being drawn back.

I swallow my nerves and look my intruder dead in his soulless eyes, body still submerged in the water, gun aimed at his head.

"Well, well. If this isn't a fantasy, come to life." Bill's eyes twinkle in a malicious way as he takes in my situation. His hand rests on his gun, but he makes no move for it. "Are you going to shoot me temptress?"

I hold steady. No shake to my hands when I say, "It depends on your next words. Why are you here, at my home?"

His grin is infuriating. "You seem rather calm for a girl alone, at night, naked and vulnerable."

"Funny thing…this is not the first time this has happened." I level him with a glare.

He raises an impressed brow and says, "You are one interesting woman. Now lower that gun, and we can talk."

I grin and lower my aim to his groin. "Speak."

He nods and smiles broadly. "Okay, dear, have it your way." His eyes linger lower, but thankfully, my breasts are submerged. "I'm here to solve a mystery."

"What mystery is that?"

"I have *two* of my men missing from *my* town. One, a Mister Henry Fletcher." He smirks. "You know him right?" He continues without waiting for a comment, "Two, Kelvin Mack. Now, you see, both of these men are important to me, and I worry that something nefarious has happened to them."

"When you say they are important to you, you mean to your *business*…whatever that may be."

His lips pull back in a snarl, but he quickly shrugs and masks his face. "You're a very astute woman, Samantha. *Yes*, they do work for me, but they are *also* my friends." He stops talking and looks around the property, mainly the barn and pasture. "Where is your companion...Warren, was it?"

"He's due back any moment," I lie.

"Good, good. It's dangerous for a woman to be left all alone out here in this barren wasteland. Anyway, have you seen either of these men?"

"No." Another lie. I pray for the red not to creep into my cheeks as my heart rate continues to spike. Adrenaline courses through me in waves.

He inhales deeply through his nose and cocks his head to the side. "You can lower your gun at any moment, dear."

"No thanks."

He chuckles. "I have men perched just on that embankment...right over there." He points toward a rolling hill not far from the back of my house. "They will not hesitate to move in on you should you take a shot at me."

Fear wrenches my gut. There's...who knows how many of them, and one of me. Warren and Jake haven't been gone long. They could take hours to get back to me.

"I'll ask you again to lower your weapon so that we can talk...cordial like." He flicks his fingers in a downward motion for me to cooperate.

Reluctantly, I lower my weapon but keep it in my hand by the tub. My breath becomes jerky, and my hand trembles.

"Good girl." He licks his lower lip and smooths down his mustache. "Now, back to civilized conversation. When did you last see Henry Fletcher or Kelvin Mack?"

"I saw Henry the night of the town's celebration. Kelvin…I'm not sure."

"You know what…you are a terrible liar." He pins me with a glare. "Would you like to know how I know that you are indeed lying?"

"Do I have a choice?"

"No…you don't." He moves a step closer, and my arm raises a touch. He tsks and points to the hill. "I wouldn't do that if I were you."

"Then stay where you are," I say through bared teeth.

He doesn't move closer but begins fiddling with my wooden table's contents. Smelling my oils as he talks, "I *know* you are lying because both men had interactions with you before they went missing. Henry told some of his companions of his plan to woo you, so to speak…they heard him say, from his own mouth, that he was coming to this farm."

My face pales, and I'm finding it harder and harder to keep composure. "Like I said, I saw him that night, then never again."

"Here is an even better story for you," he continues, ignoring my comment. "Lonnie saw you at Big John's the last night Kelvin was seen alive. He left the saloon, according to some bystanders, going to see what you were up to that late at night…"

"I talked to Lonnie. We had wagon trouble, and Warren was fixing it. That's why we were there later than usual."

"Lies, lies, lies." He takes a big whiff of an oil and moans aloud. I stiffen when his hand grazes my book from Tai, but he moves past it and smells another oil mixture. "Man, this stuff can drive a man wild…make him lose all inhibitions." He winks at me and then says, "Must be why Jakey boy can't get enough of you, huh?"

"Jake is twice your size, with zero patience and a happy trigger finger. I'd watch what you say about your nephew."

He laughs outright and then whistles, "Well, well. There has been some development in your relations with my dear nephew, as I can gather from your defensive mannerisms. Wonderful. Because I'm certain that you did *not* work alone the night my men went missing."

I try to breathe in through my nose, out through my mouth. This situation is decaying fast. "I told you; we had nothing to do with it."

"We. That is such a strong word. You, Jake, and your dark friend."

"His name is Warren, and you will not speak of him without the utmost respect, or I'll take my chances and shoot you now."

His smile is knowing and sinister. "Back to our conversation then...guess who was missing from town along with Kelvin that night?"

I don't indulge him.

"A young girl, Native American, worked for Lonnie...ring any bells for you?"

I keep silent as a mouse.

"Let me break it down for you. She came from a tribe that has been on the run from reservation life for a few years now. There's money involved in rounding up savages." He stops briefly to revel in my disgust. "She was to be the bargaining chip...the one thing that could bring them out of hiding. You see, they were hunting the night my men located them, and even though that night was not a success, it was a beginning. We had her. It was only a matter of time before she led us to them, or they came for her."

Thoughts smash together like bumper cars in my skull. Every moment that led me here. *Every. Single.* Road we have taken. If Tai had brought his men to get Nalin back, they would all be either killed or rounded up in a reservation camp by now. Our intervention changed that. A small smile splays across my face.

"What's so funny, girl?"

I ignore him and refuse to answer.

"Maybe this shall wipe the smile off your face. That is the very same tribe of heathens that Jake lived with years ago." He watches my smile fade. "There's only one reason you were there late that night at Big Johns. That was to make my dearest Lonnie violently ill and then to break out that young woman. Am I getting close?" He chuckles at my silence. "Lonnie is quite enraged by the way. She didn't take too kindly to being *poisoned*." He languidly removes a brass pocket watch from the inner part of his jacket. I squint at it. His smile grows as he swings it around in a circle.

I know that watch.

"Found this on the ground, near your house. Look familiar?"

That's Kelvin's watch. How could we miss that? It must have fallen from his pocket at some point. Bill can probably read the trepidation in my eyes. It's now or never. He knows everything. He's pieced it together and wrapped it in a nice little bow. He will kill Jake or have him killed and Warren, too.

"Why the stricken look, darlin'?"

The world moves in slow motion as my fingers twitch on the pistol. Before I can raise my arm all the way up, I hear several clicks. A rifle is aimed at my head to the right, and several pistols on the left. I'm staring into the eyes of Leonard, Tom, Charlie, and Bobby.

"I may have told a little lie myself." A grin splits Bill's face. "This night was never about questioning you. No. This night is about justice. You are under arrest for the murders of One, Henry Fletcher, and One, Kelvin Mack. Now…drop that damn gun before we bury you and save ourselves the hassle of paperwork."

"They are not lawmen; you have no right to do this!" Panic seizes my body as my eyes dart around to the men surrounding me.

Where is Jake?

"I have a written agreement from the Sherrif to use whom I may to help discharge the people responsible for my men's deaths and believe you me...I have more than enough probable cause."

The six-shooter slips from my fingers and clatters on the ground.

The men move in on me, and I panic and scream. My voice echoes through the night in hopes that Jake and Warren are close enough to hear me. "Stop, stop!" I yell at them. "Please have the decency to allow me to dress...fucking assholes!" I lash out at them.

Bill chunks my breeches and blouse from the clothesline onto the ground. "Dress and make it fast."

"I ca...can't. Not in front of y'all," I stutter. Between being in shock and the cool water, I'm shaking like a leaf.

"Dress! NOW!" he growls at me, his face showing the first signs of true rage.

I stand and hop out of the bath as quickly as possible while whistles and catcalls follow my every move. I sling on my blouse to hide most of me. My back to them, and my body facing my wooden table. Just as my breeches are almost up, I see my herbs and certain crushed plants lying in neat piles. Beside them, the hair tie from Nalin. I snatch a pile of crushed herbs and the hair tie and discreetly drop them into my pocket. Bill grabs me roughly, spins me around, and holds me at arm's length. For a second, I think he will check my pocket, but his eyes are drawn to my hip— latched to the tattoo not quite covered up as it stretches above the waistband. His stare takes on a manic glaze.

"After everything, I did for that boy. He is as much a liar as you." His fingers dig into my arms. He shoves me hard backward, and it takes everything I have to stay upright and pull the breeches the rest of the way up.

The men finally descend around me, guns pressed to my skull as Bill ties my hands together with rope. "You will walk barefoot behind my horse all the way to your new cell. Come morning, everyone will know about the harlot witch who's behind several disappearances in town."

They drag me to the back of Bill's horse, kicking and screaming. One long rope binds me to Bill's saddle. There's a steady stream of tears blinding my eyes. I watch in horror as they each move away from me, leaving me with Bill. I have no clue where they hid their horses, but they are moving around my house and barn...not toward the hillside. Lanterns in hand.

"What are they doing, Bill?" I choke out.

Bill stands there and pulls a coin from his pocket. He rolls it across his knuckles in his now signature move. He walks back to the tub and flicks the coin inside. "Oh, just leaving a little reminder of why no one messes with William Evans." I look to the tub, and it clicks…he's leaving a bread crumb for Jake to find. But what are the others doing…

I hear the shatter of a broken window. Then another. Flames begin to flicker throughout the barn and house. My screams are cut short by the gag placed over my mouth. I see Clint frantically galloping in circles, grunting, and neighing. Suddenly, he bolts toward the far side of the fence and, in a brilliant show, leaps over it. I close my eyes; thankful he's free. I don't have time to worry about our livestock as Bill's irritating voice pulls my attention.

"You know the best part dear." Bill leans in close to me and smells my hair. "Jake can't and won't resist coming after you…it's only a matter of time before I have all three of you *or* several graves to dig." He presses a kiss to my tears before mounting his horse.

My thoughts immediately go back to the house, and dread sinks into me. The duffle bag. Any hopes we might've had for returning home lie underneath those rickety floorboards.

My arms are yanked forward along with my body. The ropes bite into my skin. Every stone and spiney plant attacks my bare feet, but I feel none of those things. My pain is on the backburner as I keep my head turned to what was my temporary home. All the hard work, gone. All the sweat and tears, the laughter, and the sorrows we had in building this home…gone. Warren and I held each other through everything, and this house was part of that adhesive.

The horse lurches forward, and I stumble, barely keeping my footing. I take a deep breath. Slowing the tears. I hold my head high and grit my teeth into the gag. After everything I've been through…this will *not* be the end of my story. I am going to make Bill wish he'd never met me.

I am Samantha, a warrior, a medicine woman, mischief maker Naiche, wanderer, and one of the Indee. I chant these words in my head as the rope tugs me into hell.

One Silver Dollar

CHAPTER 28

Jake

Foam gathers around Shadow's muzzle as we blaze a trail across the mountain toward the canyon. Even with the wind whipping into my face, I feel like I can't breathe. I felt something was wrong deep in my gut the farther we moved away from Warren and Sam's home, but I ignored that feeling. Now, I'm cursing myself for not listening to intuition.

Smoke billows in the distance, barely noticeable in the dark, but the smell is wafting through the atmosphere. The closer we get, the brighter the flames become. Warren rides at my side, silent in his panic, rifle in his hand. My heart plummets the closer we get. Flames are reaching towards the heavens, lighting up the night in a strange and harrowing way.

"Samantha!" Warren begins yelling the closer we get. "Sam!

I scan the area around the property as I urge Shadow to an almost unthinkable gallop. "You see anything?" I ask Warren.

"Nothing. No one," he says.

We finally make it to the edge and slide our mares to a dead stop. I dismount in a flash and run to the house, Warren a few paces behind me. "Sam!" I yell over and over.

Sweat pours down my face the closer I get. The fire has encompassed most of the house now, and it's an inferno. I dart left and run the perimeter of the home, but there's no possible entry point. My heart hammers away in my chest. I see Warren about to dash inside. Running toward him, I holler, "Stop! Don't. You'll get yourself killed!"

Warren grunts as I collide with him and hold him back. "Stop, think clearly. Sam's a smart girl. She would've found a way out. There's no way she's in there. No way." I'm not sure if I am comforting him or myself. I see his eyes water, and something inside me breaks. Anger takes over as I reevaluate the land and barn.

"Let me go!" Warren screams, and I can hold him no longer. He's stout as an ox.

Releasing him, I grab his shoulder, turning him to face me. "Listen…look around you. What do you see?"

Warren scowls as he scans everything. "The barn…it's on fire too."

"Right. Exactly. Someone set this fire."

"Who are you thinking?" Warren's eyes become murderous.

"I'm not sure," I lie. I have a good idea of the only person who harbors any ill will toward Sam. "Let's scour the area, leave no stone unturned."

Warren nods to me frantically and bolts toward the barn. I search the square around the house. "Shit!" I swear every few seconds as I kick boards, rake the ground with my boots, and sift through debris that has made its way far enough from the blaze.

Nothing. For several minutes, I find absolutely nothing. Every second that passes brings me deeper into a rage. Looking toward the barn, which is leveled to the ground at this point, I see Warren slinging shit around. He's obviously found nothing either. I can't let myself think the worst. I won't survive it; neither will Warren.

Suddenly, I glance up, and the metal tub beside the house peeks out from debris, catching my eye. Boards had fallen on it, hiding it from view with my first pass around the house. Sam was going to bathe tonight, and I know she likes to do it out here. I rush over to it. The curtains around are gone from the fire, and some of the flames lick the bathtub from behind. I can still get close enough to look in. My heart hammers away even harder…if that's possible. I hear Warren, but don't turn around as he slams to a stop beside me. We don't say anything as we inch forward. I've never been so scared. Scared of what we may find.

"Here, help me move these boards," I huff the words to Warren and then begin grabbing pieces that resemble the roof and siding. With every chunk we move, the panic inside me rises like a tide.

We move enough to see that the bath doesn't have a body in it. "Oh, thank God," I whisper. I put my hands on my knees and try to inhale, but the smoke keeps wafting our way.

"What's that?" Warren points inside the tub.

There, through the murky water blackened from ash, I see something shiny. I reach in and grab it. The moment it breaks the surface, my worst fears are realized.

"What? Why do you have that look on your face? It's just a silver dollar." Warren tries to decipher my internal monologue.

"It's not *just* a silver dollar. It's a newly minted Morgan silver dollar. A Carson City, to be exact…minted this year."

"What the hell does that mean?"

"It means Bill was here." When Warren looks at me hard, I continue, "He got his hands on several of these because they only made a small amount. He *always* carries them."

"It could mean nothing…it is just a coin."

"No. It's him. Trust me." I roll the silver dollar across my knuckles the way my uncle taught me when I was fifteen.

Warren looks up at the sky. I can see this massive man about to break. He rubs the sweat from his brow and says, "Okay, so what's the plan? Do you think he has her? And if so, where?"

"If I know my uncle, he believes himself to be a most righteous person. His bad deeds are always hidden well behind the 'law-abiding citizen' he portrays." I stop and consider everything I know about him. "He will most likely want clout for taking her in...some kind of recognition. I can only assume he believes she had something to do with the Kelvin situation, but I could be wrong."

"Where would he take her?"

"That, I'm not sure." I slip the coin into my pocket and walk toward Shadow.

"Where you going?" Warren's footsteps stomp behind me.

"To find Sam."

"Where?" Warren asks.

I stop and look him in the eyes. "He left this coin here for me to find. He has her. That's a fact. We find him...we find her."

"Won't they be expecting that?"

"Yes, they will." I worry my lower lip with my teeth as I contemplate our situation.

I sling my legs over Shadow and wait for Warren to mount. "I can track them. After that, we make a plan." Off in the distance, I hear a horse whinny heading our way with pounding hoofbeats. "You hear that?" I ask.

Warren pulls his pistol at the same time as I do. "Yeah, I heard it."

Out of nowhere, Clint's sleek, dappled coat comes into view, and the moment he sees the other horses, he launches toward us. "Well, I'll be damned. He made it out," I whisper.

"He sure did." Warren swings off Halle the moment Clint stops to sniff her. Clint arches his neck and blows from his widened nostrils. "I got you, boy, come here." Warren throws a rope over his head and ties him to the saddle. "Sam's gonna need you, boy…glad you came back."

We head off into the night, strapped with what weapons we carry. "I got you, Sam…I'm coming," I whisper.

Tea and Secrets

CHAPTER 29

Samantha

The cold wall of the cell bites into my aching back that's pressed against it. My back is actually the *least* sore part of my body. The worst being my shoulder. After having the recent dislocation and now being pulled behind a horse…the pain is unreal. My blouse is stuck to me from sweat and grime. My hand trembles as I remove the last cactus prick from my right foot. The sun is beginning to rise, yet based on the darkness encompassing me, it's not crested the horizon enough to enter the lone window behind the sheriff's desk. The lamp has already died out long ago, and Deputy Langford snores heavily from his kicked-back position. His hat has fallen off, and his short salt and peppered hair is slicked back. I look over in longing at the keys hung from his pocket.

It was an hour ago that I was drug into town and thrown, literally, into this cage. The cells are small, squalid, and depressing. There looks to be three others lining the walls—all empty, save for one. I can hear the soft humming of a man at the end but can't see him clearly through all the bars between us. There's a bucket in the corner of my cell to relieve myself. Thankfully, I haven't needed to yet seeing as how my body is rather dehydrated from lack of water and profuse sweating.

Bill left me with parting words of revenge and retribution. He has no intention of stringing me up publicly just yet. He promised I would swing from a rope in due time, but he wants *all* of us. He can't exactly use me as leverage if I'm dead.

All of a sudden, a bubbly voice I know and love so well comes strutting through the front door. Her hair in a tight bun today with the lovely gray streaks in front framing her face wistfully.

Myra smacks Langford's boot to wake him. "Get your lazy tail up, Dale." She giggles when he startles and about tumbles from his chair.

"Ah, hell, Myra, you scared the devil outta me!"

"*You* are the one that requested warm, fresh muffins at sunrise…on your late shift days, remember?"

Dale smiles and weaves his head side to side. "Yes, of course. You just startled me, that's all."

I watch but remain quiet as a mouse, afraid to let her see me like this. My hands clench and tremble, but my body is rigid. She hands him a basket and takes a seat across from him. He pulls out a muffin while they chit-chat and takes a bite, moaning. My stomach growls, and my mouth waters instantly.

Dale leans in closer to her and whispers something and she blushes and covers her mouth with a hand. Oh, my word. She likes him. He runs his hand through his hair nervously, and his blue eyes sparkle. They flirt harmlessly for another few minutes before an idea slaps me in the face, making me forget about the muffins and the flirting. It also makes me push aside my pride.

I need to talk to Myra…alone.

In the middle of their conversation, I say softly, "Myra?" as if I'm just now seeing her.

Her eyes grow wide as saucers, and before Dale can protest she is lunging over to me. "My dear Sam! What is going on? What…" her eyes search my face for answers.

Dale is at her side before I can speak. "Myra, you shouldn't be talking with her. She's been accused of murder. Come on now, back away from her."

"No, please." I beg of him. I reach through the bars and hold her soft hands in mine. "Give me just a few moments with her." I hear my fugitive neighbor chuckle three cells down and furrow my brows.

"Dale," Myra says sternly, "this here is my friend, and ain't no way she could murder a bug, let alone a human being. Besides, she's behind bars. She can't hurt me." She eyes him down until I see his shoulders slump.

"You have five minutes…no more!"

She nods and turns back to me, still holding my hands. I see her eyes well with tears before she even asks, "What happened Sam."

I debate lying or sugar-coating the truth. Myra is one of *the* most logical and straightforward people I know. Could she believe me…but more than that, could she help me?

"Okay, here it goes…and please hold any judgment until the last." She nods slowly, and I continue after a deep inhale. "Bill is accusing me of murdering Henry Fletcher and Kelvin Mack."

"Well, that's preposterous," she exclaims.

"Wait 'til the end, remember…"

"Yes, sorry."

She rubs my hands bringing warmth to them and strength to my words. "Henry followed me to my home. He…" I clear my throat and look over to make sure Dale is out of earshot as I continue whispering, "he attempted to rape me." Her eyes widen. "He's no longer with us…if you get my meaning, but I didn't do it. Thing is…I would have. He almost killed me that night."

I stop and let her absorb that much before continuing. A single tear leaks down her cheek, and I reach up to wipe it away. "That's not all." I look down and hope she believes me. "Kelvin Mack is no longer with us either." Her head tilts with concern. "He kidnapped a young native girl, one of Jake's friends, actually. We rescued her. That's what this is all about."

She drops my hands and stands straighter, holding her fingers over her mouth. She finally removes them and asks, "Is the girl okay?" she whispers.

"She will be. She's back with her family."

"Why would Bill care about what happened with the girl?" Her brows pinch together.

"They were using her to track Apache tribes that have evaded capture."

"My lord," she sighs and wipes away another stray tear.

"So, you believe me?" I search her face for the truth.

She looks deep into my eyes for a full thirty seconds before saying, "I do," then she nods and takes my hands again, giving me a weak smile. "How on earth are you going to prove your innocence? Sam...Bill is a dangerous man with ties like you wouldn't believe."

I back away from Myra and begin pacing the cell. I notice the loner at the end has changed positions and is now standing with his back against the bars. Still, I can only make out part of his silhouette, but the sun is entering the window and finally shedding light into this dank place.

I come back to her and lower my voice even more to where she has to strain to hear me. "I can't prove my innocence, and no one will believe the righteous Bill over a woman people around here barely know." I bite my lip and pray she will consider what I'm about to ask of her. "I need your help."

"What...how on earth can I help?"

"I need two things. One you probably won't have a problem with, but the second…" I dart my eyes to Dale again to make certain he's eating in blissful ignorance.

"What are they?" she asks with what sounds a little too much like excitement in her voice.

"I need you to get a letter to Jake for me…today. Now, if you can find him. The sooner the better."

"And the second thing…" she cocks an eyebrow.

"I need some tea."

"Tea?" Her nose creases when she scrunches it up.

"Yes, tea…"

I spent the last few minutes we had explaining the details to include in the letter and what time she should return to me. I ask nothing of her except for food and tea when she returns. Might as well have a decent bite to eat before my fate is sealed. Light has pushed all the way into our cells by the time Myra leaves, and Dale returns to snoring. I wrap my arms around myself and pace the floor. My stinging feet are aggravating, but I can't relax right now. I have to keep my wits about me. There's a chance this won't work and an even bigger chance that Bill will remove me from here for nefarious reasons before the plan goes into action. The way his hands roamed my body before he tossed me in here makes me want to vomit.

A chuckle sounds out again from the man at the end of the jail. I walk to my bars, press my face to them, and finally see him clearly. "You're the quickdraw guy…from the festival in town," I muse.

His shit-eating grin is there, just like the last time I saw him. "That may be me." He looks me up and down brazenly. "Who. Are. You?" he draws it out in time with his eyes raking over me.

This guy looks like he's still a teenager. What the hell did he do to end up in here? "Names Samantha Thorne. What's yours?"

His tongue rolls across the edge of his teeth before he replies, "I'm *everyone* and *no one*."

I grin. "Fine, keep your secrets." We all have them...I think to myself.

He taps on the bars with his fingers as he eyes Dale, who's still snoring. "People who whisper in jails, tend to be planning an escape."

My mouth drops open. This little shit. "I have no idea what you're babbling on about." I smirk.

He winks at me and says, "*Fine*, keep your secrets."

Letter from Jail

CHAPTER 30

Jake

We hide the remnants of the campfire and mount our horses. I followed the trail of horse shit and prints. Along with them were drag marks and human footprints—small ones. They lead straight to town. We camped for a few hours, divulging a plan to rescue Sam. The problem being, we are, now, fairly certain she was brought...or dragged straight into town. Which can mean only one thing...she's in the jail.

We head out, traveling parallel to the trail made in the land that most people take—keeping our distance enough to *see* it but not *be* seen.

Warren speaks up, bringing my mind out of the hell it's been in for hours now, "Where will we go if we find her?"

I inhale deeply through my nose before answering, "We can make a stop at my childhood home, but only long enough to get cleaned up and restock on…things." I think about my father's collection of guns hidden in the cellar. "Then, we need to get far away from here."

Something about that last statement has Warren shifting restlessly in his seat.

Suddenly, my eyes catch a dust trail off to my left, near the worn path that leads to Tombstone. "Hey, look there." I point.

"Let's check it out," Warren whispers.

We dismount and crouch down as we make our way to the ridge separating us from whoever is traveling and peer over. My eyes squint. It takes a minute or two before the person is within a distance, where I can make out their face. "Holy shit…that's Myra."

"What about it?" Warren mutters.

"She never leaves town. And I mean *never.*"

"You think it means something?"

"I think we need to have a talk with the baker," I say as I jog back to Shadow and mount in one leap.

We follow her for several minutes, making certain she's not being followed. It's just past sunrise, and her wagon is jostling as she pops the reins against her mule's bottom. She's moving at an unnatural speed for her. "Stay here and be my lookout." Warren nods and pulls out his rifle. I speed away.

I run Shadow along the ridge, making sure to get ahead of the speeding wagon. Just as Myra is about to come around a curve, I trot out in front of her, causing her to yank back on the reins. Her mule slides to a stop and her wagon's contents tumble around aimlessly.

"Jake! Thank heavens!" she squeals, dismounts, and runs to me.

I hop off Shadow, and before I can stop her, she rushes to me and throws her arms around me. Tears stream down her cheeks. "Hey, hey, hey. Calm down, where is she?" I ask, knowing instantly that's why Myra's out here. "Where's Sam?"

Her eyes grow round as she looks me over. "She's in the jail, Jake." Her voice cracks with her falling tears.

My heart drops to my stomach. Assuming is one thing, but hearing it is another. How the hell will we pull off breaking her out? I hold Myra at arm's length as she wipes her eyes. "Tell me everything…who's on duty, what other prisoners are there…"

She interrupts me with a shake of her head. "No, Jake! You can't go there."

"Nothing will keep me from her!" I say a little too forcibly, making her flinch.

She smiles through her watery eyes. "I knew there was something between the two of you…I just knew it." I am about to yell that this is not the time to play matchmaker when she says, "You can't go there because she has a plan."

I shake my head in wonder. "Why does that not surprise me?"

Myra quickly pulls out an envelope that has my name scrawled across the center and hands it to me.

Her fingers don't release it just yet as she says, "Sam said to tell you this…uhhccuum," she clears her throat dramatically, "Jake Evans, Do *NOT* come for me. Listen to Myra and read the letter carefully." She releases her grip on the envelope.

My normally steady hands shake as I open it…

Dear Jake and Warren,

First off, do NOT come for me. I've instructed Myra to emphasize that. They wait for you to find me. I can't have either of you endangering yourself for me. So, don't! Second, I have a plan to get out of this. I'm innocent and justice will surely prevail. I need you to hear me and understand. I am fine. Tell Warren he means the world to me and for him not to worry. He needs to keep ahold of that strong faith he has that everything happens for a reason. Tell him that he can yell at me later and that I love him.

For you Jake, think about the good times we had. Like the day we rode Silver or the day we had that weird leaf tea. I could use some tea right now, that's for sure. One day…one day I will see you again at our special place. And Jake…I'm not sorry I met you…quite the opposite actually.

Love Sam

My mind shuts down and blanks out on everything she said except for those last two lines for a moment. I stare at the paper. Reading it over and over several times. Most of the last paragraph is complete nonsense.

Myra's eyes water again when she says, "She told me everything that happened. I'm so sorry, Jake."

I don't respond right away. A barrage of ideas and worrisome thoughts push through my mind. Finally, I say, "I can't just wait around and do nothing...I failed to protect her."

"Oh honey, is that what you think? You can't blame yourself for what these bad men did. They are at fault here...not you." She places her warm palm against my cheek.

"What's her plan, Myra? Surely, she told you. This letter...doesn't make much sense."

Myra worries her lower lip before she sighs, "She was specific in saying that I would be in harm's way if I knew her plan. She has instructed me to make another visit to her when I return. This letter," she takes it from me and scans it then hands it back, "was dangerous enough, Sam was afraid I would get caught with it if Dale told Bill I came by."

Deep down, I can understand Sam's line of thinking. She would never forgive herself if someone else was harmed while helping her. Behind all the walls she builds to make people believe she's tough, a soft heart is there. Hell, she came up with a convoluted plan to rescue Nalin just to make sure there was no bloodshed. And she did that for a stranger. How far would she go for someone she cared for?

Can I forgive *myself*, though, if I don't go to her now?

Myra startles. "Oh! I almost forgot." Myra fast walks back to the wagon, talking over her shoulder and fumbling around inside. "Judith, the poor dear, is not doing well. She's ancient, you know," she giggles at her inappropriate comment, "don't know how the old bird lived this long."

"What is it, Myra?" My patience grows thin as the need to get to Sam burns me alive.

"Hold your horses...it's here somewhere." She pulls out a small box wrapped in cloth and brings it to me. "Judith asked me to give this to Sam, but I haven't seen her for a while, so I've held on to it." Her eyes grow solemn. "She said for me not to open it...it's for Sam only. I figured I better bring it now... considering..."

I get her meaning. Considering she may never see her again. I crinkle my brows and flip the tiny box around in my hands a few times. "Isn't Judith a little...you know?"

"Crazy as a loon...yeah." Myra grins. "But, she has been more lucid lately. People tend to get that way when their time is nearing an end." She pats my hand and says, "If...no, when you are back with Sam, give this to her and tell her we wish her the best in life." Tears roll down her face again. "Tell her I'm proud to call her my friend."

"Aren't you going back to see her?" I ask. Confused as to why she can't tell her that in person.

"I don't want to upset her face to face. Sam's not much of the hugging kind and right now she needs strength. And you know how this goes, right Jake?" When I nod, she huffs out a breath. "She will not be able to come back around here, *ever*."

She's right. If we get her out, we will be on the run from that point on. We'll have no choice but to flee Tombstone.

Myra bids me farewell a few minutes later. I sit with Warren after telling him all about the conversation. His hat is off, and he's running his hands over his hair again and again. Agitation and nervous energy permeate from him. I'm sure I look the same, haggard, and lost.

Warren speaks up, "If I know Samantha…and I *do*, she has some outlandish scheme up her sleeve."

"So, you think she can pull it off? Escape?" I hate to sound skeptical, but it's highly unlikely, and many have tried before her.

Warren laughs, and it catches me off guard. "Yeah, Jake, I think she might. But we do need to figure out what she meant in that letter." He folds out the letter again, and his eyes widen at a part he reads. I can tell he's figured something out, but for whatever reason, he holds back the information. He masks his features and then asks, "What can she possibly be talking about…riding Silver?"

"I don't know." I smile. "She named my horse Shadow 'cause she said every good horse needed a name." My smile fades, and my brows furrow deeply. "We've never rode a Silver."

Warren reads the letter again and again, then points to another few words in it. "Leaf tea? Could she mean the peyote?"

"Don't think so. She knows that peyote is from a cactus," I say flatly. I toss a rock in frustration, and it streams through some wildflower vine growing randomly, twining through a bush. Suddenly, I sit up straighter and inhale deeply.

"What is it?" Warren's eyes dart side to side, checking for danger.

"Holy shit," I mutter.

"What is it?!" he asks louder.

"Silver…Leaf." I say it in awe. "Sam once told me about a plant that knocked her out cold as a child. It had some big fancy name, but she said it was also called Silverleaf Nightshade.

Warren chuckles. "Damn that girl. You think she's about to poison another unsuspecting victim?"

"I think she might be," I whisper, then I re-read that letter in a different light.

Cell Life

CHAPTER 31

Samantha

It's later than the agreed-upon time, and I am chomping at the proverbial bit to see Myra's face. Where the hell is she? I clench my fist repeatedly and pace the cell, unable to relax.

The door swings inward and my heart kicks up a notch, ready to see Myra waltz through, but it plummets to the depths of hell when Bill strolls in with an overly dressed Lonnie at his side. Her snarky face finds mine instantly.

Dale straightens from his slouched position. "Bill...didn't expect to see you this evening. Thought you had to be at the town meeting?" Dale says while tipping his hat to Lonnie, who smiles demurely.

Fake bitch is what comes to mind.

Bill's eyes find me, and he smiles ridiculously big and toothy. "I do; however, it *is* running a tad late. Thought I'd come check on the lovely natural disaster that is Samantha. She behaving herself?" His eyes never leave mine as he speaks to Dale.

"Of course, what's she gonna do? She's locked up," Dale says matter-of-factly.

Bill cuts his gaze to Dale. "*Don't* underestimate her," he spits.

"No sir…of course not." Dale cowers and glances my way.

"You seen any strange activity today? Anyone come by?"

"No, sir," Dale says but then cocks his head to the side as if he remembers something. "Only Myra."

My stomach drops to my knees. Shut. The. Fuck. Up. Dale. I chant it in my head.

Bill looks murderous as he leans his hands on the desk and pierces Dale with slanted eyes. "What the *hell* was Myra doing here?"

Dale seems to realize his mistake. "Oh, no, it's not what you think. Myra comes to see me." A blush creeps up his neck as he admits it. When Bill doesn't release his stare, Dale says, "She brings me goodies… sometimes."

"Goodies." Bill sneers, and Lonnie snickers. "Did she talk with the prisoner?"

Dale visibly hesitates, and in that moment, I pray his feelings for her are more than his respect for Bill as he says, "No, um…she dropped off muffins."

I release a breath with his lie.

Bill doesn't seem satisfied with that. He pushes off the desk and storms over to me—Lonnie a step behind his every move. I can hear my cellmate singing as if this is the best day ever. What a psycho. Bill leans into the bars at the same time that I back away. "Your luster fades. That type of thing happens in captivity." He grins, looking at my ragged appearance. "By the way, your fate will be decided by morning."

"You mean my trial?"

He laughs, and so does the cellmate. What the hell is this guy's deal? "No, dear, I mean your fate."

I feel nauseous all of a sudden.

"Why the fallen face, dear? Did you think your lover would rescue you in time?" He smacks the bars and presses his face to them. "I wish he would try…we are waiting. He has less than twenty-four hours before I have a hanging time set for you." He waits for a response from me that doesn't come. He moves toward the door and levels Dale with a glare. "No one visits this jail tonight…you hear me? No one."

While he chastises Dale, Lonnie remains at my cell, close enough I could reach through and grab her. The thought is provoking.

"He's right…you look just awful." Her cat-like eyes narrow on me. "If these bars weren't preventing it, I'd rip you to shreds for what you did to me."

I don't deny my actions. Instead, I lean close against the bars and bare my teeth like a wild animal. "I would like to see your prissy ass try...*please* don't tempt me with a good time."

She backs away a step, looking down her nose at me. "You and Jake will get what's coming to you." Her eyes burn with rage and something else.

"Is that jealousy I see?" I whisper low enough for the men talking to my left not to hear. "It's unbecoming of you...you are a *whore*, after all."

She takes a step back toward me. "You wretched little bitch! I could have Jake if I wanted him...*anytime*, *anywhere.* Her jaw is clenched hard. She then takes another step placing her in reaching distance.

Before she can open her mouth with another retort, I reach through the bars, grab her by her hair, and yank her face to the bars, my grip brutal and unrelenting as her face smacks into them. "He would *never* have you...and that's why you hate me so." I know I'm right from the change in her eyes as she fights for release. I hear the stomping of Bill's feet, so I say, "I hope the thought of us together keeps you awake at night."

I am laughing in her face as Dale and Bill jerk her away from me in a rush. I have no idea what just came over me...but I *love* it. My adrenaline is soaring through my veins.

Screw her.

Bill kicks the cell, cursing loudly. "Tomorrow, *dear* Samantha...tomorrow you meet your maker. *You* let that keep *you* awake tonight!"

Then he slams the door on his way out. My laughter mixed in with my cellmates. Now, I begin to wonder if I'm as crazy as him.

Once I have calmed down and Dale is battling his own inner demons from lying to Bill, I begin to come to my senses. Worry creeps back in. What will I do now? I need to see Myra come through that door. I need to know that she got the letter to Jake, but Bill said no one was allowed in.

Hope…that bitch. Every time a little hope creeps in, it gets doused with fire. Psycho cellmate in the corner is still laughing, albeit quietly.

Time seems to speed up. The upper portion of the hourglass in my mind draining rapidly. The heat of May is horrible here, and even though night has fallen outside, sweat makes my clothes stick to me like glue. I haven't had anything to eat or drink in almost twenty-four hours. My body grows weak with exhaustion. I plop down on the floor and lean my head back against the cool wall, and before long, I'm asleep.

Well Laid Plans

CHAPTER 32

Samantha

A smack of the door closing wakes me, and I lurch to my feet. My heart leaps from my chest with joy when Myra's face comes into view.

Dale stands fast and tips his hat to her. "Myra. How are you this evening?" He blushes.

"I'm very well, and you?" She grins demurely.

He fidgets with his belt and clears his throat. "I'm good…but I have something I have to tell you."

"Well, what is it?" She looks him up and down curiously, still not making eye contact with me.

"You can't be here tonight." He looks down at his boots as if he cannot make himself meet her eyes.

"Why the hell not?"

"Bill doesn't want any visitors, especially none to her." He jerks his head toward my cell.

"Dale," she bats her lashes and gets close to him, "Bill doesn't have to know *everything*…now does he?" She places her hand on Dale's, and he looks like he's a man torn apart.

He fumbles for words. "I…I can't."

She leans in and brazenly kisses him. Shocked, he timidly brings his hands to her face and returns the kiss with a groan. I watch, astonished. Is she playing him, or truly into him? I have no idea, but these two widowers have a definite connection. I hear my quickdraw celly whistle. It causes them to break apart, realizing they have an audience.

Myra caresses Dale's cheek and then says, "I am only here to feed them. No one needs to know that. Look at them, Dale." She waves her hand toward us. "They haven't eaten in God knows when. Let me drop off the food…and, of course, something for you, then I'm gone. I was never here."

He cocks his head to the side, then looks our way and huffs loudly. "Be quick."

Myra shocks me by walking past my cell and to the young man at the end. "Here." She hands something in cloth to him and then pulls out a cup of tea for him with a wink. "Enjoy."

She comes to mine and fakes digging around in her basket as she whispers, "I gave Jake the letter."

I glance at Dale, who isn't watching us at the moment. "How was he?"

She shrugs. "As you can imagine…going crazy with worry."

I smile, not at Jake's worry, but because he cares enough *to* worry. She hands me a pastry and the tea, and I reach through the bars and grasp her hand before the tea reaches me. I place a finger over my mouth, asking for her to be silent. I reach into my pocket and bunch the crushed plant leaves I swiped before Bill took me. I pinch some in my fingers and pull them from my pocket. Myra's eyes widen when I drop them in the tea and swirl it around.

She begins shaking her head. I place the cup back into her hand and whisper, "He will only pass out...I nod toward Dale. I promise."

She's stricken. I can tell that I've quite possibly compromised her trust in me. It breaks my heart, but this is my only shot. I have precious little hours left to figure out how to get the hell out of here.

I jump when Dale says, "Hurry up now," he rushes Myra.

She stares me down, and her eyes fall to the tea. I think she may walk out right now and never return. That is a strong possibility, after all. I'm asking her to drug the man she obviously has feelings for. She shakes her head as if to clear it. Without another word, she turns to leave.

"Myra." I stop her in her tracks. "You were my only friend here...you and Judith. I love you both. Always remember that."

I see her shoulders shake with sadness. When she turns her head to me, I see the tracks of tears down her cheeks. She heads for the door but stops short. She takes a deep breath and goes back over to Dale. She leans down to where he's sitting and kisses him gently on the lips. His whole body melts. "I almost forgot yours," she says sweetly, but I can hear the trepidation in her voice bleeding through.

"Oooo, what do you have for me tonight?" He grins from ear to ear.

She grabs a tin of muffins and sets them down as he salivates and praises her cooking skills. She ignores him and looks at me with concern and then back to Dale. "Oh, and I brought you a new tea I've been meaning to try." She places the tea down in front of him and quickly kisses his cheek. She moves fast exiting the building, leaving Dale looking after her curiously.

I hear my cellmate snicker, and I cut my eyes to him. He's leaning against the bars stuffing his face with whatever it was Myra gave him. He looks at me knowingly, like he can see into every devious thing traipsing through my mind. I roll my eyes to his amusement and turn to watch the deputy.

He eats one, then two, then three, then four muffins. Damn, I think. Is he ever going to get thirsty? I keep watching as I rub the remnants of the herb onto my pants, hoping none leak into my system. Then take a few bites of the pastry with the other. I close my eyes as the flavors burst in my mouth. Good lord this is amazing. I can see why Dale's stuffing his gullet. Damn…Myra can bake.

I look up just as Dale's hand eventually grasps the cup. I hold my breath. I notice my cellmate has grown quiet. He watches, too. Dale doesn't taste the tea; he downs it in a gulp. His face twinges then he curls his mouth in disgust. He pushes the cup away and kicks his feet up.

I slide down until my bottom hits the floor and watch Dale as he adjusts himself for his nightly nap. I only hope he doesn't wake up until morning.

It's been three *fucking* hours. I'm not sure what time it is, but if I had to guess…maybe midnight. It was already late when Myra came by. Why has he not passed out yet? I cringe as Dale trips on this hallucinating high. His focus in this state of mind has mainly been the voluptuous Myra. If I wasn't in dire need of his absence, this would be hilarious.

A hysterical laugh comes from the end of the jail. "What?" I ask in frustration.

My loner cellmate places his forehead against the bars and gives a manic smile. "Seems you had the dosage wrong."

"I didn't…it just works different with everyone." I'm no longer trying to hide the fact that I drugged him. It's glaringly obvious.

"Hey, I'm not hating, but...can get I the recipe for that tea...you know, after we're out of here." He winks.

"*We?*" I ask, annoyed.

His smile turns scary, but then he masks it. "Yeah, *we*. Seeing as how I know what you've done. You never know...the sheriff may let me go for that kind of information." He sees my rage and adds, "Not to mention the letter you sent out to...who was it again, oh yeah, Jake." He smooches the air, mocking me.

I grit my teeth and swear under my breath. Do I even have a choice here?

He sees my face beginning to give in and says, "So what's the master plan?"

I turn back to watch Dale, who's now dancing with a broomstick, but mutter over my shoulder, "I wasn't sure I would even get far enough to implement the tea, let alone move to part two."

"What's *part two?*"

"Well, we need those keys, don't we?"

He looks to Dale's belt and nods in agreement. "How do you propose we do that?" he says, clearly enjoying letting me take the reins in this escape.

I stand and lean against the bars and smile. I yell over to Dale, "Dale, sweetie...come dance with me." I keep my voice soft like a siren as I entice him to come closer.

Dale's glazed expression finds me, and he takes one step and staggers. "No, no, no," I say in a panic.

He drops the broom.

Does a little shimmy with his hips.

Takes one more step.

And falls flat to the floor with a thud.

My irritating cellmate is hoarse laughing as I curse, "Shit! What the hell am I going to do now?"

"*We*," I hear him say smugly.

"Whatever…*we*. Do you ever take anything seriously?"

"No." He smirks.

I look at the keys attached to the drugged man, passed out snoring ten feet away from us. I would kick the wall if my feet didn't *fucking* hurt so much. In defeat, I slide down the wall until my ass is on the ground again. Something immediately digs into my hip. "Owww," I complain and pull out my turquoise hair tie. I recall grabbing it…in case I had the opportunity to stab Bill with the sharp metal spikes that lay behind the stone, but with my hands bound, that opportunity never presented itself. I press the tip of one of the sharp spikes to my finger now and marvel at it.

I suck in a huge breath.

"What's going on in your head wielder of poisons?" His voice is sneaky and devious.

I don't answer him. I bolt up to standing and dart to my cell door. Reaching around the bars, I stick one spiked end into the keyhole. I begin to wiggle. My shoulder protests violently, but I don't falter.

"Don't just jostle it around…find the notches inside and lever it."

"You picked many skeleton locks?" I question angrily as sweat beads down my temple.

"A few." He chuckles, then adds, "You need to find the notches, then turn in a circle to disengage the lock."

Two minutes roll by. My arms and hands are cramping. I blindly flick the thin metal spike around, catching ahold of something. I hold my breath until I feel the lock give and hear an audible click. I move a step back and push the door with my hand. The heavy door moans as it swings open.

"Holy shit, lady," I hear my cellmate say in awe.

Adrenaline pumps through my veins as I look toward my freedom looming two feet in front of me. Without any more hesitation, I race through the door.

"Hey, what about me?" I pause and turn back to him.

"Ugh," I groan. I feel I may regret this. This guy could be a rapist, a murderer, anything. Another thought hits me as I look at him. He could be like me. Wrongly accused of something he had no part of. Somehow, I feel that's unlikely.

I rush to Dale and grab his keys off his belt. I drop his pistol into the back of my breeches. I stand before Quickdraw's cell. "If I let you out, you have to help me disappear?"

He smiles his characteristic shit-eating grin. "I'm at your service, madam." He bows ridiculously.

I unlock the cell, and he barrels through it and plants a kiss on my cheek as he rushes past me to shuffle through Dale's drawers.

"What are you doing?"

"Looking for supplies."

"No! You are not stealing anything from him…it's bad enough what I did."

"Did I not just see you swipe his gun, missy?"

My cheeks burn. "Okay, but you don't understand. People are out to kill me."

"Yeah, not fun is it." He giggles.

He's wanted for something bad if they want him dead too. I begin to regret releasing him again. He stops riffling through Dale's things and huffs, "Spill it. What is it you want me to do?"

I roll my lips together, not sure how he'll take this request. I roam my eyes down my cellmate's filthy clothes. He wears a brown shirt with suspenders attached to dark breeches that end with some riding boots. He's on the shorter side, maybe a few inches taller than me. I look over at Dale's attire next. He wears a normal frock coat with a dark vest and linen shirt beneath. His black breeches and boots are as average as any man's. Finally, I blurt it out. "I want you to put on Dale's clothes and give me yours."

"You're kidding right?"

I cross my arms over my chest. "We need to hurry…and no, I'm not joking in the slightest. I'm rather noticeable in this." I rake my hands down my blouse. "Maybe, if we disguise ourselves…we can ride right out of town without anyone batting an eye."

"It's after midnight." He looks out the window. "No one will be up but drunkards."

"Not tonight," I admit. "Bill would have posted men all around by now just *waiting* to see if anyone comes to rescue me. I doubt very well he'll believe me capable of escaping. They won't expect us. Two men just riding casually out of town."

He debates for a few seconds, raises an eyebrow, and smiles, then grabs Dale and begins undressing him. I turn away. Soon, a shirt flies over me and lands at my feet. As nervous as it makes me to undress right here, the thought of being caught spurs me to move and not concern myself with the eyes burning into my back. I toss my shirt to the side and hear a groan from behind me but ignore it. Once the shirt is on, pants fly over me next. "I could just die," I mutter with embarrassment. I peek over my shoulder and catch him looking. "Turn away!" He does, but the moment I turn back and drop my pants, I'm certain he's watching.

A few minutes pass and we are dressed—down to the too-big boots I wear of Mister Quickdraw's. The clothes are smelly, but I'm sure I'm no rose myself today considering we've been locked up with no way for cleanliness.

He appraises me as he saunters closer, and his hand moves toward my face, causing me to flinch. He ignores me and then pushes a stray piece of my hair back up into the flat-brimmed hat we found hanging on the wall. "One more thing." He runs to an old fireplace that clearly hasn't had use since winter. He drags his fingers through the soot, then rushes back to me, and his fingers go for my face with that blackened hand. "Mustache and beard…" he mutters.

"Oh," I muse. He paints my face and then steps back to admire his handy work. "You're still too beautiful to be a man, but it'll do. This is fun, isn't it?" he asks.

I cock an eyebrow at him. "You seem like this isn't your first time with disguises."

He leans in too close to me, his blue eyes alight with humor. "That's because it isn't."

I can't help the smile that breaks out on my face. To have been a fly on the wall in this young man's life. I laugh to myself. We move to stand side by side at the door and peer out. The street seems utterly lifeless. I begin to step through the door to look down the streets, but he wraps me in a hug, stopping me. I stand there, shocked, and unable to move. "I could just kiss you right now," he says ecstatically in my ear, and I shove him away.

"Save that for the end of this shit show." I grin as he laughs.

He moves from the window and the door and back again two times, attempting to see who lingers about. "There's a man by the alley, drunk maybe, but he could be faking it." We both continue surveying the area as he says, "There…" and points toward him. "You see him?"

"Yeah." I can see he's close to us but doesn't face the window. His body is partially obscured by some barrels.

"To the left, there's another."

I look in that direction. Sure enough, there's another man slouched on the ground, his back against the adjacent building's wall across the street. I open the door a few inches and look down the right side of the street. "Shit," I mutter.

"What is it?"

"We have another sitting in a rocker along the porch a few buildings away." That man is *not* drunk. It's dark, but I swear he looks a little like Tom Whitmore from here…Bill's other lackey. His eyes never look worried. Instead, they beam with mischief and what seems like excitement. "Does any of this bother you at all?" I ask.

"No, not really." He smirks at my worried brows.

"This isn't even your first jailbreak, is it?" I muse.

"Nope." His crooked grin has some of the tension leaving my shoulders.

"Alright then, it's now or never. We need some horses." I take inventory one last time of the streets. "We have Dale's horse," I point to the palomino tied out front, "and over there, by the store, there's a bay."

"Sounds good to me," he whispers and starts to open the door.

"Wait…we can't just waltz out of here and jump on the horses. Those men are probably working for Bill. I highly doubt that the ones that look passed out are *actually* passed out." I think for a few seconds. "They will shoot us dead before we even mount. We're going to need a distraction."

"What do you have in mind, poison wielder?"

I roll my eyes at my new nickname. I've lost count of how many I have acquired in the last few months. My brain fumbles around for a solution. I glance back to the fireplace and see a few jars and bottles lining the mantle. I rush over to scour the mantle some more. "Here we go," I mumble.

Suddenly, Quickdraw is at my side. "What is it?"

I hold up a jar. "I need some liquor."

"I could use a drink too, but I don't think now's the time." His eyes dance with merriment.

Then, I shake the matches at him. "*We* need some liquor," I emphasize by tapping the jar with the matches. He smiles broadly, and we both start digging through Dale's drawers. My heart deflates when we find nothing.

"What now?" he asks.

I shrug in frustration then slam the jar down a little too forcefully on the table and curse under my breath. I hear a faint rattle underneath the center...where there are no drawers. My eyes grow wide. I drop down to my knees and snake my fingers around under the belly of the huge desk until I feel it. I can't hide my sly smile as I pull the hidden lever.

"Damn..." he says as he watches the hidden drawer release.

I stand fast, looking down in triumph. There's a stack of banknotes, some coins, and an amber bottle full of what looks to be liquor. "I don't know many lawmen that don't keep a little drink hidden." I smile and snatch it up, moving to the window. I pour the liquor into three separate jars. I rip a few strips of fabric from my tattered old blouse and soak them before leaving a trailing piece hanging from the lip of two of the jars.

After a few minutes of scanning the area outside the window, I say, "One of us will have to climb out, sneak over to that empty shed, pour the one jar along two walls, and then light the remaining two jars and place them in the corners." I start eyeballing him pointedly. "They need to be placed gently in the corners, allowing the fire to start slowly. If we break them, someone will hear us." He nods repeatedly as I talk. "We have to wait it out for the men to move towards the fire. Once they are far away from the front of the jail...we bolt for the horses and ride in the opposite direction."

"Which one?" His brow raises.

I catch his meaning and swallow hard. Should I go or him? Doubt strikes me in waves. What if he sneaks out and isn't seen? Would he bother lighting the fire for my escape? What if this doesn't work at all? What if someone comes into the jail to alert Dale of the fire? So many problems can arise from this plan. Our options are to run or cause a distraction and then run.

One thing is for certain...I will *not* be here come morning.

"I'll go," I decide. "You keep watch for me, and if you see someone moving in my direction." I take my hand and wave it in front of the lantern on the desk, causing the light to flutter. "Do this to signal me."

He nods. My heart races as I quietly open the window. Night air hits my flushed face and I breathe in deep through my nose. This is a one-level building; therefore, the window is low enough for me to drape a leg over and step out to the other side with ease. A hand grabs my arm, and I look back at my nameless cellmate.

"Be careful," he says.

I nod. It's the first time I've seen concern of any kind grace his face. Before nerves can get the better of me, I drop to the ground and stay crouched. I cut my eyes right and left, seeing no one. I'm just out of eyesight of the man leaning against the barrels. I creep on the balls of my feet, which is almost impossible in these boots. I cling to the shadows, wishing I could disappear entirely. After a full two minutes, which feels like an hour, I make it to the shed. I finally breathe a sigh of relief when I find it empty. Looking back to the jail, I can see the room lit by lantern light but no futtering.

So far, so good.

Quickly, I douse the walls with the jar of booze. I pull the matches from my pocket. Just as I am about to light the first jar...I see a flutter. I suck in a breath when I look toward the jail. The signal. "Shit, shit, shit," I whisper. Sweat trickles down my spine as I hunker down in a corner and attempt to slow my breathing. Looking to my right, I see a shovel and grab it, squeezing it in my sweaty grip. I have no idea what my cellmate sees—no idea *where* someone is moving to or from. A minute passes.

Nothing.

The scraping of a boot to my left has my heart about to leap from my chest. I jerk when I hear a cough near the shed. I can tell the man is close. The wood planks creak, and it sounds like he is leaning directly on the wall to the other side of me. The side facing the window of the jail. You have to be kidding me…I think to myself. I can smell a pipe and see smoke waft by every now and again. More time passes, and I'm beginning to think he'll never leave when the wood groans with the weight of his body pushing off it.

His steps move *toward* the shed door, and I hold my breath. A tall, slim figure moves inside. Fear locks my body up. I pray the shadows have me hidden in their murky depths. The man moves to the opposite corner, leans one hand against the wall, and I hear a steady stream of liquid. He's pissing. A sliver of moonlight streams through the cracks, illuminating just a portion of the man's face. My original fear only heightens. It's Tom Whitmore.

Tom shakes and then pushes off the wall and turns to leave. He hesitates at the door and reaches into his pocket, pulls out a flask, and takes a big swig. I don't take a breath until I hear his steps growing faint as he moves farther away from me. I peep out in both directions and find that the coast is clear.

My body is shaking by the time I stand and strike the first match. I light the cloth in each and place the jars accordingly, making sure the cloth touches the wall.

A few minutes later, hands are grabbing me as I scurry back through the window. "Holy shit, woman! I thought you was a goner for sure."

"Thanks for the warning," I pant as I try to catch my breath.

"No problem." He winks, but this time, it doesn't look sincere. Instead, worry lingers behind it.

"You ready for this?" I ask.

"Born ready."

We watch the shed. It takes several more minutes before smoke begins to billow through the cracks. For the first time, I feel a margin of regret. What if this fire spreads and ruins someone's business? The closest store adjacent to the shed is the general store. Marvin Jennings owns it. I never knew the quiet man, but still…my actions have consequences too.

My worry is interrupted by, "It's time, Sam." He points. I see a man walking toward the shed that is now becoming a full raging fire inside. He yells, and I see the other man from the alley jogging behind him…clearly, not a random drunk who was 'passed out.'"

We rush to the door and peer out in time to see Tom's silhouette turning the corner toward the commotion. "Now!" I whisper fiercely.

We slink out of the doors and split up when our feet hit the dirt. I grab the palomino of Dale's, praying she's not a rowdy mare. I swing up in one swift move, trying not to put much weight onto my left arm. I see my cellmate leap onto the bay horse from behind, startling it. The horse rears a little, but he holds on. I don't wait for him; I kick the mare's sides and bolt toward the opposite side of town.

All thoughts of casually riding out of here leave me. I dig my heels into the mare's flank again, forcing her to move faster. I keep my focus forward, not sure if the bay is anywhere near me. The wind whips my face, and I struggle to hold my hat on. I lean forward becoming one with the horses every lunge. I see the edge of town that gives way to the desert. To my right is the paddock and barn where I once told Jake that I wished I'd never met him. Those words fester in my soul. All I can think about right now is his face and how meeting him changed me in so many ways. I wish I could take back those words.

I pass the boundary of the town in a flash of hooves and dust. Behind me, I can hear more hoofbeats. I assume it's my cellmate. Just in case, I lean my head over my shoulder in time to see a horse racing toward me. I squint, but it's too dark to visualize. Finally, the horse gets closer, I'm just about to yell back to my cellmate when I see the color of the horse. It's white…not a bay.

Time slows as the white horse gains on me. The horse's coat gleams in the moonlight, making it look like a ghost streaking toward me. The light from the moon also reaches the rider's face…Tom's face. I see rage and sheer determination. He was tasked with one job tonight, and he intends not to fail Bill. I reach for Dale's pistol only to find it's missing from the back of my breeches. In all the frenzy of lighting that shed on fire, I must have dropped it somewhere. I kick my horse, urging her forward at a breakneck pace. I can hear his guttural yell for me to stop or he'll shoot. I close my eyes and picture Jake and Warren waiting for me.

I can't stop. I can't.

A single shot pierces the atmosphere and echoes.

I wait for the pain. My hand moves to my chest and abdomen, but I find no blood. The pain...it doesn't come. Tears blur my eyes as I look back and see Tom slumped over the saddle. My cellmate a few paces behind him, eyes locked on the lifeless body.

I slide my horse to a stop when I see him do the same. Without hesitation, he grabs the reins of Tom's horse and ties it to his saddle...staring at me the whole time. I'm bewildered—completely at a loss for words. This man just saved my life, and I don't even know his name. I look down to the gun he's holding. "That's Dale's gun." I furrow my brows, but then my eyes widen. "When you hugged me...you took it when you hugged me," I state, not really in anger, but in awe at the fact that I never felt him remove the gun. That sly little shit!

He doesn't deny it, just tips his hat to me, and then says, "I'll get rid of him...GO! Get out of here."

I choke up, wanting to say so much more, but I bob my head and just say, "Thank you." He winks at me in his usual way and grins. "What's your name?" I ask.

He smirks. "Like I told you before…I'm *everyone* and *no one*. Have a good life, poison wielder."

He rides east as I ride southwest. After only a minute, I can't see his silhouette or the white horse anymore. It's too dark. I have so many questions that may forever remain unanswered about my strange companion. How did he get *behind* Tom? What kind of life created such a cunning thief? Who is he? He could have left in a different direction tonight and I would likely be dead. He didn't. I no longer feel the guilt for releasing a potentially dangerous person into the wild…no, I'm grateful.

I kick the mare, and we dart off into the night, letting the thoughts of seeing Jake and Warrens face spur me on. By morning, I'll be a wanted woman, but I don't give a shit. The only thing driving me forward is the thought of the two men in my life out there waiting for me.

A New Favorite Feeling

CHAPTER 33

Jake

The sun is just beginning to rise as I swipe a hand over my face. Warren and I took shifts sleeping. He's curled under a blanket, down by the horses a good ways away from me, while I'm perched on this rocky ridge that overlooks the trail. It's been over a day since I last laid eyes on Samantha. As much as it has pained me to stay away, I listened to Myra and heeded her words. Doubt creeps through my body as daylight brings life back to the land. What if they've touched her, harmed her? What if she needs me right now? My life hasn't been the same since I laid eyes on her. I no longer feel the need to disappear. She makes me want to be seen. She makes me want to be a better man.

I hear Shadow pawing the ground nearby. She's showing signs of agitation. Her ears are laid back, and her neck is arched as she swings her head left and right—her black mane swaying ominously.

I lay on my stomach and aim my rifle in the direction of Shadow's gaze. At first, I see nothing, but then a figure appears in the distance. A lone horse and rider. The closer they get, I can make out the rider's features, but only slightly. It appears to be a thin man on a palomino horse. I keep my aim on him. He does something odd and veers off the trail and heads straight toward where we camp. There's nothing out here and no reason he should be headed toward us, but he doesn't let up and even kicks his horse into a gallop. The closer he gets; I make a quick decision. I can't take any chances. I fire a warning shot, hitting the ground at the horse's feet. It rears back, but the rider keeps his seat. I see Warren from the corner of my eye, awake now, gun in hand, but he's too far away from me to be any help. The rider's hat flies off as the horse rears again, and a thick braid tumbles out.

I have to pick my jaw up off the ground.

"It can't be," I whisper. The rider calms the horse and holds up one hand in surrender. I stand, making myself visible, and see the rider's raised hand move to cover her mouth...*her* mouth. "Sam!" I yell. My body moves into motion on instinct. I rush down the ridge in a frenzy to get to her. My feet sliding and shuffling as I stumble over stones. She's dismounted and bolting toward me at the same time. I hear Warren yelling her name from somewhere in the distance behind me.

The feet between us disappear with each stride we take. She slams into me, and I lift her until her legs twine around my waist and squeeze her to me. A sob breaks from her chest. I can't think—can hardly breathe. It's not only the fact that she's alive and found us...it's an indescribable feeling ripping free from my heart. She's never embraced me with such vigor. This is different. A current moves between us, and we meld together. "It's okay, I got you. It's okay now. I got you." I whisper over and over into her hair. I don't release her for what feels like a long time. Her heart beating against my chest may be my new favorite feeling.

She pulls away to look into my eyes. "You shot at me." Her voice is crackling from the tears, but there's that unmistakable humor in her eyes.

"Wasn't the first time I've aimed a gun at you, witch."

"It *was* the first time you've shot at me, though...I guess this means our relationship is progressing."

"I like the sound of that." I laugh as I lean into her again and kiss the top of her head before finally setting her down to standing. She doesn't release me until she sees Warren, and then she's launching into his arms next. He spins her around, both of them beaming.

I'm finally able to get a good look at her attire and stare...stunned. What the hell has she been up to? She's clearly wearing men's clothes—all the way down to the boots. The breeches sag off her, only held up by suspenders. Her face in smeared with some black substance. I see her flinch when Warren squeezes her around the shoulders.

"Are you hurt?" I ask.

She moves out of Warren's grip and wipes at her teary face, which only smears the black substance more. "My shoulder hurts." She hesitates, but then says, "Bill tied me behind his horse when he half dragged me to town. Asshole."

I can't remove my eyes from hers. The last day catches up with me, and all I can think is that I almost lost her. "He will pay for what he's done."

"Damn straight," Warren adds.

"I know," she says confidently. She eyes the cactuses nearby and the rocks stacked up surrounding their bases. She darts her eyes between us. "You're both here…at our *special* place." She looks at Warren a bit longer before she says, "I was scared you wouldn't understand what my letter was saying."

"One day I'll see you again at our special place…that part was easy enough. We knew you meant here and hopefully in one day" Warren smiles as he says it.

I don't bother telling her about the confrontation I had with Warren. He had finally admitted he knew where she wanted us to meet. That had been the recognition I'd seen in his eyes when he read the letter. But I'd figured it out, too. I once asked her about this spot, and though she refused to tell me *why* it was their special place, I still remembered what she called it.

Warren chuckles and asks, "The next part was sketchy. Jake did some memory searching and thinks he figured it out…who exactly did you poison with Silverleaf tea?"

She tries to hide her grin. "It's a long story involving kidnapping, poison, jailbreaks, cross-dressing, and even arson." She grins lazily as if she didn't just floor us both with her comment. Then she says, "Not sure if you boys can handle it."

"At this point, nothing that comes out of your mouth could surprise me." As soon as I say it, she looks to Warren, and they have a silent moment. A moment that tells me, I don't know the half of it.

"Look, I'll explain what happened, but first, I need to get cleaned up, and I'm going to need some clothes." She pats her hands down the front of the shirt she wears, and dust billows out.

I had already told Warren where I intended to go, but doing it is much harder. I don't like what I'm about to say, but before I can back out, I let the words leave my mouth. "You can come to my house…to get cleaned up." I look to Warren. "Both of you, I mean." Samantha stares at me, brows furrowed, confusion all over her face so I add, "I do have a home, contrary to what most may think of me."

"Okay then." She stares me down as if she can pull my own secrets out through my eye sockets and then says to Warren. "We're off to Jake's house."

I can tell by the expressions on Sam's face that she has as many questions as I do, but we refrain from delving into it. She spent ten minutes loving on Clint before we loaded up to make our way to my childhood home.

Home…that's a strong word for it. I've only been back there a handful of times over the last several years to make repairs. I'm not even sure why I've bothered to keep it up. I should've sold the damn place years ago.

Bad memories haunt every room, but here I am…going home.

Haunted Eyes

CHAPTER 34

Samantha

Warren shakes with laughter when he says, "Dale was dancing with a broom."

I told them everything that happened over the last day and a half—leaving nothing out. "It's funny now, but at the time, I was dying for him to pass out." I laugh, too, then slap a hand to my forehead. "I feel so bad for breaking Myra's trust in me. What if Dale blames her?"

"They'll be alright." Warren sighs. "If he's as smitten with her as you say, he'll understand why she did it."

"Still, I feel horrible. She's my friend, and I've gotten her caught up in something she was never meant to be entangled in."

We are silent for a beat. Warren is watching Jake and rolling his lower lip into his mouth as if he wishes to say something, then he says to him, "You wanna ride ahead...make sure we're in the clear?" Warren points to some rolling hills that could hide riders easily.

Jake nods and moves in that direction.

"What is it?" I ask, knowing deep down Warren needed the privacy for some reason.

"Jake gave me something...Myra left it for you. It's from Judith."

I crinkle my brows when he pulls out a box from his saddle bag. My heart speeds up when I inspect it. The scent wafting off the checkered cloth wrapped around it smells like Myra's bakery. "You didn't open it?"

He shakes his head, and I immediately tear into it. Inside is a letter, but as I pull it out, I gasp loudly. I glance up to make sure Jake isn't in earshot.

"What, Sam?" Warren whispers. "What's in there?"

I don't say a word as I pull out a cassette tape. I flip it over to the cover and see that it's the band *Whitesnake*. Warren's demeanor matches mine. We are tense and in awe of what we are looking at.

"Read the letter." He ushers me into motion.

I clear my throat and break the wax seal, folding open the yellow-tinted paper.

Dear Samantha,

Nice damn day today. Sun is bright and so is my spirit. The Lord's work will do that to you. I need a drink, but Myra keeps hiding it from me. I wonder where you are. Did you pay your debts traveler? My mother always said you must pay your debts before returning home. I hope you find your home. This was my mother's case tape. A strange thing to be sure, but she could never part with it. Love Sam. Love kept her from finding her home. She always seemed happy, though her eyes sometimes lingered too much on the sky. Her mind elsewhere. Anyway, it's a nice damn day. Think I'll get to see her and my dearest Ray soon.

Tears roll down my cheeks as I read the letter to Warren. My hands tremble and I have to quickly fold it up and shove it in the box.

"You okay?" he asks.

"Of course not." I wipe haphazardly at my wet cheeks. "She sounds like she's dying and…I wish I could be there with her."

Warren looks off into the late evening sun. "I always thought she was one crazy bird, but I guess she has found some clarity in the end. Myra even said as much to Jake."

"Yeah, I guess she did."

Warren puts the box back in the saddle bag and turns to me. "This means you were right…this has happened to someone before us. This means there may come a time when we'll need to say goodbye to this place," he looks toward Jake's silhouette, "say goodbye to these people."

So much turmoil is eating away at my insides. Of course I want to go home, need to. I have my family, and Warren has his. We can't stay here, but that thought that used to be ironclad in my heart is now chipping away at the edges. "He means more to me than I intended," I whisper to Warren.

"I know."

We ride in silence for a few more minutes before some of my unanswered questions of the night of the fire return to me. "What happened to the rest of our livestock? Our belongings?"

His eyes sadden. "Some perished. A few animals made it out into the night. The house...it's gone."

"What about our...you know, stash."

He smiles, but it doesn't quite reach his eyes. "Jake and I went back before we came to our special place. I made it clear that I needed to salvage anything I could. Jake fought me on it, but he couldn't stop me, so we went." He reaches for his other pack tied to Halle and pulls out something wrapped in an old shirt. "I was able to save your book from Tai that was outside on that table. The duffle bag was gone. The only thing left inside it was this and your Colt."

What he hands me is light as a feather, but the weight of it is immense as I take the corners of the singed shirt and pull them back. My family's face stares back at me. Those Christmas lights twinkling in the background.

My mother. My father. My sister. My whole world.

He continues talking while I examine the photo. "I have the Colt in the pack too, but Sam…everything else is gone. I was lucky to have my old rifle with me at the time. You understand what that could mean, right?"

I do understand. Even though, just a few seconds ago, he was saying how we *must* go home…we can't. Not if everything is gone. It's obvious enough that we need a total solar eclipse, something from that exact year, and possibly a sacred spot on Earth. We're still unsure about that part. But it seems likely that the cosmic event caused some kind of linear path to cross time for a brief few seconds during that eclipse.

Warren looks at my family photo. "When was that taken?"

"I shrug…not 2017…Christmas 2016. I point to the Christmas lights in the background and sigh. I remember the day well, but not when it was exactly taken." The glass is covered in soot from the fire, and I'm continuously wiping at it. The frame is warped. I'm surprised it held out this long and especially shocked it made it through the fire. I turn it over and swivel the brackets holding the frame together and eventually am able to slip the photo free. I have to do it carefully because it is almost plastered to the 5x7 glass inside the frame.

The moment the photo gives a little, and the back of the picture comes into view, my mouth drops open.

There, on the back, is a handwritten note from my mother. Just a few lines. Warren moves Halle as close to Clint and me as he can without pissing her off, and then he leans in to read it with me.

New Years are for new beginnings. Here's hoping you read this one day and all your dreams have come true. I'm so proud of you baby girl. I love you more than life itself.

Love Mom
1/1/2017

"Holy shit," I cry, fresh tears leaking down my cheeks.

"Holy shit," Warren says.

While my mother's words tug at my heartstrings, I can't take my eyes off the date. "I assumed with the Christmas lights that it was closer to Christmas day," I say in wonder. "I completely forgot that Ryan took that photo of us the day he proposed to Jenna...*ON* New Year's."

Jake begins riding back toward us, so I drop the photo back into the frame, wrap it, and hand it back to Warren. Warren smiles at me, and I smile right back. This changes everything. If the thing with Nalin was really my debt, and now we have this photo...the possibility solidifies in my mind. We *even* know the exact date for the next total solar eclipse. Even though we are unsure about the debt Warren owes to the past, we have more to go on now than ever before. It's been almost two years that we've spent here and never once have I felt as sure as I am now that we're on the right path. A fated path, maybe, who knows. I've also never been this torn apart in my life as I am when my eyes travel over the handsome cowboy riding up who has stolen a piece of me.

I'm a jumble of nervous energy by the time Jake is by my side. His eyes dart to me every now and again as if to make sure I'm really here. I feel guilt gnawing at me like a thousand piranhas. I've kept so much from him, and for good reason, but it's killing me. Something deep inside me is begging for the truth to be set free.

The thought is lost when we crest a final hill and see a river. My mouth drops open, and I can't seem to catch my breath. Trees line one side of the winding river while an open expanse of land juts out in front of it. Settled in the center is a very old house, large, twice the size of ours. A massive barn and pasture are not far off to the right. One enormous tree grows adjacent to the house. I recognize it even from this distance. It's a Frémont Cottonwood tree. I can tell by the base and warping branches that seem to reach in odd angles toward the sky. It's the same type that stands like a beacon for my special place.

"Jake, this place is absolutely beautiful." I glance his way, but he isn't looking at me or hearing a word I said. He's looking at that tree…

His eyes are the most haunted I've ever seen.

Scars

CHAPTER 35

Jake

Sam is trying to say something to me, but it's muddled. My head freezes and inside becomes a still picture of a life long ago. Scars run so deep through me. Is it crazy that I'm grateful for the pain? I think of the people riding beside me and know that all paths, even rough ones, can lead you to better destinations.

"Jake, are you okay?" Sam touches my arm, bringing me out of a trance.

"Yeah," I lie.

Her eyes bore a hole through me, but she must sense that I had nothing to add to that one word, so she just smiles sadly. The closer we get, the more her eyes light up with wonder. It really is a magnificent property. The house is very old, but for whatever reason, I've kept it up all these years. The porch I hand built wraps around the entire front and sides. It's two stories with three bedrooms. I added a washroom last year. The barn's held up well and is large enough to hold ten horses, with a loft for supplies and feed. I can see a few posts in the fence that already need repairs again. I'll get to them soon.

I listen to Warren and Sam go on and on about the river and how beautiful everything is, and I think they may be right. To an outsider, this place is everything a family home should be. That is, if you leave out the tragedies that accompany it. After we stalled the horses and put away any supplies we had stored on us, we make our way to the house.

I reach for the front door and stiffen, but when Sam looks at me with concern, I shake it off and enter.

"Jake this place is really something," Warren says, walking from the living area into the kitchen. Both are open with no barriers between them.

I nod. Words seem to be failing me at the moment, but finally, I speak, "The rooms are upstairs." I point up looking at Warren. "You can take the one to the far right. Theres not much here, but I did stash some preserves in the cellar out back. We can hunt or fish later after we rest."

Warren asks me some more questions about the place but eventually excuses himself and heads in the direction of the stairs to get some rest.

"I know we just got here, but I need to get cleaned up…badly." Sam gives her clothes a look of disgust.

"Of course." I stand still, looking anywhere but her face for a moment. I realized, before we even got here, that she has nothing left. All her clothes burned in the fire. "You can have my mother's clothes…if you want. They are in the bedroom to the left upstairs."

She watches me carefully as if she knows she is treading on new and strange grounds with me. "I appreciate it, Jake, thank you."

I tip my head. "You'll need to wash them down by the river. I think there's still a washboard somewhere around here and a mangle and dolly. The clothes have been here a very long time, but I kept them in the chest up there, so they should be usable."

"You mind going with me?"

I look at her now and see something new. She doesn't want to be alone. I feel like an asshole. Why would she want to be alone? The last time we left her, she was taken. "Not at all," I tell her.

I take her small hand in mine feeling the immediate warmth it brings and lead her through the house. After the tour, we take stock of what we have and what we may need. We gather the chest and some lye soap along with the washboard, mangle, and dolly. I had my own stash of clothing here, so I take a set. Warren was able to salvage some of Sam's smelly stuff she makes from their house, only because they were outside at the time. We gather those, too, and head to the river.

Sam takes out each piece of clothing and begins dipping them into the water and scrubbing the soap against the board. She flits her eyes to me in between washing. "You want to tell me why this place makes your eyes harden?"

I take a pair of my old breeches and begin washing with her. "You know how this works with us, Sam. If I give you all of me, can you give me all of you?" I wasn't expecting to say that out loud, but it just came out.

For some reason, her face shows fear. She thinks about it far too long before saying, "It will change everything."

My brows furrow. "How so?"

She stops her downward motion on the washboard and freezes as she says with more vigor, "We will never be the same in your eyes. It will change *everything*."

I sigh loudly. "I'll ask you again...If I give you all of me, can you give me all of you...someday?"

Unexpectedly, a tear streams down her cheek. She viciously wipes it away, smearing what's left of the soot covering her face. "Okay, Jake, give me all of you."

Her words do something to me, something impossible to ignore. We continue cleaning each piece of clothing. I'm silent as I build the courage to expose my past. I never cared to tell anyone, never *wanted* to...until now.

"I was born here," I say. Sam doesn't look at me. She keeps her eyes down as if I may stop talking if she looks at me. "Born right on my parents' bed. I was the oldest. My sister Anna was born three years later, and my little brother Kurt, one year after her." I see Sam pause, but she still doesn't look at me or ask anything, so I continue. "My mother's name was Abigayle, and my father's name was Charles."

We move as one, hanging clothes up to dry, then beginning on another item as she listens intently. "My father beat my mother," I say matter-of-factly. Sam tenses at that, and I can understand why. She's mentioned her bad relationship before. I'd love to put a bullet through the man who laid hands on her. I grit my teeth and continue, "When he wasn't beating her, he took out his aggression on me. Every time that son-of-a-bitch went after Kurt, I'd get in the way. The only one that was ever spared his fist was Anna. Mainly because she stayed secluded and hidden from him by my mother or me."

"I'm so sorry, Jake," she whispers.

I shake my head. "It's all in the past. Nothing for you to be sorry about."

"I *am* sorry, though. No one should go through that—be hurt by the person who is supposed to love them."

She continues cleaning. I can feel the gates to my soul wanting to open. She makes me *want* to tell her everything. So, I give in to that feeling. "The beatings continued for years. Nothing we ever did was good enough for that man. He was always drunk and always pissed off. You see, my mother was a beautiful woman, and he couldn't stand another man talking to her. If they went to town and even *one* man did, she would catch a beating for days." I laugh sarcastically. "Funny thing was, he was sleeping with every whore from here to Tucson."

We hang up the rest of the pieces of clothing. Sam gathers her things to bathe with and I can see how weary she is. "I'm sorry. You need rest and food. You want me to go get some salted pork and whiskey?"

"That would be lovely, but...can you tell me more when you return?"

I nod and leave her to bathe. The sun beats down upon us and I have no doubt the clothes will be dry by the time we both get cleaned up. I don't know what I expected to feel when I told Sam about my family, but what I *do* feel is relief. I feel it down to my bones.

She hasn't heard the worst yet. Time will tell if that will make her see me in a different light.

All of You

CHAPTER 36

Samantha

I'm burning these clothes as soon as possible. I drop the suspenders and peel off the filthy, grimy top. The heat from the sun, as blistering as it is, feels absolutely amazing on my skin. I kick off the boots and lean my head back a few more seconds to soak it up.

Once my breeches are dropped, I wade into the water. I'm far enough away from the house and surrounded by a few trees that no one can see me. The river has a steady current, but not fast-paced. It caresses my skin, flowing and swirling in time with my emotions. Overwhelmed would be a good way to describe me at the moment. From being kidnapped and put in jail, to the whole hair-brained escape plan, to reuniting with my two favorite people. And now...seeing Jake's home. Hearing just a little about his childhood makes me understand him so much more now. All the stalker behavior in the beginning might have been worrisome and a bit exciting, if I'm being honest, but I get him now. He's a lone wolf for a reason. It must be why he's pushed away relationships—why he also fought what was happening between us.

He watched his mother go through horror at the hands of a man who was supposed to take care for her. That has lingering consequences and obviously left impressions in Jake's heart. It's why he took me from Henry the night at Big Johns and why his face showed rage when I told him just a snippet about Trevor. It's why he said he doesn't frequent the brothels, most likely because his father did. He has strived to *not* be like him in every way. Everything in me desires to protect that little boy Jake used to be—take away his pain. And that thought scares the shit out of me. I may be his next disappointment.

I scrub my teeth with the mint paste I made. I'm so thankful I left several toiletries I handmade outside the night Bill came for me. Warren grabbed them when he and Jake went back to salvage whatever survived the fire.

After bathing, I stay in the water. I let it wash away the last two days. The evening is growing late. The clothes look stiff in the tree, indicating they must be dried. His mother's dresses are in decent shape. Most of them are plain, neutral colors with high necklines and lace around the hems. While they're not practical for working or being on the run, they'll have to do.

Just as I lay back to float, I hear a throat being cleared. I gasp as I drop my body into the river— peeking only my head out. "What the hell, Jake! You scared me to death."

He's standing on the bank. A blanket lies stretched out behind him. He swallows and I see his Adam's apple bob as if his mouth has suddenly gone dry. He holds whiskey in one hand and a basket of food in the other.

"Is your tongue tied?" I raise an eyebrow.

He licks his lips, and I think he's finally going to form words, but instead, he sets everything down and begins removing his clothes.

"What do you think you are doing?"

He doesn't even look up at me as his shirt hits the ground and his boots next. "Bathing, what does it look like."

"I…you…Jake," I stumble over my words.

"Is your tongue tied witch?"

I tilt my head and glare at him but suck in a breath as his breeches are dropped. My face burns red, but I don't turn around. I refuse to shy away from his brazen actions. I'm at a loss for words, tongue-tied as it would be when my eyes catch sight of his very naked form. His body is thick with muscle but lean at the same time. His legs are built, and his arms are corded with strength—veins showing in his forearms. His dark hair hits just below his ears now, and his beard is short but thick and curves with his sharp jawline. I try to keep my eyes from lingering in his other magnificent areas.

He's beautiful…and this time it's not peyote Sam thinking it.

He shows no shame as he saunters to the water's edge and begins wading in. I've seen bits of his chest before, but never all of it. Scars, some small and some large are in random places on his chest and back—strewn about like a map of his life. Suddenly, the scar through his eyebrow now carries more weight to it. *Now*, I understand all the hesitation. *Now*, I understand why he was unwilling to talk about it. And like an idiot, I'd pressed him about where it came from several times.

He has my mint paste on his finger, rubbing his teeth thoroughly. I'd let him use it after the whole Henry thing happened, and he fell in love with my products. Next, he picks up the amber soap and brings it to his nose, inhaling deeply before he starts scrubbing.

I see the laughter in his eyes when they finally meet mine. "You could at least pretend not to stare."

This time, the blush creeps from my neck up to my face. All of me is burning. "You're an ass."

"Maybe, but your rosy cheeks tell me you like what you see little witch." He winks.

I start to retort but notice he's about to put the amber soap in his hair. "Wait, don't use that…" I wade to the bank and grab the shampoo I made. "This lathers and cleans the hair better." I close the distance between us and hand the jar to him, keeping my body submerged as much as possible, which isn't hard because I'm short. His taller frame has almost his whole chest showing out of the water.

He smells it and closes his eyes with appreciation. The mint mixed with the creeping rosemary made for a more clean aroma. Before he has a chance to drop some into his palm, I do something brazen myself. "Can I?" I ask timidly.

He faces me fully. "You want to wash my hair?"

I roll my lower lip between my teeth before nodding. "Can you tell me more...about your past?" I ask as I move behind him. Once he can't see me, I stand up fully, my breasts out of the water. I lather some shampoo in my hand and take my container to the bank. His body is tense when I wander up behind him, and my fingers meet his scalp. He moans, and I feel that sound reach all the way to my toes. He still hasn't answered me, but instead, he just continues from where he left off earlier.

"After years of abuse, my mother had decided she was going to leave him. She told me, but not my brother or sister. She felt they were too young to understand. She was probably right. The week before she was to leave with all of us, Cholera hit the town hard. Anyone passing through was likely to contract it, and my mother did. All it takes is one day to change the course of your life."

No statement could ever be more true. It brings me back to the day I left Trevor. That one day drastically changed my life. I continue to massage his scalp. I can tell he wants to stop there. His hesitation to finish the story has my curiosity peaked.

He takes a reassuring breath and continues, "One day, I came home from hunting. I knew Mom, Kurt, and Anna had all been sick. She'd been making me stay away as much as possible so that I could provide for them and not catch it, too. My father was out whoring as usual and left me to fend for myself and feed my sick family. I was around twelve at the time. The house was silent. I lay my kill on the table outside and went in. I went straight to my mother's room to bring her food and water, but when I got there...they were all three dead."

I gasp. "Oh my God, Jake," I whisper, not knowing what else to say. Tears well in my eyes, and I strive to hold them back. He hides any emotion as he dips into the water, rinsing his hair. He's still not facing me. I place my hands on his back, tracing some lengthy scars and feel him shudder.

He takes a shaky breath. "My father came home two days later, drunk and looking for a fight. *Two* whole days...I had three graves dug out by that big tree there." He points to the one near the house, the Frémont Cottonwood that held his gaze, leaving his eyes haunted when we arrived. "When I told him what happened, he blamed me. Said I killed them. Said I should have taken care of them. He never once cried or even went to look at the graves. He screamed and yelled in my face...then the beating started. I don't remember all of it, just that it was bad. At some point, his fists weren't enough. He took out his pistol and struck me in the face."

He turns to me, then takes my hand in his and brings it to his eyebrow. I graze the scar with my trembling fingers. Knowing its origin makes my heart wrench inside me. I can hardly breath.

He reaches up and moves some of my wet strands of hair from my face, tucking them behind my ear. I can feel his emotions rolling off him in waves. I'm caught in their wake when he says, "That's the night I shot my father."

This time, I don't bother trying to hold back the tears. I just breathe through them.

His thumb drags over my cheek slowly as he wipes them away. "I dug a fourth grave that night. Buried my whole family." He doesn't stop caressing my face as he talks through his past horrors. "Bill came by for a visit a few days later. I was covered in dirt and sitting by the graves—hadn't eaten. After I told him what happened, he took me in. I knew some of his dealings were shady. Mom used to tell me about it, but I needed a place to go. I lived with him for a time, then grew tired of it and ran off to join the infantry."

I piece together the rest in my mind when he stops talking. The horrors of war. The years of loneliness. The need to be a part of something, but the fear to ever get too close to anyone. Tai's words come back to me now like a punch to the gut. *Take care of Chato's heart. He is a broken wanderer too.*

There's so many things that I could say, but none seem strong enough. None would leave the impact I need. You can't mend a person's broken past with words of kindness and sympathy. Sometimes, those pieces take time to move back into position. To meld together again. So, I stay silent.

"You owe me all of *you* now, Samantha," he whispers.

I'm just about to panic. The shift from sorrow to fear in brain almost gives me whiplash. He stops those thrashing thoughts when he leans down, our lips are but an inch apart, when he says, "But first, I need all of your body...you can offer me your mind and soul later."

His words strip me of my armor. They lay me bare and leave me reeling. The need in him is astonishingly apparent. I can tell that he wants nothing more than to forget everything he just told me. So, I let him forget for a moment. Jake's mouth presses against mine, and I melt into him instantly. I've dreamt of this kiss—his kiss. It's never ventured far from my thoughts. It's like it was imprinted on my soul from the very first time our mouths touched. Somehow, this is different. The barrier between us, the one we both built, tumbles and crashes to the ground.

His lips part, and his tongue languidly teases my own to open. The taste of mint and whiskey is mouthwatering. A slow burning ache engulfs me. The world around fades into nothing. I willingly press my body into his and feel his hands roam my back, moving slowly to cup my ass. Suddenly, I'm lifted out of the water until my legs are wrapped around his waist, our mouths never parting. My breasts are pressed against his chest, and I can feel his rapid heart rate thumping haphazardly. It's like a drumbeat, a rhythm pounding between our bodies, and the song is beautiful.

He pulls his mouth away long enough to look at me. His golden and amber eyes seem to glow from within with the setting sun. "I need you," he says softly against my lips, and those words are so weighted. Not I want you, but I *need* you.

He nibbles my lower lip and then smashes his mouth back to mine. This kiss becomes brutal and unrelenting. Not soft and hesitant but frenzied. Our bodies are moving through the water. I can barely register the air hitting my legs before we're on the bank. He lowers me to the blanket, his mouth now exploring my jaw and trailing to my neck.

Jake lifts off me enough for his eyes to travel the length of my body. He finds what he's looking for on my hip. I intake a sharp breath when he snakes down my torso until his mouth is there—hovering. Gently, he presses kisses all along the edges of my tattoo and then to the center. His hands grip my hips as he looks up through his lashes to watch my reaction.

"I've wanted to taste you since the moment I laid eyes on you."

I tremble, my mouth open slightly. I can form *no* words. My breath halts altogether as he moves to position himself between my legs. His hands grip my hips tightly while his face is turned to mine. He gives me a sinfully wicked smirk and then his mouth is on me.

The breath I was holding rushes out of me, and a moan rumbles in my chest. I throw my head back and squeeze my eyes together as the rapid sensations ruin my senses. He devours me as if I am a delicacy and he hasn't eaten in days. His tongue has me writhing, whimpering for a release I can feel coiling inside far too quickly. He takes his time torturing me with his mouth. I catch him watching me again, reveling in my reactions. Just when I am about to go mad, he pulls away and crawls up my body, settling his hips between my legs.

His gaze is dark and sultry when he whispers against my lips, "This changes everything. You're mine now, witch. We will *never* be done."

I don't have time to contemplate his favorite quote to me, everything in my head is a befuddled mess. My core is throbbing, and without hesitation or reservation, he presses into me. He pauses with his mouth hovering over mine. A tremble runs through him, and he closes his eyes briefly as if he's barely holding it together. My mouth opens more, and he takes the opportunity to kiss me fiercely, stifling the noises coming from me. I can feel our connection throughout my entire body—not sure where one of us begins and the other ends. My legs wrap around him instinctively when he begins moving in and out. This is not slow and easy lovemaking; this is a claiming, and

I'm here for it. He breaks the kiss and braces himself with one arm, watching me. He holds my head captive with the other hand that's entangled in my hair. I arch my back—my body unable to cope with the ecstasy streaming through.

Suddenly, he drops his mouth to my breast and flicks my nipple with his tongue before taking it fully into his mouth. I tense and feel the familiar building inside my core. His teeth bite down gently, and I lose all control. I arch my back again as stars blind my vision, and reality becomes a distant memory. My orgasm blasts through me, and I begin to tremble. His hand is suddenly over my mouth, covering what was surely an embarrassing amount of noise this time.

He doesn't stop slamming into me with every wave of pleasure still flowing through me. His body slows and tenses as he watches me. I can tell he can't hold back any longer. He thrusts into me one last time and as his release takes hold of him he drops his mouth back to mine. He's shaky and breathing erratic but doesn't stop placing sweet kisses along my jaw and neck.

When he finally raises his head to me, we stare into each other's eyes, panting, sweat rolling down my temples. Our chest move in time. My heart feels different somehow. *I* feel different. It's overwhelming in the best way.

I caress his cheek with my hand and say, "I needed you too."

Devious Plans

CHAPTER 37

Samantha

After washing up, eating, drinking, and putting away all of our clothing, it was time for a conversation. One I would rather shoot my toe off than have...especially after what we just shared together. Over the last few weeks, the thought of being honest with Jake has crossed my mind daily, but each time, it sounded preposterous in my head. How do you tell someone you are from the future? The old me would have laughed in someone's face at that.

Jake and I are sitting at the dining table of his family's home. Some preserved food spread about, no doubt from Warren. Jake pours us two fingers of whiskey and passes my glass over. He's hardly said a word since the river, just stares at me unabashedly. There's a light in his eyes. I wonder if the weight of what he carried inside him feels lifted somehow. Maybe, all he needed was one person to unpack it. I'm grateful it was me. Maybe I can carry just a little of his burden for him. I'm more than willing to shoulder it all.

I'm stalling.

I'm sure the blood has drained from my face as the worry creeps through me like spiders. I have no idea what his reaction will be to my outlandish claims. I promised him all of me, but can I ever really keep that promise? I think, deep down, I've always known I'd leave one day. That's why it was so much easier to refrain from closeness with anyone.

I open my mouth, just about to say something, just about to begin my story…

The door bangs open, startling us both as Warren says, "Good, glad y'all in here." He smiles. His brown shirt clinging to him. I can tell he's been washing by the river. "We need to discuss what's next."

I huff out a long sigh. Jake is still looking at me and not Warren. Does he realize how close I was to laying it all out there? I nod to Warren as he sits. "What are you thinking, Jake?" I ask.

Jake runs a hand through his hair and looks to Warren, finally taking his intense eyes off me. "I plan on taking down Bill and the rest of what's left of his gang."

I raise an eyebrow at that. "How so?"

He nods repeatedly as if he's encouraging himself to continue, "After the war and my time spent with Tai,

I was sought out by men who needed people found. It was my specialty…tracking, scouting. I made my money doing this for a few years." He lifts his eyes to me, and I wonder where this is going. "I'd been lingering in Tucson for a bit, passing time. I became friends with the Marshall there, Tucker Jones. He hired me to find some information on someone—someone who's been skirting the law for years. William Evans."

Warren's brows crease at the same time my mouth drops open.

Jake continues, ignoring our shocked faces. "He knew that Bill was my uncle, knew that I could turn him down and run straight to Bill and tell him everything…but he also knew me personally and knew I *couldn't* do that. Not in good conscious."

"Why was he after Bill?" Warren asks before I can.

"That's the thing." Jake shakes his head. "I haven't figured it all out yet. I'd planned on breaking into his group, becoming one of them. That way I could learn from the inside out, but Bill has kept me at arm's length. I think he knows me too well. I'm not like him. So, he's kept his dealings relatively under wraps from me." Jake pauses, his eyes turn to me. "After running into you two in Tucson, I got…sidetracked."

Sidetracked indeed. We turned each other's lives upside down that day.

Jake takes a swig of his whiskey before saying, "Bill has a safe in his office. I saw a stack of documents in there and…other stuff. I'm certain that whatever's in there will be incriminating. I need to get into that safe." He taps his pointer finger on the table.

Warren makes a grunting noise, and his face hardens. "After what that son-of-a-bitch did to Sam...I want him dead, not in a jail somewhere. This girl is like a daughter to me! He dragged her behind a damn horse!"

"I want him dead *too*; that will come, but I need to do this final job. I need to make sure his name is slandered for everyone to see. It's not good enough to just end him...not for me."

Warren looks down, and I can see he's contemplating that. I chime in, "Well then, let's break in there." The men look at me and humor plays at the corner of Jake's mouth. "What?" I ask knowingly, "You want to ruin him...so do I. Let's ruin Bill's name and then be done with running. Once all the players are eliminated, we can clear our names—be free."

Jake smiles at that. "We could leave here, go anywhere...never come back."

Jake misses the look that passes between Warren and me. The one that says...we *can't* leave.

Warren turns back to Jake and nods once, but it's not a yes nod...it's more of an *ugh okay* nod. "I'm in as long as Bill pays for what he did." I grab Warren's hand and give it a squeeze.

"What's the plan, Naiche?" Jake's lip pulls up a little in the corner as he uses my mischief-maker nickname.

I'm simultaneously impressed that both men haven't barked orders for me to stay away from this, but also concerned that they may be putting too much faith in me. I contemplate Jake's question. What is the plan? That's a tough one. We're a half a day's ride from town or more. Bill has several men at his disposal, probably scouring the earth for us and likely heading here at some point. Bill knows Jake—knows we would have *nowhere* to go. The advantage of that being, maybe…just maybe, they're not *all* left near the town limits. If some or all of them are out searching for us, that gives us a better chance of getting into that office unseen.

I rattle that off to Jake and Warren as I brainstorm aloud. "So, now is our best time. Where is the last place they would think to find us?" I ask through a grin.

"Tombstone," Jake says, eyeing me proudly, and it makes me blush.

"Exactly. They'll never expect us to come back. We need to change our appearances. It would be better if we had someone with us, someone unrecognizable to drive a wagon, but since we don't…"

I fade off as Jake interrupts me, "I might…have someone that is."

"Who?" I tilt my head confused.

"I have this friend. I helped him out once a long time ago. He loves an adventure."

I scoff. "Who would possibly want to put themselves in danger for something they know nothing about?"

"Benjamin, that's who." Jake's smile broadens. Memories must be flashing in his mind of this friend.

"I've never told anyone this...*anyone*," his eyes flick to mine, "*but* today has been full of revelations, hasn't it?" I soak up his meaning as he continues, "Benji was a Buffalo Soldier..."

Before Jake gets *any* further, I see Warren tense up and become completely engrossed in whatever is about to leave Jake's mouth. I sink back into a memory of the day of the eclipse. That's the day Warren told me about the Buffalo Soldiers—the day he told me about his ancestors passing that rifle down for generations.

Jake flicks his eyes between us but continues, "He was in the forty-first regiment. However, it was later consolidated into the twenty-fourth infantry regiment. We became friends, had each other's back more times than I can count. He eventually moved to Tombstone. He had some family ties binding him to Arizona and Texas." Jake's eyes grow distant. "He found a girl one night, beaten to within an inch of her life. He took care of her, healed her over time. She asked him to keep her hidden, to keep her secrets." He glances up to me briefly. I felt the meaning behind it. He's let me keep *my* secrets.

His jaw clenches slightly as he continues, "The only reason I knew about her being there was because I showed up one day to visit and found her working a garden at Benji's house. I recognized her olive skin and black hair instantly. It was Henry Fletcher's wife...Miriam."

I gasp. "Wait...what? I thought she was dead. Henry said as much." I recall Henry saying, "God rest her filthy soul," the night he almost raped me. I assumed that meant he killed her.

"Henry thought she was dead too. He left her for dead out in that desert. Benji happened to be in that exact spot, at that exact time, hunting."

"It was fate," I mutter. Every little road that brought us to this moment flickers through my mind. It's all tied together, like an infinity sign looping in on itself. "I thought that you had a fight with Henry over him beating his wife once?"

"I did, but that was the first time I found out he laid hands on her. I never knew if she stayed with him or that the beatings continued. Anyway, Benji fell in love with Miriam over time, and she fell for him. They're still together, and I've kept his secret for years."

Secrets are scary business. I know from personal experience that, eventually, they catch up to you.

Warren is still staring at Jake, but his mind is clearly somewhere else. He shakes his head as if he's waking from a dream. "Why does he owe you? Still don't make sense that he'd put himself in danger over this."

"He hates Bill, for one. He did him dirty over land once. For two, I kept his and Miriam's secret. For three, I saved his life on the battlefield. Took a bullet for him." We watch, stunned, as Jake lifts his shirt. I traced several of those scars today but never knew the one on his side was from a bullet. It's more rounded, so I should've known it wasn't from a knife. Looks like it went straight through him. My chest hurts just imagining it.

Jake drops his shirt. "I'd never make him repay me for anything, but I know my friend…he'll want to help, not because he feels he owes me, but because it's the right thing to do."

I lace my fingers together as I say, "Okay, step one. Collect an unsuspecting Benji. Step two, pick a date and time." I pause to think, then add, "How close does Benji live from here?"

"Not far, a couple hours ride north," Jake replies.

"We could leave out in the morning, meet up with him, then try to be back in town in two days."

"Why two days?" Warren asks.

I grin. "Just so happens that Tombstone is throwing a Wild West Showdown by the paddocks…in two days." They both look as if they aren't understanding so I add, "Myra mentioned it to me. Everyone who is left in town will be at that show…on the other side…nowhere near that office."

The smiles broaden on both their faces. I smack my hand down on the table lightly. "Rest up boys…we have one more adventure to go on." I wink at them and head for the stairs.

A Buffalo Soldier

CHAPTER 38

Jake

I need to get my shit together. We're almost at Benjamin's home, but the only thoughts rolling through my mind involve Sam naked. We made love two more times last night and nothing seems to satiate the need I have for her. Something in me has snapped and repositioned itself. I no longer feel like the man I was before her. I'm better somehow for just knowing her.

This morning, when I held her, faint sorrow lingered in her eyes. She never told me anything about herself yesterday, and I can only assume that's what's weighing on her. Pressing her for details about her life is something I would've done before, but now...I don't want to give her a reason to run. And I have that fear imbedded in me that she will do just that.

She rides ahead of me now with Warren stuck by her side. Every now and then, I can see them whispering.

How bad could their secrets be?

I used to pride myself on being able to find out any information on a person. It's what I'm good at. With these two…it's like they fell out of the damn sky. Either way, I've made up my mind. I'll not live without her, so whatever she's done, I'll deal with it.

She looks over her shoulder, her braid swishing behind her, and catches me watching. I lick my lips and wink just to mess with her and see her blush prettily. I never thought I could have this with anyone, but here she is…ruining me in such a spectacular way.

She turns back, facing forward and I see her excitement when she catches sight of a house in the distance. I ride up beside the two of them.

"That's it. That's Benji's place," I say as we pick up the pace.

Sam's eyes are all light and mischief as she kicks Clint's sides and takes off, yelling, "See you there losers…"

Warren glances at me, and we both grin and dig our heels in. Shadow lunges forward, making my hat drop behind me, only held on by the string. We race across the plain, dust flying. I inch closer to her. She laughs playfully, and suddenly, she and Clint are on another level. I've never seen this side of her. It's intoxicating. Her dress flies around her in the wind, swishing in time with Clint's long black mane and tail. Warren's mare is right behind me as we rush to catch up, but she's too fast. The joy and free spirit radiating from her is contagious. I see her slide to a stop when she enters the open gates to the property. She spins Clint in a circle and then makes him rear as she blows us each a kiss. We slide up beside her in awe.

"I had *no* idea he was that fast," I say, breathless.

Sam just laughs some more, patting his thick neck, and says in a childlike voice, "We knew…didn't we, boy."

Warren's Mare is slinging her head, ears pinned back. "She okay?" I ask.

Warren and Sam say in unison, "Yeah, she's just bitchy."

We're all three chuckling like fools when I hear the click of a hammer on a gun. I spin Shadow toward the sound, pistol already aimed, but I release it and point skyward instantly.

Miriam's dark, shocked eyes meet each one of ours. Her long, pitch-black hair is rolled on top of her head. Behind her, Benji has also lowered his gun, and a big grin splits his mouth. His short, black, curly hair is sticking out of his gray campaign hat. I see he still doesn't part with that one. His button-up top is tucked half in, half out of his navy breeches as if we interrupted something.

"Holy shit, if it isn't Chato himself. I hadn't seen you in sometime." He props his rifle on his shoulder and dusts off his shirt as he looks at our group. He must notice something in all of our faces. His head shakes side to side, "What've you gotten yourself into, man," he says, seeing *too* much with only one glance. Miriam's shocked face has softened as she slips closer to Benji.

"You gonna invite us in first?" I say, already dropping off Shadow's back, throwing the reins over head so she can wander around.

He nods. "Of course, of course. Come on in, and you two are?" he asks, looking between Warren and Sam. Warren has an odd look on his face, almost as if he is speechless when he looks at Benji.

Sam nudges his shoulder curiously. He blinks and finally says, "We're friends of Jake's. I'm Warren, and this is Samantha." He shakes Benjamin's hand, and there is a moment when I think he might not let go.

"Real nice to meet y'all folks. Jake here don't really have any friends, so this is…well, this is something." He laughs lightly. "I'll lead the way, don't mind the mess. We are adding a bedroom onto the side there." He points to a rough-cut side of the house—framing pieces lie around the area.

"What are you adding on for?" I ask as we pass the boards on the ground to head inside.

Benji casually looks over his shoulder. "A baby."

My eyes widen and a grin splits my face as we enter the house. I give Miriam a once over. She's tiny until you reach below her bosom to see the bump there. "I had no idea. Congratulations."

"We were very surprised, but we have been trying for a long time now. Can you believe we are going to be parents?"

I shake my head. A ping of jealousy hits me unexpectedly. My friend is getting the life he deserves, finally. I never wanted anything of the such but looking around their home now. I'm not so sure. Everything in here is what a home should be. You can practically feel the love radiating off the damn walls. It's nothing like my hell of a childhood.

Miriam takes Sam's hand and leads her through the house, introducing herself and showing off some handmade baby clothing. Warren is taking in each and every detail of this family's life. He wanders around aimlessly in awe. It's got me questioning the things I *don't* know about him.

Once alone, I catch up with Benji for a while. We share stories from the past few years and some memories from our time together. I give the couple time to get to know Sam and Warren before laying the truth of our visit on them. It's beginning to feel like a mistake. He's becoming a father. I can't ask this of him now.

After another hour has passed, I decide to come clean with the predicament we've found ourselves caught in. I tell him *almost* everything that's transpired since meeting Samantha and about the job I was hired for before that.

"Never thought I'd see the day that Jake Evans was a wanted man." Benji sighs and laces his fingers on the dining table. I raise my brow, nodding as he stares me down. "Of course, I'll help you, you know that." I immediately shake my head, but he says, "That's why you're here right?"

"Look. *Yes*, that's why we came, but seeing you now…starting a family. I won't ask it of you." Doubts plagued me from the time we arrived here. His picture-perfect family beginning leaves me in turmoil. I feel like an asshole for coming. "Miriam's pregnant, Benji." I remove my hat, laying it to the side, and run a hand through my hair. "I *can't* ask you to do this. I thought I could, but not now."

"What's the plan. Tell me that and let me decide for myself."

I lay out our plan for him, doing a quick run-down of any obstacles we've thought about.

"So, you're asking me to ride you into town, not have a damn shootout. Besides," he smiles, "I trust you. If you say this needs to be done, then let's finish it…finish Bill."

"I don't know." I run a calloused hand over my face with a long sigh.

"Well, I *do* know. You're a good man." I shake my head at that, but he interrupts my attempt, "You are. I wouldn't be here if it wasn't for you. I wanna help."

Sam walks past us with Warren, heading toward the door to take care of the horses. My eyes trail after her all the way until she disappears through the doorway.

Benji snickers when we are alone again. "I also never thought I'd see the day Jake Evans was in love."

I scoff at that and grunt, not meeting his eyes. He laughs. "I see the way you look at her. It's the same way I look at Miriam. I'm happy for you, truly."

Even though I neither confirm nor deny his words, he sees right through me. I spend the next several minutes trying to talk him *out* of going, but to no avail. That's just the kind of man Benjamin is. He's there for people when they need him—fiercely loyal.

After our talk, I excuse myself to check on Sam and let her know that Benji's in. I make my way to the barn, but before I make it around the corner, I overhear Sam asking Warren something. Her voice is strained and nervous. I know I shouldn't, but I don't budge from that spot. I listen.

"What was carved into your rifle? Was it him?" Sam asks.

"No, I almost expected some connection, but no…it wasn't him," Warren replies.

"The day we left, I remember you trying to tell me, but I never thought to ask again. Who's name's on it?"

Warren huffs, "Tobias. That's what's carved into the stock."

There's silence between the two of them, then Sam says, "This is all so frustrating. We are what…close to six weeks or less away from the eclipse."

"Let's just take this one step at a time. No need to put the cart in front of the horse." Warren's voice lowers to a whisper. I can barely make out what's being said, so I step closer. "Have you decided…about Jake?"

Sam breathes a long exhale. "No, I was sitting there at that table, in his house, and I was so close to letting the words come out, but then you walked in, and I lost my nerve. What would you do, Warren?"

"What wouldn't I do if it was my person?"

I hear her sniffle at that. I back away slowly. Confusion is an understatement of how I feel. She was close to telling me what? What could be so bad that she would torture herself about it? What the hell are they discussing a carving in a gun for? What did Warren mean when he said, "*Have you decided...about Jake?*" I could barge around the corner and confront the two of them, but I won't. I said she could keep her secrets, and I meant it. I refuse to force her. Besides, we have this business with my shitty uncle to deal with. Now's not the time.

All I know for sure, with absolute certainty, is that she's mine. She could never be anything but mine. If that makes me selfish, then so be it.

The Safe

CHAPTER 39

Samantha

We stayed for several hours with Benjamin and his wife. All of us took time to sleep later in the day, knowing we'd have to ride all night to be in town in the morning. I can see why Jake is so fond of them. I loved them instantly. In a different world, I could see Miriam and me being great friends. She was funny, understanding, and kind. I never mentioned Henry, and neither did Jake, but I wanted to. I wanted her to know that he's dead. Maybe, one day, we can give her the peace she deserves. Jake didn't think it was the right time. We were running off with her husband, after all. She wasn't too happy about him leaving, but she seemed to have complete trust in Jake that Benji would return to her unharmed.

As we ride along behind Benji's wagon, heading to Tombstone, I can't stop the parade of thoughts crushing my brain. It's all becoming so heavy. The doubts about today, the worries about tomorrow, and our lack of understanding of what the cosmos has in store for us. When I think about it...it seems ridiculous. How the hell did we end up here, about to rob someone? It's ludicrous. I giggle quietly at our predicament because otherwise...I may cry.

The blazing sun has just risen and is already blasting us without mercy. We are close. The energy is changing in our group with every mile we cross. Everyone is quiet in anticipation. We make it to our rendezvous point...the same one we used the night we rescued Nalin. The large desert willow is blooming with magenta-colored flowers. It's such a stark contrast to the surrounding neutral shades of plants.

We begin unloading the wagon and tying the horses to the tree. I adjust my breeches until they are tucked inside the tall riding boots and pull up my suspenders. I'm dressed in Benji's clothing. Miriam and I altered them a bit to fit me better. I'm wearing one of his old infantry hats. The front of the brim is smashed upward the way many men are wearing them these days. My hair is hidden neatly inside. I have a bandana around my neck, one of Warren's peacemakers strapped to my hip, along with the blade Jake gave me. Just in case, I gathered some more Silverleaf Nightshade in a vial inside my jacket pocket.

Warren and Jake are dressed as they usually are but carry both pistols and rifles with bandoliers lined full of ammunition. Benji is wearing his infantry uniform…figured he would look more respectable that way.

"Y'all ready for this?" Benji asks.

We all nod. Warren, Jake, and I hunker down in the wagon. Benji tosses blankets over us and then begins stacking crates of goods all around. Sweat streams down my back and over my brow. The heat, coupled with being covered like this, is smothering. Jake reaches out and grasps my hand.

"You okay?" he asks.

"Yeah, I think so." My breathing is shaky, even to my own ears. I hate being confined. I'm not sure if it's claustrophobia exactly, but it's making me panic. I feel the wagon start moving and try to slow my breathing.

Jake reaches up and creates a peep hole above us in the fabric for me. I sigh heavily, "Thank you."

"Anytime," he says as he fumbles his hand around in one of the crates.

My brows furrow. "What are you doing?"

He gives me that side smile that makes my tummy do somersaults and pulls a bottle from the crate. He pops the top and takes a long swig of whiskey. "Anyone else need some encouragement?"

"Hell yessss," Warren draws it out as he takes a swig himself. I laugh as his face scrunches with the burn.

I grab the bottle next, downing a shot. It's horrible, but *damn*, it does seem to help calm my nerves. We pass it back and forth once more before putting it away. The time drags on until I finally hear the commotion of townspeople. Jake reaches up to cover my peephole, no longer being able to chance it. We are jostled around with each and every bump. I can smell leather, horses, food being cooked, and hear the laughter of children. It's the Wild West Show. Gunshots ring out and I hear more laughter.

The wagon stops abruptly, making me tense up. Jake holds onto one of my hands and Warren the other. We give each other a squeeze before releasing and placing our hands at the ready on our pistols.

A man's voice startles me, "Hello there, we're asking anyone coming through today if they've seen any of these three individuals." The sound of crinkling paper is followed by, "They're wanted for murder, amongst other things. You seen'um anywhere?"

"No, sir. I stay to myself with my wife on our farm. We don't get out much. I sure hope you find'um."

There's silence, and then the man says, "Whatcha got in the back?"

"Um, Oh…that's just some goods. I'm here to trade."

The man's boots scuff the ground as he circles the wagon. My heart kicks up a notch and I feel Jake stiffen beside me. One of the crates wiggles and I think the man is lifting out a bottle based on the clanking sound. "You make this whiskey?"

"Yes, sir. You're welcome to take that one for yourself…if you'd like," Benji says calmly.

"Don't mind if I do…much appreciated. You can head on in, but just so you know, you picked a bad day to trade. Everyone's at the show."

"I didn't realize. That's alright. I may just check out the show then. Have a good day, sir."

The wagon jolts as the horses move forward. We collectively breathe a sigh of relief. "Shit, that was close," I mumble.

"Too damn close," Warren adds.

Several minutes later, the wagon comes to a halt. We don't move. We wait for Benji's confirmation.

I hold my breath until I finally hear him mutter, "All clear." He moves the crates off us. "Now," he says. I peep over the wagon's edge.

We are tied up in the alley beside Bill's office. No one lingers about. Jake and Warren jump out and Jake grabs two sacks before he lends a hand to me. When my feet hit the ground, he pulls me to him and kisses me quickly then he pulls my bandana up to cover the lower half of my face before doing the same with his. Something about him with that bandana has me forgetting where we are and what we are supposed to be doing.

"You good witch?" He winks knowingly.

I roll my eyes and push past him, my smile hidden by the bandana thankfully.

Benji remains by the wagon, sifting through items—playing as if he's trying to find something. We move to the side door in the alley that's one of the entrances to Bill's office. Warren pulls the handle, but it doesn't budge…locked. I expected as much. I'm prepared, though. I grab one of the sacks from Jake and pull out an entrenching tool. It's made like a modern-day trowel. I hand the sack back to him and shove the end into the door beside the mortise lock. Warren taps it in for me further, and then he begins to pry it back and forth. I hear the crack as the connecting wood splits on the other side. I smile up at him.

We move, one at a time, me last, as we enter. My heart thrums inside me. Light streams in from nearby windows. There's a seating area and a bar along the back wall. A set of stairs curl to the right of me. Jake points us in that direction but stays in front of me and places Warren behind me.

It looks empty. No sounds are made other than our boots creaking on the wooden staircase. We reach the top landing, and Jake visibly relaxes. No one is here. He motions for Warren to keep watch as we go into the office. Warren nods and heads back down the stairs.

A large desk sits in the center near the window, with a chaise lounge in the corner. The safe is across from the desk, beside the door we entered. Hanging above it is a lasso slung over the horn protruding from and massive bull skull.

I rifle around the papers on Bill's desktop while Jake searches for the key. I bite my lip, but a laugh bubbles out of me, and he cuts his eyes to me. I hold up a wanted poster. "We are quite the lookers on paper," I say sarcastically when Jake's eyes see the shitty sketches of our faces. "I have to say, I'm not so worried about being caught now...these are absolutely horrible." I laugh again.

"That's not how my face looks right?" Jake asks smiling.

"Of course, not...this one's *much more* handsome," I say tapping the sketch.

He grimaces, but I see the humor in his eyes. I fold it placing it in the sack while he continues his search.

"He kept the key in his desk," Jake says as he flings open each drawer. "Shit," he mutters.

"What is it?" I ask, rifling through Bill's papers some more.

"It's not here."

"It has to be."

"Well, it's not." He slams the last drawer in frustration.

I hear a rattle in the center of the desk. My mind immediately goes back to the night of my jailbreak. I drop down on the floor and scoot underneath the desk.

"What are you doing?" Jake asks.

"Just give me a second...there." I hit the hidden latch under the desk and then pop up excitedly. I reach my fingers under and slide out of the hidden drawer.

Jake grins. "How'd you know?"

I wink. "Not my first time, cowboy."

He bites his lip to stifle the smirk as we both eye the contents inside the drawer. There, in all its glory...is the key. A golden, elongated skeleton key.

We stand in front of Bill's safe. It's at least three to four feet tall, and a deep shade of green paint covers the steel it's made of. The word "Century" is across the center in gold lettering with a shiny gold handle and keyhole. Jake flits his eyes to mine briefly before inserting the key and turning it.

I was devastatingly unprepared for this. Inside is a stack as tall as the safe and several rows deep of gold bars. I suck in a breath at the sight. "What the hell?" I mumble as I pull out one and turn it over and over in my palm. I jostle it up and down, feeling the weight in my palm.

"Yeah," Jake says while shuffling through papers. "Not no normal amount for any one man to have." Jake reads through several documents, and eventually, he freezes. His jaw clenches as he eyes a yellowed paper in his hand.

"What is it?"

He shakes his head in disbelief. "He's stealing land. Forging documents." He flips through more papers, scanning as he talks. "You heard of the Desert Land Act they passed last year?"

I shake my head, unable to remember that from history.

"It provides land to people willing to work it, to develop the arid land, but if you don't show improvement after so long, it's taken from you. If you do show improvement, it becomes yours."

I look confused. "What does that mean? What was Bill doing?"

"He's sending in forged documentation to Congress, stating these families did develop the land in the time allotted…It looks like he's taking it from them after the deed is given. For some reason, all these deeds look as if their properties were *sold* to Bill. The owners signed off on them. That's not all…" Jake rubs his face and curses. "Some of these deeds belong to people who went missing."

My blood runs cold. "You think he killed them?"

"That's *exactly* what I think. I think he killed them, took their money, belongings, land, everything. Faked the signatures, and boom…free land for him to do as he wishes. There's several false settlement claims in here, dummy entries."

"How could he do that and not get caught?"

"These were people living on the fringes. New pioneers with no family around other than the ones they brought with them. He probably chose them based on where they lived and who would miss them…or wouldn't." Jake points to a name on one of the papers. "This man here, Julias, he moved here alone with only his wife. I met them once. They had *no one* here but each other. People assumed they just…moved away."

I look down at the signatures and sure enough, it looks like they signed over their land willingly to Bill.

Jake smiles, and it catches me off guard. "*Why* are you smiling exactly?" I ask.

"This will ruin him. It's everything I hoped for, but wished weren't true." Jake starts shoving all the documentation into the sack. "I need to get a letter out today. Two actually. One to Tucker Jones in Tucson and one straight to Washington. I have some loyal friends there that I served with. They can destroy him and hopefully take our names off that wanted list."

We work faster, loading up one sack with everything inside except the gold. Once it's done, I move to shut the safe. Jake stops the door before it closes. He cocks his head to the side, looking at me mischievously.

"Are you implying what I think you're implying?" I place my hands on my hips. He tips his hat to me and smirks. I'm not sure what he thinks I'll do. Maybe he thinks that I'd be opposed to stealing gold...he's wrong. Bill doesn't deserve a cent...but I can think of *several* who do. "Alright then...let's add gold robbers to that wanted list."

His eyes widen slightly. "You surprise me, witch. Didn't peg you for this sort of devious atrocity."

"Maybe you don't know me...Chato."

His eyes darken at that. He bites his lip and nods. "Maybe not, but I *will*...know every last inch of your mind, body, and soul."

I feel hot all of a sudden, his words curling into my stomach. Our little standoff we are having with our eyes is abruptly put to a stop when we hear Warren yell for us to hurry up. Jake looks around the room and finds what he's searching for. A steamer chest sits in the corner. Its aged appearance has me wondering just how ancient it is. Jake dumps the chests contents onto the floor. I help him fill it with the gold. Brick by brick, we load it down. Then we take the remaining sack and do the same.

There are two windows in here. One behind the desk facing the streets and one to the right facing the alley. I peek out the side window to see Benji. He's still there. Still alone. Relief washes over me. We start to lift the trunk, but it's too heavy for me to help so we call for Warren.

I point to the rope hung across the bull skull on the wall. "We can lower them down from the window." They both nod in agreement. We loop the rope through the lateral chest's handles and move to the window. Benji pays us no attention when we open it, so I take a Silver Dollar off Bill's desk and toss it down. It smacks Benji in the back and he curses, swatting his hands to his back, but then looks up to see me grinning. I motion to him our plans and we heave the large chest onto the windows ledge. Ever so slowly, we lower it, inch by inch. Benji backs up the horses a touch to make sure the safe lands directly on the back of the wagon and not the ground. Once it does, he unties it, and we quickly bring the rope up, repeating the process one more time with the two sacks.

"Okay, that's it. Let's get the hell outta here," I whisper.

"Wait." Jake looks around. "I want to make sure there's nothing else here."

Warren walks back downstairs to be our lookout again. We scurry through the room, leaving a mess in our wake. I rip back portraits and anything else that may have hidden secrets, but after a good five minutes, we find nothing.

Just as our feet are moving toward the office door, we hear a clatter downstairs. The hairs on the back of my neck rise. Our eyes meet then we are moving towards the sound. We remain silent as a mouse as we dart toward the banister that overlooks the sitting area below.

I feel like I'm being gutted from the inside out. A cold sweat breaks out on me as I look down to see a young man holding Warren from behind…a gun to his head. Lonnie Graves cowers in the corner, her hand over her mouth. The man is Bobby Mack, Kelvin's brother. I think I yell Warren's name, but it's more of a screech. Panic overwhelms me as everything moves in slow motion. I barely register Jake beside me. His rifle is aimed down at Bobby over the railing.

"What do we have here?" Bobby asks smugly. He backs up more, pulling Warren with him until Bobby's back is positioned at the side entrance. "Of all the places y'all could have run off to," he laughs menacingly, "you waltz right back into the place you are *wanted*. Not. Very. Smart."

"Let him go," I scream.

"Tell me where my brother is bitch!" he yells, sending more chills down my spine.

I register again that Lonnie is here. It takes me a few seconds to realize she holds papers in her hand and a bundle of what looks like banknotes. They were dropping off more of Bill's dealings to the safe possibly.

Jake never flinches or even shows emotion. He lifts his head slightly as he says, "You have one chance to leave here alive Bobby."

Bobby chuckles and presses the barrel of the gun in harder. Warren's jaw is clenched tight. "On the contrary, Jakey boy...y'all won't be going nowhere but jail or six feet under by the end of this! Tell me right *NOW*! Where is my brother!" His face blooms red with rage as he snarls. Warren is a big man, bigger than Bobby, but the hair-trigger pressed against his head keeps him still. Warren's eyes hold anger, not fear.

Jake lowers his head to aim again. My heart stutters.

The sound of glass breaking jolts my body. In a matter of seconds, Bobby moves his pistol to point toward the sound at the same time that the side entrance door slams open, knocking both Bobby and Warren to the ground.

Two guns go off.

Lonnie screams bloody murder and backs herself further into a corner, dropping down to her ass, crying. I'm seeing this playout like a movie scene. My brain trying hard to keep up. My feet have already been moving without me realizing it. I'm halfway down those curling stairs when I see Warren roll and jump to his feet. Benji, who'd burst through the door just moments ago, is standing in front of Warren. Warren grabs Benji from behind and yanks him backwards as Bobby gets his bearings and raises his gun.

I slide to a stop, pull my pistol and aim. Three guns go off simultaneously.

Both Warren and Benji hit the floor.

I see Bobby holding his chest. Blood seeps through his meaty fingers. His face, which was once red, is now losing color fast. The blood is coming from several places. One of those holes was from me. The others, no doubt from Jake upstairs.

I struggle to breathe through the chaos. Warren is covering Benji like a shield. "No, no, no, no, no…" I rush to their side, holster my gun, and pull Warren to me. Both men are eyeing me. Blood is everywhere. I can't tell who's injured. Warren and Benji groan and move to a sitting position. I look to Bobby, making sure he's not trying to finish us off. Bobby's gun dangles from his fingers as he begins to fade. Jake's somehow made it downstairs without me hearing him and has his rifle trained on Bobby's head.

"Where is my…brother," Bobby gargles.

Jake kicks his gun away and leans in close. I hear him whisper, "You'll see him soon."

Bobby's eyes widen for a second, but then his lids lower slowly. We don't move until he's dead.

Then we are *frantic*.

Benji is standing now, yelling at us to move. Warren stands, but I hear the grunt he makes. I stop in my tracks. My eyes fall to where his hand grips his side.

Fresh blood oozes through his fingers.

My ears are ringing, everything is a blur. Not Warren. Oh my God…not him. I can't. I can't lose him.

"Sam!" Warren grabs me, shaking the sense back into my head. "We have to go *now!*"

A thought slaps me in the face. "*No*, we can't leave her." I point to Lonnie. "She'll go straight to Bill. Half the damn town will be after us by nightfall."

"We can't worry with that now! Someone's bound to have heard those shots!"

I vaguely hear Jake saying the same thing. "Tie her up!" I yell at Jake and rush over to a jug of liquor on the bar, grabbing a glass and pouring some in it. He's still yelling at me, so I scream, "TIE HER UP! I pat my pocket and feel the gritty contents still inside then I empty the vial of Silverleaf into the liquor and stir.

Jake binds her arms quickly. She is crying and violently kicking when I walk over to her and slap her hard enough to make her see stars. I don't say a word as I hold her mouth and gag her with the contents of the liquid. My emotions are null and void at the moment. I take my bandana off my face and gag her with that, too, making sure she can't scream for help before the herb takes effect.

Her eyes are slicing and murderous. I get in her face and bare my teeth, then whisper, "Have a nice trip."

Jake is pulling me through the door and onto the wagon. Warren is already there, breathing heavily, clutching his side. Benji haphazardly tosses things over us.

The wagon lunges forward before I can even get adjusted, Jake is passing the whiskey to Warren. Before he can drink it, I snatch it and jerk his shirt up, dousing the bullet hole. I keep my face placid. I don't let the emotions take over. We still have to make it out of here. I hand Jake a cloth to rip for me and then soak it in the liquor, too. I hold it tightly against his wound. We stay silent but share a sip of the whiskey. Our breathing is ragged. Jake reaches across to me and squeezes my arm. I'm not sure he realizes just how much that small gesture helps ground me right now.

We lie there, sweaty, disoriented, not knowing how far we are from freedom. I can only pray that the loud shooting from the show drowned out the shots fired in that office. I hear the distant laughter of people as the town fades into the background. Jake leans over and kisses my cheek fiercely as I hold onto Warren for dear life.

1876 Winchester Lever Action Rifle

CHAPTER 40

Samantha

The trip back to Benjamin's home was never-ending. Jake retrieved our horses and tied Halle and Clint to the wagon because I refused to leave Warren's side. Watching him go in and out of consciousness was gut-wrenching. I probably checked his pulse a thousand times to reassure myself he was sleeping... not dead.

I ensued chaos back at their farm. I enlisted a panic-stricken Miriam to boil water in two bowls and to place torn pieces of cloth into one and boil them, too. I refused to slow down to eat or rest and instead became a drill sergeant—shouting orders. I sent Jake to find specific plants and bark. I drew them out and explained where they were likely to grow. I tore through what remained of my stash from after the fire and kept Tai's native medicine book handy. Once I had some mesquite tree sap, I boiled it down to use for its antiseptic properties. I flipped through Tai's book and found that the Natives used, quite often, what they called the sacred four. Cedar, sweetgrass, tobacco, and sage. I already had sweetgrass and sage. Benji provided the tobacco, and with luck, Jake found me some cedar.

I got Warren cleaned up. While washing him earlier, I found that the bullet went clean through the left side of his abdomen. It's too far to the side to have hit any organs, thankfully, but the risk of infection is a real threat. He's no longer soaked in blooded clothing, and neither am I. I put on one of Jake's mother's dresses and left Warren in only a pair of clean breeches. I had him lie down on clean linen outside. With the amount of blood he lost, I thought he would pass out before now, but he is strong. He fought closing his eyes until the last second. Miriam had some Laudanum for his pain, and I was more than willing to use it; thankful to see his face relax into a deep sleep.

The sun has set, and the night is still warm, but we no longer have the heat of the day beating down upon us. I got curious glances from the others earlier as to why I wanted him outdoors. Without modern medicine, I'm relying on my *little* knowledge of herbal properties coupled with healing rituals from the medicinal journal. I made a poultice with antimicrobial and antiseptic plants once I had the bleeding under control with the yarrow.

Warren is out cold now but moaning softly every now and again in his sleep. "You're going to be okay…I need you as much as you need me. Remember telling me that in Tucson?" I whisper to him as I press a cold cloth to his forehead. I bend, kissing his cheek, and then sit cross-legged, facing the open landscape around us with my back to the house.

"What are you doing?" Jake startles me as he kneels down looking at the ingredients I have lain around me. I drop some of my mixture of willow bark tea into Warren's mouth. It'll ease the pain some since the laudanum will be wearing off soon.

"The Apaches believed that to restore balance and harmony, you must connect with the spirits," I say without looking his way. "Do you think I'm insane right now?"

Jake plops down beside me. "You're forgetting I spent several years with them." We make eye contact, and he smiles down at me. "No, you're not insane. You're scared."

I turn back to the items placed around me. "Will you help me?"

"Of course." His voice is low and soothing.

I light the tobacco, and we take a few puffs together and then I flip to the page I'm sure is the one I need and ask Jake to translate. From what I gather from Jake, tobacco is supposed to carry messages to the spirits. While he can speak the language very well, his translations are a bit sketchy, but we make it through the basics.

We stand together and smoke the tobacco and waft it toward east, west, north, then south, before sitting cross-legged, one on each side of Warren. I grab the smudge stick I made from the tobacco, sweetgrass, cedar, and sage. I light it and immediately inhale the strong herbs curling around me. I weave the bundle over his body as I silently pray. The smoke seems to grab onto Warren and roll across his body before finally rising.

"The tobacco is to carry our message," I whisper. "The sage is to purify and cleanse, cedar is used to create a protective space, and the sweetgrass promotes balance, harmony, as well as gives a blessing." Something inside me opens up—like a flower to the sun. Something I didn't even know existed. My ancestry, while diluted, is still strong. I feel a connection in my soul to it, like an unbreakable thread spinning through time.

We repeat the chant we found in the book and then finish our little makeshift ceremony. We spend the night by a fire Jake built for us. I wrap Warren and myself tight into a cover and rest my head on his shoulder as he sleeps.

We spend a week with Benjamin and his wife. Every day I go through the process of cleaning Warren's wounds and getting him to move and drink water. I don't leave his side day or night. By the third day, he could stomach food. By the fourth day, he was walking without hunching over. By the fifth day, he was helping Benji around the house. By day six, he was laughing again. My heart could burst from the sight of it.

Today is day seven. It's late, pitch black outside, other than the moon and all her brilliance. We have to leave in the morning. We fear that our being here could bring trouble to this beautiful family, and so…it's time to say farewell. Before we go, we decided to have a night of drinks and celebrate our success by the bonfire the guys have raging outside.

"Here, witch." Jake nudges me and passes the whiskey. "Have another." I roll my eyes but grab it taking a long gulp.

"Why does he call you 'witch?'" Miriam asks, her olive skin practically glowing from within beside this firelight.

I roll my lip between my teeth, trying to decide how best to answer that.

"The ritual she did on Warren…look at him. He's right as the rain," Jake interrupts her, saving me from answering.

"That was not witchcraft!" I elbow him. "That was a native custom. Besides, if you think about it…witch folklore isn't that much different than what natives believe and utilize today."

Warren cocks his head to the side, jumping into our conversation. "How so?"

"Well, they believed in gods and goddesses. They might have named them different names, but it falls along the same lines. They use what the earth gives them in the form of plants and animals. They both faced persecution for their beliefs." Everyone is silent, contemplating that as I take another swig.

"You are one interesting woman Samantha." Benji laughs, breaking the silence.

"You have no idea," Jake mutters, where only I can hear him.

We laugh and talk for hours. Every sip brings us closer to being drunken lushes, all except Miriam, of course. She's with child. The moment that thought hits me I ask, "Oh, yeah! What will you name your baby?"

We all watch as she smiles down at her growing belly and holds it protectively. "If it's a girl...we will call her Mirella because my name is Miriam, and Benji's mom's name was Ella."

Before she can finish, I gush, "Oh my goodness, that is so perfect!"

She beams at me and then looks at Benji cocking a sassy eyebrow. "He wants a boy. *If* it's a boy, we are calling him Tobias after my father. He'll be Tobias Benjamin Mathews."

Jake is still grinning but stops when he sees us. Warren and I have frozen, our eyes flit to each other's.

"Your last name…I never thought to ask. It's Mathews?" I mutter.

Miriam's brows furrow. "Yes, of course, I guess we failed at decent introductions. Is everything okay?"

I shake it off, knowing now is not the time to freak out. I can see Jake sorting out the last name matching Warren's. I'm hoping he assumes it's a coincidence. "Of course. I'm so sorry. That was a relative of Warren's. Someone he…*lost*," I say, hoping that will be enough to move the conversation elsewhere.

"I'm so sorry," she says.

Warren clears his throat. "No, no. No need to be. He was a wonderful man, and I think you couldn't have picked a better name for that baby."

Miriam glows again as she says, "Still sorry for your loss, but good to hear it's a worthy name."

"More than worthy," he adds.

I hope I'm the only one seeing his eyes water. He excuses himself to use the privy. The day of the eclipse replays in my mind, and now I can clearly see the name Tobias carved on that gun stock. Warren told me after the fact, but I'd never been able to see it. It's as if it was wiped from my memory, waiting for the perfect time to reveal itself.

We continue drinking for two more hours. Warren stopped a long time ago. Due to his wound, he only had a few. Benji, Jake, and I have a little too much. We dance by the fire with Miriam, talk about life…them more than me, of course. Jake and Benji even shared some war stories with me.

I fall absolutely in love with them. Some, more than others…I watch Jake laugh, and it rips through my heart. His whiskey eyes catch mine, and he winks. He's killing me. Why does he have to be so perfect? I'm suddenly wishing he was the *Jakeass* that used to call him.

When I laid my spinning head down that night, it was beside Jake instead of Warren. Warren had ushered me off, saying he was fine. Jake ran his fingers through my hair in a soothing pattern. I knew morning would bring a new kind of heartache because *now* I know in my heart, I will have to leave these people one day very soon…

For good.

Running Bind

CHAPTER 41

Jake

We've been camping out, changing locations every week. It's near the end of July. No matter how many times I press Sam to leave—to flee Arizona, she refuses. I don't know what holds her here. I wish I could read her mind.

Before we parted ways with Miriam and Benji, I had some strict instructions for him. I packaged up the documents after going through them carefully. He's to mail certain ones to Tucker Jones and have the others delivered straight to Washington. Among forging documents, selling land that didn't truly belong to him, thieving, and possibly murdering, Bill had some banknotes that were stolen a year ago from a train outside Prescott. Seems he dabbled in serval nefarious dealings. He was also the reason many renegade

Apache tribes were located and killed or captured. While that is, unfortunately, sought after and not a crime...everything else is. Bill will go down for what he's done, and that brings me some small amount of peace.

Samantha was adamant that we leave some of the gold for Myra and Judith, along with an apology note. She cried a lot the day she wrote it. Miriam gifted Sam a fountain pen and paper for her to take notes on plants she may cross paths with.

I left Benji and Miriam a large portion of the gold. They tried to protest but I wasn't having it. We added a note to Tucker Jones about the rape and kidnapping of Nalin and a list of missing people for him to look into. I can only hope those packages have already arrived and we are well on our way to being cleared. It feels like we are running blind.

Sam asked me to bring her back to the cave I once brought her to the night I got her away from Henry. So, here we are. The cave is my solace, my secret place of refuge—has been since I was younger, but this is the last place we should be. It's far too close to town for my liking. No matter how hard I pressed her and Warren to reconsider, this is where they wanted to go. We have a fire built and some kill roasting over it. Warren's been healing at an astonishing rate thanks to Sam's care. He's out hunting now, leaving us some sorely needed privacy. We haven't been truly alone since our time at my childhood home. The river will live in infamy inside my brain forever.

"I need to show you something." I watch her eyes grow curious. The dress she's wearing—one of my mother's—is dirty from traveling. She's been relatively fine until today. She's guarded and quiet. There's an anxiousness about her tonight, and I'm dying to relieve it.

"What is it?"

I stand and offer my hand to her, and she takes it without question. "You'll see." I toss my hat to the ground and pull her along behind me through a narrow gap in the cave at the far end.

"Oh, no, no, no." She pulls out of my grasp. "I can't. That's too narrow."

"If I can fit, so can you." I grab her hand again.

"Jake," she whines.

"You trust me, right?"

"I...okay," she huffs.

I pull her through the gap and into the darkness. She begins shaking. "It's okay, Samantha. I've been coming here for many years. Place your hands on my back, and don't let go." She does as she's told and grips my shirt in her tiny hands. I run my hands along the wall as we go. Several minutes later, I can hear it, and so can she. The trickling sound of water. We reach the end of the crevasse. Whisps of light stream in as we squeeze through the remaining gap.

"Oh my." Her voice is low and breathy.

The cave widens to another vaulted area, but this one has an opening in the top allowing the moonlight in. Her hand is covering her mouth when she sees the small, slow-moving river running through it—a tiny waterfall on one end.

"Jake, this is incredible. Why didn't you show me this the last time we were here?"

"You hated me then…or at least pretended to."

She rolls her eyes. "Still do."

"You were also tired and scared."

She doesn't respond to that. Instead, she immediately goes to the water, sitting, she drops her feet in. I ease down beside her and while she takes in the beauty of it all, I take in the beauty of her.

I untie the small sack I had strapped to my belt and handed it to her. She rifles through all the smelly-good products she made and smiles. "Thank you. My body aches horribly from all the riding…I really needed this." Without hesitation, she stands and unlaces her dress at the top and then lifts it over her head.

My throat bobs as I try to swallow.

She drops her shift next and stands there naked with a devious smile. The moonlight on the water leaves waves dancing on her tanned skin. Her eyes glow and rival the color of the water.

"For a big, strong man, you are subdued quite easily." She saunters to the water, and my mouth goes even drier, if that's possible. I watch her hips sway as she slips in.

"Not easily…willingly," I say as I stand and undress quickly. Sam's eyes never leave me. She watches appreciatively. The only sign that she's affected by me is the red blooming on her cheeks.

When I enter the water, she immediately lathers her hands and motions for me to turn my back to her. Her fingers curl into my scalp, making me groan. I have half a mind to say the hell with it and take her right now, but I keep my patience in check. We continue washing each other in silence.

There's something to be said about the intimacy shared while bathing one another. It's personal and special. Two people baring all to each other, completely unashamed.

She turns to face me when we are finished, reaches up, and pulls my head down to hers. She kisses my scar. It brings a pang to my chest. "I want you to remember tonight, Jake. Keep it locked away in here," she places her hand over my racing heart, "forever."

"How could I ever forget," I say, my voice sounding low and gritty.

There's a moment where her eyes show signs of that anxiety from earlier. There's clearly something she wants to say, but for whatever reason...she won't.

"Just do it...keep me in your heart," she whispers.

My brows furrow, but I give her what she's asking for. I would give her the world if she desired it—lay it all at her fucking feet.

"I'll keep you in my heart forever..." I whisper back.

The Cave of Dreams

CHAPTER 42

Samantha

Jake crushes his mouth to mine, gripping my hair in one hand, his other arm clutching me to him as if I may float away at any second. We become a frenzy of hands and mouths. My nails drag down his spine, and he groans and nibbles my lower lip. His hands move to grip my ass, and then I'm lifted out of the water. Déjà vu hits me from our day in the river and I welcome it. I wrap my legs around his waist. My heart picks up as he moves us out of the water completely. A few seconds later cool stone hits my back when he presses me into the cave wall.

It's so dark in here. That trickle of moonlight illuminates the center of the area, leaving only a faint glow on Jake's back. His features almost blacked out to me. He really looks like a shadow. He repositions me, his mouth never leaving mine, and in one swift move, enters me. I moan out loud, the sound echoing off the walls. One of his hands holds me up while the other wraps into my hair again and pulls my head back. He trails kisses down my neck with each thrust, eventually licking his way back to my open mouth. My fingers sink into his wet hair, and I open for him, giving him every single piece of me tonight. I hold nothing back.

This is what dreams are made of. The electric connection buzzes between us like a live wire. Every cell in my body wants to meld into his and become one. Close isn't close enough.

I can feel the coiling inside me. My bodies reaction to this man is instant. He is like a potent elixir I can't get enough of. One of his hands snakes between us. His fingers find my center, and I whimper against his lips. His pace increases, and I throw back my head, no longer able to hold on. A moan leaves my lips just before I call out, "Jake." His mouth finds mine again as wave after wave washes over me. I tremble with the force of the orgasm.

Jake slows his rhythm slightly and grasps my chin, forcing me to look at him. "Beautiful," his deep voice rolls across me, "so damn beautiful." He presses a gentle kiss to my lips and then says, "I like watching you lose all control."

Why does his words light a fire inside me? If a match was struck near us, we would surely combust. I can't form any kind of response. I smash my mouth back to his as our tongues explore each other. His pace becomes brutal, and I revel in it. I can feel his body tensing. He groans, the sound rumbling in his chest as he finds his release. He holds me there while our labored breaths begin to ease, our foreheads resting together. I'm not sure how his legs haven't given out at this point. His head finally rises, and those eyes hold so much adoration. I press one last kiss to his lips before he settles me onto my tiptoes.

We don't say a word as we get cleaned up for a second time, but he watches me carefully. He's a smart man. He knows something is wrong, but he doesn't ask. I almost wish he would yell at me, demand to know what's wrong. It would make things easier.

Half an hour later, we're back by the fire. I make drinks for us while Jake pulls some meat off the fire. Curiously, but also thankfully, Warren isn't back yet. That would've been quite awkward had he returned. I'm sure we could be heard from here.

I've done everything in my power to shut out my thoughts—to keep my emotions at bay. Tried and failed. Today is July 28.

Tomorrow is the eclipse.

Warren and I have talked very little about it, mostly because Jake's been around every day. So, my thoughts have gone from anticipation to worry to fear to extreme sadness. It's been a roller coaster. There's no option for me or him. We have to at least *try* to go home. I have my family, and Warren has his son.

I watch my rough-and-tumble cowboy as he moves around the cave. I want to cement his face and body into my brain; Implant it so deeply that no surgery could remove it. I may lose him, but I refuse to *ever* lose these memories we've made. I will stitch them in my heart and every time I think I'm forgetting, I'll mend that stitch.

Life here before Jake wasn't living. We were just surviving. He's taken up so much of my heart that I fear it will rip apart if I do leave.

"What's wrong, Sam?"

I wipe away the single tear that I didn't realize was falling. "I'm fine."

"Come now, witch, I know you better than that. What is it that you're trying so hard to keep from me?"

My eyes shoot to his, and my brows furrow deeply. I guess he's done waiting me out and wants answers. I'm sure my face has given away the torment inside. I look down at the two whiskeys I poured and give Jake's another swirl before passing it to him. I almost don't release the glass. "I just…I," I stutter, not able to give him this closure.

His hand wraps into mine, and he pulls it to his mouth, kissing my knuckles. "Keep your secrets, Sam, if that's what you want. I've told you that…they're yours and yours alone. I just don't like seeing you like this." I watch as he takes a long swig of whiskey.

"How did we get here?" I chuckle lightly, wiping another damn tear. "The old you swore to unveil all my secrets."

"The *old* me didn't know *this*, Sam."

I swallow the lump in my throat. This man is killing me. He's ripping my soul to shreds.

"You like this Sam *now*, but what if you don't even know her?"

He moves to sit beside me and pulls my hand to his lap. "I know you, witch. *This* Sam is a woman who would risk her life for a girl she didn't even know. *This* Sam is a woman who was strong enough to survive a dangerous relationship. *This* Sam is cunning and smart. She escaped a jail cell after less than twenty-four hours. She cries for her friends, doesn't judge people by the color of their skin or by their cultures. *This* Sam loves deeply and shamelessly."

I'm biting my lip slightly when I turn to him. Full-on crying now, I grab him to me and kiss him as if it is the very last kiss we will ever share. And it likely is. When I finally pull away, I can see that he feels it too…like an impending doom settling around us. Sadness darkens his golden amber eyes.

"I like *this* Jake, too," I whisper.

"Like…"

I hesitate. The words are there, I'm just not sure If I can say them, but I don't want to lie. I want him to have *this* truth. "Love," I whisper against his lips.

"I love you too, Samantha." Jake pulls me to him, and we kiss for what feels like forever.

It's been two hours. We stayed up half the night. It won't be long before morning. I make sure that Jake is out cold. I gather what few things we'll need and place them near the cave's exit. Warren's been back for a while but stayed outside to be our lookout. When he finally comes into the cave, and the firelight hits him…he's covered in dirt.

"What were you doing?" I ask, looking him up and down.

"Nothing, just…hunting before and then sitting on the ridge," he mutters, smacking a dust cloud off his pants.

"What hunting involves rolling in the dirt?"

He rolls his eyes, but I see a smile play on his lips. "Quit eyeing me, Sam, shit, I'm just a little dusty."

"More than a little," I mutter.

I show Warren how to get to the river that runs through the cave. He starts to leave but then looks down at Jake and sees a letter folded neatly, sitting beside him.

"What the hell is that?" he whispers, coming over to me. He gets close so that if Jake wakes, he won't hear us. "Is that what I think it is?"

Red blooms in my cheeks. "I couldn't face him and tell him such a ridiculous story, Warren."

"You think a letter is the way to go. You should give it to the man straight. He deserves that...and he deserves the choice."

"What choice?" I whisper back, although I know exactly what he's saying.

"He should be able to choose whether or not he goes with us." Warren cocks his head to the side, eyeing me.

"It's a ludicrous notion." I shake my head. "He couldn't...wouldn't."

"I think you're scared."

"Scared of what?" I lower my eyes angrily.

"Scared he might choose you. Maybe you're scared that you'd feel guilty if he did."

I roll my lip between my teeth and hold back my retort. Truth is...he's right. I'm scared he would leave this place and then one day regret it. Our time is so vastly different, busy, and loud. Why would he leave this peace for that chaos?

"By the way, he's normally a light sleeper and takes watch early...why is he sleeping so hard?" Warren shifts his eyes between Jake and then back to me.

I fiddle with my nails and look *anywhere* but into those eyes drilling into me.

"Tell me you didn't, Samantha," he grinds out.

"Okay...but listen..."

"Oh my God." Warren runs a hand over his face. "You drugged your boyfriend."

"First off...he's not my boyfriend. Second, I *had* to. I *had* to give us time to leave in the morning. What if he wouldn't let me go? *And* that letter tells him everything, but also where we are going to be tomorrow. I *did* give him the choice, Warren, just not face to face."

Warren surprises me by nodding in understanding. He sighs, "I'm off to wash up. At daylight, no matter what, we're gone, Sam. I love you, girl, and I know you too well. I can tell your heart is hurting, but if he loves you, he'll be there. And I think that man loves you more than you know." He squeezes my hand before leaving me.

I'm a mess. A fucking sobbing mess. I drugged Jake…he may never forgive me for that. I should have grown a set of cojones and told him everything. I pick up the letter and head to the fire. I almost drop it. I clutch it so hard in my hand, leaving crinkles all over the paper. I curse under my breath, stomp back over to Jake, and place the letter beside him.

Hope really is a bitch.

I brush his hair back from his face, admiring his sharp jawline. "God, I'm going to miss you. Come find me, Jake."

The Letter

CHAPTER 43

Jake

I groan and flinch as my body adjusts on the hard stone floor. Everything hurts. I sit up and immediately feel an absence in the room. I jolt to my feet even though my body violently disagrees with the act. Sam's nowhere to be seen, and neither is Warren. I freeze as I take in the cave. Several of their things are missing.

"Sam!" I call out.

"What the hell? Don't do this to me Sam…" I mumble as I dart over to the crease in the wall and move through it. I check the river area thoroughly before coming back to my pallet on the floor. I'm just about to rush out of the cave when a folded paper catches my eye beside the blanket. Sam's sad eyes come back to me from last night. Her desperate kiss. With shaky hands, I grab the note and unfold it. Taking an uneasy breath, dread falling over me, I begin to read.

Jake,

I have so much to say to you, so many things that you will not fully understand. Before I give you all of me...all of my secrets, I need you to know that what I said last night was real. I do love you. I'm not sure when it happened, but I feel it deep in my bones. You have changed me in so many ways. Meeting you was fate and I'll be forever grateful for that run-in in Tucson. You came into my life and gave it meaning again.

You remember the day we met? You asked me about my gun. It's a Colt 1911. It really was my grandfather's. He died in the year 2000. I got the tattoo on my hip when I turned 21 in the year 2016. The symbol in the center is for my birth month...May. It's called Taurus.

I know that sounds insane. It's the reason I was scared to face you and tell you the truth. You wanted my secret Jake, well here it is. We are from the future. The year 2017 to be exact...

I fist the paper in my hands. "What the hell is this, some kind of joke?" My chest rises and falls as I debate reading the rest or just tracking her down right damn now and demanding the truth! "Shit," I curse and open the letter back up.

My mother's name is Camille, and my father's name is Jamie. I have a sister, Jenna. She looks so much like Nalin. There's a reason for that. Turns out Tai and Nalin are my ancestors. Warren and I were brought here for a reason. We think it was meant to be. Our being here was essential to both our family's survival in the future.

We were at Warren's shooting range the day of the total solar eclipse on August 17, 2017. I'm not sure what happened exactly, but we were both holding a very old gun, passed down for generations in Warren's family. The eclipse rolled over us and when we woke...we were here. The gun we held was the 1876 lever-action rifle made by Winchester. There was...is an engraving on the stock of the first family to own that gun. The name was Tobias, Miriam and Benji's unborn child. We came back to 1876. We've been here almost two years.

By now you are probably ready to shake me and yell at me. I know how this all sounds but try to keep an open mind. I had no hope of going back like Warren. I assumed that whatever brought us here, would keep us here. I was wrong Jake. After meeting

Judith, it all started making sense. You see, her mother was a time traveler too. Judith seemed crazy to everyone except me. I saw her truths eventually and she gave me hope again. She said you needed to pay debts to go back home. I believe saving Nalin and Warren throwing himself in front of Benji, catching that bullet, was our debts. Judith also said not to fall in love like her mother did. I can't say that I listened too well to that advice.

Today there will be another total solar eclipse. It's happening in a few hours and Warren, and I will be there...at our special place where we landed in this time.

I feel as if I'm torn into two pieces. One that wants to see her family again and hold them, and one that needs you more than the air I breathe. I love you Jake now and forever. I'll never love again. You are it for me.

I will give you a choice, it's only fair. Live your life out here in your time, or don't.

If you choose the latter, come find me Jake. You know where I'll be. Until then, keep me in your heart as I will surely keep you in mine.

All of my secrets belong to you and all of my heart

Love, Samantha Camille Thorne

P.S. I do need to apologize for something...I drugged you last night.

I stand there stunned. I could throttle her right now. That's why it's so damn late in the morning. I slept the night and most of the morning away. "Damn it, Sam!" I yell into the cave.

Do I believe a word of this...I don't know. One memory sticks out to me, the night Sam was on peyote. I recall her saying something about people not traveling on tornadoes. She mentioned some words I'd never heard before and that song she was singing was odd too. This is crazy. I'm not...there's just no way.

It takes me *very* few thoughts and seconds to decide. I begin throwing my shit together. I may not understand or believe this shit, but one thing is for certain...she is *not* leaving me like this.

I douse the fire and load up Shadow. Her hooves rip the ground apart when I sink my heels into her sides.

"I'm coming Sam. I'm coming," I whisper to the wind.

Out Of Time

CHAPTER 44

Samantha

Warren faces me and holds my hands in his. I'm shaking uncontrollably. The eclipse has already begun. Only a sliver of the sun is covered. It's hot as hell out here. Sweat beads on Warren's brow and mine.

"You ready for this?" he asks.

"No," I say honestly.

"He'll show," Warren says as if he can read my thoughts.

Will he though? Why would anyone after reading that letter? I wanted to burn it—almost did. I knew I could never convince him face to face. Leaving the letter seemed like the right thing to do at the time, but now...I'm not so sure.

I keep thinking back to all the times we crossed paths. Would I take it any of it back? No...probably not. My life is better for knowing him and I hope that I'll leave some kind of positive impact on him. He deserves so much more than my chaotic life. He deserves peace after everything he went through. If anyone in the world deserves it, it's him.

It makes me question fate though. Was this God's plan or just a cosmic loophole, either way, I can't fathom fate would have me meet the man of my dreams just to lose him so soon. That's exactly what's happening. I may never see him again. The ache in me almost has me doubling over.

I fight for composure and ask Warren, "Remember that night under the stars…after we ran into Bill and his gang for the first time?" I ask quietly.

"Of course," Warren replies.

"You asked me what I missed, and I evaded the conversation as usual. Well…I miss my family. I miss my mother, father, and Jenna. I even miss Ryan her fiancé. I miss my creature comforts from our time. I miss so much."

"*But*," he says knowingly.

"I'm going to miss him more and that makes me feel guilty." I look down at our entwined hands.

"Don't feel guilty Sam. The love you have for your family is a given. The love you fall into with a stranger is a gift. It's different."

My heart breaks with his words. "One day, we'll sit under the stars together again and I will know exactly what I'm missing out on. It terrifies me to live without him."

"He'll show Sam." Warren squeezes my hands.

"Even if he does…he can't go with us Warren. He can't leave everything behind for me."

"He's a man who can make up his own mind. You need to let him do that."

There's still a chance we're wrong, and lightning doesn't strike twice—this could very well not work today. Who knows when the next eclipse is.

I'm pondering those possibilities when Warren says, "It's getting closer to time, and we need to say our goodbyes." Warren releases me and steps toward Halle.

This is a whole other heartache. My loyal friend of two years stands beside Halle, lovingly sniffing her neck while she lays her ears back in warning. A giggle breaks free from my chest, but it's broken like me. I drop the saddle and bridle off Clint and loop the reins over his neck to lead him away. Warren follows with Halle doing the same. I knew that if I ever left, I would need to release him.

"You get to be free now boy." I lay my head against his mane and sob silently into it. "You and Halle can run together forever. The earth is your pasture now. Thank you for taking care of me." I kiss his muzzle and before I can take the reins off his neck he leans in and scratches his head up and down my side making me stumble. I smile through the tears and kiss him once more dropping the rein.

At first, the two walk around, noses to the ground nibbling on plants. Then Warren pops the leather rein he holds and waves his hands, causing them to blow from their nostrils and crow hop before galloping away.

We watch them stop several yards away and I swear Clint turns toward us one last time. His big dark eyes find me, and then they take off again.

"They'll be okay." Warren pats me on the back.

"What if they get separated, or someone mean catches them?"

"You can't think like that, so stop."

"But, what if this doesn't work? We will be stranded out here."

"*If* this doesn't work, we *will* find them."

"Ughhh," I groan and walk back to the center of the large cactuses. "Your positivity is nauseating."

Warren chuckles. "One of us has to be! Damn woman, between you and my horse, your gonna make me cry."

I give him a side smile that doesn't reach my eyes. We sit in the center of the circle we've made marking this spot with those stacked stones around the base of each plant. I tuck Jake's mother's dress under my bottom and stretch out my legs. We left everything in the cave other than our necessities. What little we are taking back is laid between us in a sack. Warren's gun with Tobias carved on the stock, along with my Colt 1911, the gift from Nalin, my dagger from Jake, and my medicinal book from Tai. Our other belongings were burned in the fire. Warren wears his brown vest over a blue shirt today and dark pants to match. His hat is tilted down in the front, blocking out the sun. He pulls a pipe from his pocket and lights it and offers me some.

"Sure." I take one puff making me cough. The rich tobacco is sweet on my tongue. "What will you miss about this place, Warren?" I ask.

He grins and takes another puff, talking through the smoke. "Halle, for sure. I'm buying a horse as soon as we get back." He laughs then thinks about my question more before saying, "I will miss the quiet."

I know exactly what he means. There's no hustle and bustle or hasn't been for us anyway. We worked hard, but it felt rewarding making a life here. It didn't feel forced like 9-5 jobs in the future. "Me too," I say.

"I hope I always remember each and every person we crossed paths with. I don't want to ever forget them."

Tai's face comes to mind, then Nalin, Myra, Judith, Benjamin, Miriam, and even the unborn Tobias. And of course, Jake. "I don't think that's possible. They'll be with us forever." I nod with certainty. I pull out the picture of my family from 2017 and flip it around in my hand nervously.

We sit there, quiet now. Waiting.

Out of nowhere, a loud explosion rocks the earth nearby. Dirt flies over us as we duck, covering our heads. My heart pounds in my chest. My ears are ringing. I can feel Warren on me, but not sure when he did that. I'm panting and coughing. We scramble up in unison, watching the dust settle. My eyes dart everywhere. Warren and I both hold our guns now aimed at nothing. The lone tree that used to be my location point from a distance, the Frémont Cottonwood tree, is blown to bits. Branches are laying haphazardly all around. I open my mouth to say something to Warren when I hear a familiar voice, causing goosebumps to break out along my skin and the hairs rise on the back of my neck.

"What do we have here." Bill laughs manically. He sits on a bay horse, shadowed by the position he is to the sun. He's flanked on either side with a few riders. One is Butter Teeth Leanard Sands, one is Charlie Mack, and the other is Denver.

Warren doesn't lower his weapon; he just steadily aims at Bill and no one else. I shift my aim to Charlie. We killed his brothers; he will not miss if he goes for me or Warren.

"Dynamite was a little much don't you think? What do you want Bill?" I grind out.

"I like a good entrance. Impressions are important. I'd like to leave a lasting one with you." He moves closer before he says, "*And* that is a funny sort of question coming from you." He bares his teeth to me as if he could eat me alive. "What do I want?" He mocks me. "What do *I* want?"

"Spit it out!" I yell.

He pulls a silver dollar from his pocket and rolls it across his knuckles, not even bothering to aim a weapon at us considering he has his three men locked on. "I want what you took from me...*everything* you took from me you hussy!" My mind goes straight for the gold that was left in the cave, but he interrupts those thoughts, "I want my life back!"

My eyes widen. The documents had to have made it. They made it. Thank you Benjamin! I chant in my head. He's ruined just like Jake wanted. That's why he's here. But how on earth did he find me?

"I don't know what you're referring to?" I lie.

All of a sudden, Bill jumps from his horse, pocketing his coin, and stomps my way. Before he can reach me, he points to Warren. "Put that gun away right now, or I give the order for them to shoot her and you! You'll watch her die first! There's three of them and one of you...she WILL die!"

I immediately lower my weapon when I see Warren hesitate. One or both of us could die here today...only minutes away from the eclipse. I decide to keep my gun aimed at Bill only. Warren cuts his eyes to me, and I look to the sky. He squints but gets my meaning. The eclipse is close. We just need to be holding that picture when it happens. Warren lowers his weapon as Bill saunters closer but stays a few feet away.

"How did you find me?" I ask, trying to prolong the inevitable.

His one brow raises, he points to the ground for me to drop my gun completely. Against my better judgment, I lower it. Bill eyes the modern pistol with interest. "You don't think Jake was my only tracker, do you?" he chuckles. It was easy enough to find the prints. We simply waited for you to emerge from that cave this morning, followed you here. I thought you were a smart girl Samantha. Why on earth did you stay around these parts? Why not flee? *Anyway*, glad you did stick around. I have to say though, I'm surprised to see that Jake isn't with you."

My mind falters. "How do you know about the cave?"

"I raised Jake, girl! I knew where he ran off to as a boy," he says, as if I should already know that. "Where is Jake?" he asks through gritted teeth.

I'm suddenly grateful for the letter I left…for drugging him. It could keep him from being here right now unless he chooses otherwise. "I don't know," I say honestly.

"You two haven't left each other's side in months, and all of a sudden, you don't know where he is!"

"I don't…I swear! We parted ways."

He looks me up and down, not buying what I'm selling. "You took everything from me. I curse the day I crossed paths with you…or *maybe* you cursed me." His eyes dart to my covered hip that has the tattoo.

"I can't help you get your life back. You did that damage all on your own." I hear Warren grunt in disapproval at me mouthing off to him, but suddenly I can't hold back. "You're responsible for forgery, the kidnapping and rape of a young girl, the encampment of several tribes, the murder of innocent people. *I* didn't ruin your life. You demolished it all by yourself."

He sneers at me. "You've done your research. However, the body count is not quite finished."

His sinister words trail like spiders down my skin. I know in my heart he will *not* let us live, even if it meant getting his gold back.

One way or another…it ends here.

The thought barely graces my mind when a shot pierces the sky making us all flinch and flit our eyes toward the ridgeline. The second shot comes fast, and I see Lenard hunched over his saddle then sliding sideways as he falls to the ground with a thud. Everything slows down as if we're moving through quicksand. Bill ducks and darts for me, staying out of Warren's line of sight. Charlie and Denver drop from their horses and head for cover.

Another shot rings out as Bill slams into me, taking me to the ground. My breath is knocked out for a moment. I gasp…then again, trying to regain air. Bill rolls until he's under me, his arms banded around me. He stands up, dragging me up with him. He has my back to his front and my pistol in his hand. Warren is aimed at us, trying to get a clear shot at Bill.

Like a shadow descending on us, a figure emerges, hidden in the rocky ridge. I recognize that silhouette the moment I see it.

It's *my* shadow…Jake.

His black cowboy hat is hung low over his eyes and his long duster jacket opens with the breeze as he walks closer, revealing his bandolier full of ammunition and weapons. He looks like a reaper come to claim his souls. Although one he's already laid claim to. Mine.

Jake keeps his distance and weaves behind some boulders, no doubt waiting for Denver and Charlie to make a move. "Let her go, Bill!" Jake growls.

"Not a chance, Jakey boy. She's my ticket out of here, and you know it. The moment I let her go, you'll shoot me dead."

"You want your gold...I can get it back to you. Release Sam!" Jake yells again.

It's strange how your mind can divert quickly to different things happening around you, even in dire situations. My mind races to process the scene. Unexpectedly, I see Shadow in the distance, running with two other horses. Is that Clint and Halle? Shadow's dark massive form recognizable anywhere. It's a majestic sight mixed inside a horrible moment. The world around us grows darker.

I look to the sky...It's coming.

Wind from nowhere whips my hair loose from the braid. The atmosphere becomes electric with tension. I know by the way Bill holds me that Jake and Warren don't have a clear shot to him. His back is towards the direction Denver and Charlie are hiding...but I know something Bill doesn't know.

He holds *my* gun. A gun he knows *nothing* about. He shifts it between Warren and Jake's location. They're my everything. My people. It gives me the strength I need to make a move. I hear the men arguing, but it's muffled. A familiar humming sound permeates the air along with buzzing in my body. It's now or never.

We're out of time!

I look Warren in the eyes and shake my head, silently pleading for him not to shoot. "Not yet," I mouth without saying the words aloud, hoping he can read my lips.

Right when Bill shifts the gun back to my temple, I slam my head backward, crushing his nose on impact. His finger pulls the trigger at the same time...or tries to.

My semi-automatic pistol falls to the ground, useless with the safety on. I had flicked it on after Bill eyed my gun, figuring he'd try to take it from me. Bill grasps for me causing us both to tumble backwards. I hear rifles firing in the distance. We hit the earth, and I scramble away from him just in time to see Warren's rifle aimed for his head.

"Don't shoot!" Bill pleads. "I'm unarmed. You can keep the gold; I'll leave, and you'll never see me again!"

I watch Warren's sweet face turn cold as ice.

"You fucked with the wrong people," Warren says calmy, then squeezes his trigger. Bill's head is flung back from the impact. Blood sprays out and covers my dress, my face...everything. His eyes are wide from shock as the life flows out of him.

Shots still ring out behind us, bringing me out of a state of shock. I dive for cover, feeling Warren tackle me at the same time. Our guns fall to the ground as we wrap our arms over our heads. Bullets fly past, sounding way too damn close.

I peek up in time to see Charlie Mack's lifeless body sitting at an odd angle against a cactus. Denver is scrambling to mount his horse. He's a good distance from us, it would be a hard shot to make from here. I snatch Warren's rifle from where it fell. Warren is dazed, the humming noise most likely becoming unbearable. He's shaking his head as if to clear it. Jake sprints for us, I can't make out what he's saying. I raise the rifle, take a deep breath, and when I release that breath, I squeeze the trigger.

The shot sounds like a crack of lightening. Denver jolts in the saddle. I can almost make out the blood staining his white shirt...directly over his heart. He slowly slumps forward, his horse rears and sends his body flinging to the ground.

I stay there, rifle aimed, chest rising and falling fast.

Warren clears his throat as he stands and looks towards Denver's limp form and whispers, "I told you... you could shoot a hair off a possum's ass from a mile away." A weak smile pulls at my cheek through the hurricane raging in my head.

Jake grabs me from behind startling me, spinning me to him. He clutches my trembling body tight to his as I drop the rifle. The humming gets louder, and I hear Warren yelling for me to move. I shake out of Jake's grip and force him to hear me, "I love you, Jake Evans! Now and over a hundred years from now. I'll love you! Forever Jake, keep me in your heart forever!"

"Don't you say your goodbyes! Damn it, Sam, what are yo—" he yells.

I kiss him hard and pull away from his grip, grab the rifle, then dash towards Warren. I snatch my Colt off the ground and shove it in my dress pocket. Warren's waiting for me in our special place. He takes the 1876 rifle and slings it to the ground between us, so we aren't touching it. He shoulders the sack with our few belongings. Tears pour endlessly down my face as I try to catch my breath. I shuffle through debris on the ground and find the picture, gripping it tight. Warren's eyes are squinting. He must hear the humming growing louder too. He latches his fingers onto the photo as well.

Pain lances my nerve endings as the light of the day fades. Our bodies are trembling violently. I vaguely hear Jake screaming for me. I think I'm screaming too. It feels like I'm being ripped apart from the inside out. Each minuscule cell in my body is stinging and on fire.

Just when I feel like I can't take anymore...like I'm about to combust, something slams into us.

Back to the Future

CHAPTER 45

Samantha

I heave and gag, clutching my abdomen. The world around me is blurry when I force open my scratchy eyes. Stars dot my vision and have to blink rapidly to focus. I'm trembling, feeling as if I'm severely hungover. My head pounds to the sound of distant music. I close my eyes again and breathe in through my nose and out through my mouth for several minutes until the nausea subsides. I feel like I've been hit by a damn bus.

On shaky limbs, I try to rise but stumble and fall. "Warren," my voice croaks out.

I hear the shuffling of dirt near me. "I'm here." His voice sounds as bad as mine. He vomits somewhere nearby making my nausea return.

The music comes back to me. It's *Coming Undone* by Korn. The beat blaring loudly and thudding along with my nerves. My heart skips a beat, and I push and fight against my weak legs until I'm finally standing. Sweat makes my torn dress stick to me in places as I stagger several steps. I see Warren hunched over not far from me.

"You okay?" I ask.

"Almost," he mumbles.

My eyes adjust, and I inhale in a deep shocked breath. A variety of targets are scattered around an open field. I almost don't believe it. Standing there, both my hands over my mouth in shock, I squeal an unusual sound. I spin left and right a few times to take it all in and then squeal again. I'm facing the gun range. I turn and see the armory behind me in all its glory. "Warren, we did it!" I holler the best I can as my voice tries to adjust.

He must hear it too—the music. His body tenses. He looks over his shoulder from where he's crouched to see the range. "Holy shit," he pants, "we did it!" He scrambles to his feet and rushes to me. He's bent with his hands on his knees when he says breathlessly, "I'd pick you up and squeeze you if I could."

Tears spring to my eyes, and as soon as Warren is standing upright, I wrap him in a gentle hug. "I can't believe it," I cry. "We're back."

Instantly my euphoria fades when my last moments in the Wild West return to me. I release Warren, and a stunned, silent ache seeps into my stomach. Jake. He came for me, saved our lives by showing up when he did. I ran from him. He was pleading for me not to go. I could only catch a few of his words. The damn humming was so loud. He was devastated…that much was obvious. But he came for me. I grab my chest as if my heart could actually burst and kill me dead right here and now from the pain.

Warren wraps me in his arms again and pulls my head to his shoulder. "We had no choice Sam…we had no choice."

I know he's right, but it doesn't make this any easier. It's like a piece of me was torn at the seams and tossed to float in the wind.

Warren pulls away and lifts my trembling chin until I face him. "You did what you had to do for your family here. This pain you feel. I felt pain like that once. The loss of my wife, Birdie, almost killed me. You know what, though," he pauses until my watery eyes meet his again, "you have me to lean on."

I nod my head, even though I feel like curling up into a ball and disappearing.

"We need to go inside and check the date and time." His brows furrow.

He's right. I can wallow in self-pity later. We need to know the date.

We take a few steps toward the back entrance. I freeze. I stop breathing, and my mouth drops open when I hear someone else groaning. Warren's eyes meet mine, and we turn back around and dart toward the sound.

There, hidden behind one of the targets, is a body. We can only see a boot stuck out. We both creep up silently. A black cowboy hat is lying on the ground, not far away from the man. My heart pounds with adrenaline, but also with that damn hope. We move around the target and see *him*.

"Oh. My. God," I whisper. "Jake?"

He eases onto his knees and then sits back on his heels, swiping a hand over his face. I can tell his vision is just beginning to clear. "Sam?"

I bound to him in one leap and slam my body into his, almost tipping us over as we are both now on our knees. He holds me tight and then squeezes even tighter. The last minute of the eclipse was a blur, but I thought something had hit us. It was Jake. He's here…in my arms. I shake with the sobs coming from me and try to form words. "Jake, why did you…what are you doing here?"

He pulls away to take in my face. His eyes travel over it as if he's trying to make sure I'm not injured and then finally they meet mine. "I told you…you and I would *never* be done, witch." He kisses my forehead and pulls me against his chest. "What the hell happened?" he asks into my hair.

I take in a deep breath. "A lot happened."

Warren interrupts us, "Glad to see you in all Jake, but we need to check the date Sam." Warren ushers me to rise, bringing Jake with me.

"The date?" Jake asks, brows raised.

Warren and I glance to each other. "We'll explain everything," I say. I hold out my hand to him and he takes it. We all turn to walk toward the armory. I find Warren's gun, my dagger, the medicinal book, and my family photo and bring them along. Jake stops dead in his tracks, finally taking in his surroundings. His eyes widen, and then his brows crease. I tug him along. "Like I said, a lot has happened…in around a hundred and forty years." He cuts his eyes to me, but I keep moving. Now is not the time to have the *long* talk.

We step foot into the back entrance, and immediately, the air-conditioned room slaps me in the face, and I let out a moan. The large shopping area looks the same. Guns and bows line the walls, shelves full of ammunition, and the long glass counter displays various knives and pistols inside. Jake stands outside the door, touching it gently but not moving. He shifts his head around until he locates the speaker that's still blaring Korn. I tip my head toward the Bluetooth for Warren to shut it down.

It's too much to take in for him. I remember well my feeling when I woke up in 1876. Thinking of dates brings me back to the present.

We let Jake wander around but keep an eye on him as we head to the counter. There, still in the last place he left it, is Warren's cellphone. He immediately kills the music and turns it to me, showing the date and time.

It's August 17, 2017.

"It's the day we left," I whisper.

"Sure is *and* only an hour past the eclipse." Warren grins.

Rightness washes over me. It's a feeling that's hard to explain. I shake my head, looking around. "Everything is just how we left it." Except us, I think to myself.

"Even down to the glasses we sipped from before we went out to shoot." Warren points to them on the little table.

I smile. "I don't even know who that Sam was anymore."

Warren pulls a bottle from behind the counter and walks over, pouring three shots instead of two this time. He pulls out some peanuts that he must have had stashed under the counter and sets them in the center. "Well, I do remember her. And you two are not as different as you'd like to think." He motions for me to sit. I notice Jake catches my eye and he comes to sit too. Still completely shell-shocked. Warren continues, "That Sam was brave enough to leave her shitty boyfriend and strong enough that I knew she would have *never* gone back."

I choke down the knot in my throat and look between Jake and Warren. "I'll drink to that." I tap their glasses with mine, and we all down them. Warren and I laugh when we see Jake's reaction to Jack Daniels Fire…or lack thereof, considering how weak it is compared to the whiskey he's used to.

"I'm gonna need y'all to catch me up on…everything," Jake says, sounding defeated.

I nod and purse my lips. "Let's start with a hot shower, tons of food, and new clothes. Then we can talk," I say, looking down at the dried blood splattered all over my dress. Bill's blood. I shudder. Then a thought hits me, one that I've had many times before. It's why I was terrified to tell Jake about me or to ever have him *try* to come with me. "Are you sure you did the right thing by following us?" I ask, not able to meet his eyes for fear of what I'll see lingering in them. Instead, I toy with ripped fabric on my dress. I have strong guilt forming deep inside, and I knew I would.

Jake towers over me with his tall frame even when we are sitting. He leans in, brushing a stray hair from my face. "I'm right where I want to be, beside you."

We spend another hour there, shelling peanuts and sipping whiskey before we finally decide to tackle the hard stuff. The hard stuff being deciding where we'll stay for now and getting Jake acclimated to this strange new life. Not to mention, we eventually need to get our hands on some illegal documentation for him.

First things first, we need a place to stay. I ran from Trevor, and he owned the apartment. Therefore, I technically have nowhere to go other than my parents' farm...and that is *not* happening today. After throwing out ideas, Warren offers up his place, and we readily agree to stay there temporarily.

I let the guys finish talking over a few things inside, and I excuse myself. I tuck my dagger into the leather belt around my waist. I head straight for the parking lot and break into a run when I see my Chevelle is still there. I slide to a halt admiring her beauty. "Damn girl, I missed you," I say as I run my fingers down the flat black paint, now dusty from the desert breeze. I notice something is missing and look up to see the cottonwood tree is gone. "Oh, shit," I say, "the dynamite."

I open the heavy antique door to air out my car when I hear tires screeching. I dart my eyes to the road just as a blue BMW, I know all *too* well, slides to a stop and then spins into the armory's parking lot. This is definitely unexpected. Not even two hours back home and *this*...ugh. I look up to the sky and ask, "Is this some kind of joke?" Then my eyes fall back to the car, "How did *he* find me?" It makes me wonder if he'd been tracking me all along.

I clench my fists and stand tall. This time not feeling the least bit afraid of him. I cross my arms over my chest and wait for him to come to me.

Trevor slides out of the car and slams the door as hard as he can. He's not as big as I once thought him to be. I guess being with someone more intimidating will have that effect on your perceptions. His sandy blond hair is tucked under a black BMW hat, and his polo and khakis look too pristine for this setting.

"What are you doing here?" I ask pointedly as if he's a major inconvenience to my day…which he is.

Trevor stops when he gets within a few feet of me, anger is blazing in his eyes. "Is this a fucking joke, Sam?"

"That's so funny, I was just asking the same question," I mock smile.

His jaw clenches and he waves his hand gesturing to the building. "What the *FUCK* are you doing here?" he snarls. "Are you…" He trails off as his eyes finally take in my appearance.

My dress is dirty, tattered, and covered in dried Bill blood. My half-braided hair is tan from dust and I'm sure there's blood there *too*. My skin is much darker than last he saw me…a few hours ago for him. The makeup I wore that day, gone, along with the bruises he left all over me. And not to mention the black eye. From my skin to my clothes, and everything in between…

I'm sure it's quite the shock.

"I'm exactly where I want to be, Trevor. Away from you. You need to leave if you know what's best for you."

He shakes his head, looking at the bloodied dress. "What the hell happened to you?"

"You mean to tell me; my appearance bothers you *now*? You hit me in the face, remember? Where was your concern then?" His lips pull back, but I just love to add salt to wounds. "You are nothing but a small-minded narcissistic man who could never *truly* love a woman the way she deserves."

He takes a step forward. "Is there someone else?"

"You always were the jealous one." I roll my eyes and dust off my dress, ignoring his hostile tone.

"Fucking hell, Sam!" he yells, making me flinch. "I came here to get you back. I love you. I will *not* fucking leave here without you! Get in the car! You can explain yourself later."

I grin when he gets closer to me and tilt my head like a predator eyeing its prey. This douchebag has no clue what I've been through over the last two years. I'm not the same woman nor even the same damn age that I was before. "I owe you *no* explanation, and Trevor...you have no idea what love is. Don't go throwing words around that you don't understand."

I hear the door to the armory swing open, indicating my guys have finally heard the commotion. But this is my fight...no one else's. Trevor takes a step closer, his eyes darkening, not caring who's headed our way. I wait for him to lunge for me the way he used to. I know it's coming. "I *do* love you Sam. I need you to come home." He steps closer again.

"The thing is Trevor, I don't need you anymore...nor do I want you, so no. The answer is no." I say flatly.

He lowers his voice, "I'm not leaving without you." He grabs for me and when he does I dodge his hands causing him stumble.

My dagger is drawn and the tip pressed to his neck as quickly as he spins to face me.

He laughs and then sneers at me, "What is this? Huh? You gonna stab me Sam?"

Sweat rolls down my spine and my jaw hurts from clenching it tightly. I don't answer. Something has taken over me. I press the tip closer, and he tries to back up, but bumps into my car. Blood dots his neck.

"What the hell Sam?! Have you lost your mind?" Trevor has his hands up in surrender now.

Through my quiet rage, I hear Warren talking to me. His words finally making it through to my foggy brain. I don't even know how long they've been standing there. "We're in a different place now, Sam…you can't kill him." He tries to soothe me, but my thoughts dart back to each and every time this motherfucker laid a hand on me.

"He'll do it again…they always do. I won't be his last." My voice sounds strained even to my own ears.

"You still can't kill him," Warren says, trying to reason with me.

Trevor's eyes move from me to the men at my back. "Put the it down Samantha," He asks more calmly.

My hands, which were steady moments ago, begin to shake as I force myself to pull the blade away.

Before Trevor can begin to speak, Jake has him by the neck and slams him to the ground. Jake's knees press into him and his hand remains around his throat. Trevor lets out a string of choked out curses.

"Let him up Jake," I say. "He's learned a lesson here today. One I hope he never forgets."

When Jake releases his grip on Trevor's neck, he scrambles to his feet. Jake moves to me checking me over from head to toe before wrapping an arm around my shoulders. I can see the wheels turning fast in Trevor's mind, trying to decipher what cowboy reenactment I've gotten myself into. Hatred oozes from him as his eyes linger on the arm draped over me. Trevor rubs his neck and says, "Who the hell are you?" His eyes dart to Jake, then me. His face reddens. "So, this is who you're fucking! I *knew* it. I *knew* there was someone else." He growls.

Jake's arm moves from me. "Can't kill him…but" Jake grins, shrugs, and then haymakers Trevor. The crack of knuckles on bone is cringe worthy. Trevor falls onto his ass with a grunt. Blood streams from his broken nose as he moans and spits.

Warren steps up beside Jake and says to Trevor through gritted teeth, "You're done here, boy. If we *ever* see your face round here again…well, let's just say it won't be the first body I've buried lately." Warren spits at Trevor's feet, and I see Trevor's eyes widen.

Trevor stands and backs away from us—confusion marring his features. His eyes linger on mine a little too long. I can *almost* see that side of him trying to come through, the one that always came through after a fight. The fake side that liked to say sorry and buy flowers to make up for the abuse. Gut punch…here's a flower, Slap…let me buy you dinner. What a loser.

I wink at him and then lift onto my toes and kiss the side of Jake's cheek just to piss him off more. Jake looks on at him murderously without flinching, and so does Warren.

Trevor sees that kiss for what it is. Finality. He's done...like Warren said.

It took us a while to quit laughing after he left. My heart felt lighter than it ever had inside my chest. Warren and Jake...my guys. The love I have for them threatens to implode inside me. They joked nonstop about me being terrifying now after the dagger scene. When the shock of the Trevor episode wore off, we had the shock of cars to explain to Jake. We did so for a good thirty minutes before saying screw it and told him it was time to go. He was just going to have to go into this blind.

I pull out of the armory heading away from the sunset and leaving the past behind me. I slow, then downshift, releasing the clutch and smashing the gas pedal simultaneously, I burn the tires off my Chevelle, making Jake grab onto the dash and holler, his eyes the widest I've ever seen. Warren laughing hysterically from the backseat.

Might as well break him into the twenty-first century the right way.

Warren waits until we are a few miles from his business and says, "Oh, by the way," he smiles smugly at me in my rearview mirror, making me wonder what the hell he's about to say, "buying a place of your own shouldn't be a problem."

"How so?" I ask. "That sounds nice and all, but I'm kinda broke," I say, laughing.

He winks. "How does buried treasure sound?"

Movie Night

Epilogue

April 7, 2024

Samantha

Life is a cataclysm of events that alter your course *and* your destiny. No one knows this better than me. We've been here for almost seven years now. *Seven.* Sometimes, I have to look in the mirror and remind myself that this is real. Happiness can seem like a fantasy that's just out of reach, but it's there looking back at me in my reflection.

I brush my long hair, leaving it down tonight. My skintight brown patch wranglers sit low on my waist. I lace my leather belt through the loops and tuck my Ariat boots inside the flared jeans. My baby blue tank top sits just above the top of my jeans. I gently touch the line of bracelets ringing my arm, given to me by the

Apache children. I wear them almost daily. I head for the porch, stopping to grab my phone, tucking it into my back pocket. It's nice outside this evening. We have company coming by for a movie night. Warren helped Jake build and set up a lounge area out by the barn. It's a covered patio, with rock pillars and a fireplace. We have an outdoor cooking corner and bar with a hidden fridge. We light up the projector on nice evenings to watch movies and crack open a few cold ones. It may be our favorite place on the farm now. We spend as much time in that barn as we do our house.

I lean against the railing of our wrap-around porch, crossing my arms as I watch Jake. He just finished getting dressed before me. Now, he's sweeping the lounge area. His taut muscles defined through the white tee he's wearing. His cowboy hat hung low as usual. He's so handsome it hurts. He still manages to make me blush and fluster me to no end.

He got used to the clothing fairly quickly, although he'll not part with some of his signature pieces, like the hat and the duster. I wouldn't have it any other way. They're a part of who he is.

The sound of tires on gravel catches my attention. I see Warren pulling up in his brand-new Ford F250 with Carla by his side. They get out and I'm shocked when his son Miles and Mile's wife Gloria hop out, along with Warren's first grandchild, Benjamin Tobias Mathews. A smile pulls at my cheeks. I blot my watery eyes, not wanting to ruin what little makeup I have on. Warren shared their unique ancestry and connection to

Benjamin and Tobias with his son. Miles became a little obsessed with the history, and when they knew Gloria was having a boy…Warren may have put a little birdie in Miles's ear about what to name him. Thankfully, Gloria loved it, and that was that.

I keep watching them, not wanting to join just yet. They walk over to Jake, and little Benjamin, who's three now, walks straight into Jake's waiting arms. We visit the graves of Benjamin, Miriam, and Tobias once a year now. The rifle of Warren's will one day pass down to his grandson.

Life goes in a full circle, doesn't it?

Can you die from happiness, I wonder? It sure feels like my heart has reached its peak of fullness. Like it would be impossible to squeeze in one more blessing. I close my eyes and remember what it took to get us here today. Not just everything that happened in the past but everything since coming back.

The day we left the armory, we could all feel the shift in the air. It was palpable. Our lives were forever changed. We stayed with Warren, but not for long. Turns out, Warren was not just filthy from hunting our last night in that cave. His sneaky ass had buried the gold Jake gave to us, along with a few other things…just in case we *actually* made it back. We had enough money between us to do whatever the hell we wanted. The thing was, Jake and I didn't want…nor need a huge mansion on a hill somewhere. We wanted a farm, and I knew the perfect one.

We purchased my parents' farm from them, giving them plenty of money to do what they have always dreamed of doing…traveling the world. We, of course, built them a house on the property for when they *do* decide to return from time to time. We also purchased Jake's old family land and built a log cabin out there. The house was long gone, but Jake seemed at peace about it. We have proper grave markers under the tree where he buried his family. It's serene out there, and it no longer holds bad memories for Jake. No. It holds so much more than that now.

It's where we spend most of our summers fishing, hunting, riding horses, and simply living. When we get a few moments alone…we go to the river. To the place we first made love, and we fall back into each other, the passion never subsiding.

I had to make up quite a few lies in the beginning to family members, like where Jake and I met, what happened with Trevor, and why I looked different. We went with a simple explanation. Jake stepped in when Trevor raised his voice to me in a bar. I was unhappy with Trevor and after a few more dates, Jake and I hit it off. Jake and Warren were friends from the range. So…not all lies. I did actually see Jake for the first time *in* a bar and Warren and him *are* friends. And Jake saved me the moment I met him, maybe not from Trevor, but in every way a soul can be saved. As far as my looks go, I told them I'd been tanning and lightening my hair. It was enough to stop all the questions.

My mother's Porsche pulls into the drive next. She and Dad are overdressed as usual these days. Once they started traveling, their wardrobes began to match whatever country they'd been to last. Tonight, they look Italian...and *too* expensive for a barn party. Mom hugs Jake's neck and kisses his cheek. She absolutely loves him. I never told my parents about everything that happened with Trevor. I figured it would break their hearts and cause unnecessary pain, seeing as how I've moved on and am better for it. I guess I should be thanking that loser because if it weren't for that fateful day that I ran from him, none of this would be possible.

Jenna and Ryan pull in next in Ryan's older restored Bronco. Their daughter Camille is six now. She bolts from Jenna and makes a beeline for her Nanna. Jenna named her after Mom and *wow*, those two are inseparable. Her pink frilly dress flares out as Mom spins her in a circle.

My cell rings from my back pocket, and I answer it quickly, seeing it's from my employee Rachel. "Hey, what's up?"

"Just checking to see if you want me to open up for you tomorrow. I know you have a family gathering tonight, and I figured you could use the rest."

Damn I love her. "Oh, Rach, yes. Please. That would be wonderful." I sigh with relief.

"No problem, girl, have fun. See you whenever you get there tomorrow."

"See ya, bye." I hang up and slip the phone back into my pocket.

Rachel has been such a lifesaver. I immediately dropped money into remodeling and revamping Emerald Moon Apothecary once we purchased the farm. By 2018, it was up and running. It's everything I dreamed of and more with the Western/hippie/dark witchy vibes. The front room is large and open with shelves lining every wall full of herbs and tinctures. Plants for sale and some for looks hang in each window and some vines line the walls. Every gemstone known to man is displayed and labeled in glass cases. One corner houses my hanging dried herbs and bundles for smudging. Once you step into the back room, down a set of stairs, it opens up to a coffee bar and floor-to-ceiling bookshelves. The rust-colored plush chairs and rattan ottomans are strategically placed for people to stay and read while they enjoy the view from the large back glass windows overlooking the desert. Out back, I have a covered deck with round tables and chairs and a wine bar. It's perfect. Some days, Jake and I stay there past closing and sit under the moon, basking in her glory.

Being there reminds me of Tai and Nalin. If it wasn't for the knowledge in his book, I wouldn't have half the recipes I do now. I dedicated one area to them, displaying Native American traditions and relics.

A week after we were back home, I met up with Jenna for lunch at Joel's Pizza Parlor. I think I ate an entire pie myself that day. I remember almost choking on a piece when I saw the necklace she was wearing. It was the one that I gave Nalin, the one that used to belong to me. The large Labradorite stone was practically glowing. When my eyes raised to hers that day, I could see Nalin looking back at me. Tears sprung to my eyes, and I recall quickly wiping them away. Nalin had to of passed that necklace down through the family line. The odd thing is, that necklace was purchased by my mother from a gem mine when she was a teenager. Now, that iridescent stone has made it full circle…like us. Jenna recognized the pain in my eyes, even though it was brief. She was the one person that pressed me the most. Sisters have a keen eye when it comes to their siblings. She knew something was off about me, but I could never tell anyone the truth, not even her. Still can't. These are my secrets and mine alone, as Jake used to tell me. Some things are truly best left unsaid.

I walk back into the house to grab my flannel in case it gets chilly tonight. Leaving our bedroom, I pause and look at the framed wanted poster hanging above the nightstand. Really horrible sketches of Warren, Jake, and I stare back at me. I giggle, covering my mouth with my hands. We keep this here for laughs but tell everyone it was a joke, and we had it made in a tourist shop for old-timey pictures. It was packed away along with all Bill's gold.

Well, *our* gold now. Bill's name died out long ago. I managed to find a few records of his traitorous and unthinkable deeds, but not much. His band off assholes were never mentioned. I guess the shootout at the OK Corral later on was more dynamic and wiped away Bill being the biggest outlaw to have ever ridden into town. William Evans is a name long forgotten by everyone except us.

I shrug off the past and go back to the porch to watch my family laugh and clink drinks. It looks like from here that they're selecting a movie. I begin heading that way. I get a whiff of some pastries my sister is passing out to the kids, and it immediately takes me back to Myra's bakery. I could never find her grave, nor Judith's. I assume they were buried on their own land, like many people did back then. I always wondered if Myra forgave me for drugging Dale and if they ever married. I'll likely never know. I *was* able to find records of a missing woman from 1990. Her name was Patricia Lambert. When I saw the photo I *knew*, without a doubt, it was Judith's mother. She looked just like her. Same eyes, short stature, and hair. She disappeared on an eclipse that year and was never seen again. But I know where she went and that it was love that kept her there. Sometimes I wonder if I hadn't had Warren with me, would I have stayed too?

I would like to think that this version of my reality is what it was meant to be.

I reach my family, and we all talk over each other as we say our hellos and share hug after hug. Smiles and laughs are abundant as we catch up on life. Camille's wiggly loose tooth, remodeling woes in Ryan and

Jenna's house, work stories from Deadeye Armory, foods in Italy, and everything in between.

My eyes naturally scan the area for my shadow, but he's nowhere to be seen. Warren walks up to me while no one is around and hands me a beer. "I brought you something."

I side-eye him. "Really, what's that?"

He pulls a novel from his jacket pocket, handing it to me. I flip it over. The cover has flames licking up the sides, with a man carrying a, what looks to be, an unconscious woman. The man carrying her is standing in front of an old Mustang. "Looks interesting." I say, brows raised.

"This couple came to the range today to shoot. I got to talking and bullshitting with them. Names were Callon and Maisy. They were maybe mid-forties or so." He takes a swig of his beer. "Anyway, he used to be in the service, and so we shared some stories, but his wife, Maisy, she wrote this here book. Said it was based on her life when she was younger. I thought you might like it. I know how you like to keep your nose in a book."

"Warren, this is really cool. Thank you." I flip open the book to see that it's signed to me, Samantha Camille Evans with love…Maisy Wolfe.

Warren taps his finger to the signature. "She signed me a copy too."

"I've never had a signed novel before. This is kinda awesome." I hug him for his thoughtful gift and place the book on the bar.

He's quiet for a beat, then says, "It's a nice damn day, isn't it?" He grins, clinking his bottle to mine.

I slap my hand over my mouth, laughing and remembering my dear old friend Judith. "Why yes, it is...a nice damn day Warren."

"Where is Judith, by the way?" Warren asks. "I haven't got my chastising from her yet." I laugh, and my eyes dart around the yard and out to the pasture. "She's been with her daddy all day. You know how she is...a daddy's girl through and through."

Warren and I walk to the edge of the barn and look toward the back pasture. Jake is laughing at something Judy's said, probably something she *shouldn't* have said. She's a feisty one. Jake is squatting down, picking a flower, and he sticks it behind her ear. The yellow of the petals contrasting drastically with her long, dark brown hair. She has her daddy's hair for sure, but my blue-green eyes. She just turned four.

Behind them, I see Midnight and Dirty Harry, our mare and gelding. Midnight is as black as Shadow was. I bought her for Jake a year after we got the farm. I knew how much he missed riding. I got Dirty Harry from the same ranch so that they could remain together. He's not a dappled gray like my Clint was. He's a buckskin, but he has every bit the heart Clint had. I named him that from one of the Clint Eastwood movies I grew up on. Everyone hates the name but me.

Just then, I see Kurt carrying a bucket toward Midnight.

"Jake," I call to him and point toward our son.

Jake smiles but doesn't stop him. Kurt Warren Evans is a menace to society. He's a Taurus like me and every damn bit as stubborn. His dark hair is ruffled, sticking out every which way, and his golden eyes are alight with mischief when he looks at me from a distance. He places the bucket beside Midnight and hikes up his little wrangler jeans as he climbs, first onto the bucket, and then gives a big leap and hangs half on her and half off. Jake is laughing when he tosses Judy on his shoulders and goes over to Kurt, lifting him the rest of the way. Midnight stands there, used to the kid's abuse by this point.

He's almost six now—born around eight months after we got back. One day, we'll tell him about the uncle he was named after. Jake's little brother...gone far too soon. What he'll never know is that he, too, was a part of the Wild West. We just didn't know it yet. I was terrified when I found out I was pregnant. All manner of dreadful thoughts had me up at night. I was so afraid that the travel through time would have affected him in some way...but it didn't. Jake and I married right after the birth.

"Man, they're just perfect, Sam," Warren says, bringing me out of my thoughts.

"No kidding." I lean against him while we watch Jake lift Judy onto Dirty Harry. I thought I loved Jake before but seeing him with his children...that's a different love—a deeper love.

I let them ride for five minutes before it's time for the movie. All the kids are piled around a fire, roasting marshmallows with Mom and Dad. Warren is tucked in a chair with Carla. She blushes when he whispers something to her, and I look away from the intimate conversation. Jenna has her head on Ryan's shoulders. Miles is eating his burger, and Gloria is snapping photos of the kids.

I'm lying across Jake's lap as we watch the movie. Warren decided we needed a Western. I could disagree, but what the hell? The movie Young Guns kicks off. The more I watch, the more engrossed I become. Emilio Estevez plays the role of William H. Bonney...better known as Billy the Kid.

A while into the film, I start seeing some strangely familiar mannerisms from the lead character. I sit straight up in the chair, shoving off Jake. My brows furrowed deep.

"You okay? What is it?" Jake asks.

Everyone's eyes shift to me. "Oh, no, just remembered...I need to make a phone call...work thing." I rush out of the barn making subtle eye contact with Jake and Warren as I go, hoping they get the gesture. Once outside and hidden from ears and eyes, I drag out my cell and type in William H. Bonney. My heart skips a beat, and my mouth hangs open. The first photo I see of him sends me back there. The day of the townwide celebration, the young quick draw, my partner in crime escaping jail.

"Holy shit," I mutter.

"What is it?" Warren asks, fast walking to me, Jake on his heels.

I flip my phone to them so that they can see the old black and white photo. "*This* is Billy the Kid."

Jake looks confused, but Warren's eyes widen. "That's the kid from the gun show…the one that winked at you."

"Also, the one that I helped escape…*and* he later saved my life."

"Damn, that's heavy." Warren rubs down his beard.

My mind is reeling. If I would have known who he was…would I have released him? I'm not sure. I'd probably be dead now if it wasn't for him, so I'm glad I did. Also, glad he never gave me his name, just always said "*I'm everyone and no one.*" It makes more sense now. He was always wearing disguises with fake names attached to escape the lawmen.

"I always wondered what happened to that guy after you told me about him," Jake adds.

"Yeah, me too. I *aided* the escape of Billy, the *freakin'* kid!" I say trying to keep my voice down. I'm frozen in place as I recall each and every detail of our time together.

The guys stare at me, but then the seriousness is lost. I break and start hoarse laughing, causing them to join in. I hold my tummy, doubled over with the giggles. Through tears of laughter, I say, "I got *undressed* in front of him…and wore his clothes."

Jake stops laughing, cutting his eyes to me, which only makes Warren, and I become more belligerent.

It's nighttime. Everyone has gone home, and the kids are tucked in bed. Jake and I sit on the back porch, watching the horses in the moonlight. It's so quiet here. Peaceful. Reminds me of my time in the past.

"Tomorrow is another eclipse," I say softly.

"I know, heard your sister talking about it," Jake says.

"They asked if we wanted to get together again and watch it," I say lightly.

"And…" Jake asks, his full attention on me now.

I snort. "I said no, of course, but Warren overheard the conversation and said *HELL* no."

Jake sighs in relief. "Good, I'd hate to have to tie you down in the basement until it's over."

"Jake…don't tempt me with a good time," I say, trying to be sexy, making him grin.

Jake is quiet for a while, and then I hear him snicker.

"What is it?"

"Did you know that your daughter told Warren that he should've brought her a BB gun today?" Jake asks.

"My daughter, huh?"

"Yeah, when she gets mouthy…she's yours. Sounds just like you."

I chuckle. "What did Warren say?"

"He's bringing her one tomorrow."

"Oh my God, what a pushover." I roll my eyes.

"She hid white sage in Kurt's underwear drawer today, too."

"What?" I dart my eyes to his.

He laughs, running a hand over his face in exasperation. "She said it makes negative energy go away, and her brother was *negative* energy."

I wheeze laughing, hand over my mouth, trying to be quiet so I don't wake the kids. When the giggles finally subside. I groan and compose myself. "She needs to stop going to work with me."

"I agree…I think *one* witch in the family is enough." Jake smirks.

I drop my mouth open feigning being offended. "If I was a witch, I would have cursed you long ago." I smirk back.

Jake jumps from the chair and grabs me before I can flee. My squeal carries on the breeze when he throws me over his shoulder, walking fast until we reach the barn. He tosses me on the hay as I swear under my breath. "You are an exasperating man." I huff.

He plops down between my legs, lowering his body onto mine. The weight of him pinning me down. My legs automatically wrap around him. He playfully bites my lower lip, his eyes growing darker. "You know, I think you *did* put a spell on me long ago, woman."

"Just now figuring that out, huh?" I kiss him softly and then pull away to watch the glow from the moonlight in his whiskey eyes.

"I would gladly stay spellbound to you for eternity." His voice is low and gravelly.

"The feelings mutual my handsome cowboy." I give him a wink.

"Is this peyote Sam talking?"

I laugh, "No this is *just* Sam talking." I kiss him softly and then ask, "You ever miss it? Your time."

Jake's side smile pulls at my heart. I've asked him a thousand times. Always insecure…as if I stole a life from him.

"Never," he says, "but you know how this game is played between us, right? A truth for a truth."

I purse my lips, tilting my head when I ask, "Okay, what is it you want to know?"

"The night we met, until now. Do *you* regret any of it?"

I roll my lip between my teeth, and Jake's eyes fall to my mouth, making my body temperature rise. I lift his hat off his head and toss it aside. Running a hand through his short beard, I whisper, "Not one bit."

He crushes his mouth to mine, and I moan into his. I could kiss this man every second of every day. His scent lingers on me when he pulls away and says, "You stripped away the darkness that hung like a cloud over me. You are my light. The day I met you, I was reborn, and my true life began. The one I was meant to live. I think I've loved you for a long time, and maybe I was waiting for you to find me."

His deep words penetrate my heart and settle there, taking root. "How am I supposed to top that?" I whisper as I drop little kisses onto his cheek and then his lips.

"No need. You can owe me one." He smiles.

My brow raises and heat flushes my cheeks as the day we met floods my memory. "A debt huh? How will I ever repay you?"

He becomes ravenous as he gives me a wolfish grin. "I can think of a few ways."

I bite my lip and then lean in for a long kiss.

This is one debt...I *don't* mind paying; I think to myself.

The End...

Turn the page for a short bonus chapter ;)

Bonus Chapter

December 2017

Jake

"This is not funny Sam." I try to make my voice serious, but she's making it hard for me to be convincing.

Her giggles subside, but only slightly. "It's kinda funny."

She taught me how to drive one of her old farm trucks a few months back. It didn't take me too long to master the automatic. I've been obsessed with cars and trucks since the day she forced me into hers outside the armory my first day here. But…*now* she's got me in her rolling death trap of speed. I *love* it…but she doesn't need to know that. We've been on this dirt road for an hour practicing shifting gears. I just stalled it out…again.

Warren's also been with me several times a week to give me a run-down of historic events or to teach me tools and their uses. I even learned all about tractors and can handle ours pretty well on the farm.

This car though…it's insane.

"Oh, come on…try again." Her sickly sweet smile has me wanting to bend her over my knee.

I huff and roll my shoulders. I press in the clutch like she showed me, keeping one foot on the break, and then turn the key. The engine roars to life. I swear this thing is part beast.

"Put it in first and slowly relea…"

"I know, I know," I take a deep breath. I ease the gas pedal down while slowly releasing the clutch. We move forward. "Okay, this is good." I say it more to myself than to her. I hear the peak the engine gets too, indicating it's time to shift and I do so smoothly.

I do this three more times until I reach fifth gear, and we are cruising at a decent pace. My knuckles turn white from my death grip on the steering wheel.

"You're doing wonderful babe!" She yells over the loud engine.

A grin splits my face. I glance over as she closes her eyes. Her right arm is hanging out the window—fingers dancing on the wind. Her left hand makes slow circles on her belly. She's due sometime around May.

If someone had told me a year ago what my life would look like now…I'd have laughed in their face. It's unimaginable, but it's real. I'm with this amazing woman who is about to be the mother of our child, driving a muscle car in the year 2017.

Every night, before bed, I give thanks for my blessings because they are plentiful.

I stall out one more time on a hill, before finally getting the hang of it. After another hour, Sam has deemed me worthy to borrow her baby to drive sometime.

"Your turn." I say as I hop out of the car and switch places with her. I give her backside a firm smack as we pass each other making her squeal.

She knows what I'm wanting. I don't need to ask.

She situates herself and straps on her seat belt, then looks to me and waggles her eyebrows, "Do you have the need for speed?"

I grab her chin pulling her lips to mine for a sensual kiss before letting go, but keeping my lips against hers, "Yes, please." I growl against her mouth.

She raises one brow and bites her lip, turning to face the open desert. "Okay cowboy...hold your horses."

I barely have time to grip the dash before she's dropping the clutch and spinning dust clouds in our wake. The car lurches forward. We barrel down the road at a break-neck speed. Gears shifting, the world flying past our windows. After a few minutes she asks, "You ready?"

I nod grinning from ear to ear. Sam slows the car down when she reaches a certain open area of dirt with no cactuses or debris around. She stops, then revs the engine to screeching. As she's releasing the clutch, the wheel is turning. The car slings in a circle and then another and another. She is whooping and hollering while I hold the dash with one hand and my cowboy hat with the other.

She calls these doughnuts. I don't give a shit what they're called...I need this every day!

Suddenly, she stops the car, flinging me a little sideways with the abruptness of it. Her face is lit up as she grabs my hand and places it on her belly. My face goes slack for a moment. Little bumps meet my hand. Kicks. The first she's had.

"He likes it," I say as I lean down to place a kiss to that spot.

"He? What if it's a girl?"

"Either way, this little devil seems to have the need for speed too."

She cackles and we both hold her belly together, waiting for the next kick. She gasps when we are rewarded with another.

"Have you thought about names?" I ask.

She nods. I move away and lean back in the seat to watch her as she takes off again, this time heading home. She clears her throat before saying, "Kurt for a boy...Judith for a girl. That is, if you're okay with that."

I pride myself on being a strong man, but damn. I try to swallow what feels suspiciously like a lump in my throat. She wants to name our boy after my late brother. My voice comes out gruff when I say, "It's perfect Sam."

She smiles knowingly and adds, "I was thinking...Warren for Kurt's middle name and Anna for Judiths."

I can't do anything except nod my approval. I'm glad she's honoring two people I loved and people she loves. Judith was a brief part of her history but made such a lasting impact on her life. If it wasn't for her, where would we be now?

She breaks the heavy thoughts swirling in this car when she asks, "Wanna go one more time?"

"Hell yes! Don't hold back this time."

"Hold back!" she scoffs. "I never hold back!"

And with that, she spins us into a massive circle. I hold my hat out the window, swinging it wildly.

"It's a nice damn day isn't it!" She yells.

"Yes…nice damn day." I holler back. Silently, I whisper to myself, "It's a nice damn life."

Acknowledgments

First and foremost, let me thank *you*…my reader. You make it possible for my stories to be heard. You bring life to them, and I will forever be grateful.

I want to thank my editor, Maryssa Gordon, with Pocket Editing, for being there for me a second time. She's responsible for my line editing and formatting of the interior. Her patience and attention to detail are unmatched. Kudos! You are wonderful.

I want to thank my family and friends for their endless support. Writing comes naturally to me, but it's also time-consuming and can pull me away from them. They stood by me through it all.

My biggest thanks goes to my husband Mitchell and daughters Megan, Cameron, Emily, and Amelia.

As I said on my dedication page, this book cannot be dedicated to just one person. The strong women in my life are truly the real FMCs. My mother, Judy, who passed away in 2022, and my mother-in-law, Mary, who's the backbone of the family. Two strong females that shaped my life in endless ways. The character Judith, and later, the daughter of Sam and Jake, is specifically for my mother. She said what she meant and meant what she said. She was feisty! Unfortunately, she never had the chance to go on this book journey with me, but I know she's watching. Love you mom.

Growing up on horseback was as natural to me as writing. The free spirit of the horse lives inside still and shows in my daughters. It's an untamable, wild strength and sense of adventure.

Many people ask me where I come up with these stories. The best answer for that is in my dreams. I had a dream one night about a girl drinking Jack Daniels Fire in a saloon. She was sitting beside a man, and he passed her a flask, but when I woke up, I stopped my husband as he was getting dressed for work. I told him about the saloon and the whiskey, then I said, "She was *not* in her time...she wasn't from there."

Alas...*Out of Time* was born.

About the Author

K.D. Elledge is a voracious reader with a passion for writing, crafts, and classic cars. She spends her days working in healthcare as an X-ray and CT Technologist. She spends her nights plotting her next imaginary characters. She's a wife and a mother to four inspiring daughters. Her family is living in the foothills of rural North Carolina with their two normal cats, one psycho cat, and two eccentric dogs.

Find me on my socials…

https://www.tiktok.com/@author.k.d.elledg?_t=8r22OdbE1bb&_r=1

https://www.facebook.com/share/19UNd5sB48/?mibextid=LQQJ4d